MW01611978

THE TRUTH ABOUT LOVE

....The Whole Truth Series

Book One

By T L Fisher

Dedication

My parents proved that you can be a friend to your child and they turn out ok. My husband, who may not have been my first love...but he will certainly be my last. And my four daughters, who are all fairy princesses in my book, I love with all of my heart. This book is for you.

Acknowledgements

A special thanks to Hunter, my very first fan and first to critique this book. To Pam and Kristin who helped me mold the final draft. And to Melanie...the best, most honest, most brutal beta reader EVER!! Thank you for making my story better.

Finally, to friends and framily both old and new who have touched my life and my stories ...thank you for making my life entertaining and interesting. You are my therapy and I love you ALL!

There's always that one stupid mistake that changes everything.

TABLE OF CONTENTS

PROLOGUE

The memory is etched forever in my mind, like lovers initials carved deep in the bark of an old oak tree.

It was my twelfth birthday when my dad, Randy, decided to move us to the country. Our washed out silver pickup truck crept its way up the rutted rock lane. I still feel the vibration. The lane was so overgrown with scrub trees, branches ripped down the side of our truck, like fingernails skating across a chalkboard. I had to bend over and press my ears firmly between my knees.

When we arrived at the end of the lane, I lifted my head and there she stood. —The ugliest house in the entire fucking world.

My eyes pinch shut while I squirm my way out of the confined back seat. This is all a bad dream, I think to myself. My dad kills this theory when he asks the stupidest question on the face of the planet.

"What do you think?"

My focus shifts to his face. For the life of me, I can't twig his giddiness. Tears begin to build in my eyes, but I force them back. I have an answer for his question, but my throat has imprisoned all forms of sound.

"She needs a little work, I get it. But look at all of this room you and Ben will have to run and play. Cool. Right?"

1

A little work? The place is a dump, with a bold—underscored—capital— **D**. Who on earth lived here? And were they human? Room to run and play. What am I, five? My eyes see nothing except a cloud of monotonous boredom ahead.

My dad's face mutates into a creepy clown smile as he unlocks the back door. As the door swings open, shreds of yellowed paint forfeit their lose grip of the weathered wood and float to the ground like dirty feathers. So. Fucking. Creepy.

"Welcome home," he announces, stepping over the threshold behind us. I suddenly have a strange sensation I live in a Steven King novel.

My inner smart ass manages to escape and claws her way between my lips, "You can't be serious. This place is so far beyond disgusting, I don't have a word in my vocabulary to describe it."

The sunshine drips off of my dad's face when those words dance across my lips. Every ounce of happiness that beamed from his existence is destroyed. I feel dreadful, but can't unearth anything encouraging to say to make this better.

My eyes canvass the kitchen, and all I see are filthy windows filled with huge flies—some dead, some still buzzing with life. Old metal cabinets hang crooked on the dingy peach walls, heavily soiled from years of use and abuse. The brown tile floor is busted in places and scattered with a smorgasbord of dead insects and dirt. His glow has burned out and it's entirely my fault. Not even a white lie will make this better.

Self-pity sinks its ugly fangs into my flesh while my dad shares his deranged vision of grandeur. *This can't be happening.* I draw in a heavy breath and hold it in my lungs for sheer contempt—he doesn't notice. Nobody notices.

My mom, Angie, grabs his hand in support, but her eyes tell me a different story.

My arms cross over my chest and I roll my eyes so much I'm dizzy. Room ...by room ...by agonizing room he paints us an image. I try, I really do, but I can't envision his reverie. The fly the size of a small dog, buzzing in the window pane of the front door is distracting, so it isn't entirely my fault.

He muddles through our obvious skepticism, "Raising cattle on my own farm has been my dream." His tattooed arm waives toward the grime covered window, "Look at those rolling hills! A creek runs through the valley in the center, and there's a barn. I've always wanted a barn."

Most of his speech skates by me, because I'm still stuck at *cows*. After I consciously choke back my laughter, I realize this isn't only my nightmare, but my father's dream, and who am I to quash it.

I sleep on the dining room floor that night, on a blow up mattress in the corner. More than a few tears saturate my pillow. The following morning, I accept my fate with uneasiness—*E.I.E.I.O.* The house is actually the least of my concerns. My new anxiety is loneliness. Making friends has never been my forte, in fact, I completely suck at it. As much as I want to be one of "*them*", the chirpy, way to fucking fizzy people that radiate

3

popularity, I'm not. Cute and fun are not adjectives I can claim, more like neurotic and defensive.

She knocks on my door as the milk from my cinnamon toast crunch dribbles out the corner of my mouth. The back of my hand quickly wipes it away. The cold tarnished handle turns slowly in my hand while I peer through the curtain-less window.

"Hey," she smiles, "I'm Natalie." Her mouth is full of metal and a long blonde braid hangs down the center of her back. She is one of *"them"*…and she's at my door.

"Hi." I fight the urge to hug her. "Brianna."

"Brianna, cool. I live across the street from you. We will be great friends, I can already see that. So, do you want to come hang out?" *Score!*

In those ten brief seconds, Natalie changed my life forever. After four years, she is still one of my best friends.

CHAPTER ONE

I squeeze into my favorite faded jeans. The pair with the little tattered hole right above my knee. The brush pulls through my long chestnut hair one last time while Natalie stands at the bottom of the stair case and bellows up to my bedroom.

"Jesus Bri, we're going to be late! I don't want to miss tip off. You have like two minutes and I'm leaving!"

"Hop off Natalie, I'm coming!" I pull on my North Face jacket and stuff my cell phone deep into my pocket before I fly down the staircase.

"Finally," she huffs.

Daggers shoot across the room from her chocolate milk eyes while I quickly peck my mom's cheek. "Bye Mom, be home after the games." With her face still buried in her recipe book, she smiles and nods.

"Let's roll," I smirk.

If you look up jock in the dictionary, I'm sure you will find a picture of Nat. Her life is everything sports; playing them, watching them, and constantly talking about them. Makeup is for phonies and her idea of doing her hair is to pull it up in a squirrel on top of her head. The frequent wait for me must seem completely ridiculous. Natalie isn't what I would call gorgeous, but she has a certain vivacious charm that sucks people in. She is never without a boyfriend, unlike me.

Natalie opens her driver's side door and through the dimly lit interior of her car I can make out Adrienne sitting shotgun. Adrienne lives next door to Natalie. They have known each other since kindergarten. I'm an awkward third wheel flung into their pre-existing friendship. Being a third wheel, escaping into my own backseat reverie, is totally ok by me—at least tonight.

The passenger door flies open and Adrienne half-heartedly offers to take the back seat. Her offer is for appearance sake. Adrienne isn't the type to take a back seat to anything, or anyone. Her circle of friends is limited, but this deficiency isn't because she doesn't look the part. Except for the way her tiny nose points up at the very tip, Adrienne is flawless. Her quest for perfection pushes people away. Everything about Adrienne has to be spot on. She wouldn't dream of stepping foot out of her house without her designer clothes, perfectly applied makeup, and every shining raven black hair in a perfect position on her petite head. Only those who truly know her, which would be me and Nat, realize under this layer of perfection is a teenager who struggles to find love and acceptance. Her constant search is an exhausting battle to watch.

"No thanks princess, I am completely comfortable with third wheel status," my long black eyelashes bat back at her.

Before I have my seatbelt fastened, Natalie begins to ramble about the tournament. Eight teams compete today, we are the third game. The winners will face off tomorrow. I breathe a silent sigh of relief knowing I am busy tomorrow.

6

Adrienne struggles to change the subject to her latest male addiction. Like me, Adrienne isn't into sports. Unlike me, she is totally into guys. She looks at every social event as an opportunity to sink her claws into some new non-expecting victim.

The conversation between them is grueling. They struggle to come up with anything to discuss on common ground. I silently cheer, because as long as they try, I don't have to say much myself. My own thoughts are a much more relevant escape.

Lately my mind has been preoccupied with my grandfather, my dad's dad. He suffered a stroke over the summer. My Saturdays are spent helping my grandparents out. Gramps has a good day, now and again. On these happier occasions, he knows who he is. He sits up in his wheel chair with little help from his family. He tells jokes, or recounts stories already often shared.

On bad days, he transforms into someone barely recognizable. Gramps will call out to me, but the name is not one I'm accustomed to. In his mind I might be one of his sisters, who died many years ago. He will ask for a hammer, or a hoe, and proceed to nail imaginary boards in the air above his head, or tend to a garden that doesn't exist. I guess he is in another place and time in his mind, a happier place perhaps.

Then we have the really sucky days that leave him motionless in bed retracing memories through the old wavy glass of his picture window, mumbling indistinctively. His face is a snapshot, empty and dead. None of us exist in this shadowy world.

My mind is completely engulfed in everything Gramps when Natalie interrupts my thoughts. "Hello!! Are you going to get out of my car?" she barks while she slams her door shut.

Adrienne holds her seat forward for me. I slide out submissively.

"I'm not waiting on you two, see you inside," Natalie rants, while she runs towards the gym.

A vision of Forest Gump pops in my head, "Run Natalie, run!" I roll my eyes while Adrienne and I stroll to the double glass doors which lead to the gym corridor. "Does she realize how ridiculous she looks?"

"Please—you think Natalie cares? Missing tip-off is right up there with missing your period. Oh my god, the guy over there is so staring at me," Adrienne divulges while she eyeballs her petite reflection in the gym door when we approach it.

Adrienne executes her typical examination of potential suitors while her eyes cruise through the trophy filled corridor. Her eyes peruse the sea of faces to see if there is one that stands out and captures her interest. She turns to me, "Oh, forget it. You would think out of eight schools, there would be at least one cute guy here. Let's go find Nat."

I chew on her words before answering, "You go on ahead, I'm going to grab a soda."

Don't take this wrong, I'm really not desperate for a relationship. Oddly, I don't mind not having a boyfriend.

My friends are much more concerned about my social health than I am. However, just because I'm not concerned doesn't mean I don't want to check out the goods myself, and this is not an option with Adrienne around. Adrienne is an eyeball magnet, so I disappear like an unfocused background.

Adrienne disappears from the corridor. I scrutinize the faces while I shuffle back and forth on my feet in line for my soda. Like Adrienne, I'm not feeling any wow factor. But, unless you're a peacock, physical appearance is a ridiculous way to pick out a boyfriend anyway. I've seen some pretty kickass covers on some pretty lame books.

I walk down the sideline of the gym and sip on my soda, in search of Natalie and Adrienne. The dissonant screech of sneakers and the thunderous hammer of the ball up and down the pale wood court is deafening. The smell of sweat and spicy deodorant smack my nostrils when I walk the edge of the court.

Spotting Natalie and Adrienne isn't tough. Natalie is center court barking commands to our players. That's my Nat, spectator, coach and cheerleader all wrapped into one. I scale up the few flights of bleachers where Natalie's arms flail around like an octopus, so I take the empty seat next to Adrienne. Soda drenched jeans are not something I am willing to put on tonight's agenda.

"We're kicking ass!" Adrienne boasts. Funny, neither of us is into sports, but we still desire to be the winning team.

"That rocks, but the game just started, we have a long way to go."

"So, did you spot any keepers?" Adrienne questions with one eyebrow cocked into her forehead.

Embarrassed, I lower my focus, "You caught me, but to answer your question, no." Satisfied, Adrienne smiles and continues to watch the game.

My eyes wander left and then right while our boys travel from one end of the court to the other, each team scoring equally as well—like the pendulum of a clock, never-ending. *This can not be over soon enough.*

My mind again drifts; I picture my Gramps, motionless in his bed with his artic blue eyes glazed over in a nebulous stare. His cheeks are hollow and dark, his skin pallid and lifeless, with course grey whisker stubble scattered across his jaw and chin. He is turned away from me, facing the distorted glass of the picture window. What temptation is hidden beyond the glass? Why does this mysterious place pull his consciousness away from the people he loves? Why does he—

"What the fuck!" Natalie shrieks and intrudes my thoughts for the second time tonight. The room gasps in chorus before falling completely silent.

One of our better players, David Hampton, has taken a fall and lands flat on his face. A crimson river of blood gushes from his nose, and trickles down his chin and drips onto the pale wood floor. The image turns my stomach.

"What the hell happened?" I whisper to Adrienne.

"Hell, I don't know. I was looking at the guy over there in the red jacket."

"So Nat, what happened?" I ask again, louder.

"Umm seriously? You two fail, you're not even watching the game, are you?" Natalie hisses.

"Yeah, sort of." I fudge on my response and sink further into the bleachers.

Adrienne rolls her eyes, which are still anchored on Mr. Red Jacket.

"Oh my god, some freaking douche bag on the other team tripped David. What a jerk!"

David gimps his way off the court with the help of some team mates. The gym buzzes once again, louder than ever. The uproar of their screams and the thunder of clapping are all enough to give me a headache.

Adrienne, obviously bored, strikes up a random conversation; there is no escaping back to my own reality. She must have assumed where my mind was.

"So, how's your granddad doing, Bri?" she asks with her liars concern.

"Some days he's fine, or almost fine. Other days, he's not even my gramps, but he's hanging in there."

Adrienne carries on, "Bri, I get you love your grandparents, and all. Giving up your Saturdays to take care of him is kind of crap, just saying. Your sixteen, you should be hanging out with hot guys, not old people. I mean, one of these days you will wake up and be old. You will look back on all of this time you wasted while you were in your prime."

My prime? I chuckle, because her comment strikes me as funny...in a ridiculous sort of way. I have no doubt Adrienne sees the complete seriousness of her concern. "Oh good lord Adrienne, we're sixteen! I think I have a few more years to find the man of my dreams. Besides, right now, my grandparents need me. They won't be around forever," I enlighten her with a satisfied smile.

"This is not funny Bri, I'm totally fucking serious. You're a junior and you've never had a boyfriend—a real one I mean. What will you do after high school, when you don't have me or Nat helping you out anymore?"

I feel my mind flatten in a corner. Adrienne is right, of course; I have never had a boyfriend—not really. My pathetic attempts at dating were guys from other schools introduced to me through Natalie's sports connections or Adrienne's frequent guy patrols. Without them, the whole dating torment would be non-existent. I don't feel like dealing with it...facing it, not tonight.

"Adrienne, I'm not concerned about diving into the high school dating cesspool, not like you and Nat. Most guys are either jerks or boring anyway," my inner fairy princess emerges, I call her Jezebel because she's kind of a slut. She covers her mouth to hide her smirk.

Adrienne's eyes narrow to a slit—she's so damn cynical. I can only assume her deduction, they aren't boring ...I am.

Now guarded, I continue, "Besides, that would be so sweet of me Adrienne, to let my eighty year old, exhausted grandmother do this solo."

"How many of the cousins your age help?" she drills, "And why isn't your mom helping?"

"Shut up Adrienne, Jesus! I help, because I want to help. I love spending time with my grandparents," I retort and shift my eyes to my hands not understanding why I feel ashamed.

Adrienne, in a tone that tells me she wants to lay this conversation to rest, ends, "I'm just saying, this shouldn't be your responsibility. You should be hanging out with me at the mall and shit—or making out with cute guys on Saturday nights. This is your grandmother's responsibility and the responsibility of her children, not her grandchildren. You shouldn't be the one dealing with this shit."

This is far from shit! Her debate is decidedly over, so a response will be futile. Adrienne didn't grow up with any grandparents; I don't expect her to understand.

My body slouches in the wooden bleachers. My mind tries to drown out the constant rumble of the game. I can't help but mull over Adrienne's observations. Finding a boyfriend *has* been one hundred shades of complicated for me. Adrienne and Natalie appear to ease their way into relationships, over and over again.

My friends are a mile ahead of me when it comes to dating. My pudgy, late blooming body hung with me until my sophomore year. Now, I am taller, twenty pounds lighter and have curves in the right places. Somehow, this new *me* is still overshadowed by the awkward inner child who refuses to leave. Of course, it is entirely possible my catch-22 has little to do with my physical appearance. Following in the shadows of Natalie and Adrienne on the path to adulthood has stifled any personality traits I could have developed on my own. How I wish I could have Adrienne's confidence, or Natalie's outgoing personality.

BUZZZZZZZZ........The first half is over and the buzzer startles me out of tonight's endless daydream state.

Adrienne slaps my shoulder, her gunmetal gray eyes lock in a hawkish gaze, "Get a load of the sex magnet at ten o'clock!"

As she continues to point, my instinct doesn't take long to decipher which victim she is referring to. Without doubt, he is her precise type.

"Let's go ...Let's go ...Follow him!" she demands in a muted voice.

Natalie and I grin at each other while Adrienne climbs down one of the bleacher levels in front of us.

"Keep up Nat, if she loses him in this crowd, we'll never hear the end of it." I stretch my neck above the crowd and try to keep her in sight.

"He is a hottie; maybe he has some cute friends!" Natalie chirps and flips her ponytail from side to side.

We trail twenty people behind Adrienne while she pushes through the crowd in a way that makes her look important.

"Do you think he has friends on one of the basketball teams?" Natalie's voice takes on a new level of excitement.

She continues to talk, but my focus is set on Adrienne, so we don't lose her. I also wonder what his friends might be like. Princess Jezebel hovers overhead and shakes her long skinny finger. *Here you go again, dumbass. Instead of searching for your own prince, you're settling for a tag along boyfriend.* My lips pull into a scowl, a tag along is better than no boyfriend at all.

While Adrienne vamps her prey, Natalie and I absorb her every move. She makes some excuse to ask him a question when we approach her.

"Excuse me; do you go to school here? I'm looking for the restrooms," her smoky voice asks nonchalantly, while she pushes her short black hair behind her ears.

What? Seriously, is that the best she could come up with? Natalie and I glance at each other in complete disarray.

Adrienne never loses her touch, so maybe he is too cute. *Doubtful!* Anyone would have difficulty denying he is cute, but I don't think *too cute* is a concept Adrienne could ever begin to grasp. She continues to the restroom in

15

the direction he guided her, so we follow puzzled. When we walk by Adrienne's victim, I notice he has a large scar on his right cheek. His imperfection doesn't appear to be old. The wound still looks fresh—pink, like it hasn't been healed very long, a car wreck perhaps.

He smiles at me when I pass by. Princess Jezebel blows him a kiss. I shift my eyes to the floor while heat rushes to my cheeks. The mystification all becomes clear. Adrienne's lame question had a purpose after all. She isn't interested. In her eyes, he doesn't measure up to her over zealous expectations. Pity, he might be nice. He has a great smile.

Natalie ditches us in the restroom. She wants to go talk to some of her jock buddies, before the game resumes.

Adrienne doesn't mutter a word about her hot pursuit for Mr. Right; she appears bored and ready to go home while she ogles herself in the mirror.

Adrienne and I wander through the corridor and make small talk with a few people from school. Nothing meaningful, just babble about the game and our winning half-time score. When our break draws to a close, we wander back into the gym. The seats we occupied the first half have been taken. We climb a few more flights of bleachers to find replacements. Natalie wanders over about the time we sit down.

"We are beast, and so going to win!" Natalie roars, while she pulls her latte blonde hair out of its ponytail and shakes it around. The scent of her citrus shampoo spills into the air around us.

"Watch out, Natalie's going into beastmode, it's about to get real," Adrienne chuckles in my ear.

I nod in agreement and return the smile.

The buzzer sounds and our boys are off again. I find it easier to focus on the game the second half. Natalie is louder than our cheerleaders, so having a conversation at this point will be difficult. Returning to my day dream state might even be a challenge.

Excitement builds in the gym when the score begins to even up. When we approach the end of the third quarter, the opposing team has pulled ahead by eight points. Because Natalie takes her sporting events more serious than her chemistry exams, you can watch anger build in her expression. One of our players, Josh Gray, fouls the other team again—their streak is over.

Natalie lunges from her seat, "Josh, what the hell are you doing!"

A voice from behind me declares his annoyance, "Hey blondie, you make a better door than a window!"

Natalie's upbeat personality can transform into scrappy Nat on a dime. Attempting to keep it light, I turn to the guy and blurt the first thing that pops in my sarcastic mind, "I don't know, I think she's pretty transparent." I smile.

A surge of emotion sweeps over me when his deep dark espresso eyes burn right through my soul. His eyes are so three dimensional they suck me in, I barely notice the rest of his face. They are brown, but not like any brown I have ever seen. Brown is boring. No, these eyes are deep and mysterious. The center sparkles like a precious topaz that fades to an outline so dark, it is nearly black.

My body is frozen in place; like the world has stood still and we are the only two people that exist. I want to break free from this self-imposed restraint, but can't find the strength. We connect somehow. Not like a magnet, but more like a wide rubber band has been woven and twisted through my guts while he pulls me inside of him. I think we both recognize something incredible is about to begin.

His eyes hold something familiar. Not reminiscent of a prior encounter, I am certain I have never met him before. Instead, I am overcome by a feeling of déjà vu, like I knew I would meet him someday. He looks at me with such intent, I feel like I am absorbed right into his pores. After what has to be a full sixty seconds, he breaks his gaze and his eyes become softer and friendlier. He smiles and winks ...I nearly pee myself.

I smile back and let my hair fall over my face. I quickly turn around in my seat and bite my lip. Princess Jezebel grabs my shoulders; her eyes are wild with excitement. Embarrassed by my reaction to someone I don't even know, I sink deeper into the bleachers. As humiliated as I am, all I want to do is turn around and soak more of his image into my brain. I chew on my nails and try to come up with an excuse to turn around.

I hear Adrienne and Natalie talking, but their voices blur in the back corner of my mind. I think they want to leave after the game if we lose. *Leave, no I don't want to leave, how will I ever meet him!* Since they are both aware I haven't watched much of the game, how will I ever convince them to stay? For what seems like hours, my mind races. *Think Brianna, think!*

A tap on my shoulder from behind startles me, I nearly slide off of the bleacher. His eyes lock with mine for a brief second, then his face pulls into mine and he whispers in my ear while he climbs down the bleachers past me, "You are a girl who could haunt my dreams, I'll be back. Please don't go."

Goose bumps fall over my body like cold rain. His warm minty breath fills my ear. Princess Jezebel swallows hard, while a whimper pushes up her throat. I watch every step he takes down the sideline until he fades out of site, like he never existed.

"Leaving!" I hear Adrienne's impersonal voice summon me.

I don't realize our game is over. I don't want to leave yet. I don't know his name. I don't know where he goes to school, and most importantly, I don't know if he has a girlfriend. *God, I hope not!*

"We can't go yet," I plead.

Natalie's eyes narrow, "What do you mean we can't go yet? We lost."

"Because, he's coming back. I have to know who he is," I answer.

"Who's coming back?" she questions.

"The guy that was sitting behind me."

"Guy, what guy?" Adrienne zones into our conversation.

"The one that smarted off to Natalie."

"You are too funny, great comeback by the way," Natalie smiles.

Great comeback, really? Not that I meant to insult Natalie, but my off-the-cuff retort should have pissed her off. Natalie could really blonde out sometimes.

She adds, "Are you talking about Sean Gentry? He's weird."

"You know him!" I exclaim. *Of course she knows him!* Natalie knows everyone.

"No, not really, but I know who he is. He goes to school with my cousin, Tyler. I've seen him at the water park in Lamar before. He shaved his head in a mohawk last summer because of a stupid bet. Come on—who fucking does that? Freak, just sayin!"

"He's not a freak, he's super cute. Come on Nat, how many times have I hung around waiting for you or Adrienne to check out a guy."

"Ok, whatever, ten minutes. If he's not back, we're leaving."

Adrienne doesn't say much about my infatuation, but through her pursed lips and slanted brow, she does manage to toss in her two cents, "Bri, really? He was kind of a jerk."

He may have been a jerk to Natalie, but he was certainly not a jerk to me. I sit patiently while my gut does somersaults—ten minutes pass. I talk Natalie and Adrienne into another ten minutes. They agree to not leave, but won't sit around and wait, so we set out in search of him. We walk the entire gym and search through the corridor—nothing.

"Come on, the next game already started. He's obviously not still here. Lamar already played today. They played before we did," Natalie informs me. Of course, she would know this.

"Yeah, I'm ready to go," Adrienne adds.

"Fine," I pout.

We push through the exit doors. I search the students in the parking lot, he is nowhere in sight. I know a look of anguish shadows my face when I climb into the back of Natalie's car.

Natalie is still in a bad mood since we lost. She hops a curb in her huff when we pull from the school parking lot. Adrienne and I remain silent. Natalie bitches about losing the entire drive home. I am good at tuning her out, but poor Adrienne has to listen to every bad play our team made and who didn't have their game on. Her desperate eyes keep glancing back at me, hoping I will join their conversation and change the monotonous subject. *You're the one who needs to sit shotgun, princess.*

All I am capable of is recalling my life changing experience. I have an image of Sean burned into my memory. This is an image I don't see disappearing anytime in the near future. All I can picture is his toffee colored hair falling around his face, framing his dark espresso eyes. Everything about him intrigues me. He is a puzzle I definitely need to solve.

Finally, Adrienne manages to garner my attention, "Ok Bri, snap out of it. Don't get me wrong, I'm glad you finally have an *interest* in someone—but why this guy? He obviously isn't interested or he would have asked for your number."

"Yeah, like seriously," Natalie adds. "Trust me, he is a jerk, from what I know of him."

Natalie and Adrienne's opinion, for the first time I can remember, mean nothing to me. Princess Jezebel raises her upper lip, offended. Sean is interested, I am sure of it. Even more significant, I am interested. He is a novel I can't wait to read—and read—and read again.

"He would have asked for my number, he told me not to leave," I argue.

"Well then, he shouldn't have left," Adrienne finishes and turns her focus back to Natalie.

Not sharing my enthusiasm, their conversation returns to the game. I nod and smile in the appropriate places. Their chatter floats somewhere over my head like a dense fog. All I want to think about is Sean. I have a name for him, this makes me happy.

Natalie skids into my driveway, obviously still trying to cope with her loss. I give them both hugs and say goodbye. They both look me over like I am a lost cause.

After Adrienne is back in the car, Natalie pulls me aside. "Bri, sorry—I can have my cousin Tyler give him your number if you want," Natalie offers.

That seems childish. Not that I'm beyond childish tactics, but maybe they're right. Maybe he doesn't really want my number, "No, it's ok. I'm probably making a big deal out of nothing," I answer and hug her again.

I head into my house, yell at my mom to let her know I am home, and head straight for my room.

"Hold up a minute, get back here," my mom yells out.

Ugh, I don't want to waste another minute, I have to sift through everything spinning through my head.

"Yeah Mom, what's up?" I answer, straight faced while I walk into our living room where she sits, TV on and magazine in hand.

"Did they win their game? Talk to me, how was your evening?"

My mom doesn't care if we won or lost. Her show of interest is predictable. This crafty form of interrogation is her way to analyze my appearance—have I been drinking, doing drugs. Her questions never bother me. I have nothing to hide. I am a *good* girl ...or boring, it depends on whose perspective you view me from.

"Uneventful Mom, we lost our game and came home—boring," I reply. I spin to go back upstairs to my room before she drags the conversation on.

I slide off my white scarf and slip out of my royal blue turtle neck—my feeble attempt at school spirit. I throw on my favorite hello kitty pajamas and turn my stereo on a sleeping volume. The sound is just enough to break the silence. Tonight's reality is a foggy dream I grip as tight as possible. My stomach is in knots. All I can think about is the way he stared at me, so intense, so mysterious, and so significant. I picture over and over in my mind his perfectly sculptured face ...his shrewd deep-set eyes. When he left, he whispered in my ear—I still feel the heat of his breath.

You are a girl who could haunt my dreams. What did he mean; does he feel a special connection too? He noticed me in contrast to Adrienne, which never happens. He doesn't go to my school and this is good, because he won't remember me as the short pudgy nobody. He goes to a school thirty minutes away ...and this is bad. How will our paths ever cross?

I must have thought about him for hours, because I don't remember falling asleep.

CHAPTER TWO

Bzzzzzzzzzzzzzzz "Ugh ...already," I say while I slap my snooze button and sit up in bed.

I can't remember what I dreamt last night, but I know my dream, without doubt, was about Sean, because he comes to my mind the instant I pull my face from the pillow.

I kick my dirty clothes into a pile in the corner of my room. Laundry sucks. I hurry around and finish my chores, wishing I would have done this last night. Then I realize, going to the game last night was possibly the best decision of my entire meaningless life.

"Brianna, telephone!" My mom calls out.

My heart skips five beats when I consider the possibility of Sean on the other end of the line. *Stop it!* I stumble down the staircase almost falling.

"Hello," I say, in the softest sexiest voice a sixteen year old can muster on short notice. *Oh good lord, did I seriously just do that?*

"Hey Bri, it's Sam, will you spend the night tonight? My parents are going out and I am so freaking bored."

That is a no brainer. An evening with Samantha is exactly what I need. Samantha is a different kind of friend than Natalie and Adrianne. I haven't known her as long, but we relate better. We built our friendship on mutual interest. Our conversations are easy. Samantha can help me make sense of this whole Sean intrusion.

"I need to help my grandparents today, but I can swing by about six."

"Six? Bleh, I'm bored now ...but whatever, I'll settle for six."

Sean fades into the back of my mind while I drive the road to my grandparent's house. My thoughts, like usual, shift to my Gramps.

My gramps is a funny man, short and stocky with a tiny half ring of grey stubble connecting the back of his ears. His eyes are as blue as the Caribbean Sea. Before his stroke confined him to bed, he always wore bib overalls and had a plug of chew in his mouth. His smile will melt even the hardest of hearts.

Grams is a wise woman. She has taught me how to cook, how to garden, and about the importance of family and faith. I can talk to her about anything. With five kids and nearly sixty grandkids and great grandkids, I suppose she has already heard pretty much everything. She is beautiful, even at eighty. Her hair is still leather black with a freckle of grey at her temples. She always has it pulled back in a bun.

I climb the long gravel driveway that leads to my grandparent's house. No one else is here. This makes me happy.

"Bri! How are you today? Come give your grandma a hug," she beams, as soon as I step through her kitchen door.

While I hug her, I ask, "How are you and Gramps today?"

"I'm great, go check on your granddad. I think you'll be happy."

I walk into their living room, where his hospital bed is set up.

"Hey Gramps, how are you feeling today?"

"Riny," (his pet name for me), "I'm great. If I could get out of this bed, I'd be even better."

Grams steps into the livingroom, "He has begged to be out of his bed all morning, I'm so glad you're here Bri, you can help me lift him into his chair."

I pull down the rail on my Gramps bed and slide his legs off the side until they dangle an inch above the floor. Grams stands on one side of him and I stand on his other side, we carefully lift him up to a standing position then lower him into his chair.

"Much better, huh Gramps!"

"You bet your britches its better! Now clean me up and we'll go dancing!"

My Gramps makes me laugh all afternoon. "Did I ever tell you about—" escapes his lips more times than I can count, while he shares his most treasured stories. This is one of the best days I've seen him have in a long time.

"Hey Riny?"

"Yep Gramps."

"Do you know what's great about being old?"

"No Gramps, what's great about being old?"

"Nothing is left to learn the hard way, ghaaa. You know what else?"

"What else?"

"Your joints are more accurate than the weatherman, tehehe! Do you know what's bad about getting old?"

"What's that?"

"The only thing you can sink your teeth into is a glass, ghaa-haa-haa. You know what else?"

I giggle and shake my head, "What else gramps."

"It takes you longer to rest than it did to get tired. Speaking of tired, I think I need to go lay down for awhile."

My Grams follows me to the living room and we lift him back into his bed. After we tuck Gramps in, Grams sits down at her kitchen table and gazes out the dusty old window. I pull up a chair at the other end, across from her, and watch her for a minute. She is so beautiful, but the dark circles divulge her exhaustion.

"Bri, your granddad and I have so many great memories," she says, still focused on the window. She slowly shifts her eyes to me, "You're at an age you need to make your own memories, not hang out with your grandparents every weekend."

Grams hesitates for a minute, but continues. "You are the same age I was when I met your granddad. I remember those days like they were yesterday. Bri," she hesitates again for a few seconds, "Bri, don't ever settle. You need to make sure he's the one—the special one you picture yourself with, when you're my age. Make sure he loves you so much he would die for you," she insists, and pats her chest with her frail hand.

She gazes out the window again for a few seconds then turns back to me, "Bri, you have to promise me you won't settle."

I respond the only way I can, "I promise, I won't settle." *Shit, what is this all about?* "Can I ask you a question?"

Grams loves to share her wisdom, "Sure, anything dear."

"How did you know Gramps was the one? How did you meet him?"

Retracing old memories, Grams looks up and a warm smile fills her face. "Bri, I met your granddad one cold winter night by chance ...or fate. I was sixteen years old. Your granddad walked to town from his farm to court Ella Hanks."

Chuckling Grams continues, "Ella's dad was a banker; she was a little better off financially than most of us. I remember the air was bitter that night. Every star in the sky shined bright, but the wind was as brisk as a bee sting." Staring out the window, I watch my Grams lose herself in her memories.

"An unfortunate—or fortunate, depending on your viewpoint, accident led your granddad to our doorstep instead of hers. Taking a shortcut through the woods, your granddad had to cross a creek he thought was frozen over. The ice gave way and he fell into the freezing water. He showed up at our door shivering and wet. My daddy pulled him into the house and Momma wrapped him in a warm blanket." Shaking herself from her reverie, my grams turns back to me.

"My daddy made him strip out of his wet clothes and put him on the couch. I think he piled every blanket we had in the house over him. Momma stayed in the kitchen and warmed up some left over soup. Bri, I remember this memory like it was yesterday. My momma told me to take the young man some dinner, and when I handed him the soup we stared into each other's eyes for what seemed like an eternity. I knew that very moment; your granddad was my destiny. I can't explain to you why I knew, I just did. Your granddad was on our sofa for three beautiful days. He later admitted he probably could have been on his way the following morning." She smiles and shakes her head at his audacity.

"We never looked back from that first night we met. Poor Ella was doomed and never had her opportunity to be courted by your granddad. Bri, I believe in fate, and we all have a true destiny. As long as we follow our heart, it will lead us down the path we are meant to travel. Sometimes people don't follow the path of their heart, these are the people that grow old with regret. I can honestly say I have never regretted a single day I've spent with your granddad. When he meets our maker, I hope I will be right behind him."

I want to tell Grams about Sean, but she looks too happy reliving her memories with Gramps, I can't bring myself to ruin this moment for her. My story will have to wait for a more appropriate time. Speaking of time, I promised Samantha I would be over around six.

Grams still basks in her memories and returns her gaze to the window. I walk over and wrap my arms around her shoulders, "Thanks for sharing your story with me Grams, I love you and Gramps more than the world, but I need to go home now."

She smiles back, "Thank you for pulling those old memories out of this dusty old mind."

Gramps is fast asleep when I walk into the living room. I kiss his forehead and whisper, "I love you Gramps—thanks for a good day."

CHAPTER THREE

My overnight necessities are stuffed in a bag that is slung over my shoulder while I skip down the staircase. Mom is making beef Manhattans from last night's leftovers. "Would you like a sandwich before you go, Bri?"

"Sorry Mom, gotta go. I'm running late, plus Sam always has gobs of food." I hug her goodbye and fly out the door.

Samantha is amazing to hang out with for a long list of reasons. She is easy to talk to and a great listener. Sam doesn't feel the need to control every situation; our conversations always flow. Those awkward moments of silence are non-existent between us. Samantha has a spiritual side, more so than the rest of my friends. Our conversations can dive pretty deep without becoming uncomfortable.

My intrigue with Sean is above Natalie and Adrienne, but Samantha will totally understand. She will help me interpret this feeling taking up permanent residence in my gut.

The drive to her house is the first real chance, in hours, I have to replay last night from start to finish. My constant nagging obsession with him is driving me completely crazy, still I don't want to lose his memory—if that is even possible.

My mind drifts back to that surreal moment, hypnotized by his eyes, like I peeked right into his soul. I have goose bumps thinking about it. *Those damn eyes!*

Still, there has to be more to our encounter than his eyes. What else is hidden beneath the obvious surface? Somewhere behind Sean's intense stare is a force. He sucked me in, like he was some sort of black hole.

Did fate throw us together? The jury isn't back on this theory yet. The only thing truly certain, I have never felt anything like this before...ever. Plus, I should mention, he is unbelievably fucking hot.

I fan my face with my hands when I come to a stop in Samantha's driveway. It is apparent her parents have already left for the evening. I catch a glimpse of her dimpled smiling face and her long sunflower blonde hair while she waves at me through her bedroom window upstairs.

Sam's house is way cool to hang out at. She is the youngest of all of her siblings and the only one left at home. Her parents go out a lot since Sam is older; it is not unusual for her to have the entire house to herself. We crank up the stereo and listen to music without objections. No annoying little brothers or sisters are around to interrupt us all night—just us.

Sam meets me at the door and grabs my overnight bag. I follow her to her bedroom empty-handed.

"How was the game last night?" she pries and tosses my bag in the corner next to her bean bag chair.

"We lost, you didn't miss anything."

Sam's gazed look is unable to hide the rejection in her expression. She might be sad because we lost—but I know better. She is sad because I didn't invite her to come along—I should have.

How do I begin to explain to her my fear? Do I tell her the truth and admit *I don't want you to hang out with Adrienne and Natalie, because you might like them better?* I am aware my actions are completely childish and self-serving. I choose to forego embellishing at all, unless she brings up the subject again.

"Hey, are you hungry? Mom picked up a frozen pizza and a few movies. I think we have some popcorn and soda too, we can watch a movie," she says, her sweet tea smile returning.

Their basement is a teenagers dream—Sam is so lucky. The basement has a media room with a huge TV screen and all of these super comfy chairs made for watching movies. They even have cup holders in them. *Seriously badass!* They also have a game room with a pool table, dart board, and video games, the type of games you might see at a retro arcade.

"Actually, I'm kind of hungry. Can we do pizza for now and fast forward through all of the prerequisite bullshit gossip? We can watch a movie later," I toss her my opinion.

Sam smiles, her dimples dig deep into her cheeks, "Sounds like a plan."

Sam and I aren't really gossipers, so we don't have any exciting news to share. Instead, we sit at the breakfast bar and discuss a book of short stories we are reading in literature class. We only discuss them because they are creepy. One of the stories is called The Monkeys Paw, the other The Landlady.

We don't solve world hunger or develop a cure for diabetes, but our conversation is pleasant. Sam takes the pizza out of the oven and cuts it into squares. We both throw a few pieces on our plate.

I decide this might be a good time to throw my dilemma out there, "Sam, something happened to me last night. I could use your opinion."

Her brow creases, like I have completely changed the aura of the room, "Sure Bri, what's up?"

I start my recollection of my evening to her and try not to leave out any important details, "Last night at the tournament, this guy is sitting behind me, right. I guess his name is Sean Gentry. Sam, I have never seen him in my life. I didn't notice him when I sat down, but he made this smart ass comment to Nat, so I turned around to say something to him ...and Jesus Sam, it was completely insane. His eyes fell over me like some sort of fucking force field, I couldn't move—I couldn't speak—I was frozen. That's not all, I felt dizzy...like I couldn't breathe. Has this ever happened to you before?"

"Are you kidding me? Seriously no, but that is way cool. Did you say anything to him?"

My focus falls to the slate tile that covers her kitchen floor. *I should have said something—anything.* "No, well not unless you count my smartass comment about Natalie. He did say something to me when he left. He tapped me on the shoulder when he climbed down the bleachers and whispered to me, you are a girl who could haunt my dreams—or something like that. What do you think he meant?"

Sam's soft green eyes grow wide, unlike the look I remember from Natalie and Adrienne. I knew Samantha

35

would understand. "Oh my god, like he will dream about you, shut the fuck up? Wow, that is over the top romantic, or he wants in your pants," she laughs.

"Cause I'm such a slut...right! I don't know Sam, it could have meant, I was his nightmare. He did say haunt."

"Bullshit! No, this is not a bad thing. He felt something too, oh my god. Bri, do you believe in fate, or destiny?"

"I don't know, I guess so—maybe. It feels like I was supposed to meet him, like I knew he would be part of my future."

Sam flips on her serious button, "You know, most religions believe in divine intervention. Our life is some predetermined course of events. Everything that happens is part of some natural order, or divine order. Some people believe destiny is inevitable and unchangeable while others believe we choose different paths throughout our life, but will still end up at our predetermined fate."

She continues, "Brianna, maybe there is a reason he sat behind you last night. Maybe this all is meant to be. I guess you will know soon enough—you know if things start to develop between you. Are you going to call him?" she pumps, while she stacks our plates in the sink.

"Sam, how can I call him? For one, I don't have his number, but if I did, what would I even say?" I seriously ask myself this question. "Hey, remember me, I'm the mouthy bitch who sat in front of you at the basketball game. Wanna go out sometime? God, that is so lame."

"Yeah—I see your point. Are you going to wait and see if he calls you?"

Is that what I'm waiting for? "He doesn't even know my name. God damn it, why did Natalie and Adrienne have to be in such a hurry last night."

"Bri ...trust me. If he wants you, he will find you. I still think you should call him, lame or not."

"I don't know Sam, we'll see. I've never been good at calling guys, or asking guys out. Probably why I never have a boyfriend," I chuckle.

"Well, if he's your destiny, you need to figure this out. Now, I want details, what did he look like?"

I see a clear image of him, yet the words won't come. "Sam, he's hard to explain, that's the whole thing. Whatever I say will not do him justice. He has this wavy toasty brown hair that falls around his face. Sweet Jeezus, his eyes are like coffee brown gemstones, piercing...you know. Then he has these totally sexy lips that make me want to grab him and kiss him." I suck in a deep breath and push the image of kissing him out of my mind.

"He has these tiny little dimples in the corner of his mouth when he smiles. I don't know he is totally fucking hot. Now, I'm getting all sweaty talking about him."

"I'm kind of sweaty too." Samantha giggles.

"The weird part, as hot as he is, I don't think his looks are what sucked me in. The way he made me feel— sweet jeezus, and the way he looked into my soul. I fucking melted. He is special Sam, almost magical. I'm not sure what our connection is, because I don't know anything about him—but I feel it. He's deep and mysterious and intriguing, and his eyes are intelligent and see what others miss. He's not like any guy I've ever met. Please don't ask me how I know this, I just do."

"Wow Bri, that's a lot to know about someone you've never had a real conversation with, I hope you're not disappointed when you actually do meet him."

She is right. Her observation shoots a hole through my balloon that is now a mile high and I slowly descend back to earth. Maybe I am creating an illusion of someone I want him to be. What if he does find out who I am and calls me? What if he is like every other jerk I have met up until now? What if there is no real magic? *Too many fucking what if's.*

"Brianna, this is all super cool. I envy you right now, because I don't think I've ever been this excited about a guy I *have* dated. You have me super psyched to meet him, so he better freaking find you ...and call you," she chuckles and weaves her blonde hair through her long slender fingers.

We talk, listen to music and watch movies the remainder of the evening. My time with Samantha is always enjoyable. She makes friendship easy.

We shut up and go to sleep about three in the morning. We don't talk about Sean anymore that night, but he is on my mind and in my private thoughts. I am glad I spent the night with Sam; she always helps me put things into perspective.

CHAPTER FOUR

What is school? For a few of us, school is a place to absorb. I am one of those spongy nerds. Although I despise homework, I honestly like to learn. For others, school is nothing more than a glorified Facebook page. This is Natalie; school is simply another place to socialize.

I have limited friends, but I'm ok with that. Friendship, to me, is meaningful and goes beyond hanging out and comparing the latest slut report, or planning trips to the mall. I prefer my time with friends to be one on one and have some real purpose.

I feel lost when I am thrown into a situation where crowds of people are everywhere, suffocating me—like school. I think daydreaming has always been my way of escaping the masses and I have plenty to daydream about these days.

A million questions run through my mind every day, while I think about Sean. What is he doing at this particular moment in time? Is he reading a book? Is he walking down an empty corridor? Is he in his car listening to music? Is he thinking about me, like I am thinking about him? The questions are endless, because all week, while in and out of class, I come up with more reasons why I have to know him.

I pay just enough attention to the teacher to know the answer to the question she may ask. Seven times, I catch myself doodling his name onto my notebook, my homework, and pathetically…my geometry test.

Lunch is the only thirty minutes of the day I can focus and push his haunting memory to the back burner...to simmer. I eat lunch with Samantha, even though I share my lunch period with Natalie, as well. Natalie surrounds herself with hordes of jock buddies, a place I will never fit it. Samantha is like me; we don't need or want a crowd of endless chatter. We are comfortable in our little corner of the lunchroom, joined only by Emily.

Emily has been a friend of Sam's since grade school. She still clings to Sam, much in the same way I still cling to Natalie and Adrienne. Emily is tiny, much like Adrienne, but ordinary by comparison. She is the only person I know, more quiet than myself.

"Bri, I assume you still haven't heard from Sean?" Samantha grills for the third time this week.

"No ...nothing," I stare into a white blob that might be mashed potatoes. "I am completely ridiculous, this is hopeless. I knew the fairy tale was a long shot, but still I hoped my prince would ride up on his white horse," I bite my lip now and try to mask the twisted pain in my gut. "Those things just don't happen to me. I should have known better."

"I hate to say this, but that is probably for the best. You're making yourself *crazy*," she comments and grasps my head between her hands, shaking it from side to side. "He probably isn't near as kick-ass as the guy you've created in your head anyway."

I chuckle, "Yeah, I don't think anyone will hold a candle to my dream guy, I'm so doomed."

I continue to pick at the mystery meat on my plate while images of Sean continue to haunt me. My confession to Sam is complete bullshit. These fantasies are going nowhere—at least not yet. I will have to hide the crazy better and keep my infatuation buried and protected.

I suddenly remember a conversation with Adrienne in the hallway earlier today. She invited me to check out a new dance club in town and extended the invitation to Samantha. This idea completely sucks, because I'm a grudging bitch and I don't share well, yet Samantha is the one missing out because of my fear and insecurity. I'm completely selfish, I admit it.

I chew on my lip, *oh, what the hell,* "Sam, I forgot to ask you if you want to go to Parazzo's Sunday Night. Emily, you're welcome to go too," I finish.

"What the heck is Parazzo's?" Sam questions.

"It's some new dance club in town Adrienne wants to go to. I guess since Monday is a holiday, they're going to open it up for teenagers Sunday night. Kinda fierce, right? Anyway, Adrienne wants to go check it out, or check out guys, or whatever it is she does. Who knows, it could be fun. Maybe there will be a guy there so freaking hot I will forget Sean ever existed." I sigh because his name runs over my lips again.

"I can't go, we're going to our cabin this weekend," Emily answers, her eyes glued to her history book.

"Yeah Bri, that sounds freaking fabulous, but you know my parents won't let me go to a club, even if it is only teenagers." Sam slams her tea bottle onto the table, "Damnit!"

Now I feel awful. I don't understand why her parents are so strict and mistrusting. Samantha has never been in any trouble, that I am aware of. Maybe her parents' over protectiveness is a result of the older sister syndrome. I bet her sisters did bad things when they were her age; now Sam pays the price for their mistakes. This is completely unfair. *Bullshit.* If Sam isn't going, I'm not going either.

"Fuck it Sam, forget I mentioned it. This isn't a huge deal; I seriously don't care if I go. It will probably be a room full of Aberzombies anyway. I spent the night with you last weekend, why don't you plan to spend the night with me Sunday, instead."

"Oh my god Bri, I love you! You are freaking brilliant!"

Ok, it is a decent idea, but nothing to deserve a brilliance award. I must have the deer in the headlights gape on my face, because she feels the need to explain.

"Don't you get it? Hello! I'll spend the night with you, then we can go and I won't have to tell my parents."

"Whoa ...Samantha, you're lying to your parents?"

"No, it's not *really* lying. I *am* spending the night with you."

This scheme feels like a total lie to me, but the lunch bell rings and interrupts my apprehension. "Well ok, sweet! I'll see you Sunday." I gather my books and head to class.

CHAPTER FIVE

I am dumbfounded how things can change so suddenly in a week. Last weekend I walked into Grams' house and felt love and happiness. The aura was good; all of the colors of the rainbow were waltzing around the room. I couldn't see the colors, but I could feel them. This weekend everything is different. I walk in and the house feels black and cold, like I am walking through a dense fog. The air is heavy, making it hard to breathe.

Grams sits at the kitchen table. She looks tired. She seems to be caught up in deep thought. She doesn't notice me walk in. I slide into the chair next to her, "Grams, what's wrong? Is Gramps ok? Are you ok?" Grams slowly shifts her eyes to mine. She is confused and frightened. I have never seen her like this. Panic sets in, *sweet jeezus, something has happened to Gramps!*

"Grams, please answer me ...is something wrong?"

"Brianna, they are coming to take your granddad away from me. I feel them, they're here."

I examine Grams' expression, she is terrified. I pat her hand to reassure her and walk into the living room to check on Gramps. Gramps is having his typical bad day. I approach his bed and startle him.

"Molly, what are you doing here? I thought I told you to stay away from this place. It's not safe for you here," his croaky voice mutters.

"I'll be ok, don't you worry about me." I reply, like I'm Molly, his sister who has been dead for nearly twenty years.

43

I kiss Gramps on the forehead while he gives me a lecture that doesn't make sense. Confused, I head back to the kitchen were Grams sits and once again scoot in next to her. Days like this are not uncommon for Gramps. Why is she so freaked out?

"Grams, what's going on? What are you frightened about?" Her eyes are large and filled with confusion. I have to wonder, has she had a stroke, or a mental breakdown. I debate whether to call an ambulance.

"Brianna, they are coming to take him away from me. I can't live without him. I don't want to live without him!"

"Who's taking him away Grams? Who are you talking about?" She doesn't answer. I lean in to hold her. I think maybe the embrace will calm her down long enough for me to call someone; my aunt perhaps.

"Bri they came last night. They were here," a single tear slowly trickles down her cheek.

Her mental state begins to scare me, but I manage to hide the anxiety from my expression. I start to ask who again, but she continues. "I was watching TV in my bed last night. I was watching The Late Show, like I do every night. Someone was playing the piano downstairs; I could hear the music as clear as I hear your voice right now. I can even tell you what song they were playing."

"Go on Grams, who was here …who was playing?"

"I walked down the stairs and thought maybe it was your cousin David, because you know he comes to check on your granddad sometimes and he plays the piano." She sucks in a long breath and her tense stance loosens a bit.

"The music didn't stop until I walked into the living room ...and Bri, no one was there. I know this is hard to believe, but it's the honest to god's truth. I will swear it on my mama's grave."

"Grams, I'm sure there's a logical explanation. Maybe the noise was someone playing their car stereo to loud, or maybe David was playing the piano and he slipped out the living room door instead of going back through the kitchen."

Grams' amber eyes burn through me. She senses my doubt and doesn't like it. "Bri, don't you think I already thought of that! The song on the piano was Satin Doll. That's an old song Bri; I don't think anyone would be playing that on their car stereo loud enough for me to hear." I nod in agreement.

"No one uses the living room door, what point would there be." She makes valid arguments. Her driveway is a long lane that ends at the back of her house, where her kitchen is. No one ever uses the front door that faces the road, because they would have to walk around the house to end up there...pointless.

"Besides, there's more. At first, I thought maybe it was all my imagination getting the best of me. I brushed it off and sat down at the piano myself and started to play. I plunked through Satin Doll and a few other songs. I must have played for ten or fifteen minutes."

The color begins to fade from Grams' face while she continues her story. "Someone put their hands on my shoulders Bri, like they were standing behind me watching me play. I could feel their touch, only their hands were cold, like they'd been outside. I could feel their breath on my neck. I remember thinking, crazy old bat, it was

45

David. He must have gone outside to grab something and he came back and listened to me play."

Grams swallows, her eyes are wide. "I turned around Bri—nobody was there," she whispers. Her frail hands tremble more than usual. "I know you don't believe me, but I felt their touch as plain as I feel your hands on mine right now. Bri, whoever's hands those were, they care about me. I think someone is here, waiting to lead your granddad home. What else could it be?"

Oh good lord, this is a lot to take in! First of all, do I believe Grams? I know she believes what she tells me is the truth. If she is telling the truth there has to be an explanation.

I search my mind for answers and grasp at straws. I can't work out anything logical until a revelation hits me.

"Grams, I do believe you, but maybe it was all a dream."

Her golden eyes shoot me an irritated glance, "Bri, I was not dreaming."

I can't come up with anything else to say, so I give her a hug and tell her it will all be ok. We go about our regular Saturday routine without another word about her encounter. This entire day will remain our little secret.

CHAPTER SIX

Tomorrow can't get here soon enough, but tonight I have nothing but time ...time to think, time to dream and time to evaluate my obsession.

Collective Soul resonates from my speakers and pulls me under its spell. I grab my sketch book from my desk drawer and let a pencil flow across the empty page. A face begins to form; nobodies face in particular ...just a face. My mind is a million miles from my room while my fingertip blends the defined line of the bottom lip by pure instinct.

My day with Grams was weird at best. I feel guilty not telling my parents, but repeating my concerns would feel so much like tattling. If Grams wants to share her story ...it's her story to share. What if she is right? Not about the ghosts ...*ridiculous*, but what if Gramps time is drawing near? Am I ready for the inevitable? Worse, is Grams ready for it?

A whole week is gone and I haven't heard anything from Sean, the stranger who ruined my simple—happy—predictable life. Down deep I guess I never expected to hear from him, but I hoped, just this once, life would deal me a royal flush.

My mind replays that bizarre evening—over and over. And over. The image is painful, not because it is hard to remember, but because the memory haunts my soul. These fleeting glimpses of his perfect face are like holding a glass of water in front of someone lost in the desert. The glass is there, right beyond your reach, beads of sweat trickle down the edge and drip onto the hot dry sand. Too weak to move, you lay there ogling and know its moisture will never touch your lips. This makes your thirst unbearable.

A part of me, however small, wishes I had never met him. I have to put this all in perspective, but I can't. I have never felt like someone is physically part of me before, like a piece of him is permanently connected. I want to peek through his eyes and view the world like he does. When his eyes locked with mine, he could really see me. Not only the image of me, but somewhere deep inside of me.

I glance down at my sketch only to realize I'm staring into Sean's deep inquisitive eyes, the soft honey waves of hair that frame his face, and the lips that blush like they are feverish. The image is him alright. Not precise, but close enough to bring me comfort.

My fingers scrawl a few finishing touches and doodle his name across the bottom of the picture. I rip it from the pad and place it in a scrapbook Adrianne and Natalie bought me for my birthday last year.

When my room goes silent I yank myself from my reverie, before I go totally wacko. One foot in front of the other, I glide down the staircase to hang out with my parents. Distraction.

My Dad is on the road most of the time. He plays guitar in a rock band, so he bounces from town to town playing gigs. He's pretty cool to hang out with, but since he's gone a lot, I try to give him and my mom their space.

My dad had a recording contract when I was born, but he gave up his career to raise his family—noble, I guess. My mind often wonders if he regrets that decision, but he never once made me feel like he did. Now that my brother and I are older, and his cattle debacle is dead and buried, he hits the road more and more, trying to rebuild his career. My dad the rock star, I guess that is kind of cool, in a social acceptance kind of way.

My mom is a hybrid cross between a housewife and a trophy wife. I call her a trophy, because she is totally gorgeous …and way younger than my dad. But, she's also a housewife, because my dad isn't rich.

My mom has had a few part time jobs here and there, her idea, but most of her married life has been spent taking care of my brother and me and keeping my eccentric father in line.

My mom is ultra cool, even more than my dad. My friends all love her. She knows when to ask the right questions, but doesn't pry to the point of annoyance. She trusts me and Ben and allows us to make mistakes, as long as we learn and grow from them.

"Hey Mom; hey Dad."

"How's my favorite daughter?" Dad grins.

"Dad, I'm your only daughter, so that doesn't count."

"How was your granddad feeling today?" Mom asks.

"He was in a different decade, but other than that he was ok." My dad pulls up a smile, but it is masked by a layer of sorrow. He isn't ready to lose Gramps either.

"Mom, do you care if Samantha spends the night tomorrow? We are going with Natalie and Adrienne to

Parazzo's for a special dance they are having for high school kids."

My dad's eyes slice right through my flesh, "Parazzo's! That's one of those new clubs that plays fucking canned music, right? You know Bri, your dad is a musician, I would think you, of all people, wouldn't patronize that kind of bullshit. Fucking DJ's make it harder and harder for a musician to make a living. What happened to the days of live music—dancing to a real band? It wasn't this way back in my day. What a fucking shame."

I am anxious for a minute he won't let me go, but he just needs to vent about the perils of his career.

"Will only the four of you be going?" Mom pumps, ignoring my dad's tirade.

"As far as I know, although I haven't talked to Adrienne or Natalie today. They didn't mention inviting anyone else." I pray my mom won't press whether Samantha's parents are good with her going, because I won't be able to lie if she asks.

"That's fine, but make sure you and Sam are back here by eleven, and not one minute after." I smile, because I have escaped the one question that could put an end to our completely innocent, yet devious plan. My mom rocks.

I am still skeptical about Samantha hanging out with Adrienne and Natalie. Natalie and Adrienne have been my friends since seventh grade. I love them like sisters, but I see we are becoming different people as we grow older. Sam is special, she understands me. I have only been hanging out with her since the beginning of my sophomore year, when we were lab partners in chemistry. She saved me from my lunch hour debacle …and for that, I will always owe her my life. As ridiculous as it may sound, my biggest fear is losing Samantha to Natalie and Adrienne. What if she likes them more than me, after all, they are way cooler than I am. My insecurities are selfish, but they are also legit.

I flip my stereo back on and turn it down to my sleeping volume. I slide an oversized tee-shirt over my head and crawl into bed.

I close my eyes and images of Sean tango through my mind. Will I ever see him again? Once again, finding a boyfriend has become a ridiculous struggle. He belongs in my world, every ounce of my soul whispers this to me—everyday.

It's time to break out the goofy high school tactics. I smile while I drift to sleep.

CHAPTER SEVEN

I wake up to the smell of bacon drifting up my staircase. Not even the aroma keeps my mind away from Sean. Is he still stretched across his bed with blankets pulled over his beautiful face? Do I still haunt his dreams like I'm sure he haunts mine?

The time has come to make a move. I waffle back and forth whether this is the right thing to do. Something about it feels like a mistake. Our first real encounter should be special, memorable. Yet, I am convinced if I don't make some kind of move I will never know if we have something special. These feelings are too real to erase from my memory. I need to speak to him, if I have to phone every Gentry in Lamar.

I stare at my phone for a full three minutes and decide I will give this one more week. Princess Jezebel rolls her eyes and shakes her head in annoyance. While I make my bed I wonder if he will be at Parazzo's tonight. He doesn't seem like the dance club type, but anything is possible. A vision of Sean standing in the back of a crowded room with a beautiful girl in his arms explodes in my brain.

"STOP Brianna ... freaking stop!" I say to myself aloud. "Pull your shit together."

I decide to call Adrienne and finalize our plans for the evening. This is her gig, so it makes sense to let her map out our evening.

"Hey Adrienne, this is Bri—what's up?"

"Finishing up my homework, tonight will be freaking awesome."

"I know, right! Yeah, so you mentioned inviting Sam; do you care if she tags along? She's spending the night with me, so you won't have to go pick her up, or anything."

"I told you to invite her, so of course its fine. I can't believe you finally asked her. I've tried to include her in our plans several times. You're the one who never wants her around." Adrienne holds on for a rebuttal from me, but never receives one, so she continues, "They open the doors tonight at five. I'll pick you both up about four and we can grab something to eat before we go."

"Five o'clock, seriously? Why so early?"

"Yeah, they have to have us out by nine. That's the stupid law." She explains.

"Cool, then I'll see you at four."

I am pumped about the early start. I was dreading a long boring day filled with anticipation. Now I can have Samantha come over early and we can get ready together.

I decide to give her a buzz, "Good morning princess. Rise and shine!"

She moans, "I'm trying to sleep in, so we can stay up late."

"Well you need to drag your butt out of bed! I talked to Adrienne and the doors open at five. I think you should come over early and we can get ready together. She's picking us up at four."

Samantha chuckles, "Oh Bri, you are so predictable. You think you need to look extra hot in case Sean is there, don't you?"

Samantha is intuitive, she knows what I think, even if I'm not sure.

"I can't lie, the thought has crossed my mind," I can't stop the giggle from escaping, "but mainly, I'm bored."

"Oh hold up, I've got one better!" she replies. "How about I come over now and we can go out to the mall and buy new outfits for tonight."

"Yes, that's genius!"

Not an hour later Sam shows up at my door. I work it, "Mom, you look really, really pretty today. Here let me take the trash out for you."

"What do you want Bri?" she pulls up a crooked smile.

"So ...Samantha and I want to know if we can run out to the mall to buy something new to wear tonight, pleeeaaasse!" The task is easier than I anticipate, but I haven't begged for a while. She digs in her purse and pulls out her Macy's credit card. "One hundred is your limit, understand Bri?"

"Understand Mom, love you!" I answer and give her a quick peck on the cheek.

Sam and I put on our coats, ready to walk out the door, when my dad corners us. He offers me thirty dollars to go have a nice lunch, on him. I have a feeling, since my brother is at a friend's for the weekend; my dad's motive is to keep us out of the house a little longer—*eww*! But, the extra money for lunch is gladly accepted.

As I walk out the door, I'm reminded, "Bri ...forgetting something?" I smile sheepishly and grab the kitchen garbage.

We pull into the mall parking lot about ten. Searching for the perfect look, we scour through the racks at Macy's. A dozen different outfits die a slow death on the dressing room floor while our piles dwindle. Sam looks gorgeous in everything. When you are built like a model your choices are endless. Pair that with a magazine cover face, and you're unstoppable. Sam is perfect in every way...*bitch*.

She picks out a spaghetti strap top that is bright yellow with huge white polka dots. It flares at her rib cage and hangs down to the tops of her thin thighs. The look is completely Sam.

My quest isn't as pain free. Mirrors in dressing rooms completely suck. They should seriously make them so they make you look thinner and more tan. They would sell so many more clothes! I am certain the mirror I'm staring at has the opposite effect. I look like a cotton ball. *And I'm not pudgy anymore—damnit!*

My entire weight loss passage is a bittersweet memory. It is righteous that the baby fat that plagued my childhood is finally gone—but, the circumstance that led to the journey, not so much.

My biggest fear became my reality my sophomore year. Neither Adrienne, nor Natalie shared my lunch period with me—I know, right! Since they were my *only* friends, I was in a serious predicament. I completely suck at meeting new people, so I did what any other shy nerdy teenager would do. I hid. I locked myself in a bathroom stall and read...everyday. I. Am. A. Loser. That is, until the last quarter when Samantha, my lab partner, mentioned having B lunch. I searched for her that very day. No lunch for almost a year had a definite impact on my figure.

After I try on fifteen different shirts, I huff, "Ugh, really! I can't find what I'm looking for Sam, this is so fucking ridiculous!"

"You are way to picky, Bri. Everything you've tried on has been super cute," Sam taps her finger impatiently on the arm of the chair.

"I wish I looked more like you—this would be so much easier."

"Jesus Bri ...seriously! You have a great body, at least you have a shape. I look like a freaking board."

My search continues while I try to pull my Jezebel confidence back to the forefront. When I am about to give up, I find a blouse that is ivory eyelet and laces up the front to a princess neckline. The three quarter length sleeves are shear, as well as the triangles of fabric that flow over my hips in staggered layers.

"Oh Bri, that is perfect, love, love, love it!"

"Yeah, I kinda like this one too," Princess Jezebel smiles and runs her fingers through her hair.

"It's the right mixture of sexy and innocent. You look like a smoking hot virgin," she laughs. "

We both sift through some jewelry to go with our new shirts and head to the register.

"Hey, since we have some time to kill, we should *so* have a makeover," Sam grins.

"A makeover, I've never done that before."

"Really? They are so fun, we *have* to do this!"

"Well ...ok," I follow her, my *I'm a dork* grin stretches across my entire face.

Sam and I sit at the cosmetic counter waiting for a consultant to approach. Three of them glare at us from across their glass bubble ...waiting for us to get bored and leave—we don't. I swear I catch them playing rock—paper—scissors. Finally a young woman with short fawn colored hair approaches us, she must have lost. Her makeup is perfectly painted, but way overdone.

"What can I help you girls with today," she pumps, her eyes fixed and unfriendly.

Sam responds with a smile still pulled from ear to ear, "We would like to learn more about this MAC line, would you possibly have time to give us some makeovers?"

The consultant breaths a heavy sigh while she starts to pull out samples to show us. I eyeball Sam, uncomfortably, and wonder what she has pulled us into. Sam gives me a reassuring smile, my shoulders ease there way into their normal slump.

The consultant, whose name is Krysten according to her name tag, describes the makeup line and its benefits, while we sit and listen patiently. She dabs a few samples on Samantha, but only in small patches; she isn't trying to make her look gorgeous. The disappointment is painted clearly in Sam's expression. Her brows pull together and she glances over at me ...I've seen this look, Sam's about to get snarky.

"Ok, Krysten ...that's your name, right? I have a confession to make; we're not here to learn about the MAC cosmetic line, as much as we are to get a makeover. You see, my friend here met this guy a couple of weeks ago and she's over-the-top into him. It is imperative that she looks totally beast tonight. I would be grateful if you could do that for her, and while you're at it, if she looks hot, I need to look hot too."

"The consultant's inconvenienced expression finally pulls up into a smile that seems genuine. Still smiling, she turns to face me. "So what's your name?" she asks.

"Brianna."

"Well Brianna, this guy is pretty special, huh?"

"If you only knew," I reply.

"You know, I remember your age ...I miss those days sometimes. Sit down; we will make you look irresistible."

Kristen works on my face for nearly half an hour, when I look in the mirror I barely recognize myself. My bright turquoise eyes have never been so vivid, my lips are perfectly defined and my complexion is flawless. I can't help but smile when Princess Jezebel lifts her pointy nose to the air.

After she finishes my face, she works on Samantha. I feel guilty for consuming so much of this nice woman's time, so I reach in my purse for the Macy's card and ask for one of the eye shadows she has used on me, which is all I can afford and keep under my hundred dollar budget. Samantha buys some foundation and eye shadow too.

After we leave the mall, we hit Sonic for lunch before going back to my house. We fix each other's hair and change into our new shirts. When the clock strikes four, we both feel confident.

"Brianna, Adrienne is here!" my mom yells up the staircase towards my room.

"Ok, we'll be right down."

My dad gives us a wink when we walk by, "You girls are far too gorgeous to leave this house."

"Yeah right, thanks Dad, love ya bye!"

We both rush out the door, like my parents might change their mind. Natalie is already sitting shotgun. As usual, Adrienne is over dressed. She is wearing a white silk blouse with a long black blazer that hangs down to the knees of her black skinny jeans. They are tucked into tall black leather boots. Sam and I glance at each other and don't think we look all that hot anymore, but smile anyway.

Natalie is dressed like she always dresses, in blue jeans and a sweatshirt. That look works for her. Natalie is Natalie; she doesn't put on any false façades.

"What's up? You all know Samantha don't you?" I ask, while I climb into the backseat.

"Sure, hey Sam! I didn't know you were going with," Natalie admits, while Samantha slides in beside me.

Adrienne feels the need to make a much more dramatic production. "Well, it's about time Brianna brought you along. I was beginning to think she didn't want to share you. It will be way cool hanging out with you."

Does Adrienne have me figured out? My motives must be totally transparent. I wonder if Samantha suspects this. How embarrassing. If she didn't, I'm sure the thought is going through her mind now that Adrienne has planted the seed.

Adrienne, being the attention whore that she is, plays twenty questions with Samantha the entire time we eat, and the entire ride to the club. Funny, the questions seems to annoy Samantha. This is oddly refreshing. The attention to Sam annoys Natalie, as well. She typically has Adrienne's ear to absorb her latest ankle biting gossip. I see Natalie's skank face start to unveil.

I'm not mad at Adrienne. I know she is trying to make friends with Samantha. Samantha has the façade Adrienne can be friends with—and Adrienne, like me, doesn't have many real friends. My only concern is the *threes a crowd* thing. Natalie, Adrienne, and I have been best friends since seventh grade. We always have a third wheel, and that spare wheel is usually me. I don't ever want to become a third wheel with Samantha.

Samantha's jaw drops when we pull into the parking lot, then a smile creeps up into her eyes. I know this has to be the first time she has ever participated in anything remotely like this.

As for me, the only light in my tunnel will be spotting Sean's face in the crowd. I scour the parking lot and dissect every face I approach, but none of them resemble the face I search for.

"Oh my god Bri, are you fucking serious! Are you still hung up on Sean Gentry? He doesn't strike me as the dancing type, so get over it already," Natalie's crass persona sermonizes as we walk towards the door. "A million other cute guys are here—focus."

Am I that obvious? Sam's lip pulls up as she studies me with sympathetic eyes. She sees the gouge Natalie inflicts, but isn't willing to debate her view of my infatuation. Samantha is sweet and naive; Natalie can be a bit intimidating.

Over three hundred teenagers are here. Most of them I don't recognize, I guess they are from other schools in the area. Maybe Natalie is right and I will meet some other guy that will take my mind off of Sean.

I am glad Samantha is with us, because Natalie and Adrienne spend most of their time being social whores. Natalie is especially good at that. She has the courage to walk up to perfect strangers and start a conversation without hesitation. With Nat it doesn't matter if they are drop dead gorgeous, or the average Joe, nothing shy emanates from her.

Four wheels work to my advantage. Everything feels in balance tonight. As Adrienne and Natalie bounce around and mingle, Samantha and I hit the dance floor. After we dance to our fourth straight song, we head back to our table. Samantha offers to grab us both a soda from the bar.

While she's away, I concentrate on each face in the crowd and hope to catch a glimpse of Sean. About half way around the room, I lock on a pair of eyes. They are vivid blue beneath a blonde brow—and are totally fixed on mine. I look away quickly and heat flushes across my cheeks.

Samantha sets my coke in front of me and I take a long sip and empty nearly half of the glass. I quickly glance back over my shoulder and those same blue eyes are still in a penetrating stare. This time I gaze back and pull up a soft smile. He smiles. I turn back around.

"Shit." I say under my breath.

Samantha pulls her face back, "What?"

"Some blonde guy behind me is staring," I explain.

"Oh," she smiles. "You mean the one that is heading this direction?"

"Are you kidding? Fuck!"

"He's cute Brianna, run with it," her smile spreads across her face.

I don't have time to argue, because he approaches our table. "Hi," he says.

"Hi," I blush.

"So, my name is Cory, do you care if we sit with you two girls this evening?" he asks. His friend stands quiet in the background.

"These seats are actually taken; we have two other girlfriends here." I say while Samantha kicks me under the table. *What?*

"You're welcome to sit down," Samantha adds. "They won't be back for a while."

"Thanks," Cory smiles at Sam, but then turns towards me. "So what's your name beautiful?"

I feel the blood rush to my cheeks again. "Bri" I answer quietly.

Cory talks above the music, "I couldn't hear you. What's your name?"

"Bri," I yell, louder.

"Would you like to dance Bri?"

"Not right now," I smile and let my eyes sink to my awesome shoes.

Samantha jumps up, "I'll be right back, I have to use the restroom. Bri, come with me."

I look at her confused, but stand up to follow.

"We'll be right back," Samantha says to Cory while she drags me by the hand behind her. Once we step into the bathroom, she spins me around to face her, "What in the hell are you doing?"

"What?"

"Why won't you dance with him, he's hot," Samantha reprimands and slams her hands on her hips.

"I guess, if you're into blondes," I shrug.

"What's wrong with blondes?" she glares.

"Kidding. It's nothing personal Sam, I don't like that song."

"I don't care if they play The National Freaking Anthem when he asks; you need to go dance with him. He's cute—and you need this."

"What do you mean—I need this?" I ask, puzzled.

"You need a distraction from your Sean obsession. Give this guy a chance Bri."

"Ok, whatever." I smile, but the mere mention of Sean overrides any real interest that might develop with blondie.

We wander back to the table. Cory and his friend both still sit where we left them. I dance with Cory on the very next song …and the next …and the next. We finish up with a slow song. I can't breathe, he squeezes me so tight. I look into his eyes, they're not Sean's …but they're here. In front of me. Close enough to touch. Damnit, why do I feel guilty?

We finish swaying to the music when the DJ announces that it's time for us to go. Cory grabs my hand and walks me outside. Samantha lags behind with Cory's friend at her side. Natalie and Adrienne are god only knows where. Once we are at Adrienne's car, Cory pushes my body against the door and bends his head towards mine. Sweet jeezus, he's going to kiss me! I role my head to the side, quickly. Cory pulls his face back, annoyed …embarrassed …I'm not sure.

I should be all over this. He seems nice, he's pretty fucking cute. What the hell is wrong with me? Something inside of me doesn't sit right, this all feels wrong. I think I feel guilty and I know I have no reason to. How can you cheat on a guy that doesn't know you exist? *Stupid Bri, seriously fucking stupid!*

Cory still has his body pressed into mine, but his face gives me space. "I'd really love to take you out sometime Bri, what are you doing for the rest of your life? This weekend in particular."

I crack a smile, but try to squirm my way out of his grip. "I'm not sure what my schedule is like, but I'll give you my number and I'll let you know in a day or two," I answer. I see Samantha out of the corner of my eye, glaring. I push Cory back off of me and dig through my purse for a piece of paper and a pen. I right down my number and turn to face him. When I start to hand over my number, I ask, "So, where do you go to school Cory?"

"Lamar."

I am certain I stop breathing. I drop the piece of paper. My legs collapse underneath me and pile up into a tangled wad. I have no idea how long I sit there with my mouth gaped. Drooling. I lose all sense of my surroundings. *This has to be a dream. A really, really fucking good dream.*

Cory and Samantha pull me up from the parking lot.

"Jesus, are you ok? What the hell happened?" he asks.

"La …La …La …you go to school in Lamar?" I stutter.

Samantha throws out a laugh that roars above the crowd. She bends over and grabs her gut. "Burn dude …and you almost had her."

"What are you talking about, what the hell is going on?"

I still cling to the door handle with a death grip, but I manage to stay upright. Here it comes! "Do you happen to know Sean Gentry?" I grill.

"Sean? Yeah, he's my best friend—why?"

Why? Why? What the fuck do I say? I stand there speechless while Samantha saves the day.

"Cory, I'm afraid my best friend has been secretly in love with your best friend since the dawn of creation. You don't stand a chance in hell. Will you please—please—please give her number to him and have him call her, before she drives all of us crazy."

I half expect Cory to be mad, instead he laughs along with Sam. I'm glad to see they're having such a great time at my expense. I bend over and pick up the piece of paper I dropped and shove it into Cory's hand. My hand trembles. *Stop it, you look like a freak!* He shoves it in his shirt pocket and stops laughing long enough to give me a sincere smile. "It was nice to meet you, Bri."

"It was nice to meet you too. Don't forget to give him my number," I plead.

"No worries," he slaps his friend on the arm and points across the parking lot. Cory turns back towards me when they start to walk away, "Sean …really?"

66

I hear Samantha's words from last weekend echo through my subconscious. *Bri, if this is meant to be, this will be.* Is my intervention happening; is Sean Gentry my fate?

CHAPTER EIGHT

Three weeks pass since I gave my phone number to Cory. With each passing week my expectations dim. Sean Gentry has no interest in me. I keep busy with school and my grandparents, but the aching feeling in my gut will not recede no matter how hard I try to suppress it. Sean is still etched permanently in my mind, even after a month of not seeing his face again. I feel my obsession will never wear thin. He has stained my soul forever.

My friends don't bring up his name. They understand, like me, Sean Gentry has no intention of calling. Grams does not speak of her haunting ever again. I have to wonder if she keeps her pain buried, like I am. Gramps hasn't had a good day in weeks. I miss our conversations more and more, as the weeks skate by. It is like all of the clocks in my life have stopped. Nothing moves forward. Another boring Friday night alone, I think to myself while I sit in bed and listen to Taylor Swift.

"Good god Bri, snap out of this, you are absurd," I sigh. *"You've never even had a conversation with him. He's some guy who glanced at you for a few seconds at a god damn basketball game."*

Everything I feel seems so insignificant, like a speck of dust. I am nothing more than stagnant air that floated through his mind for a brief second. An image he forgot about the night he walked out of the gym. My recent behavior is ludicrous. Enough. Is. Enough. I jump off of my bed and put on some upbeat music. I need to hear lyrics that don't talk about love, or losing ...or asshole ex-boyfriends.

68

I grab my sketchbook and decide to draw something that will take me to a happy place. I begin to sketch a seashore. I pencil in a few sea oats that sway in the breeze, while the surf laps up onto the sand. I am ready to start on a lighthouse when my cell phone rings.

"Hello," I answer.

"Hey Bri, its Sam. I've been thinking. Tomorrow is your birthday and you need to be happy on your birthday, so I called Adrienne and Natalie and we decided we're all coming over to spend the night tomorrow. Don't try telling me no, because that's not an option."

"My birthday? I totally forgot tomorrow was my birthday. Sam, I'm fine," I lie. "Who needs a bunch of Sean Gentry anyway?" The words sting my tongue.

"Brianna, nice try …but cut the shit, I know you're not fine. I know you immersed yourself in a sea of Sean and it hasn't worked out. That completely sucks, but tomorrow is a new year. A new beginning."

"Sam, I appreciate what you're trying to do, but I need to go over and help Grams tomorrow," I argue, happy to have an out.

"Nope, I said no excuses …already taken care of. I talked to your mom and she will help your grandmother tomorrow. We will all be over right after lunch and that's that, so suck it. I have all kinds of surprises planned; this will be your most fabulous birthday, ever! I promise," Sam finishes.

"Whatever Sam. I'll see you tomorrow."

Ghaa ...this sucks royally! The last thing I want is to be the center of some pity party, and that is precisely what this sounds like. Obviously, they have all planned it together. All I want is to bask in my misery. Alone.

I finish the lighthouse and place the sketch pad on my bed next to me. I fall back on my pillow and stare at the blank white ceiling. I picture Sean and I walking down a beach, our fingers wrapped together in a braid. We stare into a sunset of vivid reds and orange. The warm soft glow of the sun that fades into the horizon warms my skin. He turns his focus to me and gently kisses my lips. I feel the ocean move beneath our feet.

CHAPTER NINE

The morning sun peeks through the window of my bedroom and gently lands on my face. This feels familiar. I'm still in my jeans and sweatshirt when I finally open my eyes. *I must have fallen asleep. What time is it?* When I glance at my clock, I spot my sketchbook that lies next to me on my bed. *Ah, now I remember ...the kiss. The beautiful, warm, passionate kiss that was all a fucking illusion.*

These fantasies are my self-inflicted curse, yet somehow they make me smile. I peek at the clock, it reads nine-thirty. *Time to drag my ass up.* My friends are coming over in a few hours and I have a lot to do. My depressed mental state has robbed me of my ambition. My room is a total sty. I kick together piles of shoes and clothes that have gathered on my floor for weeks. By the time I have my last load of laundry folded and put away the doorbell rings.

"Hey Sam, come in."

"Happy birthday! I'm so sorry for this, but please don't be mad, we will have fun, I promise!" she reiterates while we climb the staircase to my room.

"I know. I should thank you for caring enough to do this. I haven't been much fun to be around lately. I should be the one apologizing."

"Its fine, we totally get it ...*but* it is time to turn the page."

"Yeah, I know ...and I will. Promise."

Sam reaches over and gives me a reassuring hug and continues. "I hope you don't mind and I know I should have called and asked, but can Emily stop by today too? She's not spending the night, but she wants to come over for a makeover."

"A makeover?"

"Yeah, I thought we'd do each others makeup and hair, I brought a bunch of stuff with me." *Did Miss Natalie approve of this plan?* I laugh.

Emily doesn't wear much makeup either, but I'm guessing she doesn't despise it ...like Natalie. I have a feeling she has never had a friend, a sister, a mother, or even a magazine show her what to do with it. "Sure Sam, she could have spent the night, it would have been fine."

"Hey, besides the makeup, I brought over a boatload of CD's. We'll be fabulous and freaky."

I don't see the point of looking "fab" if we stay at my house, but I ride on the wings of her enthusiasm.

Samantha and I sprawl across the bed and sift through some of her fashion magazines. We save mental snapshots of makeup and hair ideas when the doorbell rings again. This time it's Natalie. She totes no makeup, but has an entire grocery bag full of snacks and CD's. A shiny wrapped present sits on top of her load.

"Whose birthday?" I joke, while I carry her sleeping bag and pillow upstairs.

"Ha-ha Bri, I thought you could use a present, considering your pissy-ass mood lately."

"Thanks. You're so kind."

"Whatever," she scoffs.

As we climb the staircase, I have to wonder if Natalie will partake in the makeover session of Samantha's agenda, she never wears makeup. I am kind of curious to see what she will look like. We no sooner have her bags set down and put on some music when Adrienne waltzes into my room.

"Hi everyone, I walked in with your mom Bri, she said to tell you she's home."

The whole sleepover bash pulls me back to my junior high days. No one tries to be the attention whore, not even Adrienne. I realize, possibly for the first time in my life, how blessed I am to have such amazing friends.

Natalie volunteers to be first ...miracles never cease. Adrienne works her magic on her long blonde hair while Samantha applies her makeup with artist precision. This glimpse of Natalie with loose curls that fall around her face, and shades of blue and brown highlighting her eyes is wicked cool. The new façade doesn't look at all like Nat. She looks so much older and really beautiful. She, of course, thinks she looks ridiculous.

Adrienne is always so picture perfect; I decide to try something different. I spike up her short black hair with some mousse, while Natalie plasters on heavy dark eye makeup. Nat isn't familiar with applying makeup, hers or anyone else's. I'm not convinced the Goth look she creates is intentional. Adrienne could pass for Joan Jett when we finish with her.

I gently apply Samantha's makeup, while Natalie weaves her hair in a set of several French braids that all merge into one. Samantha's hair is gorgeous, I'm so jealous.

When it's my turn, everyone hovers around me in a circle. Samantha begins to pull my hair in a loose updo with curls that dangle around my face. Adrienne, with the skill of an artist, begins to apply makeup in ways I would never think of. Natalie even paints my toenails. When it is over, I don't recognize the face that stares back in the mirror. I look way to awesome for the Snoopy flannel pajamas I sport.

We all dance and sing around my bedroom until my mom screams up the staircase, "Bri, you have a visitor."

I turn down the music. "Someone else is here, shit!" my eyes glance around the room at my friends.

"Oh crap! I bet it's Emily, I so forgot she was coming!" Samantha confesses.

"Fail!" Natalie blurts, her eyes reveal her inner smile.

Natalie is such a bitch, but she's right, we did fail ...in catastrophic proportion. Emily is smart enough to figure out we forgot about her. I hurry down the staircase to meet her; while everyone else drags the supplies back out. When I turn the corner towards the kitchen I gasp and almost trip over a bar stool. My visitor isn't Emily at all.

Sweet jeezus! Standing before me are the espresso eyes that sucked me into the abyss of his soul one month ago. *Over kill ...yeah, maybe.* Air goes stale in my lungs, because I am unable to breathe. Fainting is literally seconds away. I'm certain, because he slides his hand underneath my elbow to keep me from collapsing. A smile gently pulls at his beautiful crimson lips and he stutters, "It's...it's you."

I can't escape his penetrating gaze, but I really don't want to. I could stand here and stare at him from now until the end of eternity. He's so beautiful I want to cry.

"Are you going to say something?" his smooth voice pleads, still smiling but with a hint of concern in his deep jewel like eyes.

With all of my might I try to think of something to say, but I can't make my lips move. He is far more gorgeous than I remember. He is perfect ...fucking perfect. If he knew the thoughts that spin through my mind, thoughts like gluing him to a chair, or handcuffing him to my bed, he would run in terror.

I catch a glimpse of movement out of the corner of my eye. Someone approaches the door from outside. This time it is Emily. Thank god she arrived when she did, because if she hadn't I may have stood here in humiliating silence forever. I turn to open the door for her, not taking my eyes from Sean's. "Come on in Emily," I mumble.

"Sorry I'm late Bri. My mom wouldn't let me come over until I helped her clean the house. I've already missed the makeovers, haven't I?" she asks with disappointment that blankets her voice. A rush of color floods my cheeks when I realize I stand before Sean with the face of a glamour queen, wearing gaudy snoopy pajamas. The hundred different shades of red that swathe my face must give me away, because he tries to hold back a laugh and fails.

"No Emily, they're ready for you, go on upstairs." My shaking finger points her towards the staircase. She smiles at me and squeezes through the small space between my back and the kitchen cabinet and glues her eyes on Sean.

"So Bri, that's a nice name," Sean says and releases my arm.

"Brianna, actually."

"Well, Brianna," he smiles. "I see you're busy. I'm sorry, I should have called first. I'll catch up with you another time."

Our eyes lose focus of each other, when I narrow my concentration on his full crimson lips. Lips I want to kiss now, but I know that would be stupid.

I suck in a deep breath to push the panic away. "Um …no, you don't have to leave," I plead. *Think Brianna, think!* "You should come up and meet my friends. Today's my birthday, so they're hanging out with me." I roll my eyes. "But they'll be leaving soon," I fib.

"Wow, I have great timing, happy birthday Brianna. No, it's ok. I think I'll take a rain check on whatever you have going on up there. Besides, I already had a makeover this morning. Can I call you tomorrow," he asks in his smooth hypnotic voice.

"Um yeah, sure, please call me tomorrow," I beg, like a desperate loser.

"Tomorrow then," he flashes me one last smile and turns towards the door.

I chew on my nails while I watch him walk across the patio. I want to run after him, I want to grab him and tie him up. I don't want my illusion anymore, I want him.

I watch while he turns the corner on the sidewalk and walks towards the driveway. I watch when his car backs slowly out of the drive, until it disappears from my view.

My mom's brow furrows, "Bri, are you ok? Who was that?"

"Oh. My. God. Mom. That was my future, and the most incredible guy I have ever met in my entire life." My mom shakes her head and smiles while I stagger up the staircase, feeling intoxicated.

Emily must have filled everyone in when she arrived upstairs, because when I walk into my bedroom everyone is silent. All eight eyes lock on me.

"Well?" Samantha finally pumps.

"Was that Sean?" Adrienne continues the grill.

I smile, one of those cheesy painful smiles. They all lunge from my bed screaming and tackle me with hugs, with exception to Nat.

"Come on, come on, what did he say?" Samantha presses, nervously twisting her hair.

"Um …I don't know. Oh my god, I think my brain shut down."

"Bri, he is freaking hot," Emily chirps.

"Damn it, I want to see what he looks like," Samantha adds. "I should have snuck down there and checked him out."

I feel Natalie's unrelenting stare from across the room. Her face tells a different story than the rest of my friends. She taunts, "Well, it's about time he got in touch with you."

Natalie is used to guys that fall at her feet; she would never have the patience to wait on a guy, no matter how special he might be. Of course, she also unearths a valid point. What is the reason he took three weeks to contact me? I must definitely be reading more into our special moment than he is.

I defensively snap back, "He said he would call me tomorrow; he didn't want to interrupt our party."

"Mmmkay," Natalie snips. "So you've waited like a month for this guy to call you, and he spent what, like five minutes with you. I hope you don't go another month before you hear from him again—that's all I'm saying."

Natalie's skepticism is a cancer that eats all of my happy thoughts. I feel her tension tug at my features. My thoughts about Sean will have to remain locked away. Where no one will destroy them.

"Emily, are you ready for your makeover?" I ask, while I turn my back to Natalie's opinion. Her pessimism has drained the room of exuberance. Everyone welcomes the abrupt subject change.

We give Emily her makeover and spend the rest of the evening twerking around my room like a bunch of idiots. After Emily leaves to go home, we all scatter sleeping bags around on my floor and talk until four in the morning about meaningless bullshit.

One by one they fall off into sleep. *Thank god.* When my room is finally quiet, I begin to dwell on Natalie's harsh observation. Why did Sean wait so long?

I am definitely putting more into our happenstance than he is. He probably already has a girlfriend, which would definitely explain the delay. God, what if I'm the reason for his reluctance? Maybe he simply isn't into me. Will I hear from him tomorrow? Will I hear from him ever again?

Exhausted, I close my eyes and fade into my dream world—*my perfect dreamworld.*

"Brianna, wake up." I feel a hand jiggle my shoulder, while I try to pry open my eyes.

"Brianna, wake up you bum!" I realize the voice that invades my dreams is Natalie.

"What ...what time is it?" I say hoarsely, while I stretch my arms and blink a few times to focus.

"It's ten o'clock; you need to get your ass up."

As my eyes dart around the room, I realize everyone has already packed up their stuff. Adrienne and Samantha sit on my bed and browse through my sketchbook. Nat sits on the floor next to me.

I see Samantha and Adrienne are off to a good start on their newfound friendship. Their camaraderie doesn't bother me as much as I thought it would, but I'm not sure why. Scrutinizing Natalie's behavior, I think the alliance is far more troublesome to her.

"You never opened my present last night, bitch," Natalie jokes and hands me the small package wrapped in shiny blue paper with a silver bow.

"I'm sorry Nat, I totally forgot," I apologize, and pull myself into a seated position on the floor.

I unwrap the box while Adrienne and Samantha slide down to the end of the bed to watch. Inside the box is a necklace. It is a silver circle with a cutout that displays one tiny gold shooting star. Around the circle are the words, "If you can imagine it, you can achieve it. If you can dream it, you can become it." I give Nat a hug. *Sounds like a Nike commercial.*

"This is super cute Nat. Thank you," I say while I hug her.

CHAPTER TEN

One by one my friends depart, until I am left alone, bored—and free to bask. I check and recheck my cell phone for missed calls to make sure I don't somehow miss his call. Nothing.

My day crawls by at a snail's pace. Tick tock, tick tock. I sit on my bed and stare at the blue screen and command it to ring—hour—by hour—by hour. I could have, or should have, found something constructive to do. My time would have passed by much quicker. The specks of lint scattered over my comforter begin to form mental pictures in my head.

I want to move, but I can't. Fear has me locked securely in place—fear that I may miss his call—fear that my mind won't be focused and clear. I know I have to impress him today. Our previous encounters have been ridiculously mute. This conversation needs to be just that, a conversation. If not, there is a good chance I won't ever hear from him again.

With every hour that passes, I fumble more and more with my phone. I check the ringer volume, the missed call log, my text messages—I find nothing. Morning turns into afternoon—afternoon turns into evening. Each passing hour brings me closer and closer to the certainty of rejection.

Natalie's harsh remarks echo through my mind. Maybe she is right; maybe it will be another month before I hear from him. Then the realization chokes me, like a wad of cotton. I may never hear from him again. Sean's brief visit with me yesterday may have told him everything he needed to know. When I look back, I can't find a reason why he would be impressed. I stood before him, a bumbling idiot, with ridiculous snoopy pajamas on—*fuck*!

As I replay our scene, something else occurs to me. How in the hell did Sean know where I live in the first place? I never gave his friend Cory my address. I only gave him my cell phone number. Everything about his visit is dejectedly suspicious. I try to put the pieces together and come up with an explanation why Sean would have my address. I can't find one—this is all too weird.

Looking back, Sean was surprised I was the reason for his visit. His comment, "It's you?" was more of a question than a statement. Everything comes into focus. My friends staged his entire visit—I am certain. When I review the facts, this mystery isn't hard to solve. All of my friends were here, gathered together. They used my birthday as their excuse. One of them is the mastermind. One of them called Sean and begged him to show up at my house—*manipulating little bitch*.

My head sinks into my lap, my palms squeeze my forehead tight. I pull my hands away and pound my fists into my mattress and search for something to throw. Everything I dreamed about and wished for over the past few weeks is now lost, forever. Who was the architect of this cruel plan? My intuition assures me it wasn't Adrienne. This isn't her style, plus Adrienne is far too self-absorbed to worry about my woes over a guy not calling.

Emily is completely out of the equation—but Samantha? I can see her convince herself she did a good deed. Was her addition of Emily to our little soirée a ploy to catch me off guard? Did she know I would assume Sean's arrival was Emily? SURPRISE!

82

But then again, what about Natalie? She has the means to contact Sean. Her cousin knows Sean; this would make it especially easy for her. Her negative energy may have been her way of saying—*dumbass, I had to pay him to show up. He's a jerk, like we tried to warn you.*

Honestly, it doesn't matter who devised the plan, it may well have been all of them—each having their own crucial part in the lie. The only thing that matters now is my delusion of Sean has been put to death—strung from the highest tree, stabbed in the heart, decapitated and de-limbed. Anything special between us is now a faded delusion—and maybe it always was. I am nothing more than some pathetic girl from Joplin who had a crush on him. He is probably laughing about me with his friends at this very moment. *Idiot!*

My cell phone slides across my night stand and tumbles to the floor. I escape the prison my bedroom has become. I need four new walls to stare at, and I need a hot bath. I stretch out in the hot water. "How can I be so fucking stupid?" I say aloud. My face is blanketed in the moist heat of a washrag. It works to sooth the burn my eyes now feel. I stay in the water until the tips of my fingers prune.

I don't often run to my mother with my issues, but tonight ...she is absolutely what I need. "Hey mom, when will dad be home?"

"Either late tonight, or tomorrow. He will be home for six days," her eye's twinkle.

Call it mother's intuition but she senses my demons before I open my mouth. "By the way, tell me about this boy who visited you yesterday; does he go to your school?"

"No, his name is Sean Gentry; he goes to Lamar."

"How on earth did you meet a boy from Lamar?" she questions.

"Remember the basketball tournament about a month ago? He sat behind me in the bleachers."

"Ah, well he is quite handsome and seems to be completely smitten by you. I swear the boy couldn't take his eyes off of you the entire time he was here."

Now, I am confused, "Really Mom, do you seriously think he is into me? I think his visit might be a setup by my so-called friends, big time bogus."

"Bri, why on earth would you think that? Why would they call some boy who lives thirty miles away and have him drive all the way down here to meet you as a joke. That doesn't make any sense."

"It's not like they tried to be mean. I think they did it to cheer me up. He's had my phone number for like three weeks and never bothered to call, so I've been kind of sad. *Kind of sad?...Liar!* Magically, he appears on my birthday while they're all here. Seems a little fishy—just sayin."

"That is odd it would take him so long to call, but I could tell by the way he stared at you, his visit wasn't forced."

"Not forced? He said he would call me today and it's like nine o'clock, not a word."

"The day's not over yet, patience Bri. You must like this boy?" she pumps and slides her arm around my shoulder to pull me in next to her.

"Yeah Mom, I've never liked anybody like this," I answer, staring down at my gnawed off thumbnails. I pull away from her grip and slowly stand, "I think I need to go to bed."

"Night Bri, everything will look better in the morning."

I pull myself up the staircase to my room, unsure what I should believe. Some questions will need to be answered by my so-called friends tomorrow, that much *is* certain. I slide under the covers and press back the tears, embarrassed, humiliated and lost. All of the magic is gone. Anything Sean may have thought about me is now tarnished ...if I was worth thinking about at all. I reach over to turn on my alarm and when I do my cell phone rings. My body slumps to the floor and I snatch it in my palm. This is a number I have never seen, but a prefix I pray is Lamar.

My heart is racing by the third ring, *pull yourself together—answer!* "Hello."

"Brianna?"

"Yeah."

"Hey, remember me? I'm the guy with incredibly bad timing that showed up on your doorstep yesterday."

That stupid uncontrollable cheesecake smile returns to my face. I am glad he can't see how school girl giddy I look right now. "Remember you?" I chuckle. "I don't think I'll ever forget you."

"Hmm—I'm not sure if that's a good thing or a bad thing, but either way I'll take it. How was your birthday? I feel stupid for interrupting."

"My birthday was fine. I secretly wished they would all leave, so you would stay longer." *God, I can't believe I said that...*

"Really?" I could hear the smile touch his voice. "I'll stay longer next time ...promise."

Next time? Score!

He continues, "I have to admit, as soon as I saw you, I was super nervous, so I'm kind of glad you were busy."

"You weren't the only one nervous," I say, with that stupid grin that digs so far into my cheeks now, they ache.

Our conversation over the phone flows much easier than I expect. I am not nearly as intimidated when I can't see his intense eyes focused on me. Our conversation becomes comfortable, like I've known him forever. Sean and I talk for over an hour about school, things we like, stuff we hate, music, TV shows, books, everything. I begin to feel confident that my friends were not behind yesterday's social call.

As we approach the end of hour two, I have to ask him, to be sure... "So Sean, I have a really stupid question."

"Shoot."

"Did my friends arrange for you to come and visit me yesterday?"

"What? No, why on earth would you think that?" he questions.

"Well a few reasons, but the big one, how in the hell did you know where I live? I only gave Cory my phone number. I sure don't remember handing out my address. Honestly, I don't think I even gave him my last name."

Sean chuckles, "Brianna, you wrote your phone number on the back of a deposit ticket. Your address, your phone number, and probably your height, weight, and social security number were on it."

My weight, no...no...no! I am horrified, but then I realize the last part is a joke. "Oh, did I?"

"You did. Now what's your other reason?"

"Well, so much time has gone by since I gave my number to Cory," I chew on my lip. "I mean, you took a really long time to contact me. I don't know—I thought maybe my friends finally intervened and begged you to come and see me. I guess I was pretty flaked out, I can't say I would blame them."

"You were flaked out?" *Oh good god Brianna, shut the fuck up!* "Really?" A smile touches his voice again, so I suck relief deep in my lungs. "Brianna, I'm not sure what you're talking about. Cory gave me your number Friday night. All he told me was he ran into some girl at a club that wanted me to call her. I had no idea you were the girl."

"Seriously? That's kind of bullshit, I gave him my number three weeks ago. Why did he wait so long?"

"I don't know. Maybe he forgot." Sean states.

"Yeah, maybe," I sigh. *Jerk!*

We talk on the phone for four hours. I reluctantly hang up the phone at one-thirty in the morning. I fluff up my pillow to go to sleep, my eyes are heavy. As my head begins to sink softly into the flannel pillowcase I realize, fate, destiny and love—are all things I now believe in.

CHAPTER ELEVEN

Four nights have come and gone since our four hour phone marathon. With each day that passes, the bright colors he painted my soul fade to black. Samantha asks everyday if he's called... today she doesn't ask. He likes me, I know he likes me, but something doesn't feel right. He has to have a girlfriend; this is the only explanation that makes sense.

So now what? Is it time to let go? Should I concede to defeat? —or is it time to put on my big girl panties and fight for him?

I can't afford to lose the few friends I have. They are growing weary of my constant mood swings, and I can't blame them. From an outsider's perspective, my behavior is absurd. My friends can't begin to understand this attraction the way it plays out in my mind. They can't feel, or see, or fathom the connection I have with him. To them this obsession is all nonsense, a crush gone bad.

Every instinct I have jabs at my heart and confirms what I already know. He is worth the fight. He is the one I'm meant to be with. I can't give up so easily.

My last class of the day feels like it will never end. My only reprieve ...today is Friday. During this final hour of my day, I sit and daydream about Sean. Is he also watching the clock, or is his girlfriend sitting at the desk next to him. Are they smiling at each other? Is he making plans with her for the weekend? I feel nauseas; the bell rings just in time.

When I pull into my driveway, there is an empty patch of gravel where my mom's car typically sits. This is weird, because my mom rarely leaves. Has something happened to Gramps? I squeeze the steering wheel with both hands and suck in a nervous breath.

The sidewalk seems longer than normal, while I stumble over a crack in the concrete. I throw open the door and toss my book bag on the counter. A note rests on the breakfast bar. My heart pounds out a rhythm in my gut, faster and heavier with every beat; I hold my breath and pray a silent prayer.

Bri and Ben,

Your dad and I are visiting your grandma and granddad. Your dad hasn't had a chance to see them for awhile. Not sure what time we'll be back. Some of the other family plans to come over. You know how they are when they all get together, it could be hours.

There's a pizza in the freezer. Don't burn the house down, finish your homework and be good!

Love Mom

The heavy breath I held breaks free from my lungs. I sling my book bag over my shoulder and climb the staircase to my room, taking two steps at a time. My book bag and jacket land in the center of my roughly made bed. I pull my favorite gray night shirt from the drawer and head to the bathroom.

My crappy day is in serious need of de-stress time. I push open the double glass doors that lead to my parent's bathroom. My mom has a huge tub—to soak away huge problems. I light some candles and dim the lights, before I slide out of my clothes. My long brown hair is piled on top of my head and I secure it with a big black clip. I sprinkle a handful of lavender bath salts in the hot steamy water and slide down into the fragrant fog.

The soft glow of the candles and sweet aroma of lavender soothe my spirit. In the dim candle light, waves of steam roll from my body like I am on fire. This trancelike state gives me insight to evaluate this constant ache in my gut, calmly. All of my fears and anxieties slowly slip away, piece by tiny broken piece. Is it the lavender and candles, or is my real remedy the decision I make, without realizing I make it?

I will call Sean tonight. I am tired of being the girl that hides in the bathroom. Somehow, I will muster up the courage to dial his number I saved in my phone five days ago.

The steam disappears, silently urging me to leave behind this feeling of quietude. If that isn't enough persuasion, now I hear a guitar screech through the wall I rest my head against. This intrusion reassures me my brother is home. Ben has only recently taken an interest in the guitar, so his riffs are more noise than music.

While the tub drains, I pat myself dry and pull my gray nightshirt over my head. I need to escape to my room, so I can muster up the courage I need to make this call. Funny, it sounded so much easier when I was floating in candlelight. I don't know what I'll say when I call, but I need answers—and I need them tonight.

Random strands of hair escaped from my clip, which left them drenched in lavender scented water. They drip onto the shoulders of my nightshirt now, and force a shiver up my spine. All I want is a blanket and the solace of my bedroom—*and for Ben to ease up on the fucking noise.* I quickly rinse out the tub and pitch my dirty clothes in a basket in the laundry room.

I start to head upstairs, but I hear Ben's guitar flail out an Aerosmith song I recognize. *Wow, my brother is getting all John Mayer on me; that's actually pretty good.* I walk down the short hall to his room to let him know I will be upstairs in case he needs anything and to tell him he's kicking some axe ass. I round the corner into his bedroom while Sean hands his guitar back to him. *Sweet jeezus!* I stumble backwards into the doorway and smack my head on the frame. "Ouch!"

"Way to go, klutz," my brother smirks, more interested in his guitar than the condition of my skull.

Sean smiles, "Are you ok?"

I shake my head yes, while I try to sink into the hole I dig around me. He turns back to my brother and demonstrates how to finger a chord on the song he is playing. *Deeper ...and deeper ...and deeper I go.* My brother picks his brain for another full minute while I inch my way back to the surface. I stare down at my hands that shake like a junky. *Stop it Bri! Damnit!* I glance up while Sean walks towards me; he licks his lips nervously and smiles. He has this little dimple in the corner of his mouth, I can't stop looking at. "I hope you don't mind I stopped by."

"What?" I shake my head and let his words sink in. "Um ...no, I don't mind at all," I reply, stuttering my way through the words. I realize I am once again dressed in pajama's, only this time it's my ragged grey night shirt, *oh god.* My hair is piled haphazardly on my head and I don't have a stitch of makeup on. *Awkward!*

"I can't stay very long, but I had to see you."

"Why can't you stay?" I plead, already conspiring to kidnap him. Images of him confessing his love for his girlfriend poison my happy thoughts.

"I have to work tonight, but I don't have to be there for a couple of hours."

"We can go up to my room and hang out," I tell him while I wince away from my brothers screeching guitar.

He eyeballs me with concern, "Are you sure that's ok? I don't want to piss off your parents."

"We can hang out in my room, my parents are cool with that." I reply, unsure if this is the truth or a lie. I have never taken a guy to my room before—I've never had a guy hang out at my house before. "Besides, they won't be back until long after you leave." Princess Jezebel raises her eyebrows and flutters her long lashes. *Take your mind out of the gutter...tramp!*

We climb the staircase slowly; he gnaws on his thumbnail unearthing his apprehension. When we walk into my room, he looks away from my bed and turns his focus to my stereo instead. "Damn, you have a ton of music," he gushes.

I explain, "My dad's a musician, so he has like a boatload of cool music. I grew up listening to a lot of the older stuff—classic rock, grunge. I totally snag my favorites from him. He has so much; I don't think he notices."

Sean pulls out Fleetwood Mac, Rumors and sticks the disc into my CD player. He turns the volume down low, like I do. *Ghaaa, we have so much in common.*

"So, you have a job?" I ask while he walks the perimeter of my room and avoids my bed like it is possessed and will levitate any second.

He slides down the wall and takes a seat on the floor next to my stereo. His knees pull into his chest. "You act surprised. Some of us have to pay for our own cars and gas, Brianna."

Because I am undeniably defensive, one of my many shortcomings, I rebut, "I pay—," but then I stop, because truthfully I don't pay for anything, at least not yet. "Well ok, I don't pay yet, but I plan on finding a job this summer," I shrug my shoulders and sit on the floor next to him and tuck my knees under my nightshirt.

He grins, his eyes wander through my soul. *That damn dimple is there again.* We sit and awkwardly stare into each others eyes—maybe awkward isn't the right word...trancelike is better. It takes exactly ten full seconds for my body to feel weightless, like I am floating through my room, watching myself through my own eyes.

I look away quickly to break the stupor. I suck in a nervous breath and continue with my defense, "You *are* older than me; you told me you were a senior. Plus …you're a boy."

"I'm a boy?" He chuckles. "You seriously want to play the gender card in the twenty first century—and older, come on," he rolls his gorgeous dark brown come kiss me eyes. "I'm a year older than you and I've had a job since I was sixteen. I do believe you are seventeen. I wanted a car and that was the only way I would have one. I would wager my next paycheck that you were given a car."

I can tell by the tone of his voice he is playing, but I don't want to continue this debate with him. Our limited time doesn't need to be wasted on finger pointing, especially when it can be spent kissing. I decide not to call foul to anymore of his responses. Instead, I attempt to change the subject.

"You didn't call me this week because you had to work?"

"Brianna, I realize you have like no responsibility, which is cool. I, however, have to work and pay for my own shit, so yeah ...I'm pretty damn busy." *Ok bullshit, how is the subject eternal?* Sean isn't angry as much as he's frustrated. "I don't have a cell phone, because if I did I would pay for that too. You live in Joplin, so calling you won't be free on our archaic land line. At least it's a better rate after nine, because I guarantee my parents will hand over the long distance bill when it comes, too. I think the four hour phone marathon we had last Sunday will be a pretty good start to that bill. This sucks that you live so far away," he leans forward and rests his elbows on his knees.

My shoulders fall towards the floor, now I feel bad. Somehow, Sean makes me see myself different than I ever have before. My parents are pretty poor, compared to a lot of my classmates. My dad's a musician, for god's sake. In Sean's world, I have a silver spoon. Maybe, I have

95

taken for granted everything I am blessed with. As much as I hate the picture he paints of me, I'm totally relieved this is the reason he hasn't called. I say the only thing I can say, "I'm sorry."

"Brianna, what are you sorry for? That's not the point. You're worth the extra effort—you're worth the extra expense," he says softly. He grabs my hands and cradles them between his own. I feel the tremble wain when he tucks my head into his chest and slides his arms around my shoulders. His touch is strong and warm like the sun, but I still can't control the shaking.

"Are you cold?" He pulls me closer.

"I'm not sure, maybe a little."

He pulls his arm away from my shoulder and pushes himself from the floor. This is not the outcome I was after. He yanks the throw from the end of my bed and turns to me with his panty dropping grin. I can't stop the obvious shivers from running the full length of my spine. Without his warmth next to me I begin to feel the chill of my damp nightshirt pressed against my shoulders and back. Then again, completely dry I probably would have chills. *God, he's so hot.*

I can't help but stare at him while he lowers himself down and takes a seat against my footboard, away from the clutter of cd piles. "Are you going to sit by me, or do I need to pick you up and carry you over here?" He teases and pats the floor next to him. The mental image of being swept off my feet is enticing, but I cast-off the temptation.

I suck in my smile while I crawl the few feet across the floor that separates us. I slide in next to him and leave a small space between us. He quickly fills the gap and wraps the throw around me and tucks every inch around every corner of my body. He reaches around and pulls me back onto his chest and caresses my shoulder gently. The blanket and warmth of his body calm my tremors, but I want the soft chenille wall between us to dissolve completely away.

"I have to work tomorrow, but I was thinking, maybe Sunday I can pick you up and we can go do something together. My friend Cory thinks your friend is cute, maybe we can all go hang out, I mean, no pressure," he offers, chewing on his bottom lip.

I pull my face from his chest to peek into his eyes, his deep dark crystal eyes. "I would love that—but which friend is he talking about? I had three friends with me the night I met him."

"Hell, I don't know. I don't think the choice matters much, Cory isn't too picky."

The situation feels a little awkward, considering I was the one Cory actually hit on. I'm sure he probably means Samantha, but will she be offended that she is his second choice?

"Samantha can be his date. I'm pretty sure that is who he's referring to."

He glances down at me and shrugs his shoulders, "Ok." He continues, "Can I pick you up around two, Sunday?"

"That works for me, where are we going?"

"I think I'll surprise you, if that's ok."

I giggle, "You don't know, do you?"

"No ...no fucking clue," he releases his laugh.

"That's ok, I like surprises."

We talk...and talk ...and talk some more. Time rushes by and I want it to slow down—or stop altogether. I am not ready for him to leave, but I know he will.

When it's almost time, his warm fingers slide beneath my chin and pull my cheek from his heart until our eyes meet. My body is tense while he runs his hand up the back of my neck...goose bumps swathe my entire body. *Sweet jeezus!* His fingers lace through my hair until his grip is firm on the clip that holds my hair loosely piled on my head. He pulls it free and my hair tumbles down my back and over my shoulders in thick feral waves.

He has sucked all of the oxygen from my room. I can barely breathe.

He leans into me until his lips meet my forehead. My lips are like radar—they hone in on their target. I am afraid to move my head. I don't need to, because his mouth slowly works its way to mine. The closer our lips pull together, the harder my heart pounds in my chest. When they finally touch, it is like fire and gasoline—that explodes in unison. Not only does he kiss my lips, but he kisses my soul, like I have never been kissed. His hands cup my cheeks while his fingers begin to weave in and out of my hair. At that moment, nothing in the world exists or matters, except him.

CHAPTER TWELVE

I rise from my bed Saturday morning with a huge satisfied smile that covers my entire face. This will be the best weekend of my life.

I pull on a pair of jeans and a neon orange oversized t-shirt. I can't muster up enough concentration to deal with my hair or makeup, so I gather my hair in a ponytail and tuck it under a ball cap. I know Sean works today, so there will be no surprise visit. *All he's ever seen you in is pajama's anyway, idiot!*

I quickly scan my room, and touch the spot where Sean sat last night. Did I think he might magically appear, I don't know …maybe? Instead, the carpet is cold and empty.

I skip down to the kitchen to spend a little time with my mom and dad before I have to rush off to my grandparents. They must have had a late night. Mom still has a wrinkle that runs down the left side of her face, left from her pillow. Dad's hair looks like a spooked cat. They pour their first cup of coffee.

"How was your evening?" I pry while I pour a glass of orange juice.

"Apparently too much fun," my dad answers and digs his fingertips into his forehead. "Spending time with everyone was great. I feel like I don't have time to see anyone these days," my dad grumbles. "That brings me to ask you a favor Bri," he continues. "My band plays in Springfield tonight and some of the family talked about coming out. They want your grandmother to come with us. They think she could use a night away from Dad. She is under a lot of stress," he works to convince me—like I don't already know this.

"What's the favor?" I pose.

"Can you spend the night with your granddad? This sacrifice would mean the world to me, favorite daughter."

"Of course I can. No problem."

"Well, I think your cousin Amanda is staying too. I thought you could handle this yourself, but your grandmother freaked the hell out about you being there alone. She wouldn't even consider leaving unless you had someone with you. What's up with that, Bri?" His eyes study my expression.

I wonder myself why Grams would not trust me with Gramps. I have been helping her faithfully, for months now. I am completely capable. I dig for excuses, "Maybe she thinks I'll need some help if I have to move Gramps."

"Yeah maybe, but she was really freaked. I have to say Bri, I didn't think she would give in and go. You haven't went over there every weekend to be a nuisance, have you? Please tell me you help Mom, and don't make things worse for her," his unshaven face glares at me over his coffee cup.

I feel my defensive tackle build—here it comes. I want to shout, *at least I make an effort to help her, that is more than I can say for you.* I am glad I snatch my snarky remarks before they escape.

Grams is still frightened by what happened to her a few weeks ago. She hasn't mentioned her fears anymore, so I assumed it was an isolated event. Maybe it wasn't. If this is the reason she's skeptical, I sure as hell can't tell my father. I don't want him to think she is losing it—even if she is.

"Dad, you can believe what you want, but I am helping. I love them both and I would never go over and be a burden to them. Grams is probably worried about being away from him for so long. You have no idea how much she loves him."

"Yes, I have every idea, but she needs this break Bri; this will do her some good."

"I already said I would," I snip.

I don't like the tone the conversation has taken. I make a wise decision. I am far too happy about my prior evening to let my dad's ritualistic morning pessimism bring me down. I grab my jacket and head for the door.

My mom looks up at me, "Are you leaving already?"

"Yep, I have to stop by and talk to Samantha, and I'm going to go *help* Grams, she will have a lot to do if she's going out this evening."

My dad's grumpy unshaven face eyeballs me, "Leaving this early will make for an awfully long day with your granddad."

"I have no problem spending time with my gramps, my time is certainly not awful," I say, while I close the door behind me.

I hear his faint voice through the closed door while I walk across the patio, "I never said her day would be awful, I said awfully long, you heard me right, didn't you Angie?"

I hate to argue with my dad, because I miss him when he's away. But ...he has this maddening way of provoking my defensive armor. Hell, he's probably the reason I have defensive armor. Dreaming about Sean is a much more productive way to spend my time, at least until I pull into Samantha's driveway.

CHAPTER THIRTEEN

I should have taken the time to call Samantha before I left my house, but leaving the drama my father creates is all I could focus on.

Samantha is surprised to see me. She is excited to go out with Cory, which makes perfect sense. She's the one who thought he was hot in the first place. The whole situation still feels a little awkward to me. I'm just glad I didn't kiss him.

Samantha doesn't want to complicate things by telling her parents she is on a date. She wants to come over and hang out at my house until Cory and Sean pick us up. This has become a predictable habit.

A big part of me loves knowing Samantha and Cory will be with us tomorrow. Our date should be more relaxed, especially since I can't communicate when he looks at me. Yet another part, doesn't want to share my Sean time with anyone, not even one of my best friends. Will he kiss me again with Samantha and Cory around? I begin to dislike the double date agenda more and more.

The sound of gravel under my tires tells me I am driving up my grandparent's lane. I don't remember a single detail of my trip. My mind is that far gone. When I step out of my car, I realize what a beautiful day it is. I lift the rim of my ball cap up to allow the sun to shine on my face. The glow is warm and comforting, like my evening with Sean. The temperature has to be in the upper sixties today, unusual, but not unheard of for this time of year.

I enter Gram's kitchen to find her doing dishes from last night's festivities. "Hi Grams, let me help you with those," I say, while I approach her. *I can't believe they left this mess for her, losers!*

"Oh Bri, you're here early today," Grams responds.

"Well, I heard you have a hot date tonight, so we have lot's to do!" I smile and catch the glimmer in her eyes.

After we clean her kitchen, I feed some eggs and a protein shake to my gramps. I take her rugs out and shake them, and sweep her floors. Time ticks by at a steady pace. I start a load of laundry for her, but decide to leave the rest. It will give me something to do tonight while the family gets their party on.

Grams fixes me a BLT sandwich for lunch, and we sit down and catch up on the past two weeks. Gramps days have all been bad lately. He is becoming weaker. Concern is deeply imbedded into Grams' weary face.

I thought I would escape, but her crazy talk begins. "Bri, I don't think your granddad will be around much longer, their presence is getting stronger," Grams conveys, while her eyes glare into her coffee cup. *Here we go again—more ghost bullshit.* "You know, death is ok though, I've accepted our fate. Your granddad and I have been blessed with the life we've shared. Now it's time for us to move to a better place."

"What? Whoa ...Grams, what on earth are you talking about with this we, us crap. You will be around for a very long time, forever maybe."

"Bri, no I won't, and watch your language. If something happens to your granddad, there's nothing here for me anymore. I'm not afraid to die as long as I'm with him. I've accepted this and truthfully, I embrace it. I'm tired Brianna, that's the simple hard truth."

"Please don't talk like this. I need you! It's hard enough to think about losing Gramps; I can't lose you too, especially when there's nothing wrong with you."

Grams is silent, but her determined stare reveals everything. Physically, she is in great shape. I am sure she will be with us much longer than she hopes, determined or not.

This death talk is awkward so I change the subject, "So I hear Amanda is staying with me this evening?"

"You heard right. You will not stay here by yourself."

Addressing my dad's concerns, I ask, "Grams, don't you trust me to take care of Gramps by myself?"

"Don't be silly. You are quite capable of taking care of your granddad. I have every confidence in you."

"Then I don't understand, why does Amanda need to be here?"

She thinks hard about what she wants to say before she replies, "Brianna, my concerns don't lie with you. Weird things happen in this old house. I'm not sure I even want you here with Amanda, but your dad and Uncle Rick insist I go tonight. I promise you, I won't be out late."

"Have other things happened to you, since that first night with the Piano?"

Grams' eyes are serious and strangely sane, "Let's say I believe someone, or something is here, waiting—hovering over your granddad like a damn vulture." Her eyes stare through me for several seconds before she continues. "I won't tell you everything that's happened, because I don't want to frighten you. I will tell you that you and Amanda need to stick together tonight. Play a game or watch a movie and I'll be home as soon as I can."

"Ok Grams, we will ...and we'll be fine. I want you to have fun tonight and not worry about us. If anything happens we know how to use the phone."

After our lunch, we clean up Gramps. This task takes less effort with each passing week. As time slips by, Gramps withers away and grows lighter and more frail. All of his brittle bones are exposed, with a lose layer of thin skin that barely protects them.

After I clean Grams' bathroom for her, I dig her makeup out of the drawer. When I walk into the kitchen, I see the concern in her topaz eyes. "Grams, I need you to sit on this stool. I'm going to make you look like a movie star for your big night on the town."

The sparkle returns to her eyes and she smiles at me, "This old lady is no movie star, but if you think you can make me look like one, who am I to argue. Let's go pick out what I'm going to wear first."

We climb the staircase to her bedroom and walk into the long row of clothes that hang in her eve style walk in closet. I am positive some of her outfits are thirty years old. We thumb through dozens of outfits before we pick a navy blue pant suit. We find a silk blouse with wide brush strokes of navy and royal blue on a background of white.

I dig out her navy shoes. Once she is dressed we climb back downstairs to begin her transformation.

I sit her down on the stool and rub some lotion on her already velvety soft skin. While the lotion soaks in, I fix her a cup of coffee. Over the course of the next thirty minutes I apply her makeup, taking my time. I want her to look amazing, since she has not been out for such a long time.

"Oh my Grams, you are the bomb! You will have every eye in the place on you."

She smiles in the mirror, but then frowns, "Not if we don't do something with this hair."

I pull her hair out of the bun she had thrown it in this morning. I brush through the black thinning locks longer than I need to, because I see how much she enjoys being pampered. I redo her bun for her and plaster it with hairspray, so it won't fall out.

When I am finished, she again peeks in the mirror and smiles, "Brianna, you did make me look like a movie star."

It is nice to see her happy, with all of the suffering she is silently living. Maybe a night out of this house will end this silly talk of her end being near.

We sit down at the kitchen table to relax before my uncle comes to pick her up and drop off my cousin. I refill her coffee and pour myself a glass of apple juice out of the fridge.

"Brianna, what have you been doing lately? Are there any cute boys in your life?"

Oh my god Grams, you have no idea! This feels like the perfect time to tell Grams about Sean. "I have met the most incredible guy, Grams. His name is Sean, and he's so freaking cute and smart. He makes me feel like I will faint every time I hear his voice, or see his face, or think about him."

"Well, that's lovely dear. Does he go to school with you?"

"No, he goes to high school in Lamar, he's a senior. I have never met anyone in my life that makes me feel like he does. The first time I saw him was similar to your first night with Gramps. We couldn't pull our eyes from each other. We have our first *real* date tomorrow."

Grams places her shaky gentle hand over mine, "Ah, my dear, you will never forget the moment your eyes first met. Trust me, you will never forget. Did you know your granddad was from Lamar?"

"No! Are you kidding me? See Grams, it is fate."

Her tone tightens, "Don't you dare put this boy off, so you can come over and spend your Saturdays with us. The special ones don't come along often, sometimes only once."

"That's the thing Grams, he works most Saturdays, see how perfect he is. It's a little scary."

"Scary ...hogwash, that's love. The truth about love, your first real love is the strongest. You go into your first love believing love is forever. For me, that belief came true. I married my first love. Our forever lasted a mighty long time, but I guess nothing is truly forever. He lies in that bed in there and our forever shrivels away to nothing. Even though I understand these limits, I wouldn't trade one single day of my life I've shared with him. Keep your heart open and don't be afraid to love him back, because your love for him will never die, not completely. Is he a good kisser?" Grams probes, while a mischievous grin fills her face.

I turn one hundred shades of red, "Yes Grams, his kisses are as magical as he is."

"That's important you know Brianna, can't go through life with a bad kisser." *Seriously, she didn't just say that!* "These things matter. You've made him sound wonderful, I'm happy for you. You sacrifice so much of yourself; you deserve some happiness of your own. I hope I meet this young man someday."

"I'm not sure what he has planned for us tomorrow, but maybe…"

"Not tomorrow, I'm going out tonight. I need my wits about me if I meet the love of your life."

"Another time then Grams, I promise."

Uncle Rick and Amanda walk through the door and end any further "*Sean*" conversation.

"Look at you Mom, aren't you a hot little number," Uncle Rick proclaims, while he wraps his arms around her.

"Hey Amanda, long time no see," I say to my cousin, while the conversation continues between the adults.

"We better leave if we're going to find a good table," Uncle Rick states, when he grabs Grams' coat off of her coat hook.

Grams sends one last stern glance in my direction, "Brianna, remember what I said about sticking together. The refrigerator has some leftovers you can feed your granddad tonight and there are some frozen dinners in the freezer. I'll be home early, so I prefer you stay up until I'm back, if you can manage." Grams hugs me when she walks by, "I love you."

"Love you too Grams. Have fun, everything will be fine."

I watch while my grams climbs into Uncle Rick's car, she looks beautiful. This will be a good night for her.

CHAPTER FOURTEEN

I sense Amanda's eyes on me while I watch Grams and her father back out of the driveway. She feels out of place, out of her comfort zone. Although she is older, she follows my lead.

I like Amanda. As young kids, most of my cousins and I played together every Sunday. My grandparents always hosted Sunday dinner on their farm and this was a huge family event. Amanda and I were close growing up, but now we are both at an awkward age, and we haven't seen each other for close to a year. I know she is probably more nervous than I am, since she hasn't been around much since Gramps stroke. I need to break the ice with her.

"So, Amanda what have you been doing since you graduated? I haven't seen you in forever, it seems."

Her shoulders relax and she sits down at the table, "I take a few classes at the community college and work mostly. You're a senior this year, aren't you?"

I correct her, "No, a junior, but I can graduate early next year if I want to."

We continue to chat, while I heat up some left over mashed potatoes and noodles for Gramps. I ask if she is seeing anyone, but this is a sore subject. Amanda is more interested in rehashing some of her favorite childhood memories. We share a few laughs together and rewind the clock back a year.

When Gramps' food is hot, I head into the living room, Amanda follows close behind. She spots a crossword puzzle book that sits on the end table, next to the couch. She grabs a pencil, flips through the book, and finds an empty puzzle. I lower the side rail on Gramps' bed and pull the stool up next to where his head rests on his pillow.

Maybe Grams is right. Gramps looks awful. His face is a blank colorless canvas with cheekbones that protruded far above the sinking dark holes where his jolly fat cheeks used to be. He slept most of the day, and I need to wake him to feed him his dinner.

When I wake him, his eyes are wide, startled maybe, but more frightened. He stares at me through terrified eyes while I spoon in the small bites of mashed up noodles and potatoes. I want to calm his fear, but I know he won't understand anything I might say to him. He finishes about half of the cup I fixed him before he starts to fling his arms at me, like he is swatting a bothersome fly. I bring his cup of water up to his mouth and gently pushed the straw between his lips. He still swats at me, but manages to take a few sips.

I see Amanda's reflection in the picture window; she continues to glance up at me, while I take care of Gramps. I'm not sure if the expression on her face is envy or confusion, but she never offers to help.

I lift Gramps' head to fluff his pillows back up and gently lowered him back down. He rolls his head away from me and stares blankly out the window. The sun has already set; consequently I'm not sure what he thinks he might see. I raise the rail back up on his bed and watched him while he stares out the window and mumbles in a whisper. He reaches out for something that isn't there with his feeble fingers.

As I watch him, something catches the corner of my eye in the reflection on the glass. I squint until it comes into focus. In an instant, I am paralyzed, I can't move. Fear shrouds me like a cold torrential rain that soaks your clothes, leaving them clingy and wet. I stand and shake with my hands gripping the rail of the bed.

I hear Amanda's voice whisper on the outskirts of my mind, she repeats her question, this time louder, "Bri, do you know a ten letter word for soup that starts with an M and ends in an E?" I try to answer her, but can't. I stand there and tremble.

Amanda pulls herself up off of the sofa; she must sense something isn't right. She walks to my side and examines Gramps. He still grabs for something in the air above his head. Amanda's eyes follow the path my eyes focus, because a few seconds later she clings to the rail and starts to tremble with me.

Several feet behind us, I see the reflection of a woman; her face is pale like ivory. She brushes her long black hair in slow even strokes. Her face is beautiful ...inhumanly beautiful. She stands there and watches, or waits ...I can't tell. Then, she vanishes.

I slowly turn and face the wall behind us. I am already certain I won't find anything, and my instinct is correct.

"Minestrone," I whisper while my wide eyes lock with Amanda's.

"What?"

"Ten letter word for soup."

"Bri, what the hell was that? I know you saw it too."

I take a few seconds to gather my composure. I grab Amanda's hand and lead her to the couch. I don't know if this gesture is to comfort her, or to comfort me.

"I have no idea what that was, or maybe I should say who that was, but I think we should keep this between us. Grams is under a lot of stress. She doesn't need to be scared in addition to all the worry she already lives daily. Besides, nobody will believe us anyway." I know this last part is a complete lie, because Grams would definitely believe us.

"I'm scared Brianna, I don't want to stay here. I want to go home."

"Amanda, you're free to go home if you want. To be honest, I'd appreciate it if you stayed. We could watch some TV, or work on a crossword puzzle together. I don't want to be here by myself."

I honestly don't care if Amanda leaves, *well maybe a little*. My biggest fear is Grams coming home to find me alone. She would know something went wrong. I don't need her to feel guilty for having fun tonight. She needs a night like this to move past her grim reaper bullshit talk. If she gains knowledge of what happened, she will never leave for the evening again.

"I don't know Bri, I'm scared. Aren't you scared? Isn't there someone we could call to come over, so we can both leave?"

"I'm scared too, but I don't think whoever, or whatever we saw was here to hurt us. Maybe what we saw was an angel that looks out for Gramps." This sounds as good as any other possible explanation. "We can talk about what we saw if talking makes you feel better."

"An angel, I never thought of that. What if it does want to hurt us?"

"Amanda, it didn't feel that way—besides, she's gone now. How about this, if anything else happens tonight I will call someone and I will take you home myself, but for now, let's see if we can stick it out. Grams needs this night."

"Ok, if you're willing to stick this out, I guess I can try too."

I pick up the crossword puzzle Amanda worked on and between the two of us, we finish the puzzle in no time. We fly through three more crossword puzzles together, snuggled under a throw on the couch. Neither of us moves from the sofa, not to eat, not to drink, not even to take a bathroom break. Grams said to stick together. If Amanda was any closer, she would be in my lap.

Finally bored with the puzzles, we begin to talk. I tell Amanda about Sean, but leave out all of the obsessive infatuation that would make me look pathetic. I'm not sure she is sincerely interested, but she needs the conversation to make our time pass more quickly.

Grams and Uncle Rick return home at eleven-fifteen. Amanda jumps off of the couch, like the cushion is on fire. I walk up to give her a hug, after she throws her jacket on, and whisper in her ear, "Just between us, ok?"

Amanda shakes her head yes, but I'm not sure she can keep our secret. She and Uncle Rick walk out the door and climb into his car ...and they are gone.

"How did your evening go Brianna? Was everything ok?" Grams asks, while she hangs her coat on the hook in the kitchen.

"Everything was fine Grams. I had fun hanging out with Amanda. Gramps ate most of his food and he's been pretty quite all night."

"Are you going home now?"

"No Grams, it's late, I'll stay here with you and head home in the morning ...if you don't mind."

"That would be lovely," she gives me a grateful smile. After tonight, I can only guess what kind of fear cradles her to sleep every night.

"How was your evening, did you have fun?" I ask while we climb the staircase to her bedroom.

"I had a wonderful time, thank you for being here. Will the noise bother you if I turn the TV on low dear?"

"Not at all, I usually turn on my stereo when I go to bed. The noise is comforting." *It drowns out the creepy noises my house makes in the middle of the night.*

Grams smiles back at me while she pushes the power button of the television. I slip out of my shoes and my jeans and climb into her bed. She slides in next to me, after she has changed out of her fancy clothes and into her nightgown. Grams wraps her arm around me and drifts immediately to sleep. She looks peaceful. Maybe because I am with her, or maybe she is simply wore out.

I lay awake for one...two...three...hours and listen to Grams' light snore and the soft voices on the television. Images of tomorrows date with Sean spin through my head like a leaf caught in a maelstrom. This is our first *real* date and I want it to be perfect.

Pictures of the woman in the glass interrupt my glorious illusions. Is she here to take Gramps away from us like my grandmother fears?

Grams' words, from earlier that day haunt me. Why does she feel certain both of their times are near? Am I ready to lose my grandparents—this thought petrifies me. I think about all of these things for hours, but finally drift to sleep.

CHAPTER FIFTEEN

The smell of Grams' cooking trickles up the staircase. "Oh crap, what time is it?" I roll over to glance at the clock that reads nine o'clock.

My date with Sean is a few hours away; I don't have time for breakfast.

I slide on my jeans and brush through my hair before I head downstairs, skipping every other step. "Good morning, Grams."

"Morning Bri, I made you some breakfast."

I want to turn down her offer, but after a good whiff of sausage, my stomach cries out *I'm hungry*. Amanda and I were so caught up in fear last night, we forgot to eat. "Thanks Grams."

She loads my plate with a high stack of pancakes, scrambled eggs, and sausage patties. She starts to crack open more eggs for Gramps, but I stop her. "Grams, I'm all about breakfast, but I can't eat all of this. You have enough food for three people on this plate."

I grab two small plates out of her cupboard and start to divvy up portions. "Well alright Bri, but I don't want you to be hungry."

"Trust me; I won't be hungry if I eat all of this."

I finish all of my breakfast and offer to feed Gramps, but Grams insists on doing it herself.

"Are you sure you don't need me to do anything for you, before I go?" I ask, feeling guilt ridden for leaving notably quick.

"No, you go home and get ready for your date; Aunt Rachael will be here in a couple of hours." Aunt Rachael helps my grandmother every Sunday.

I hug Grams goodbye and head out the door. When I climb into my car I notice what a beautiful day is on the horizon. The sun is intense and the air smells like springtime. "Sweet," I say aloud, while I put the car in reverse.

Sean kidnaps my every thought. The terror of last night is a distant memory in comparison.

This is our first real date. This is also the first time he will meet Samantha. What the hell was I thinking? Samantha is way prettier than I am. He has seen Natalie several times and must not be impressed. He didn't notice Adrienne the night at the tournament. But, Samantha—the golden goddess! *Damnit!*

I pull into my driveway and the sense of urgency to get ready for my date has vanished. I don't want to leave the comfort of my car. I have created a complete disaster. Sean will think Samantha is beautiful—because she is. I will pale in comparison. Rule number one, never take someone better looking than you on your first date...*amateur move Bri!* I consider calling Samantha to tell her I am sick. I can call Sean and tell him Samantha is sick, so Cory will have to hang out with her another time.

The only thing worse than bringing someone better looking along on your first date, is starting your relationship with a lie. I bang my head lightly on the steering wheel, "Are you going to hide your friends from him forever?" I speak out loud. I'm stuck—I have to go through with our plan.

I walk into our house and I don't see my dad, I assume he is still in bed from his gig last night. Mom is dusting the living room. I yell hello to her before I head for the staircase.

I glance at my clock, it is already ten. I only have three hours before Samantha will be here. I thumb through my closet and scrutinize my outfits, trying to find something perfect. This task would be simpler if I knew where we were going.

I dig through my drawers for my favorite pair of faded blue jeans, the only pair that fit just right. I grab a white camisole and toss them on my bed. I pull a faded denim shirt from my closet to wear over my camisole, since the weather can change on a dime this time of year. As long as we don't go to some fancy restaurant, this outfit should be fine.

I head for the bathroom to shower, before I change my clothes. I spend more time than usual applying makeup and brushing my hair. I laugh out loud and wonder what Natalie would say if she was watching me this morning.

I slide into my camisole and jeans and examined myself in the full length mirror on the back of the bathroom door. *God, why can't I be built like Samantha!* She is tall and has long, perfect legs. Why do I have to be short? *Thanks Randy and Angie.*

I am ready, just as the doorbell rings. I run to answer the door to find Sean and Cory, not Samantha whom I expect. *Sweet Jeezus, breath Bri!*

I feel my smile, this reaction is involuntary. I can almost see the *I Am Cheesy* sign that flashes on my forehead. "Come in, come in," I motion to them while I stand in the doorway.

"Wow, you look amazing!" Sean says, flashing his dimples down at me.

"At least I don't have on pajamas this time," I say, in a quiet voice my mother can't overhear.

He grabs my arm and whispers into my ear, "You look pretty fucking hot in old nightshirts and snoopy flannels too," he confesses, kissing my cheek before he pulls away.

"I'm sorry, sit down please," I say, pointing to the breakfast bar. "Samantha isn't here yet, but she should be here anytime."

My mother walks in to inspect Sean further. "Brianna, are you going to introduce me to your friends?"

"Mom, this is Cory." I point him out to her without peeling my eyes from Sean's. "And this ...this is Sean," I smile. "This is my mother, Angie."

"Are you kids going somewhere today or do you plan to hang out here?" she pumps, biting her lip nervously.

I suddenly understand her line of questioning. She doesn't want Sean to meet my dad—not today. He played last night and he can be especially irritable after a gig. The risk of this happening has me in a panic. My father has never met any of my boyfriends. Of course, I haven't really had any to meet. I'm not sure what his reaction would be. Would he be rude and ask all of the stupid questions fathers find appropriate? Would he try to embarrass or intimidate him? *God, what if he pulls out Gramps old gun! Samantha needs to hurry.*

"We're leaving as soon as Samantha gets here." I answer, while I glance impatiently out the dining room window towards the driveway.

"Oh, that's nice. Where are you off to?" My mom grills. This was a question I am curious to hear the answer to myself. I wait for Sean's reply.

"Mrs. Hart, I'm not completely sure, but since it's such a nice day I thought we would start out down by Shoal Creek Falls and do some hiking. Then, we'll probably stop and eat somewhere this evening. I will have Brianna home at a respectful hour; around ten, if that's ok."

I can't help but admire the way Sean is consciously respectful to my mom. I find more and more reasons to like him. *Samantha, damnit please hurry up!*

My mom continues her conversation with Sean, "First of all, my name is Angie, you may call me Mrs. Hart when I'm sixty five. No...on second thought, not even then. And Sean, I think that sounds like a wonderful day. You kids have fun."

She returns to the living room, which is a relief, yet her reaction also makes me question whether she understands how important Sean is to me. Wouldn't she want to know more about the man I will be with for eternity? Then again, my mom has never been one to hover.

"Hey, it's nice out, why don't we wait for Samantha outside?" I suggest. I don't want my dad to wake up to strange voices and cause a scene.

"Sounds good to me. So, when is she supposed to be here? I'm ready to get this party started," Sean smiles, his dimples dig into the corner of his mouth. I want to run up and kiss them.

"Well, you are early, which is a good thing. She said she would be here around one, so she should be here anytime. I'm going up to grab a jacket for later; I'll meet you on the patio."

I race up the stairs quickly, so I can spend every second that ticks by with Sean. I grab my white Northface jacket, my cell phone and twenty dollars from my dresser. I quickly shove everything in my jacket pocket and glance at my reflection in the mirror again. What does this completely hot, totally awesome guy see in me? The mirror reveals nothing special. *Ok Bri, pull yourself together now, be cool. He's so, oh my god, beautiful!*

I fly back down the stairs and out to the patio to be with Sean. When I step through the door, Samantha is walking up the sidewalk towards the patio. She looks nervous and awkward. I want to run up to her and rescue her from this feeling I completely understand.

"Hi Sam!" I call out to her.

I see her lips pull up in a smile that reaches her kind pale green eyes. I almost feel the weight of her insecurity lifted from her shoulders. *Seriously, why is Samantha insecure? She is totally gorgeous!* Her fear doesn't make sense to me.

Sometimes, Samantha and I are too much in tune. Sam is wearing a white tee shirt and a faded denim shirt unbuttoned over her faded blue jeans. Our wardrobe looks totally planned. She has her hair pulled back in a loose pony tail with a few strands that lay loose against her cheeks.

I should have pulled my hair back too, it's breezy today. If my Friday evening with Sean is an indication of how today will be, my hair wouldn't stay pulled back anyway. Princess Jezebel smiles and throws me a high five.

Samantha met Cory at Parazzo's, but Sean and I formally introduce them anyway. We give them a few minutes to reacquaint, so they won't feel so awkward together. We stand and stare at each other, smiling. He fumbles with my hands and plays with my fingers and strokes my palms lightly with his fingertips.

Cory's voice breaks my concentration, "Are we ready to rock?"

Sean shifts his eyes and glances towards Cory, "Let's roll."

Cory and Samantha lead us to the driveway and Cory approaches the driver's side door. *Cory is driving, hell yes!* This means I will have all of Sean's attention on the drive to Shoal Creek.

Sean opens the driver's side rear door and motions for me to climb in. *What a gentleman.* I am about to slide over in the seat to make room for him, but he closes the door behind me. He walks to the other side of the car and climbs into the seat next to me

My eyes fall to the floorboard. I don't want all of this space between us. Sean grabs my arm and thigh and pulls me in next to him.

His arm slides under my hair and onto my shoulder. The tiny hairs on the back of my neck stand on end when his fingers brush across my neck. He is so close; I smell the mint of his gum. My mouth begins to water. He fumbles with my hand and traces my fingers gently. Something about Sean Gentry's touch pulls me to a whole new level of consciousness.

Cory and Samantha fuse, their conversation is effortless. They talk about school and music while they flip through radio stations in search of something they both like.

Sean doesn't give two spare thoughts to Samantha. I seriously need to quit worrying so much. No words escape our lips for the majority of the drive. He gazes at me intently and traces the shape of my arm and my fingers with his, like he is trying to memorize every inch of my body. The silence should feel awkward, but it doesn't.

Samantha and Cory giggle about something, while the radio continues to scan stations. I'm not listening to their conversation, so I'm not sure what they find so fucking amusing. It is quite possible that Sean and I are the source of their entertainment. From an outsider's perspective, I'm sure we do look stupid.

The radio scan stops briefly on Drops of Jupiter, Sean and I in unison yell, "Stop!"

We both smile at each other. Sean states, "I like this song."

After the song is over, Sean whispers in my ear, "We should probably join the conversation, so they don't think we're completely weird."

I shake my head in agreement and smile.

Sean, still with his arm around me fondling my hand, asks Samantha, "So Sam, what kind of music are you into?"

"Lamo's, we've talked about music for the last fifteen minutes. Keep up."

Sean rolls his eyes at me, "Sorry, I guess I wasn't paying attention."

Sam turns her head around to face the backseat, "I don't know, I guess I like dance music a lot. Some rap is ok. I like some of the older stuff too, like Bon Jovi and U2."

"I don't really get into any of that club or rap shit, but U2 kicks ass," Sean responds.

They continue to discuss music for the next several minutes. *Ok, seriously, that is enough mingling.* Sean tries to be polite, but their conversation drags on and on. I am more than a little jealous he finds it so easy to talk to Sam, yet has little to say to me. *Oh my god Samantha, please turn around and shut the fuck up.*

We turn onto Riverside Drive; I know we will be at the falls in a matter of minutes. The scenery changes, when the roads begin their descent through the curves and rolling hills. It is beautiful, though spring only begins to open her tired winter eyes.

"Funny, I've lived in Joplin my whole life and I haven't been to the falls since I was a little kid," I say, to gather Sean's attention away from Sam. "I barely remember any of this."

"A good choice then?" Sean smiles and shifts his attention back to me. *Finally!*

"A very good choice," I smile back.

Cory pulls the car over to park in the small spots they have marked along Riverside Drive. Sean unfastens our seatbelts. I open the door and can already hear the thunder of the water that crashes over the thick layers of rock. I climb from the backseat and reach back for Sean's hand and he slides out behind me.

The weather is perfect. The sun glows like a warm fire. The sky is crystal clear and that perfect neon blue. I stand there for a few seconds and soak in the warmth of Sean's hand in mine and the glow of light that shines on my face.

"Are we ready?" Sean asks, breaking my concentration.

Cory and Samantha are already in front of the car ready to cross the road.

"Ready," I answer, my cheesy smile pulls across my face again. *Ready for you to wrap your tongue around mine!*

As we follow Cory and Samantha across the road, we both grin when we witness Cory reach for her hand. They look good together. Better than Cory and I would look. They are both tall with golden hair and pale eyes.

They look like they were meant to be. Samantha glances back at me; her dimples dig deep into her cheeks, while her stride turns to a skip.

We climb down the chunks of umber-colored slabs. The water plunges to a white capped holding pool below. Sean helps me make my way down each rugged natural step, placing his hands on my waist to steady me. He stands behind me and wraps his arms around my shoulders, while we stand and admire the falls in total awe. Tiny particles of mist drift through the air and bond to our skin.

We all stand in silence and watch, not to mask the thunderous sound of the water. I look over at Samantha, only to catch Cory's eyes on me. *Weirdo!* I turn quickly back to Sean.

"This is almost as beautiful as you are," he shares, in a breathy low voice only I hear.

"Yeah, right," I reply, biting my lower lip.

Cory and Samantha have seen enough, their need to move on is apparent. Sam anxiously twists her hair, while Cory shifts back and forth in his red converse. Sean and I are entranced by the power of this natural wonder; we could stay here all day with no discontent.

Sean, also notices their boredom. "Cory, it's fucking gorgeous out and shit, if you and Sam want to move on, you're free to take a hike, literally. We passed a restaurant called Santo's Café about two miles up the road. Brianna and I will meet you there a little later. We are enjoying this."

"Great idea, except for the hiking part. I think Sam and I will take the car and find something to do. We'll meet you at the restaurant in a couple of hours."

"Whatever man."

My mouth twitches with guilt. I want to ditch Samantha, but I see uncertainty in her expression. Princess Jezebel doesn't want to save her; she scowls at me and plants her hands firmly on her hips.

I understand how Sam feels. My conscious persuades me to be the good friend. I cave, "Samantha can I talk to you for a second?"

Sam approaches me, I interrogate her quietly, "Sam are you ok with this, because I won't throw you to the dogs here if you're not comfortable alone with Cory."

"Brianna, don't be ridiculous. I think Cory's awesome! I want to spend some time with him, where we can actually hear each other. I'm worried someone might see me. I told my parents I was with you today."

"Samantha, you seriously need to quit doing that shit. Jeez, you're almost seventeen. I'm sure your parents would have let you go on a double date with me."

"I know, I know, you're right. I don't know why I can't tell them. It's so much easier not to hassle with all of their questions and rules. I'll be fine. I seriously doubt I'll run into anyone who knows my parents."

"Ok, see you in a couple hours if you're sure."

"Don't do anything I wouldn't do," Samantha smiles and lifts her eyebrow, while she walks away and grabs Cory's hand.

I breathe a heavy sigh while they climb the rock staircase towards the road. *Finally.* Once again, I take in the beauty of the falls; the thunderous roar and the power it possesses…kind of like the power Sean has over me. My mind soaks it all in, until Sean grabs my hand and spins me around to face him. My mind empties. All other thoughts float away like fireflies that escape the jar that once held them captive.

"So, do you want to take a walk up the river with me? This rocks. I can't believe I've never been here. Then again, I'm glad my first time is shared with you—kinda puts me more in awe."

I bite my lip and try to suppress the ridiculous grin I feel building on my face again.

Sean helps me climb the slabs of rock that line the river, sometimes he grabs my hand to steady my climb, sometimes he literally lifts me to another level. *I'll say!*

We make small talk about our future, while we soak in the nature around us. Sean wants to go to school this fall to pursue a journalism degree. He writes for his school newspaper and enjoys the research and writing.

I'm not as confident. It's hard to know what you want to do, when you've never really done anything. I like taking care of Gramps. Maybe nursing? My true passion is sketching. To create fairy tale worlds would be my ultimate dream, but the possibilities seem so limited.

We continue to walk while the thunder of Shoal Creek Falls fades in the distance. The rough box shaped rocks that lead our path look like they've been carved by the hand of God. On our hike, we stumble on a small pocket of water in one of the stones. This natural pond is home to frogs and tiny little plants. We stop to study and appreciate the wonder of this tiny self-contained little world. I have to question if that is what I create with Sean, our tiny little self contained world where only we exist ...certainly not a healthy option.

About an hour into our hike, Sean bends down to pick a small yellow wild flower that grows up through a crevice in the rock. "So, do you want to kick back for a minute and take a break ...or whatever?" he asks while he hands me the flower.

Here's comes that damn smile again, my jaw aches. "Sounds good. I would love to soak up some of this sun before it leaves us today." My true motive has little to do with the sun, but everything to do with heat.

We are further up the river; you have to concentrate to hear the thunder of the falls. Our surroundings are quiet and peaceful. Only the sound of frogs and wintered dead leaves that gently rustle on the trees speak to our ears.

He grabs my waist from behind and helps me climb up the oversized mass of stone. I watch while he climbs onto the rock and maneuvers his way behind me. Not another living soul is around. We are completely alone, just he and I and the gentle rolling music of the river.

I scoot up to the edge of the rock and let my lower legs dangle down the face of the boulder. Sean scoots in directly behind me and wraps his arms around my shoulders and pulls me back against his chest. "This is amazing," he says, quietly in my ear.

"This place is really awesome," I reply.

"I'm not referring to the river, Brianna. I'm referring to how I feel when I'm with you."

Princess Jezebel, with her lips pulled up in an awestruck smile, dances a waltz around my head to the point of annoyance. I want to swat at her, but I have to hide the crazy.

I try to turn my head to gaze into Sean's eyes, but he gently turns my face back toward the river. He begins to move my long dark hair over my left shoulder bit by bit. He gently rubs his warm soft lips against the back of my neck. *Sweet Jeezus!* His hands gently slide the blue denim shirt off, one arm at a time. My hands grip the edge of the boulder and squeeze until my knuckles are white. His lips wander from my neck ...to my shoulders ...to the center of my back. I'm in a place I've never been before; not in my dreams, not in my fantasies. My body aches, I want him so bad. I can't take anymore, I have to kiss him ...I have to kiss him now.

I struggle to maneuver myself around to face him, without tumbling from the boulder.

Sean slides back further on the rock. He begins to pull me backwards, closer to him, until my legs no longer dangle from the edge. My body is almost entirely on the rock when I turn over onto my knees to face him.

Sean rests his warm soft hands on my cheeks and whispers, "Come closer."

I crawl on my hands and knees until I am merely a hands width from his face when he suddenly stops me. "Don't move. I want to look at you."

His eyes hesitate and look away. He pulls me in; he pushes me away.

After a moment, he decides, "Brianna, maybe we should start to head back ...or whatever. I don't want Cory and Samantha to think we abandoned them. They are kind of our responsibility today."

I gape at him, confused. *What the?* "Ok, if that's what you want."

"Trust me, that's not what I want, but that's probably what's best."

I'm not sure what happened, or what went wrong, but I feel rejected. He pulled away from me. What did I do to change his mood? He doesn't want to kiss me.

I sit on the rock and pout while I tie my shirt around my waist.

"You probably should put that back on Brianna, hanging down below your waist like that could trip you up on these rocks. You might scrape your arms up, too."

"Fine." I reply, confused. Princess Jezebel throws out her pouty lip and stomps her feet like the spoiled princess she is.

Sean still offers to help me up and down the rocks, while we continue to hike north along the river. He may be moody, but he's still a gentleman. This time our conversation isn't as free-flowing. Tension looms over both of us, like a disease. He smiles down at me from time to time to ensure me all was well, but something is different—and it's not ok.

"We're here, let's head up to the road," Sean states confidently, while he pulls me towards the rock above him.

"I thought you've never been here before? How are you sure this is where we need to be?" My pouty princess probes and tries to catch him in a lie.

"On the drive down, I spotted the restaurant I sent Samantha and Cory to. I know the river split right after we passed it. I also saw a tire swing that hung from an enormous tree across the bank. The tire swing is over there, can you see it?"

"Yes I do, I see the fork too. Very observant Mr. Gentry, remind me if I'm ever lost to make sure you're with me."

"You'll never be lost with me," he chuckles and tries to lighten my dejected mood. *So not true, I'm kind of fucking lost right now.*

We finish our steep climb to the road and as he predicts, the restaurant is within view. I see Cory's car parked in the small gravel parking lot. We walk along the edge of the road until we approach the restaurant.

"Santo's Café, this looks nice. Are you sure we're dressed for this?" I ask Sean, when we approach the Tuscan style architecture.

"I would think they see a lot of hikers," he replies.

"Do you think Cory's car is unlocked, I need to grab my jacket?"

"Are you cold? Today, there were times I thought it was downright hot!" he flashes me a playful grin. *Yes, it was scorching hot until you poured ice water all over it.*

"No, I want to check my phone to make sure no one's called," I fib. I am truthfully after the cash I have stuck in my pocket. This place looks expensive and I don't want Sean to fill obligated to pay for my lunch. "The door is locked."

"Come on, let's go in Brianna. I'll come back out and grab your phone if you need it that bad."

We walk into the restaurant and the atmosphere is like walking into a Tuscan farmhouse, with beautiful stone fireplaces and grand thick wooden tables that look like they were crafted centuries ago. We soon see Cory and Samantha and walk over to join them.

"Have you been here long?" Sean directs his question to Cory, while he pulls my chair out and motions for me to sit.

"Ten minutes ...or some shit, great timing," Cory replies.

We place our orders for drinks and Sean orders some toasted ravioli and fried calamari for us to share.

Cory and Sam recap their day spent in an arcade, playing video games. Although the thought of hanging out in an arcade on this beautiful day sounds hideous to me, Samantha is happy. She impressed Cory with her mad video game skills. Her little secret is safe with me; Cory doesn't need to know she has most of these games in her basement.

Sean tries to describe some of the sights we took in along the river, but Cory and Sam keep changing the subject.

"You know Sean; I told Samantha our band plays at Lamar Park in a couple of weeks, the girls should come up and see us."

"Um, yeah, that would be great," Sean's expression pulls tight.

He doesn't want me in Lamar. Wow ...really? All of this waffling today makes me dizzy.

The conversation between the three of them fades from my consciousness. My mind has other things to contemplate.

At times, Sean is indisputably into me. My evening with him Friday night is beyond words. Today was perfect, at least up to the point where I wanted him to kiss me. Other times, Sean is distant and unsure ...like he is hiding something. Why didn't he want to kiss me today? Is there a reason he doesn't want me in Lamar? And what about the lack of phone calls. Do I honestly buy into his excuse about the phone bill? I'm not sure anymore. My insecurity is fed by the quiet little secrets he keeps hidden inside. I'm not sure where I fit into his world, because I don't have full access to his world.

"Brianna!"

This startles me, I turn my head to focus on Sean, "What!"

"Wow, I thought we lost you. Where on earth have you been?"

"What? I've been listening," I fudge.

"If that's the case, what are we talking about?"

I glare at him.

He receives no response from me, so continues. "Yeah, that's what I thought. It's only five, we still have five hours before I need to have you home. We need to figure out what we *all* want to do next. If you're tired, I can take you home…no pressure," he frowns and eyeballs his hands.

"NO, no, I don't want to go home yet. I'm fine, see!" I plaster a huge cheesy smile across my face, "Come on, let's go!"

CHAPTER SIXTEEN

As I glance around the table, I feel chastised. I hear their unspoken thoughts, *"Is she mental?"* *"Man, Sean better be careful with this one."* *"Wow Brianna, you're seriously embarrassing me."* I shake my head to clear the voices and take a deep breath.

"What did you all decide to do?" I ask, shamefully.

Samantha responds first, she's conditioned to my crazy. "Well, I read in the paper that Parazzo's is open to minors every Sunday now, from five until nine. You guessed it—that's my vote."

Sean squirms in his chair like a fish out of water, "Brianna, I don't do the dance club scene, I hate the music and *I don't dance.*"

I see an opportunity to even out the score. "Well Sean, they did go do what we wanted to do, and they weren't into the whole scenic river hike. I say this half should be their choice."

After a moment of shocked silence, daggers shoot from his gorgeous brown eyes and bury themselves under my wind burnt skin, "Ouch," I say, maintaining my smile.

"See Sean, Brianna makes complete sense, plus the consensus is three against one, you're totally outvoted!" Samantha crows.

"Sam, I didn't officially vote. I'm just saying, you and Cory should decide."

Sean's jaw clenches, before he turns away from me and digs for his wallet. *He's mad. What the fuck was I thinking?* The truth is, I don't give a rat's ass where we are, as long as we're together. All I want is to shut the world off and bury myself in everything Sean.

"Well, you guessed it, we're going to Parazzo's!" Samantha gloats.

Cory and Sam slide away from the table and head towards the door. Sean tosses a twenty on the table and throws me a look so loathing, I cringe.

"Sean, I'm sorry. I don't care where we go, as long as I'm with you. If they want to go dance, let them go dance. I promise I won't make you. We'll find a quiet table in a corner somewhere. I think we have a few things we need to talk about anyway."

He opens my door for me, but irritation shadows his face. *I want his dimples back.* He walks around the car and climbs in the other back seat. This time, he doesn't pull me to the center. *This will be a long fucking night.*

I hate the gap between us, both physically and emotionally. The air between us is filled with tension. I am blowing everything, just like I feared. *How do you do it, Brianna? Think damnit.* The solution comes to me about half way to the club. *You've got this!* I unfasten my seatbelt and slide over to the center. My lips curl up into a soft regretful smile while his fingers dig into my thigh. I tuck my head against his chest and though I can't see his face, I feel his dimples return.

Cory pulls up to the club and I feel Sean's grip on my leg tighten. *What's his fucking hang-up?* Is he worried he will run into someone; another girl?

Cory pays all of our admission and we walk into the club. The music is louder than I remember. I miss the beautiful thunder of the falls and the quiet rolling of the river.

Cory and Sam head up to the bar to grab a soda; I know this is our one opportunity to find a table as far away from the noise as possible. In the far back corner, next to a pool table, is a table for four. The music is still loud, but bearable. We wave at Cory and Samantha, while their eyes scan the room in search of us.

"Why are you clear back here, away from the dance floor?" Samantha whines.

"Come on Sam, don't be snarky. We're here aren't we?" I respond.

"Brianna, you *will* dance with me tonight. That's why we're here, *to dance!* Cory and I walked down to the falls with you today, fair is fair."

"Ok Sam, fair is fair. You did walk to the falls, and stayed for like five minutes. Then you went and played video games. So, in the tradition of fairdom, I'll come up and dance with you tonight for about five minutes. I think that's about two songs."

"Twice, seriously? That's less than one song an hour!" She catches my glare, "Ok, ok, two songs." She shifts her eyes to Cory, "You'll dance with me won't you?"

"Of course I will, baby," he responds to her, but stares at me. *Baby? Barf.*

Cory and Sam look good together, but there is something dodgy about Cory. I can't put my finger on it. I'm happy for Sam, she seems to really like him, but I don't need this awkward foursome to become the norm.

We aren't ten minutes into the night when Samantha cashes in one of her dance chips. "One more," I remind her while I follow her to the floor.

I think she is more interested in talking than dancing, "Bri, I'm so happy for you. Sean seems like a great guy. You look so cute together. He's totally hot."

I look back towards our table and smile, "Yeah, he so fucking is."

Sam continues to shout over the music, "And Cory. Oh. My. God. He is the best kisser...EVER!"

After our dance, I return to our table and peel off my denim oxford, that is damp with sweat. The black lights, illuminating the room, reflect from my white camisole. I feel like a human glow stick.

Sean's craving eyes follow my every move when I lean over him to see if he wants a soda. I catch the nervous breath that escapes from his lips when my breast brushes against his arm. I am so working it.

"Brianna, shit I'm sorry, I should have offered," he apologizes and slides his fingers through his hair, exposing his mesmeric eyes. *Damit...you need to stop that!*

"Sean, you paid for my lunch, I think I can spring for a soda."

"Ok, sure," he smiles, *those god damn dimples.*

I walk up to the bar and grab two sodas. My reflection in the mirror behind the bar is hideous. My hair is a hot mess. The wind today did some definite damage. I don't even have a brush with me. *Damnit!* This will not be pretty when Sean tries to run his fingers through my hair as he kisses me later. *And he will kiss me later.*

I return to the table with our sodas and whisper into Samantha's ear, "Please tell me you have a brush with you?"

"Going with durrr on that one."

"Thank god, bring your purse and come with me to the restroom."

"Well I would, but my purse is out in Cory's car."

"Shit, ok!"

Cory and Samantha dance to the next three songs—after that, a slow song. I watch them while they hold each other. My aqua eyes become greener by the moment. I peek up at Sean, but he doesn't offer—and I can't renege on my promise. But damnit, I want to feel his body pressed against mine. I need a small fragment of security from him.

Samantha turns in her second dance chip about an hour into the night. I admit it feels good to be out of my seat, moving. The dance floor is thick with bodies. I can feel the heat as it radiates from my skin.

Samantha doesn't waste a second and she's back to the dance floor with Cory. Sean and I try to carry on a conversation, but the noise makes it a real challenge. We sit and smile at each other and watch people. *Ok, this silence is fucking awkward.*

Another slow song begins to play. I know Sean won't dance, so I pull my chair in close to him and lay my head on his shoulder. My arms wrap like a belt around his waist. He lets me sit like this a full ten seconds before he softly pulls my arms away and grabs my hands. He lifts from his chair and pulls me to my feet. Our arms cling so tight around each other you would swear we were on the edge of a cliff—and maybe we are. Back and forth, we sway with the music. His soft voice fills my ear with lyrics. I close my eyes and imagine we are the only two people in this crowded room. I feel strangely complete— like I'm finally whole. He looks into my eyes like he can read my thoughts, then he leans in to kiss me. *Finally!*

His arms tense up and he uses all of his strength to keep me standing. My legs are complete rubber …maybe from the hiking …maybe from the kiss …I don't know. Breathing the same air with him always makes my bones feel overly hollow, like they could crumble at any moment. The song ends, but I don't let him go. I gaze into his eyes, eyes that seem impossible to ever doubt, and whisper, "Grab Cory's keys."

"You're ready to go home? I just started to enjoy this," he flashes a flirty grin.

"Whoa no. They can stay; in fact I hope they stay forfuckingever. I want to be with you. Only you. Alone."

His full white smile glows beneath the black light. In less than two seconds he is down to the bar where Cory and Samantha buy their third soda of the night. I watch while he talks to them—his hands fling around like a mad man. I'm not sure what they say, but I don't particularly care anyway. He races back toward me. My heart rips through my chest. He doesn't stop at the table; he grabs my hand and pulls me behind him all the way to the parking lot. My denim shirt is still on the back of my chair, but I don't care. Samantha will see it and grab it for me.

Sean unlocks Cory's doors. He pulls open the back door and motions for me to climb in. I slide into my seat and immediately reach forward in the front seat for Samantha's purse. Sean slides into the seat next to me. He tips his head, confused, "What are you doing?"

"It's ok, I have permission. My hair is totally screwed from the wind and dancing today. I just need her brush, so breathe."

Sean sighs. *What the hell did he think I was grabbing?* "Can I brush your hair for you?"

I don't answer him, I hand him the brush. He pulls me between his legs and brushes through the back of my hair in slow gentle even strokes. I'm all about it, until an image of the woman I saw brushing her hair in the reflection flashes through my mind. A cold shiver slithers down my neck and slides down the full length of my spine.

"Brianna, you left your shirt inside, should I go grab it?"

"No, I have a jacket and I'm far from cold. Besides, Samantha will grab it."

Sean continues to brush through the tangles in my hair, "Earlier, you gave me the impression you want to talk to me about something. It's been kind of freaking me out, is there something wrong?"

I don't want to ruin this moment with my bullshit, but he's right, we need to clear up the uncertainties. I have to think carefully about what I need to ask, because I am not walking away from this night without kissing him some more. It is much easier to talk to him with my back to him, so I begin. "A couple of things have been bothering me, I guess."

"So tell me, I only want you bothered if you're hot," he jokes. I reach back and slap his leg.

"Ok, I know you told me Cory sat on my number for a few weeks. I guess I can believe that. But, how did you not know it was me? That night...the basketball game. That night was earth moving and magical, at least for me. I'm not sure the feeling is mutual. Why did you leave that night and not come back? And why wouldn't you kiss me today? On the rock.

Sean turns my body around and starts to brush the front of my hair while I free-fall into his eyes. "Ok, a compound question, let's see, B ...A ...C ...All of the above."

I sigh in frustration, he continues, "First of all, not only did Cory forget to give me your number, he said you were some cute blonde he met at a bar. Cory can be all kinds of stupid. *Or shady.* To be honest, I didn't have an interest in Cory's cute little blonde. I almost threw your number away. My mind was completely absorbed with this gorgeous brunette I met briefly at a basketball game. She haunted every dream and consumed every waking hour of my existence. No matter what I tried, I couldn't push her out of my mind. I didn't know who she was, because she left after I asked her to stay. You ask why I didn't come back? I did come back, to an empty bleacher. I realized I was crazy to think someone like you would be interested in someone like me. I finally accepted I would never know who you were. I didn't even have a glass slipper. When I walked up onto your patio that day, I had no fucking idea the girl who haunted my dreams was the door I was knocking on. I had no fucking clue I would be sitting in the backseat of a car with her now, brushing her hair and wishing with all my heart I would have kissed her that night at the basketball game...kissed her today on the rock...and was kissing her at this very moment."

Whoa. My. God! My questions are finished, at least for tonight. If all of Sean's answers are as good as this one, my reservations are ridiculous. I gaze into his eyes for a few seconds. I see the sincerity and honesty they reveal. He still has so many mysteries to solve, but for now I will be content, knowing I'm the girl he chooses to be with.

Sean takes his finger and traces the side of my face. His warm crimson lips invite me in, making my mouth water. I swallow. This time I lean in to kiss him and he allows. His arms wrap around me and pull me so close, our bodies become one. I understand the feeling I felt that first night, the force that weaves together our souls. My skin is on fire, I swear it melts off of my body. Steam fills the car and fogs up the windows. There is no part of me that does not tingle, from my head to my toes. We're on the brink of an eruption.

Sean gently pulls the back of my hair. His fingers weave through every strand. My lips tip up, at a perfect angle, to meet his. He swallows every ounce of me. His hand slides down my side, gently. His fingers work their way under my camisole and climb up my abdomen. I panic. I'm not ready for this—this is our first real date. Everything I feel right now is new to me. I need time to process. I wrap my fingers through his and gently guide his hand back to my waist not to miss one moment of our kiss.

There is an unspoken understanding and he doesn't pursue it any further. Instead he pulls my body more snugly against him until he can't take the fire between us anymore. He gently pushes back. "Wow, I think we need to come up for air. If we go any further I don't think I'll be able to control myself."

I smile. Princess Jezebel rests in a hammock and fans herself with a palm leaf. Deep within my gut is an ache that's unfamiliar. A part of me does not want him to stop. We both giggle when we notice the opaque windows that surround us.

"Sweet Jeezus, I think I probably need that brush back," I say to Sean.

He laughs again and hands me the brush he dropped on the floorboard earlier. "Yeah, I think I might need it too," he admits and runs all ten fingers through his hair.

We slowly drift back to earth and regain our composure. The sweat evaporates off of my body and sends a cold shiver up my spine. The night air has a late winter chill. I slide into my jacket and check my cell phone for messages. None. No one ever calls me. I'm not sure why I even check. The windows still conceal us from the crowd in the parking lot, but droplets of water now cling together and slide slowly towards the ground.

"You know Brianna, we should probably talk. I'm pretty sure we have it going on in the chemistry department, but there is still so much about you I want to know and understand. You're a mystery."

"Me, a mystery?" I chuckle. "I'm an open book. What do you want to know? I hate to disappoint you, but my life isn't all that exciting."

Sean asks me questions, random questions. What was my first pet, how many boyfriends have I had, what is my favorite color? I ask him the same random stupid fucking questions. Questions that help us understand each other better, but questions that are irrelevant compared to the unspoken bond we share. We don't stop talking until Cory and Samantha join us in the car. The windows have cleared just in time.

Samantha jumps into her seat and tosses me my shirt. "Forget something?"

I glance at Sean and smile. We belong. We fit. And something I learned today, we don't need anyone else. We both prefer the solace of our own private little world.

We head to my house ...wrapped in each other's arms.

CHAPTER SEVENTEEN

Five days pass without a word from Sean—our all too familiar routine. Routine, however, does not make the silence any easier. We had this super great date, well most of it, and then nothing—Zip. Zilch. Zero. Being blown off all week is starting to annoy me. With each passing day, my mood fades to a grayer shade of blue.

Today is another Friday and I am so freaking sick of Samantha's bubbly recap of her extended phone conversations with Cory—every fucking day. I don't understand the connection between them, at least from Samantha's perspective. Their chemistry is so bipolar. Cory is fun and, ok I admit, fairly good looking…but there's something about him that makes my skin crawl. I don't know why I have these reservations about him. I have no real reason to be suspicious. If I were to guess, it's the envy I am trying to slice through. *Maybe I picked the wrong boyfriend.*

Sam and I both stab at our schools repulsive meatloaf, mainly for something to do. Neither of us actually eats it. "Bri, have you heard from Sean yet?" She asks, for the fifth time this week.

"Nope, not a word," I reply, as I stare at the pinkish gray meat on the end of my fork.

"I don't understand why he doesn't call you. He acts like he's totally into you, but then, I don't know—," she stops.

"But then what—explain please?"

"Don't take this wrong, please! I'm just saying you two have a strange thing going on, too intense or serious or something. Maybe you need to lighten up. It's like you never talk, you just stare at each other. It's kinda creepy. I don't know, just my opinion."

"Wow, thanks Sam, that makes me feel a whole lot better. We talk. We talk a lot actually. We just do it when no one is around." Princess Jezebel purses her lips and turns her back to us with her arms folded across her chest. She's such a pouty baby.

Sam rolls her eyes, "Ok, I'm not trying to upset you. Maybe you do, I just didn't see it Sunday, that's all I'm saying."

I continue to stab at my mutilated meatloaf—now with more vengeance. Is Samantha right? Are we two *strange* people trying to make this *strange* relationship work? The relationship is a little *strange*—even I have to admit this. But strange is a harsh word, *unique* sounds so much more appropriate. *Yes, unique—that's it!*

The lunch bell rings and I pray for my day to die a quick pain-free death. I crawl through my next three classes and count the minutes before I escape to the refuge of my bedroom.

I jack around in my room all evening, skipping dinner. I climb in bed at seven o'clock. I see no point being awake, when my dreams are so much better than my reality. I strip off my jeans and slide under my blankets. I hope the warmth will remind me of Sean, but my sheets are cold. I stare at my cell phone that rests on my night stand and wish it would ring; I summon it to ring. *Please call me damn it, I hate this silence.* When the heat from my body finally warms the pocket of air between my sheets, I begin to imagine Sean and how his body felt pretzled with mine. I still feel the warmth as we sat on the rock last Sunday...while we danced in each other's arms, in our own little corner of the world...and when he was pressed against me in the back seat of Cory's car.

I must have drifted to sleep, because the next thing I remember is the sun shining on my face. The soft glow reminds me of Sean's hands, warm and gentle, slowly stroking my cheeks. I smile and open my eyes, but he isn't there. I turn to glance at the clock, it is only six thirty. I want to go back to sleep, but my mind won't allow it. Almost twelve hours of sleep have sealed the secret door to my dream world—for now. I sit up and stretch, sore from the extended hours in bed. I am sad, not for any particular reason, just sad.

The thought of going to my grandparents today doesn't even hold much appeal, and that is something I generally look forward to. *What is happening to me?* Is all of my self-inflicted desolation because of Sean? Or, is there a part of me that fears every passing week, because with this passage of time comes a granddad that is weaker and closer to death.

I have to set my apprehension aside; Grams needs me no matter what I might be feeling. What I am going through is minor in comparison to what she lives every day. I wolf down a bowl of cereal. I think about eating a second bowl, but the buzz of the dryer interrupts me, so I fold my clothes instead.

I yell at my mom while she vacuums our living room. "I'm going to Grams now, see you later." She shakes her head yes and continues to vacuum. *Doesn't anybody want to talk to me today?*

I head back upstairs to grab my jacket and stare at my cell phone, that still rests on the nightstand. Today I leave it behind, I mean, what's the point. I plug it in to the charger instead.

When I arrive at Grams, she isn't in a good mood either. She is fixing a plate for Gramps with some eggs and sausage gravy. "Here Grams, I can do that for you. You eat something. I've already eaten breakfast this morning."

She snatches the plate away from me, "I'll feed him!" *Well, isn't this fucking perfect?* I don't argue, but follow her into the living room. Like everyone else, in my tiny little corner of the universe, she's completely ignoring me. I feel like a damn ghost. I stand over Gramps while she struggles to shove a few bites of food down his throat.

He touches the tips of his fingertips together, over his chest. Still tending to his garden, or fixing something in his mind. In between bites he tries to talk, but the only sounds that escape are faint one syllable sounds—the sounds a baby first makes. I stand and watch him until Grams finally gives up her struggle to feed him. I'm invisible in his world, too.

I follow Grams back into the kitchen—still silence. She takes her normal seat at the kitchen table and intentionally ignores me. *Oh, sweet jeezus.*

"Grams, what's wrong?" I finally ask.

"I'm a little upset with you, Brianna."

"I don't understand, what did I do?"

"It's not what you *did*, it's what you *didn't* do. I appreciate everything you do for me. You know that."

Now I am more bemused than ever. Can my purpose in life be any more conflicted?

"I guess, but then what? Why are you mad?"

"Your uncle Rick called this week. He told me about the crazy story Amanda concocted the night she stayed here with you. *Oh, good lord.* He thinks you fed her full of stories to scare her, but you and I know that isn't the case, is it Bri? Why didn't you tell me what happened? Why did you lie to me?"

"Grams I'm sorry, I really am. I didn't really lie. She obviously made this out to be a way bigger deal than it was. I told her not to say anything. " *Big mouth.*

"Brianna, when I asked how your evening went, you said everything was fine, that was a lie. Whatever happened, Rick said Amanda was scared to death."

"Grams, it wasn't that big of a deal. I was standing over Gramp's bed while Amanda worked on a crossword puzzle and we saw something in the reflection of the picture window. It looked like a woman—a woman with long black hair. Then she disappeared and that's where it ended. The rest of the night Amanda and I did crossword puzzles and talked. Nothing else happened, I swear. I would have told you, but you didn't need to feel bad about having some fun."

The color empties from Gram's face. She is as pale as that haunting reflection. She presses, "You said this woman had long black hair. Where did you see her exactly?"

"Well, in the reflection, it appeared like she was a few feet behind me, but when I turned around no one was there."

"So the picture window is where you spotted her?" Her eyes are wide with horror. She continues, "What else can you tell me, what else do you remember about her?"

"Let's see, her face was pale, but beautiful, in an eerie way. She didn't look scary, she looked almost peaceful. This was probably all in my imagination anyway Grams, because of the story you told me a few weeks ago."

"Amanda saw her, as well?" Grams prods.

"Yeah," I stare down at my hands, clenched and white knuckled.

Grams slaps her hands on the kitchen table, "Imagination—my ass. If there was ever any doubt, it's gone now. She is real. I told you she was real! I've seen the exact same woman, only I don't think her image is a reflection. I think she is on the other side of the window looking in, pulling your granddad away from us."

The hairs on the back of my neck stand straight up and send a ripple down my spine. How many times have I stood over my Gramps and wondered what is on the other side of that wavy old glass that takes him away from us—for hours—or days at a time? Her deduction makes perfect sense, as creepy and insane as it sounds.

Grams shakes her head in disgust, "I should have never left you here alone, not even with Amanda here. I should have known better. If anything would have happened to you, well I can't even fathom the idea."

"Grams, stop—nothing happened. I'm sorry I didn't tell you. Can we forget the entire thing, please?"

"Forget it! No, I won't forget it. I don't want you to come over and help me anymore. I will make your Aunt Jenny start coming on Saturdays. She needs to get off her lard ass anyway."

Grams' bluntness makes me smile for a nano-second, but the core of this conversation rips out what is left of my heart. Rejection drowns me today—and I don't know how much more I can take.

"Don't do this! I like coming over to help. I like to visit with you and Gramps."

"Try again Bri, you haven't been able to visit with your granddad in weeks. He doesn't even know you're here. Jenny will help, and that's final. You can still come and visit, but I don't want you hanging out in that room anymore. Something bad is in there, I feel it."

"Grams, this is ridiculous, nothing will happen to me or to anyone else."

"Don't argue with me! This is the way I want it, and this is the way it will be."

Grrr ...she is so bullheaded! I feel like a child scolded for being bad. *I wasn't bad--damit!* What will I do now? Spending my Saturday here is a comfortable routine. It makes the time pass. I don't want to add these hours to the lonely hours I already live, where I sit at home and think about Sean.

Grams sits in silence at least two minutes before she continues, "Brianna, you need to spend more time with your friends anyway, and that new boyfriend. Someone your age should not sit in a sad old house and watch their granddad die. Do you understand what I'm saying to you?"

Yes, I understand you sound like Adrienne, I think to myself. What neither of them understand, I have nothing better to do. "You have to realize, my social calendar isn't exactly jam-packed, in fact, there's not even much penciled in. If I wasn't here, I would sit at home, bored."

"Well Brianna, it sounds like you need to create your fun. You're seventeen, when is the last time you hung out with your friends, or your boyfriend on a Saturday?"

"Sean usually works. I haven't seen Adrienne or Natalie for a while, I guess."

"You go home now. Call your boyfriend and tell him you want to spend time with him, when he gets off work. Or, call one of your friends and hang out at the mall. *Yeah, totally Adrienne.* That's what you should be doing on a Saturday. I'll call your aunt Jenny and have her come over and help me with your granddad today. Now run along..."

My eyes swell with tears, and I hug Grams goodbye. I walk into the living room and bend over Gramps bed. I watch him while he whispers words I can't make out. It is painful to imagine not being here with him. The tears escape my eyes now and roll down my cheeks. They land in a puddle on the edge of his bed. How I pray God will give me a miracle and bring my Gramps back, the way he was one short year ago. I bend over the rail and kiss his forehead. He doesn't notice.

I grab my jacket off the back of the kitchen chair and tell Grams goodbye.

"Bye Bri, go have fun today ...do it for your granddad," she whispers, while tears start to pool on her drooping lids.

I don't look back while I make my way to the door. I know I have to leave, before we both lose it. On my drive home, my tears could fill a river. Maybe hanging out with my friends will be a good thing, a distraction from this heavy blanket of hopelessness that slowly smothers me.

Grams said to call my boyfriend. Why have I never thought of this before? Why do I wait for Sean to call me? I am capable of dialing his number. I'll call him.

As I approach our driveway, I realize my father will assume Grams sent me home because I didn't help enough. How can I explain this away without divulging our secret? I pull in the drive, thankful to see he has already left.

I walk into the house and my mom looks up at me under a crooked brow. She will ask and I'm not sure what I'll say to her, either. "You're home early Brianna, is everything ok?"

I don't have time to concoct a believable story, so I tell half-truths. "Yes, Grams thinks I need to spend more time with my friends, she made me go home after we fed Gramps." My answer must have sufficed, because she doesn't even look at me weird—not even a little.

"Well, I have to agree with your Grams. You do spend an awful lot of time at home or over at your grandparents, for someone your age. Go have fun!"

I reluctantly head to my room. I have grown weary of staring at the same four walls, waiting for them to move or change color. I climb the staircase slowly and contemplate whether or not to call Sean. The thought of dialing his number petrifies me—which is completely ridiculous. This sounded so much easier when I sat in my car—far away from my phone. I sit on my bed and stare at the phone, that still rests on my nightstand. I don't know if I expect it to stand up and dance, or walk over to me, but it sits there—waiting. Where is this childish fear coming from? Am I still scared he has a girlfriend? Am I scared he will reject me? What fear keeps me from picking my phone up and dialing his number? *Stupid...stupid...stupid!*

I suck in a deep breath, while I gnaw on my already ate up nails. I grab the phone violently from my nightstand, like it might run away. I open the cover and let out all of the air I trapped in my lungs. I look down to see I have a missed call. He called this morning, an hour ago. *Thank god.* This strangely makes the task of dialing so much easier.

"Hello," a mature female voice answers.

"Hi, is Sean home?"

"No, may I ask whose calling?"

I stiffen, "This is Brianna, I have a missed call from him."

"Well Brianna, I'm sorry dear, you just missed him. He had to work today, but I'll tell him you called."

My wickedly beating heart stops beating. Swallowing is difficult. I feel my throat swell shut. I muster up enough voice to spit out, "Oh, ok. Bye…then."

He is working. I'm having a panic attack. Perfect. Well, life could be worse. She could have said, "He's out with his girlfriend." Yes, that would definitely be worse. But, it doesn't appear I will spend my day with him.

"Well now what?" I say to myself.

CHAPTER EIGHTEEN

I don't appreciate my lack of routine, I feel like a clumsy child stumbling through my day. Already bored, I dial Nat's number, but naturally she's not home. Her dad tells me she's at track practice, and then off to shop with her mom.

I toss my phone on my mattress with enough force it almost bounces onto the floor. This is why I need my Saturdays to remain structured. I don't want to worry about finding things to do. My Saturdays may not be exciting, but they're predictable and I need something I can count on.

"Bleh, this seriously fails," I say aloud.

I debate between Adrienne and Samantha for a full minute. I already know Samantha will babble about Cory all day. I'm not in the mood to be reminded of Cory's perfect, gold star attentiveness. Adrienne is a better choice for today's stormy mood.

"Hello."

"Hey Adrienne, it's Bri and I'm completely bored. Can I come over?"

"What, not at your grandparent's today?" she badgers. "I have a date tonight, but you can swing by now. I'm not doing anything except flipping through magazines."

"Awesome, I'll be right over. Thanks!"

I stuff my cell phone deep in my sweatshirt pocket, just in case Sean calls again. Adrienne lives next door to

Nat, so I walk. The weather is cool and damp, compared to last weekend, but the air emanates signs of spring. On my short trek to Adrienne's I replay my day in my head, that's now starting to ache.

I detest Grams over-reactive banishment, but to save face with my father and to give this nonsense a chance to calm down, I come up with a brilliant solution. Grams said I could still visit, so that's exactly what I'll do.

I kick myself for missing Sean's call, but I'm thankful I have an excuse to call him later—without that daunting, make-me-want-to-puke, apprehension. I miss him at every possible level. I need him to hold me. I need his reassurance to slither out of this feeling of abandonment that cloaks me like a tight glove.

I arrive at Adrienne's and she greets me at the door with a bright white smile stretched from ear to ear. "Hey stranger! I'm so glad you came over. Something is in the new Teenation magazine. You need to see this, you will shit," she beams.

I sigh and roll my eyes. *Perfect, we're going to spend our day looking at fashion magazines.* I strip off my jacket and drape it over the end of her bed. I climb over piles of magazines and join her near her headboard. "So, what's going to make me shit?" I ask, while I pull the hair out of my face and push it behind my ears.

"Check this out, an astrological love guide. This tiny little insert will tell you who you should be with and who you should avoid. Isn't this completely beast?"

"Beast!" I say, rolling my eyes.

"Seriously Bri, this is brilliant and kind of important."

Adrienne continues, "See, I'm a Virgo. I can see which guys fit my personality the best. Some guys will love me, but I will hate them. Other guys, I will totally love. This tells me which ones I'll have the best shot with."

Oh good lord. I roll my eyes again.

"For instance, look here what it says about Leo's. They will overlook my criticisms and I will take pride in them, feeding their ego."

Their ego? I bite on the inside of my cheek to keep the festering laughter from escaping.

She continues, "I will bring a lot of emotional heat into the relationship with them. I will satisfy and excite them. They are persevering, which will satisfy me. Isn't this the most epic thing you've ever seen?"

"That's so epic, it's sick," I giggle.

Oddly enough, as strange as this day has been, I can't help but wonder what sign Sean might be. I wish I knew his birthday.

Adrienne starts to read another, "Cancer is also a good sign for me. Our personalities thoroughly mesh. I'm practical and Cancer is emotional, but we complement each other. We are a perfect match in the bedroom— yowzah. The only drawback is we are both talkers and not doers ...but personally, I think that's a load of bullshit. I'm a doer, don't you think?"

"Yes, I would agree, lies ...it's all lies," I giggle.

She shoots me an evil glare, but continues. "Ok, the last good one is Capricorn. We both like stuff, we take pride in our stuff and how we look. We are both practical, but we're not very romantic. I don't like that part. I wish I could combine all of the good signs—or maybe I could have one guy from each sign. Yes, that would be killer!"

I'm now dizzy from rolling my eyes so much. She flips her way through the rest of them, quickly. "I've already read these and the rest of them suck. The way I see it, I need to concentrate my efforts on those three signs. This will save me loads of time."

"So Adrienne, explain. How on earth will this save you time? Now, not only do you have to find someone who fits into your mold of perfection, but he now has to be born in July, August, or whatever the hell Capricorn is? I don't see the time savings, just sayin."

"No Bri, you're not getting this. It may take longer to find him, but I won't have to waste months dating someone I'm not meant to be with. Once I find him, he will be with me forfuckingever," she tosses her hands into the air and smiles.

I pry, "Your date tonight, what's he? Who is this guy by the way?"

"He's a mega-beast that works at the movie theatre. His name is Brandon. He's ridiculously gorgeous, we're talking model material. But, that's like a seriously lame job, so I'm not getting my hopes up. Nat and I met him last weekend and he asked for my number. I have no clue what his sign is, but you can bet it will be one of the first questions I ask tonight. Right after, are you looking for a better job? If he's not a Leo, Cancer or Capricorn, I won't

163

waste my time—I'm serious. Ghaaa, this is so freaking awesome!" she basks and falls back on her pillow.

She turns and looks up at me, "Are you still seeing that guy from Lamar, that Sean kid?"

"Yeah, I guess you could say I'm seeing him." *I guess, what kind of answer is that?*

"What sign is he, we'll see if you're destined!"

"I have no idea, I've never asked him." *How could I have missed the birthday question?*

Adrienne's eyes bulge, "Hot damn, this is perfect! I can prove to you this is the real freaking deal. I want you to find Pisces and read through all of the signs. Tell me which one you think sounds like you and Sean. That doesn't mean it will be a good match ...because you might not be."

"I don't know Adrienne, I haven't been with him *that* long." I respond, skeptical.

"Ok, so you can narrow it down to three, and I bet he is one of those three picks. You have to be honest about your choices. No cheating, trying to make it better than it is." *But it is good.* Jezebel flips her off.

I snatch the book from her hand and flip through the pages labeled Pisces. The first three signs do not sound like us, at all. This won't work for us. Our relationship is unique and ok, like Sam describes, strange. There cannot be two other people, anywhere, who share the weird connection we do.

Finally on the fourth sign, enough hmm's escape my throat, I have to re-read it.

"Ok …we might have one here, Cancer. We are affectionate and sensitive to each other. I'm a dreamer; he's a worker, therefore, together we make our dreams reality. That's accurate I'd say, I spend my days dreaming and he works all the fucking time."

"This is complete bullshit; mine says cancer isn't a doer. Yours says he's a worker. I call foul," Adrienne scoffs.

"Maybe he likes me better," I giggle and quickly continue. "I provide romance, he protects me—cool. We are great in the bedroom, oh good god! I don't know about that, but he kisses great."

"What do you mean you don't know?"

"Shut up Adrienne," I smile and punch her in the arm—hard. "Let me finish, we're both sympathetic and supportive. We're a perfect fit day or night. Wow, that's a good one. I'm going to say he could be a Cancer."

I read through three more and find no similarity. Then—I come to a page that makes me drop the magazine in my lap. I am certain the words are written about us and only us.

I pick the magazine back up, and find the insert. I quickly open the page, "Adrienne, this one is completely us …Scorpio. We are a love at first sight combination. A first encounter may feel like discovering a kindred spirit. That is awesome and shit, remember the basketball game. The first time I met him! I knew the minute I laid eyes on him I had to be with him, so freaking weird."

"I remember that night, that is weird. What else does it say?" Adrienne probes.

"We are mystical and sensual. We have a magnetic attraction—Whoa. My. God. Scorpio is the most passionate sign of the zodiac, while Pisces is the most romantic. When we meet, there is immediate sexual attraction. Sweet Jeezus!"

"Keep going, this is juicy..." Adrienne prods and leans so far into me she's almost in my lap.

I suck in a deep breath, "Ok, ok, it says Scorpio's are secretive, but the soft side of Pisces brings out the soft side of Scorpio and makes them disarm. Pisces are granted a rare access to Scorpio's deep well of intensity, which opens a door to a magical bond."

Adrienne pulls back now, skeptical, "And you like that secretive shit?"

"I don't know, I like the mystery. Let me finish ...it gets better. We are both more comfortable in intimate settings, rather than large groups. So true."

"So you have no friends? I don't dig this ending, Bri. Glad it's you and not me."

"Adrienne, here is the weird and wonderful part, the part that completely freaks me the fuck out. We transcend from our physical world and share a special communion on a sensual unspoken level. This is so fucking bizarre, because most of the time we sit and stare at each other, or touch each other, like we don't need to talk to communicate. I know that seems strange, but it's like we hear each other's thoughts."

"Sounds creepy to me," Adrienne, discerns.

"The last paragraph states we are the zodiac's ultimate connection. Once involved, on a sensual level, we never truly let go. We reappear in each other's dreams for years to come. The first night I met Sean, he told me I would haunt his dreams. Sweet jeezus—if he's a Scorpio, I will totally freak the fuck out."

"Well, ok, Cancer sounds better to me, but maybe that's because I'm compatible with Cancer too. I hope he's a Scorpio, because if he's a Cancer we'll be fighting over the same dude," Adrienne ribs.

"Not if the dude is Sean, we won't be!" I say, while my poisonous eye daggers bury themselves under her skin. Princess Jezebel pulls up her fists and kicks off her glass slippers.

Adrienne chuckles at my reaction, "Ok, hop off …jeez, Sean's off limits, I understand. You think this is a tossup between Cancer and Scorpio so far …keep reading!"

I read through the last four, but none of them sound remotely close.

"That's it Adrienne, sorry but there aren't any more that come close. I told you we were kind of weird."

"Listening to that Scorpio shit, you're beyond weird. That's ok, now it will be even crazier if he's one of those two. I can't wait until we know. Call him and find out."

"I wish I could, but he's at work. I'll ask him the next time I talk to him."

"The next time you talk to him? You talk to him every day, don't you?"

"Well no, not every day," I cower, intimidated by Adrienne's rendering question. "He called this morning, I'm sure I'll hear from him this evening." Princess Jezebel tosses back her hair, confident with my assumption.

I am literally dying of curiosity. I need to talk to him now, more than ever. I can't wait to see if there is anything to this astrological connection. My guess, he is a Capricorn, or Gemini, or one of the many signs that sound nothing like us.

Adrienne and I continue to flip through her magazines and talk, all afternoon. Time ticks by swiftly and brings me that much closer to talking to Sean. I wonder what time he gets off? I could call him at work. I realize I don't know where he works. Another top ten question I should have thought to ask.

"Are you listening?" Adrienne blurts.

"No, sorry …I must have been day dreaming. I need to go home anyway; you have a date to get ready for." I pull on my jacket, while Adrienne's step mom busts through her bedroom door. The solid brass door knob slams into her wall and falls into a previous impression. I back up against the opposite wall slowly and try not to draw attention to myself.

"I thought I told you to put this shit away!" her stepmom shouts and flings the shiny metal scissors across the room, missing Adrienne's leg by inches. "I'm sick of picking up after you, next time your shit will end up in the trash ...where it belongs!" Her step-mom slams her door back shut and mumbles *like you.*

My heart aches for Adrienne. Her real mom died in an accident when she was only seven, it left Adrienne jaded and resentful. As if that pain wasn't enough for a young girl, her dad remarried almost immediately and tossed this stranger into their already dysfunctional life. Adrienne is such a daddy's girl; the jealousy between them continues to fester. The older Adrienne gets, the worse their relationship gets. They both constantly battle for her dad's attention, to piss each other off, more than anything. Adrienne treats her stepmother like a bottom feeding rodent and gives her no respect. Her stepmother treats her like the slutty blonde at your high school prom that is too close to your boyfriend. It's all painful to watch. I have to believe this is why Adrienne's pursuit for love is so determined. She needs acceptance ...and she needs escape, the sooner the better.

After a deep sigh, Adrienne mumbles, "What a fucking bitch!"

I force a smile and hug her, then head for home.

When I arrive at home, it is too early to call Sean. *Chicken shit.* I decide to finish my laundry and hang out with my mom.

"What did you and Adrienne do today?" she asks while she rinses a bowl of potatoes in the sink.

"Nothing honestly, talked and read magazines, enormously productive stuff," I smile.

"Awe Bri, hanging out with your friends is good for you. You'll appreciate the memories when you're older."

"It's not that I don't like hanging out with my friends. I don't see much of a point sitting around skimming through pictures of clothes you will never buy."

Mom laughs, "Point taken …but life doesn't need to be so serious. Not everything has to have a purpose."

I grab a knife from the drawer and help my mom peel potatoes. We continue to talk about school and my friends, but she never once brings up Sean. Odd.

I finish my laundry and put my clothes away. Completely bored, I watch a little TV with my mom and brother after we finish dinner. Sean still hasn't called and it is now after seven. I head back to my room to talk myself into calling him.

I grab my cell phone out of the pocket of my sweatshirt and stare at the screen for the longest time, beckoning it to ring. *Come on Sean, please call me. I know you have to be home by now.* Stalling, I check the battery, which is still eighty percent. I check my missed calls, but there are none. I lay the phone on the bed next to me. I need to overcome this phobia and dial his number. My apprehension is ridiculous.

Still stalling, I climb off of my bed and sift through my collection of CD's. I slide Tom Petty into the CD player and flop back against my head board. I begin to concoct excuses in my head, not to call. I left him a message today; I don't want to seem pushy. I don't want to annoy his parents by being a pest. His mother already said she would give him a message. If he wants to talk to me, he will call me back. All of these excuses are reasonable, but subconsciously I know the truth, I'm chicken shit.

"Come on Brianna, he won't bite you. Even if he does, it could be fun. Pull yourself together and dial the stupid number!" I say aloud and glare at the dial pad on my phone.

I take a deep breath and search in my contacts for his name. I pull up his number and stare at the illuminated screen for a second. My finger hovers over, but can't push the send button. The phone rings and startles me. I fumble to answer the call and almost drop the phone.

"Hello."

"Hey beautiful."

"Wow, I was about to call you. My finger was right over the send button. Weird," I explain, failing to tell him my finger may have hovered there indefinitely.

"That is weird. Hey look, I can't talk long. I'm supposed to be at Cory's right now for band practice. We have that stupid gig in the park next weekend. I hear you called earlier, so I thought I'd give you a buzz before I left, since I don't have any idea when I'll be home. I need to hear your voice, I miss you."

He lost me at *practice*. My heart crumbles into my gut. I won't see Sean tonight, or even have a marathon conversation with him. I take a deep breath and try to regain focus. "You had to work today?" I question and pull out the first topic my preoccupied mind can think of. "So, where do you work? I've never thought to ask."

"At Western Sizzlin, on the west side of Lamar. I've worked there for about a year ...or whatever. I started as a bus boy, but now I'm back in the kitchen. And yep, I worked all day today. I have to work tomorrow too, but only the lunch shift, I should be out of there by four. I'll give you a call tomorrow night, maybe we can spend some time together, or at least talk way longer."

"Good! I miss you. So, you are prepping for your big debut next weekend?"

"Um, yeah…or whatever. Cory has told fucking everybody, and this is so freaking stupid. The park is basically letting us go up and practice on their bandstand. You don't plan to come up do you? Because, this won't be worth the gas it takes to drive here? We're only playing like four songs—and we suck. I know Cory is trying to talk Samantha into coming, which is stupid. Honestly, you don't need to waste your time. I won't be upset if you're not there."

This conversation is not comforting. Is there a girl in Lamar he doesn't want me to see? Does he want to hide our relationship from someone? Sean confuses me with his mixed signals. It's no wonder I'm anxious and nervous around him.

He doesn't want me there, and this is painful. To mask my wounds, I play it off like I don't care, "I haven't given the day much thought. If Sam wants me to go, I'll be there. Otherwise, I guess I won't. Good luck with practice tonight."

"Oh, ok then …I guess I'll talk to you tomorrow. Bye Brianna, sweet dreams."

Damnit to hell! What have I done? I made a conversation closing statement, when that is the last thing I want. Has Adrienne taught me nothing! I start to return his goodbye, but the flash of Adrienne in my thoughts reminds me of something important.

"Hey Sean, before you go. I know this will sound totally random, but when is your birthday?"

"November 8th, why?"

Scorpio, sweet jeezus! The phone slides through my fingers and bounces on my bed. I reach down to pick it back up. "Oh um, no reason, I was just curious. Bye Sean. I can't wait until tomorrow," I add.

"Bye Brianna, me either."

CHAPTER NINETEEN

Sunday morning brings a bright outlook. Sean will call tonight and he's a Scorpio. This revelation still has me freaked the hell out. Adrienne will shit. Her date with Brandon last night should reveal whether he is one of her three destined choices. We have so much to talk about.

Sean won't be calling until tonight, if he has to work until four. I need some activity to fill my day, so the hours won't linger. Yesterday was enjoyable, in a weird way. The hours are definitely less monotonous when you share them with someone else.

Curiosity is killing me, I give Adrienne a call.

Adrienne's step mother answers the phone. It is apparent her dad isn't home, because I hear her scream, "If you won't pull your lazy ass out of bed at a decent hour, tell your god damned friends to call later in the day!" Adrienne is right; she is a complete bitch.

"Hello," she answers in a groggy voice.

"I'm sorry Adrienne, did I wake you?"

"No, it's ok. I'm still in bed, but awake—avoiding the bitch."

"You seriously need a cell phone girl! Your step-mom is over the top."

"You mean step-monster? Nothing motherly emanates from that creature."

Being polite, I ask about her evening before I share my personal revelation. "How was your date? Did you find Mr. Compatible?" I giggle.

"Oh, my date, hmmm, what do I say here? Let me start with the obvious. He is totally gorgeous. He is possibly the most beautiful human I've ever laid eyes on. He is indeed a Cancer, which means we will have killer sex. The night should have been epic, right?"

I sense her reservation, so I prod, "It wasn't?"

"Oh wait for it, this gets good! At first, I thought he was trying to be funny. As the night went on, it became clear—he's a fucking moron. I have never met anyone so childish ...and clumsy, OMG. He's clingy, like an annoying piece of lint. He tripped twice. The second time, he hit his head on the bumper of his car—drawing blood. The date seriously sucked ass. I don't know if I can put any faith in this zodiac bullshit."

Quashing the urge to laugh—totally out loud, I try to console her, "Sorry Adrienne, maybe he was nervous. You can be a little intimidating."

"Maybe. He is a cancer, and he's ultra-hot, so I'm giving him a chance to redeem himself next Friday. You're so right, my scorching body probably made him totally edgy," she laughs. "I've got to say, if our date is no better next week, I'm done with the whole love, according to the stars, compatibility shit, and I'm done with him."

"Wow, so sorry ...but guess what I found out?"

"Sean's birthday? Let's hear it, were we right?"

"Adrienne, he's a Scorpio. Isn't that freaky? What were the odds?"

"Well, one in twelve actually, but yeah that is pretty cool."

Adrienne doesn't seem as mesmerized by the power of her revelation today, not like she was yesterday. Her *not so great* date last night is clearly to blame. I still want to cling to the hope that there is something to this. The prognosis given to us, as the ultimate zodiac match, is totally freaking cool. Plus, everything it says is spot on!

"Do you two have plans today?" Adrienne probes.

"I don't know," I sigh. "He has to work ...again, but he said he will call me when he gets off."

"Have you already told him that your sex life, according to the stars, will be earth moving?"

"God no! I don't want him to think I'm a total freak."

Adrienne laughs, "What are you doing today?"

"Well, I'm going to pick up a copy of that magazine for starters. Then I don't know, I thought about calling Nat, I haven't seen her for a while."

"We should all go do lunch."

"Yeah, that sounds good. I'll give Nat a call and see what she's doing. I'll call you back."

Natalie, once again, isn't home. Her father tells me she is in Lamar with her mother, spending the day with her uncle and cousins. I am green with envy. I want to be in Lamar! Sean's already left for work, the jealousy is short lived.

Adrienne likes Samantha, so I give her a call. "Hey Sam, whatcha up to?"

"Absolutely nothing," she responds.

"Adrienne wants to go to lunch today, want to come with?"

"Um yeah, of course. Anything to get out of this house. I'm so bored I could die."

"We'll be by to pick you up around eleven."

I play mediator between the two until we finalize our plans. We decide on Arby's next to The Hallmark Store. I want to pick up a copy of Teenation while we're out. While we eat lunch, Adrienne recaps her disastrous date to Samantha—and adds even more drama than the story she shared this morning. Sam rolls, literally. She is bent over at the waist …in the booth at Arby's …rolling on her side.

Samantha doesn't bore me with her Cory phone call recaps all day, but does mention the gig in Lamar next weekend. The three of us need to be there—life according to Sam. *Hmmm, she doesn't include Natalie in these plans; maybe because she's not here…or maybe because she senses the animosity Natalie has for her.*

Sam's suggestion makes me cringe. She doesn't know Adrienne like I know Adrienne. She doesn't understand what she is capable of. If Sean and Cory want us to hang out, where does that leave Adrienne? She will either be a third wheel, which she isn't particularly good at. Or she will try, and likely succeed, to be the center of everyone's attention, including Sean and Cory. This is the far more likely scenario. If Samantha knew Adrienne better, she would have had the same reservations.

In an attempt to undo her naive damage, I reject her plans. "Sam, I'm unsure if I'm going. In fact, I'm more than likely not going."

"Why would you not go? Don't you want to see Sean play?" Sam grills.

"I would love to see him play, but he's given me the impression he doesn't want me to be there. He has made it clear that he sees our trip as ridiculous and a waste of time and gas."

At a complete loss, Sam continues, "Well that doesn't make any sense at all. I want to go, but I'm not going by myself. Adrienne, do you want to go with me?"

*What the...! How can she do that? How can she invite Adrienne to go to Lamar to see **my** boyfriend? This is fucking bullshit. Sam, you stupid bitch!*

Adrienne studies my face and dissects my expression, I don't even blink an eye. "Samantha, I think that sounds entertaining. You bet I'll go with you," she gloats.

Adrienne's response has me enraged. I have put up with a lot of shit from her, over the years, but this has crossed a line.

She continues, right before I snap. "But, Brianna is going too. I'll invite Brandon to come along, that way I won't be a third wheel. Oh, and I'll drive. Don't want you two wasting gas," she scoffs.

The bomb in my chest has been deactivated, but I reiterate my concern, "I'm telling you, I don't think he wants me there."

Adrienne demands, "That's exactly why you are going. You need to see what he's hiding. I see absolutely no reason for him to discourage you from going, unless he is hiding something. You need to learn this shit Bri ...never trust them, not completely. Who says he's always at work? It could all be one big front that you are too naive to recognize."

My head sinks into my hands. This is a disaster. Adrienne is right, of course. But, I don't want Sean upset with me. On the other hand, I also don't want Samantha and Adrienne to hang out with my boyfriend all day, if I'm not there. What if Adrienne is right, what if Sean is hiding something from me? As painful as that possibility is, I need the truth.

Their conversation moves on, but I'm not listening anymore. Somehow, Sean needs to have a change of heart during our conversation tonight. I seriously want to be in Lamar next week, but not if it causes problems between us.

"Hey Bri, let's go pick up your magazine," Adrienne interrupts the tactical scheme I plot in my head.

We walk next door to The Hallmark Store and flip through piles of books and magazines. I grab Teenation and make sure the insert is attached and in place.

"What's the deal with this magazine? Is there something special in it?" Samantha asks.

"Yeah, it's kind of silly, but this month's issue has an astrological love guide. You can read through the matches to see who you're most compatible with," Adrienne responds.

Funny how yesterday, with me, she thought the guide was the fucking bomb. The greatest publication since The Chronicles of Narnia. Today, with Samantha, it's silly.

"Seriously? That's killer."

Samantha grabs a copy for herself, along with two other magazines. Adrienne also has a short stack. I have one, the only one that actually interests me. We head to the cash register to make our purchases.

During the ride home, Samantha looks up the prognosis for her and Cory. Samantha is an Aries—Cory is a Libra. Of course she would know this. *Bitch!*

Samantha flips to the page and begins, "Ok, here goes. We have a powerful initial attraction to each other because we're opposites. *Yes, you are definitely that!* We each supply what the other lacks. That sounds good, so far," Sam states and flips the page. "I will try to go too far, too quick. What? What on earth does that mean? Oh no, he will eventually look for someone less demanding, and I will look for someone more adoring. A connection is possible, but only temporary. Well that isn't what I wanted to read, but I can't say I'm surprised."

"What do you mean?" I pry.

"I mean, we're different. Cory is a lot of fun. I like hanging out with him, but I can't see this like long term relationship building with him. There's no real substance. I like him ok, but I don't love him."

Samantha pauses and turns her focus to me, "What did it say about you and Sean?"

"He's a Scorpio, read it yourself."

"You're a Pisces, right Bri?"

"Yep."

Adrienne adds, "Hers is pretty fucking amazing Sam, you're gonna shit. She figured out his sign before she knew his birthday. How weird is that?"

Sam begins to read. I glance over and see the shocked surprise in her eyes—her jaw dangles like a broken hinge. "Holy smoke, that is fucking creepy. If I were to write a description of you and Sean, that would be my exact depiction. Yowzah! You so have to read this to him!"

"What is with you two? Clearly, I'm not going to read it to him! But, I kind of hope he flips through the magazine I bought and reads it himself," I chuckle.

I pull into Sam's driveway and drop her off.

"See you at school tomorrow, Bri! See ya Adrienne!" she smiles and waves, while she treads up her driveway.

Adrienne and I both wave back with wide grins stretched across our faces.

As I pull from her driveway, Adrienne's smile morphs, her lips pull straight and tight. *Here we go.* She obviously has strong conviction about the band gig subject we discussed earlier. She lectures me the entire ride home. The urgency in her voice tells me her advice isn't a mere suggestion, but rather mandatory action. In her expert opinion, if he has nothing to hide, he won't mind me being there—in fact, he will embrace it.

I am completely torn. This subject critically needs more debate tonight. I want to trust Sean, without constant doubt. I am aware, even without the seed Adrienne plants, this isn't entirely the situation.

I drop Adrienne off at her house. I think about hanging out for a while, but I have some homework to finish before Sean calls. I need to devise a plan that will turn his opinion around. I have to be in Lamar next weekend—there is no other option. I would prefer to be there with his blessing.

My day flies by quickly, it's already three o'clock. Sean will be off work in one more hour. I use this time to think about how I will approach the taboo subject.

What are my options? One. If I say nothing and don't show up at the gig, I know Adrienne. She will go with Samantha out of spite. She will find a way to punish me—and it will involve Sean. Two. If I say nothing and show up, Sean may be upset. Or worse, I might catch him with another girl and end everything between us. Although this may be smart, it also sounds painful. I don't like pain. Three. If I try to talk to him about the gig, and once again he reiterates that he doesn't want me there, won't that make matters worse? On the other hand, four. If we discuss it again, he may have a change of heart and want me to go. I don't enjoy any of these options, with exception to the last one. That option will definitely require a discussion, and maybe a little pleading. My nerves are on edge.

I need to be at that show, not only because Adrienne says so, but—I miss him so much my gut literally aches. And there lies the answer I've searched for. If he doesn't come down tonight, I can't endure two weekends without him. Waste of gas, or not …I have to be with him. If he misses me at all, he will understand this.

I work out a speech in my head, while I stare at my ceiling. I must stare too long, because I doze off.

I look down to see my fingers braided with Sean's. We meander down a dirt path through a meadow, towards a dense patch of woods. Sunlight glistens from his caramel hair. His dark jewel eyes twinkle out Morse code from rays of sunlight that beam through the trees.

The forest is dark and cold compared to the field. The air is heavy, with a foul musty odor that over-powers my senses. The earth becomes damp and the sunlight fades out of grace. We seep further and further into the soul of the forest.

Ahead, I make out a tiny stone cottage covered in moss. The windows are small and arched. Curious, we approach and peek through the dirty windows and strain to see what's inside. My fingertips circle the glass and try to remove some of the crust of gray dirt. Through the tiny portal I exposed, an image appears of a woman with long black hair. She brushes her hair as she stares right through me with soulless eyes.

I gasp and trip backward over a rotted limb. The stench in the ground around me is overpowering. I begin to choke and cough. Sean flies to my side and pulls me from the damp earth and we run towards the sunlight….and run…..and run.

I wake up and shake my head violently, trying to erase the nightmare that left me breathless. I face the clock and another form of panic sets. The clock reads seven-fifteen. I'm late for school. I missed my conversation with Sean. *Damnit!* It takes a few minutes to realize, by the lack of light that comes through my window, it isn't morning...but still evening. I grab my phone to see if Sean has called. Once again, no missed calls, I shove the phone in my pocket.

My grumbling stomach coaxes me to the kitchen. My mom has made chicken enchiladas for dinner. I scoop out a couple and put them on a plate. The growls subside, when I shovel the last bite into my mouth.

Why did I dream about that woman? It's been over a week since that haunting night. I return to my room. Two more hours go by with no call. Nine o'clock has come and gone. My patience has worn to a thin layer of delicate film. Anger and tears battle for their rightful spot in the forefront. I am tired of this constant waiting. The time I spend with him is magical, but all of the misery that comes from waiting and wondering overshadows these magical moments.

Sean is my first real boyfriend, but is that what he is? Since the day he walked through my door and into my life, he has only called me three times. He has come over only twice. I may not be an expert at relationships, but this is far from what I witness my friends sharing with their boyfriends.

The clock now reads nine-fifteen. My phone finally rings and I know who is on the other end of the line. As distraught as I am, my heart still manages to skip four beats.

"Hello" I answer anxiously.

"Hey Brianna. How is my amazing beautiful girlfriend tonight?"

"Honestly, I feel rather neglected and confused," I spit; shocked the words actually spill from my lips.

Sean is nervous now and caught off guard, "Neglected, why do you feel neglected?"

My tongue has a mind of its own tonight, I resign control, "Well, let's see Sean, where do I begin? Could the reason possibly be because you rarely call me? Or maybe it's because you never come over. I sit around most evenings and wait for the phone to ring—nothing! I mean, come on, you told me you were off at four. I hoped you would come over, but now it's after nine. Why would I possibly feel neglected?"

I suck in a breath and continue, "I have a chance to see you next weekend and you've made your opinion clear you don't want me there. I don't understand. I guess I need to know if you want me at all, because at this moment, I'm not feeling it."

I sit in silence for several seconds and wait for a response, some tiny response. I want to suck every word back through my lips and swallow it, but it's too late. They spew all over the floor, like piles of vomit. *What in sweet jeezus have you done, Brianna.* Princess Jezebel stands before me and trembles with a pistol pointed at my heart.

My heart pounds a dozen times before he responds, "Wow, not the greeting I expected. This is not the way I wanted this evening to go."

My anger had its performance in the spot light, now the tears take center stage. I hold my hand over the microphone to mask my emotional breakdown. In a taut voice, I struggle to push out the words, "Sean, I'm so sorry. I was so worried you wouldn't call me tonight, and I miss you—god, I miss you so much. I think I worked myself up into a frenzy."

In a calm, reassuring voice, Sean explains, "Brianna, I miss you too. I do what I can to spend time with you. It's all of these fucking responsibilities. Five minutes, can I just have five minutes that belong to me. I have work and school and homework and now this stupid fucking band practice. Sometimes, I want to run and hide from the world. This is the first time I've ever dated someone from a different school. If you went to school with me, this would all feel so much different. We would be with each other every day."

His calm becomes more guarded, "I guess I don't understand why you feel neglected. I came over *and* called you two weekends ago, I was over twice last weekend and this weekend I called you twice. How do you see this as neglect?

Sean puts me on the spot with his question, because to hear him recap our time together, it sounds perfectly reasonable. What makes me look at us so differently?

"Sean, I'm sorry. I guess you don't neglect me, I feel defeated because it's late. I hoped to see you tonight, and the later it got, the more I thought you wouldn't even call. I'm also concerned about this whole park gig. I don't understand why you don't want me there."

"Oh Brianna, is that what you think, I don't want you there? That's not how it is, at all. Brianna, I love to spend time with you, please believe this. Certain days, I seriously have to pinch myself to accept that you are real and that you also choose to be with me. How can you not see this? I would love to have you with me next Saturday.

186

I only feel like a trip clear to Lamar is ridiculous, because I won't be able to spend any time with you if you're here. We have to set up, play our four or five songs, tear down, take all the equipment back to Cory's garage, then I have to be at work. It will be a total fucking waste? I seriously hate Cory for talking me into this! I would have much rather spent my evenings with you, instead of practicing."

Still skeptical, I prod, "Sean, is that seriously your concern? You're afraid I'll waste gas, or time, or whatever? I would drive one hundred miles to spend ten minutes with you. This is not an issue in my eyes. Besides, Adrienne is driving. Samantha invited her and her boyfriend."

"You are kidding, right? This is totally out of control," Sean blurts.

Still confused, I dig deeper to unbury the truth, "Sean, this news should make you happy, if you're truly concerned about my gas bill. What is really going on here, why don't you want me in Lamar?" I hold my breath and blurt out the ominous question, "Do you have a girlfriend in Lamar, because I need to know the truth?"

Sean's laughter stabs at my ear, "Brianna you think I have another girlfriend, this is why you're worried?"

Irritated that he finds humor in my serious concern, I answer honestly, "Yes, the thought has run through my mind, more than once. I don't understand you. I miss you and I need you and I can't stand to be away from you. The reason is deeper than what you admit, because the reason doesn't make sense, not totally."

"Ok Brianna, you want truth and honesty, that can be a double-edged sword. I have a difficult time sharing my fears, or my feelings in general, but you do deserve to know the truth. To be completely honest, we suck. We're four high school kids that tinker around in a garage. I'm embarrassed to play at the park. I'm so reluctant; the thought alone makes me want to puke. Now I know you want to be there to watch, this makes my anxiety ten times worse. I'm not sure I can play at all, if you're there. Now I get to embarrass myself in front of your friends, too. This is all a fucking nightmare. That Brianna is the entire truth."

My own rejections blind me to the insecurities of others. "Sean, I don't know what to say. I feel really stupid, can you ever forgive me?"

"Brianna, please know you are all I think about. Not a day has gone by, since the day you walked into my dreams, I haven't thought about you, and I'm not talking briefly. I need you to be happy, *my* happiness depends on it."

Princess Jezebel tips her head like a curious puppy and smiles, "Sean, there has to be a solution. I can't go another weekend without seeing you, even if I can't be with you. If I don't go, Samantha and Adrienne will both find that strange. I'm kind of trapped here. You can play chopsticks and I'll be in awe."

"I think I might have found a way around this. Hold on—" Sean is away from the phone for several minutes. I would think he hung up, but I hear noise in the background. *What the heck is he doing?*

"I'm back. I've wanted to do this for you since our first kiss--but never more than this very minute."

I hear Sean suck in a deep labored breath and blow out through pursed lips. The warm sound of an acoustic guitar starts to fill the earpiece of my phone. Sean plays his guitar for me. I recognize the song, the melody is familiar. He begins to sing, while tears swell in my turquoise eyes.

We do it all
Everything on our own
We don't need anything or anyone.
If I lay here
If I just lay here
Would you lie with me and just forget the world.

...he continues the song to the end. I'm speechless—like I could talk anyway. My throat feels like it swallowed a boa constrictor. Tears roll down my cheek. Some end their path at my chin and pool in my lap while others continue their journey in a narrow stream down my neck. I would give anything to have him next to me right now.

Sean speaks, "I feel better now. I would love for you to be at the park Saturday, Brianna. I would also be honored if you accompany me to my senior prom in three weeks."

A bright light reflects on my world. My feelings for Sean become crystal clear. I am uncontrollably and unmistakably in love with him, every tiny significant piece of him. I clear my throat and salvage what remains of my voice, "Sean, I will be honored to accompany you to prom."

"Well then, that is settled. Can we move past the negatives, please?"

"No more negatives," I promise.

Our conversation continues ...for the next three hours.

CHAPTER TWENTY

Monday morning brings a new outlook. My fears are put to rest...for now. My late night on the phone with Sean should have left me exhausted, instead I feel oddly refreshed and alive.

I head to school ready to face my day—ready to face my week. The hours fly by while I doodle Sean's name on everything that my pencil comes in contact with. During lunch, I'm already seated at our usual table when I catch a glimpse of Samantha approaching. Her grin is stretched from ear to ear. Does this mean Cory invited her to prom, too?

"Hey Sam! I almost shout.

"Wow, you're in a good mood. You must have seen or talked to Sean yesterday," Samantha observes and sets her tray of food on the round royal blue table.

"You guessed it! He always puts me in a good mood."

"Not always," Samantha teases. Princess Jezebel sticks out her tongue.

"Ok, let me rephrase, when I see or talk to him it puts me in a good mood."

"Yeah, that I can buy," Samantha giggles and twists the cap off of her bottle of water.

"What's up? Did you talk about the park Saturday? You are going, aren't you?" her reproachful voice prods.

"Yep, it's all good now. Sean is just nervous and embarrassed about playing in public. He faced his fear and sang to me over the phone last night, can you believe that? It was over the top. He's so fucking awesome!" I smile to myself. "He feels way better about it now. He wants us to meet him at Cory's garage, about eleven. We will help them take the gear to the park and set up. Hopefully, with our help we can finish quick, and hang out for a while before they have to play," I explain.

"Fun! I can't wait, this will be so killer."

"Something else happened last night," I add, with a smile so wide it hurts.

"What? You didn't....."

"God, no. We talked on the phone, I didn't see him. But, he did ask me to his prom last night!"

"SHUT UP!!" Samantha screams. "Seriously!! Do you think Cory will ask me too?"

"I don't know, but I would assume. He is your boyfriend, and he's more into the whole dance thing than Sean is. Did you talk to Cory last night?"

"Yeah, for a little while, he didn't mention anything about prom. Maybe he will wait and ask me this weekend when we're all up there."

I glance over at Emily. She smiles, but is alone all at the same time. Maybe she's just bored with our conversation. I wonder if Emily has ever been to a dance—with a guy.

We pick at our tray, too hyper to eat. Samantha and I make plans to shop for prom dresses. Prom is even more exciting, now that I've shared the news with Sam. My first prom.

The rest of the week skates by at a steady pace; not quick enough, but the time doesn't drag either. April has arrived, spring is officially here. Summer is just around the corner, which means more free time to spend with Sean.

Saturday morning the weather is cool, but beautiful, similar to our day by the falls.

Adrienne decides to take Natalie with us instead of Brandon. She isn't confident about their future, so she doesn't want to make a commitment she can't keep. This works out for the best. Natalie knows most of the people in Lamar, since that is where her mom grew up. She and Adrienne will be the typical social leaches, which will leave Samantha and me to our boyfriends.

Adrienne and Natalie show up promptly at ten. Adrienne is always punctual, this comes as no surprise. I climb in the back seat behind Adrienne and we set off to pick up Samantha.

On our drive, I think back to my fear of losing Samantha to Adrienne and Natalie. I now realize how paranoid that fear was. Our friendship, if anything, is stronger now that the group has four instead of three. No one—*and by no one, I mean me,* is the odd man out anymore.

"Hey Nat, I haven't had a chance to hang out with you in a long time, you're never home," I say, while we follow the curves to Sam's house.

Natalie replies, "Yeah, I've been pretty busy lately since track started up." Natalie's focus turns to her track meets. *I just had to go there.* Since I'm happy to see her,

I listen politely while she fills us in on every detail of the season.

We approach Samantha's drive and she is sitting on the retaining wall next to her driveway. She is either anxious to go, or wants to leave before her parents see that she isn't only with me. The latter is probably closer to the truth.

"Hi everyone!" Samantha beams, while she slides into her seat.

"Hi Samantha," Adrienne turns to answer with a pulsating white grin.

"Hey Sam," Natalie repeats, without glancing back. Her lip push out into a pout.

I smile at Samantha while she fastens her seat belt. She smiles back, her dimples dive deep into her cheeks.

Natalie starts a conversation with Adrienne, before Adrienne can start a conversation with Samantha. If this wasn't so pathetic, it would be comical. Since they are engrossed in their own conversation, I ask Samantha quietly if Cory has said anything about prom yet.

"No, not yet, I almost said something to him last night, but you know how the zodiac guide says I'm pushy and demanding. I decided to wait for him to ask me. He might be planning something special. I don't want to ruin the moment." I laugh that she puts faith into a prediction that basically says they will fail.

"I bet he asks today while we're at the park. That would make sense. I'll bring the subject up with Sean, when Cory is around. We'll claw it out of him," I assure her.

"That's perfect, Bri. See why I love you. You're a genius!"

Natalie turns around and questions her comment, "So what makes you a genius, share please?"

"Nothing Nat. Sean asked me to prom and Samantha hopes Cory will ask her today. I'll bring up prom in front of Cory to see if I can shake it out of him. That's all."

"Oh, and here I thought her enthusiasm was something exciting," Natalie replies and turns back around to continue her conversation with Adrienne. Samantha's snarky face comes out. She glares at the back of Natalie's head. *God Nat, you are such a bitch.*

I return my focus to Samantha and change the subject, "What do you want to do for your birthday? You realize it's coming right up."

Sam stares at me, like I'm a rainbow of stupid, "My birthday is two weeks from today, that's when prom is, goof!"

"Oh sweet jeezus, I went from genius to moron, in record breaking time. I didn't think about the date, I guess. You have to go to prom now."

We talk about prom dress shopping all the way to Lamar. I'm sure Adrienne and Natalie would be bored to tears, if they were paying attention.

We pull into the town of Lamar and I explain to Adrienne how to drive to Cory's house. We are about a half hour early, but this is good. The sooner we have them set up, the sooner I can take Sean behind a building somewhere and…kidding. We pull into the drive, Cory's car is parked on the road, but Sean's car is nowhere around.

Adrienne, Natalie, and I slip out and lean against Adrienne's car. Samantha walks up to the door to let Cory know we're here. While we stand and wait, the garage door flings open. Cory is already in the garage packing cords and small items up in plastic bins. Adrienne and Natalie go on in. I head up the sidewalk to grab Samantha.

While we walk back towards the garage, a truck pulls up. Out of the truck jumps the tall dark-headed guy I saw with Cory the night I met him. Two girls are with him, two super cute girls, one with long dark hair, the other with long curly blonde hair. I suddenly feel nauseous. My insecurities fight to conquer me, but this battle I am determined to win.

Cory directs Natalie and Adrienne on what to pack when I enter the garage. Samantha and I are told to load some of the smaller tubs into his back seat. We place the last bin in his car when Sean pulls up behind Cory's friend.

My heart races across my chest when he climbs from his car. I feel the rhythm crescendo. My pulse creeps up into my throat. He smiles at me as he approaches, I feel my legs begin to collapse under their own weight. I quickly place my hands on Cory's car to steady myself.

He grabs my hand when he passes me and pulls me along behind him into the garage. He glances over at Cory, "What's left to do?"

Cory responds, "The girls already loaded all of the small stuff in my car. Jon and I have everything else loaded in Jon's truck. I think we're good to go as long as you have your drums."

Sean shakes his head in disrepute, "No, I didn't think to bring them. Cory, are you fucking stupid...or what?"

Sean turns to me, "You met Jon and Victoria, I presume."

"No, not really. I mean they were here, but I didn't know who they were."

Sean shakes his head again, "Um yeah, Cory seriously is all kinds of stupid."

Sean yanks me by the hand again, over to where the group is standing. Natalie, naturally, is already over talking to them. Is there anyone Natalie doesn't know? Sean introduces me to the couple. He introduces me as his girlfriend, Brianna. I like the sound of the word girlfriend. I think it's my new favorite word.

Sean canvasses the area and shouts, "If we're loaded, let's roll! I want this shit over with." Then he gazes into my eyes, long enough for me to lose my breath. He pulls me behind him, again. "Come on, you're riding with me."

I don't stop to say anything to my friends. I happily climb into his car. Princess Jezebel bats her long

197

eyelashes and unbuttons the top button on her blouse to fan herself.

Everyone scatters to find their appropriate rides. I catch a glimpse of Samantha, she looks bewildered and confused. She stares at me and then turns towards Adrienne and Natalie, she glares at Cory and waits for some direction. Cory climbs into his car, but so does the girl who rode with Jon and Victoria. The blonde I wasn't introduced to. Confusion and disappointment steal Sam's dimples.

"Sean, we have to bring Samantha with us, look at her."

"My back seat is full of equipment Brianna, where will she sit? Why can't she ride with your other friends?"

"She doesn't know Adrienne and Natalie all that well, she's my friend. Why isn't Cory taking her with him? Who is that girl with him anyway?"

"That girl is our singer, and it's a long story. Damnit, I want some time alone with you," Sean argues.

"I will sit on the console, super close to you," I smile and bat my thick eyelashes.

Sean's lips pull up in a crooked smile, "You better tell her to come on."

My arms wave out the window and I yell at Samantha. I see relief rush over her face, but she still glances back towards Cory's car, one last time.

Samantha inspects the seating arrangement when she approaches Sean's car. She shakes her head in discontent, "You don't have to sit on the console, I can ride with Adrienne."

I rebut, "Don't be silly, jump in. Besides, Adrienne already pulled out."

Samantha rolls her eyes and opens the door to climb in. I wrap my arm around Sean's neck to help balance myself. The park is only a few blocks from Cory's house, so the ride is short. Samantha climbs out first and heads directly to Cory's car to unload. I follow behind her.

Sean's voice cries out to me, "Where do you think you're going?"

I spin around to answer "To help unload."

He motions with a single finger for me to come back and stand next to him. I completely submit. Sean wraps his arms around my waist and leans me back against his car. His body is pressed hard against mine. "God, I've missed you. I think you can help me unload," he smiles while his eyebrows dance across his forehead.

I shake my head with a crooked smile.

He begins to laugh, "That's not what I meant."

"Yes it is," I look up, still smiling.

His hands slide from my waist, "Let's get this shit over with."

He opens his trunk, "If you grab the little shit, I'll take care of the big shit...or whatever."

I don't answer, but grab the small bins and stack them in my arms.

We go back and forth between his car and the stage a dozen times, until everything he needs sits scattered next to the spot he will set up. He starts to put his drum kit together, while I sit next to him on the edge of the stage.

"Sean, you didn't tell me a girl sings for your band. How long have you known her?"

"I've went to school with her my entire life. She's pretty good, I guess."

I continue to make meaningless small talk, while Sean works to set his drums up. I feel a freckle guilty when I look around. Everyone else works so hard, plugging in chords, setting up speakers and moving equipment. I don't feel near guilty enough to leave Sean's side. I try to hand him parts occasionally, so I don't appear completely worthless.

I see Samantha helping, out of the corner of my eye. Cory and her have not interacted, at all. Something isn't right between them. Her dejected expression breaks my heart. I was worried about Sean when it appears, Samantha is the one that needed to worry.

We still have two hours before they perform. Sean and I go sit on the trunk of his car. We sit, face to face, his warm hands laced with mine. Beams of sunshine peek through the trees and touch our faces. Sean and I try to fit as much conversation in as we can during our limited time.

Cory approaches the back of the car, "I hear you're going to prom with drummer boy. Erik Miller is having a huge party after prom; you need to be there." Good, this means Cory plans to go to prom.

This makes me smile, "Sure—"

"Try again Cory, we won't be at Erik's party." Sean interrupts. "We will be at post-prom."

"Whatever," Cory snaps when he walks away. Sean's comment leaves me confused. He's been shitty to Cory all day.

"Sean, I don't understand, why would you not want to hang out with Cory and Samantha?"

"Brianna, first of all, he's not taking Samantha, he's taking Jessica." He points to the singer in his band.

"What? Is she his fucking girlfriend? I knew something was weird today," I exclaim. "What an asshole!"

Sean explains, "Ex-girlfriend actually. In Cory's defense, they did break up before he started hanging out with Samantha. I guess he had already invited her to prom, and she already bought a dress…or whatever, and blah, the fucking blah, blah. I guess she guilted him and he decided to still take her. In my opinion, it's totally fucked up. Cory's an ass.

The second reason we won't be at Erik's party is, it's a kegger. I'm not taking you to some high school drinking party after prom. I would never disrespect you or your parents like that. I don't care if we're the only two people at post-prom, in fact, I kinda hope we fucking are."

Yes, that would be fucking epic. Princess Jezebel rests her chin in her palms and looks away dreamily.

"Oh god, poor Samantha—she will be devastated. To make matters worse, prom is on her birthday. Wow, you know Cory could have talked to her about his predicament. Sam might have understood. Jesus, he had to know we would talk about this. Now she came all the way up here to see him, and he has totally ignored her—like all fucking day. It appears he doesn't want ex-girlfriend to know new girlfriend exists. This sucks. Sean, you need to tell him, he needs to spend time with Sam today and let her know what's going on. This is just wrong! She was so excited about coming up today."

"Cory is an arrogant fucking asshat. I totally agree with you, he needs to talk to her—and he will. And he'll do it when he feels like it, and she'll grovel her way back. And you want to know why? I'll tell you why. Because Cory is the king of manipulators. This is part of the reason I can't believe he pushed you all to come up here today. I think he likes the drama. As much as I would love to sit here all day and discuss their issues, enough about their fucking tragedy, let's go for a walk."

I slide my feet to the ground. Sean follows right behind me. His fingers braid into mine and we head down the sidewalk, towards a small water park that is shut down for the season. On the other side of the water park, I see a patch of forest that is just starting to green up. The park is nice, for such a small town. We come to the forest edge and stop. I can't put my finger on it, but I'm apprehensive to take a step forward. We are at the entrance of a one mile trail. I suck in a breath and step into the woods. It doesn't take long to realize my apprehension. My body trembles while the nightmare about the cottage replays in my mind.

Something weighs heavier than the nightmare, so the dream fades. This precious time alone should be my solace, my harmony, my time to reflect on everything

Sean. Yet, I can't escape the guilt I feel about Samantha. I left her alone with people she barely knows, and a boyfriend who pretends she doesn't exist. I am a complete failure as a friend.

Sean and I have such little time to spend together. I need to put this feeling of repentance aside. I am allowed to be self-centered long enough to enjoy this tiny moment of contentment with him. I will spend time with Samantha once their band starts to perform.

With my mind clear, we continue on the path going deeper and deeper into the woods. The musty smell of the air forces thoughts of my dream back again, that make the hair on my neck stand stiff. *Let it go Brianna.* About half way through, Sean stops next to a large fallen tree and lifts me up onto the trunk. I sit and face him at perfect eye level.

"Brianna, I meant what I said earlier—about missing you. When I'm not with you, I seriously ache. I could not wait to see you today. We have to figure out a way to spend more time together. I can't keep going a week without holding you in my arms."

"I totally hear you. I'm here right now—that's a start."

"That's definitely a start," he says, while he leans into me and wraps my legs around his waist.

He crawls into my eyes like he's trying to open the door to my soul and climb in. He is growing much better at this. I can almost feel him when he enters. I love everything about talking to Sean, but I love this form of communication with him just as much—sometimes more.

He slips his arms around my shoulders and pulls me into a hug. He whispers, in his panty dropping voice, "Brianna, these moments we share together are some of the best moments of my life. Please know how special you are to me. You have invaded my soul so deeply; you have left a permanent scar. I don't ever want to be without you."

He pulls his face away from my shoulder and kisses my forehead, gently, softly. He kisses the tip of my nose and then brushes the hair away from my face. His lips move to my cheek. I feel the heat of his breath on my skin. I become lightheaded. The trees that surround us begin to blur. I close my eyes to escape the vertigo. I feel the heat of his breath as he pulls in closer and begins to caress my lips with his.

Closing my eyes has not made the dizziness disappear. I trust Sean. I know he will never let me fall. Once again I feel the elastic that snakes through both of us. It slowly pulls us together while it twists its way through my body and pulls me into his. I am so overwhelmed by its power, I want to scream.

Our lips do not want to break free—they are quite content. Ultimately, we have to come up for air, to catch our breath. He, once again, kisses my cheek with less intensity this time. "Brianna, we should probably head back. I would prefer to hide in the forest with you all day, but they might miss a drummer."

Not that I want to, but I know he's right, "I agree." I reply, breathless.

He lifts me back down from the tree and weaves his fingers through mine. Sean is my serenity, my harmony, my heaven. I can't think of one place I would rather be than with him. We finish walking the trail back through the woods. I keep my eyes peeled for a small stone cottage covered in moss. To my relief, one never materializes. I ramble on while we head towards civilization and try to keep Sean's nervous mind off of his performance.

In all of Sean's random questioning, he asks, "What's your favorite flower?"

I immediately answer, "Orchids, definately. They are perfect. When the bud opens, they are immediately unique, exotic and so full of mystery. But then, as time moves forward they slowly blossom into maturity and become more fascinating with each passing day. Everything about an orchid reminds me of us."

Sean's eyes are wide, "Wow, cool fucking choice."

We approach the outer edge of the forest. I see the gazebo stage in the distance. I see people scurry around and tweak the final details. All the stage lacks is a drummer ...my drummer.

Their band is good, even the singer, who I don't particularly like right now, through no fault of her own. They play several extra songs they hadn't anticipated for their cheering, sizable audience.

I repent by spending every moment of their performance with Samantha and try my best to make her smile. Cory broke the news while Sean and I were on our walk. A small part of her tries to understand, but the hurt and embarrassment is painted vividly in her big green eyes.

After their performance is over, I help Sean tear down his drums while the others load everything else off of the stage. When everything is packed, Sean grabs my hands and kisses them both.

Sean begins, "I wish I could spend the rest of the day with you. But I can't, I'm sorry."

"Sean, it's ok. I knew you had to work today."

He continues, "I don't even have time to unload." *I snicker under my breath.*

"Get your mind out of the gutter! I'm trying to be serious," he teases. "I don't even have two minutes." *I laugh harder.* "I didn't know I would spend so much time beating the skins." *I'm rolling now!* "Damnit Brianna!" Sean snips, but breaks out into laughter, himself. "I have to go," he insists and pecks my lips lightly, dropping my hands to my sides. "I wish I could say I'll see you tomorrow, but I have to fucking work, *again*. This is getting so fucking old!"

"Sean, it's ok, honestly. I think I will go see my grandparents tomorrow. Try to call me if you can."

"I'll try, but it might be late. Now, I seriously do have to go. Sorry about your friend." He kisses me one last time and adds, "Brianna, I'm glad you showed up today, it means everything." He climbs in his car and drives slowly down the road and stalks me in his rearview mirror until he fades from sight.

I smile. Princess Jezebel sits back in her Adirondack chair and sips her sweet tea, content.

I head out to join the rest of my friends. I think to myself while I walk towards the stage—he's mine. *All fucking mine!*

CHAPTER TWENTY-ONE

Vivid memories of my day with Sean linger in my mind, when I wake up Sunday morning. The delusions I create seem impossible to live up to, yet Sean finds a way to make my reality exceed anything I can possibly imagine. The only thing I can't bear is our time apart.

Samantha occupies what little space is left. She was so excited about yesterday, only to be let down by false hope and hidden agendas. On our drive home from Lamar, her decision to stop dating Cory came as no surprise. She was humiliated. If it were just her and I, the embarrassment may not have sunk its painful claws so deep beneath her skin. Natalie made snide comments most of the drive home. Samantha tried to make excuses for Cory's behavior, but in the end, she couldn't justify his actions either. *Taking your ex-girlfriend to prom, really, who fucking does that?*

I have a plan today, this makes me smile. Time moves at an acceptable pace when I have a plan. I am heading over to see my grandparents. Although it has only been eight days since I was there last, it feels like a lifetime ago.

I miss Grams. I miss our conversations, while I help around her house. More than that, I miss Gramps. I miss the granddad I grew up with. I miss his laughter, his smile, and the way he always sat in his rocking chair. I miss his stories, even the ones you could tell he made up. I miss his made up words like salawags and birchmisers. I miss his pale blue eyes that sparkle when the light reflects from them. I even miss the smell of his chewing tobacco emanating from his breath.

I clean my room and finish my laundry before I dress. This takes longer than I expect. *I need to quit letting my room fall into such disarray.* Depression is not the reason for my irresponsibility this time; a busy schedule was the culprit. This, at least, is a much better excuse.

I head over to my grandparents around one o'clock. Grams irrational fear might make this a brief visit, but I'm hopeful.

The dust swallows my car when I pull up their lane. We apparently have not had rain for a while, I didn't notice until now. I see Aunt Rachael is still at Grams helping her for the day. A smile pulls up on my lips, because Grams won't convey her ridiculous fears in front of Rachael.

I walk into my grandparent's kitchen and Rachael is sitting at the kitchen table, alone. "Well Brianna, what brings you here on a Sunday? I thought you were the Saturday girl," she probes.

Rachael obviously doesn't know Grams exiled me from Gramps care. I don't think she needs to know, so I play it off. "I had somewhere to be yesterday, I thought I would drop by and see how everyone is today," I answer. "Where's Grams?" I continue.

"She went upstairs to lie down for a while. She's exhausted and a bit under the weather, I'm afraid. She wouldn't eat her lunch; I hope she isn't coming down with something," Rachael explains. "Are you hungry? The refrigerator is full of food. I can fix you a plate."

"Sure, that would be great. I'll run up and check on Grams if you don't mind."

"She's probably asleep, but be my guest. I'll pull out some food."

The stairs creak when I climb the steep incline to Grams' bedroom. The dim light and the daunting groan of old wood sends a shiver up my spine. Funny, I was never anxious climbing this staircase before. I've made this same journey literally hundreds, if not thousands, of times. The rusty hinge echoes through the stairwell when I open the door into her bedroom.

Grams is stretched across her bed, her hair is combed out of its bun. It rests on her shoulders and flows down the middle of her back. Grams softly snores. I sit on the edge of her bed and watch her sleep and admire her beauty. Her face is like an angel. Her complexion is pale like ivory, her skin velvety soft. Her long black hair was beautiful once, you can tell. Age has left it thin and lifeless, exposing parts of her scalp. Grams doesn't look sick, she looks peaceful and content. I have to wonder if her dream world takes her to a better place, like mine often does.

The sun disappears behind a dark cloud and turns the sky gray and somber. In that brief instant, I see a reflection in Grams' window—a reflection of the woman with long black hair and a pale face. This is the same woman who haunted Amanda and my evening, a few short weeks ago.

When I strain to look closer at the fading image, it is Grams. Her pale ivory angelic face, the face of an angel draped with her black hair resting on her shoulders. Suddenly her eyes fly open wide and her face fills with a grimacing smile. I gasp and slide off of the bed. I shake my head and realize my edgy mind is playing tricks on me.   I kiss Grams on her head and follow the staircase back downstairs.

Aunt Rachael has a plate of food already on the table. She replaces the plastic wrap and puts everything back in the refrigerator when I sit down. "Aunt Rachael, you didn't have to go to all of this trouble. A piece of chicken would have been dandy."

"Don't be silly dear; your grandmother still thinks she cooks for fifty people on the weekends, when sadly, she and your granddad don't eat a cup of food a day."

Aunt Rachael fills me in on the latest family gossip while I pick at my chicken and noodles. After I finish, I rinse off my plate and head into the living room where Gramps is resting. His eyes are wide open, but he is nowhere to be found. His lost eyes don't even glance at me when I kiss his forehead. His focus wanders around the room haphazardly, like a newborn that soaks in his new surroundings.

I lower the rail of his bed and sit with him for a while—and zone. I love my Gramps, but sitting here— truly seeing him, I understand what Grams has tried to tell me. Gramps has already left, he is gone. This lifeless body is nothing more than a constant reminder of what we have lost.

I lean back on the bed next to him and hold his hand, his cold feeble shaking hand. I stay like this for close to an hour. I close my eyes and feel Sean's hand in mine. I see our ageing bodies next to each other, holding each other. This picture should repulse a seventeen year old. Instead, this picture is one of contentment, that reflects a life of happiness. I will be with Sean forever. I will love him just like Grams loves my granddad.

My trip today has been a waste. Neither of my grandparents will realize I visited. Still I feel satisfied. Maybe my time with them isn't for them as much as it is for me. I am copiously aware that my time left to share with them is on its final chapters.

As I sit back up, I stare out the picture window and retrace some of the beautiful memories I have of my grandparents. Suddenly a thought occurs to me. Grams would be livid right now if she caught me lying here with Gramps, staring out this same window she feels steals him away from her. Aunt Rachael is oblivious to Grams fear, or I doubt she would allow me to spend time in here. I stare at the large pane of glass and struggle to catch a glimpse of this woman with the face like ivory. I see nothing, except new leaves on the trees that sway in the breeze.

The face, "Sweet jeezus." I whisper.

The image in the window isn't a ghost at all, the image is Grams; a younger version, but her, I'm positive. But, how can Grams be here with us, yet on the other side?

I walk back into the kitchen where Rachael still sits at the table. "Is there anything you need me to do while I'm here, Aunt Rachael?"

"Everything is pretty much done, but if you want to help me turn your granddad to his other side before you go, I would appreciate that."

"Sure, I'd be happy to." Moving Gramps is important to keep his bed sores at a minimum, although the constant rearrangement doesn't do much good anymore. "Well, I guess I'll go back home unless you have something else I can do. If Grams wakes up, please tell her I stopped by."

"I sure will. Sorry you drove over and didn't have a chance to visit with her. I think I may head home myself, in a bit."

As I drive back home, I wish I could drive to Lamar to see Sean instead. I miss him already. I am addicted to him, to everything Sean. I have prom to look forward to, but that is two weeks away. I still need a dress and now it doesn't appear Samantha will share that task with me. She could still shop with me, but that idea feels like rubbing salt in a fresh wound.

Adrienne could shop with me. Umm no. Adrienne is far too critical and her taste is drastically different than mine. She would put me in something three sizes to small and way too expensive. I can't envision myself in a slutty cocktail dress, but I'm not sure what I do picture myself in. Admittedly, it isn't as much about my taste as much as my body type that plays my deciding factor. Adrienne would scoff at everything I think looks decent, and I'm just not in the mood.

Of course, there is Natalie. And then I laugh, out loud. Natalie hates anything to do with dresses. Shopping for a prom dress would be up there with having a tooth extracted.

The choice is obvious. My mom, along with my grandmother on my mom's side. Perfect. My grandmother loves to shop and she has great taste. Plus, we haven't been shopping since my Gramps turned sick. Spending a day with Mom and my grandmother will be an enjoyable change. I'm freshly excited.

After my car pulls in the driveway, I jog into the house. My mom sits in the living room watching TV with my brother when I walk into the kitchen. I yell into her, "Hey mom, what's up?"

"Did you have a nice visit with your grandparents?" she asks, when I bop into the living room.

"Actually no, Grams wasn't feeling well, she was in bed asleep. Gramps was in a different dimension. He was awake, but I don't think he knew I was there. I did visit with Aunt Rachael for a while."

"Are you hungry, I put your dinner in the fridge?"

"No, I ate at Grams, Rachael fixed me a plate. Mom, can I talk to you about something?"

"Sure, let's go in the kitchen where it's quieter."

Once in the kitchen, we both sit down at the breakfast bar. "Mom, Sean invited me to his prom in a couple of weeks. I was wondering if you and Grandma Harris will go with me next weekend to find a dress."

My mother turns as giddy as a high school girl. "Brianna, I would love to go with you. That will be so much fun; your grandmother will be thrilled! You really like this boy, don't you?"

"Mom, we've been over this. I have never felt like this. He is everything. He is the air I breathe. He is my sunrise and my sunset. He is my first thought in the morning and my last thought before I go to sleep. He is beautiful and respectful and intelligent and interesting and passionate and...

"Ok, I get the picture. We will find the most beautiful dress on the entire planet. You should be the one to call and ask your grandmother."

My mother and I continue our chat for two hours. We talk about Sean, her high school days, her days of dating my dad, my friends and the dance. My mom can be my best friend, at times, and this is one of those times. When we finish our conversation, I decide to soak in the tub for a while. Sean won't be home from work for at least an hour. I need something to fill my time.

While I soak in the coconut fragranced water, I close my eyes. I plainly see Sean dressed as a prince and me as a princess. We glide across a huge ballroom floor. Onlookers eye us while we dance—alone. My vision turns to the room full of people, mingling and chatting. Sean, my prince, grabs my hand and leads me out of the room through huge glass doors. We run and run until we are far away from the clamor. All that remains is us. We are surrounded by a beautiful meadow filled with flowers. We collapse to the ground complacent and wonder if anyone will miss us.

My brother Ben bangs on the bathroom door and pulls me from my beautiful reverie.

I head up to my room with a towel still wrapped around my head and nothing but a robe covering my body. My room feels colder than normal. I grab my sketch book from the desk and climb underneath my blankets. I began to sketch Sean and I, the prince and the princess, with their white horse gallantly standing in the background.

Sean stands and faces me with his palms touching mine. His hair falls gently around his face and his lips reveal a smile. He wears a dark suit with tales that hang slightly longer than they should. His eyes unravel every mystery my soul has to offer.

My hair flows in curls that reach the lower part of my back. Tiny flowers and ribbons weave through the strands. On top of my head rests a tiara, a small one, yet enough to transform me from a common girl into a majestic princess. The dark chiffon that splits at my waist drifts to the ground surrounding me. Underneath this chiffon is a layer of shimmery satin that kisses the ground. Lace covers my bust and three quarter length sleeves fall from my shoulders.

My drawing could easily be an illustration for a promising fairy tale—one with a happy ending. I stretch across my bed and stare at my sketch. An image of Sean riding up to my window on his white horse plays over and over in my mind. My hair and my dress flow gently behind me while we gallop across a high rocky ridge. The western sky fills with shades of red and orange and purple and pink. The horse gallops faster and faster, until we are completely out of sight.

I place my drawing on the bed and realize, I don't need to dream about meeting a prince. I already have one and his name is Sean Gentry.

CHAPTER TWENTY-TWO

Another Friday. The school year is coming to an end. Anxiety and excitement fill the halls. The noise level continues to rise while the passing weeks approach their final destination, summer vacation.

Once again, I haven't heard from Sean all week, but this is our routine and I'm *almost* getting used to it. I head home after my final class wondering if Sean will surprise me tonight. After I clean my room, I sit down on my bed and open my history book to study for a quiz we have coming up on Monday. I have a full page of notes copied when my phone rings.

"Hi Brianna, I only have a minute, but I want to ask you a favor." Sean pants and catches his breath.

"Of course, anything."

"I have to work tonight until nine. If your parents don't care, you can meet me at work tonight about eight. I can show you around and we can spend some time together when I get off. I have to work tomorrow and Sunday, since I'm off next Saturday and Sunday. I don't want to wait until prom to see you."

"I want to see you too, how do I get to your work?"

"If you come up highway seventy-one north, then turn west on one-sixty, we're right past the airport. Come to the back door and I'll meet you at eight."

"I'll be there!" I answer.

"Awesome, see you soon," Sean rushes the conversation to a close.

I have two hours to freshen up and drive to his work, which is a good twenty minute drive. I race downstairs to clear my plans with my mom. She doesn't have a problem with me leaving, but seems slightly disgruntled that I am heading out of town, by myself, that late at night. I assure her I will be home before curfew at eleven. She reads the desperation in my expression and can't bring herself to tell me no.

I jump in the shower to rinse off quickly. I dry my hair and brush through it quickly. I pull on some jeans and a ruby red button up blouse and head out the door. I glance at the clock while I drive down the highway. It is only seven o'clock. I should have taken the time to put on some makeup. Now I will be super early, but early is better than late--especially when it comes to spending time with Sean.

I drive my car to the back of the building and search for the door I am to meet him at. I glance right, and then left confused, there are two doors. I decide to park in between them and hope he will poke his head out at eight to see if I'm here.

I have a forty minute wait ahead of me. I turn on the radio to pass my time. This doesn't work, because time is still moving ridiculously slowly. I am sure the clock in my car stops working. I see pictures form in the brick façade that envelopes the building.

The moon is bright tonight, but the yellow glow of the parking lot lights masks most of its beauty. I wish I could fly above all of the illumination and buzzing. I want to be engulfed by stars and the translucent glow of the moonlight.

I begin to dream, Sean and I sit in a row boat. Our faces shimmer an iridescent blue in the moonlight. I lean with my back against his chest; his legs straddle both sides of me. I hear frogs croak, and the breeze rustles the leaves on the trees that surround the lake we drift over. Calm waves gently rock us. His arms slide around me and pull by body in close. I feel his breath against my cheek. The sound of faint music plays in the background and pulls me into a complete dream state.

The boat begins to rock gently on the waves, until it builds momentum and crescendos into full slamming seizures. Sean pulls me in tight and screams my name while our bodies slam into the sides. What is trying to destroy our serenity? Why did it ruin my dream? Like a bullet, the woman with long black hair shoots up from the water and hovers over us. I gasp.

The gasp startles me back to consciousness. My eyes scout the parking lot before I focus on my clock, it's eight forty five.

"Shit!" I exclaim.

Where is Sean? Does he know I'm here? I run to the door on my right and knock several times. No one answers. I run to the door on my left and knock, this time louder, still no one answers.

I'm not sure what to do. Do I go in the front door and ask for him? Will he get in trouble if I do? Was he sneaking me in? Since it is almost nine, I decide I will find his car and wait for him. He will be out soon.

I drive around the entire back parking lot, but I don't find Sean's car. I drive to the front of the building but it's not there either. Panic sets in, I have to find him.

Finally, I spot his car in a dark corner of the parking lot, close to the road. *Relief.*

I park next to his car and wait for him to come out. A few minutes pass before I spot a group of guys walking out the front of the building. They head my direction. All of them are dressed in black pants, with white shirts, I see the one in the middle is my Sean. *Thank god.* He stares in my direction. His lips pull tight while his coworkers poke and prod at him. When he approaches, his expression is revealed by the dim light of the parking lot. Or maybe I should say lack of expression, his annoying poker face.

"Hi" I say timidly. Even Princess Jezebel twists her hair and keeps her eyes on her really cute shoes.

"Wow, you are here. Hmmm, now I have a problem," Sean states.

"I'm sorry, it's a long story. I don't understand, what's your problem?" I plead.

"Well let's see, I had to assume your parents wouldn't let you come, or you didn't want to make the trip, or you were in a ditch dead somewhere. I told Jay and Jeff I would go hang out with them for a while."

My head falls deeper into my lap. I blew my opportunity. "Oh..." Princess Jezebel glares at me down her long pointy nose and shakes her skinny finger in disappointment.

"What was up Bri, why didn't you meet me at eight, or call, or something?"

I feel the weight of my tears tug on my eyelids. Everything begins to blur. I can't allow Sean to see that I am crying. I look into my lap and allow the tears to drip into a pile. I try to pull my shit together. I take a finger and wipe away the evidence.

My brittle voice begs for forgiveness, "I'm so sorry. I was here; in fact I was here by seven-thirty. Since I was early I sat in my car until closer to eight, but I fell asleep. When I woke up it was eight forty five and I didn't know what door to go to. I knocked on both of them, but no one answered. I didn't know what to do. I found your car and decided to wait by it." I feel my eyes start to swell with tears again.

"Have you ever heard of coming in the front door to ask for me, Bri?"

Funny, I have never heard him call me Bri before tonight; weirdly this makes me feel ordinary.

"Sean, I thought about coming in, but I didn't want to get you in trouble. I thought maybe you were sneaking me in the back door. I'm so stupid, I'm sorry. I'll go home now, that way you don't have to keep your friends waiting." I hear them shout his name in the background.

"Well, I guess I'll see you later. I will see you next weekend for sure, unless you decide to sleep through that too."

I can't swallow; my throat feels like I swallowed a toad. Now I can't breathe, either. There is no way humanly possible to keep the tears from escaping, at this point. The floodgates open and the salt river flows.

Sean starts to walk away, but turns back around and grabs my door. He swings it open and startles me, "Can I at least have a hug from you, before you go?"

I choke out, "Yeah sure," while I unbuckle my seatbelt and wipe the tears away from my cheeks.

I climb from my car and expose myself to the glow of the moon and distant parking lot lights. Sean studies my eyes, intently. The faint light is enough to reveal I have been crying. He places his palms on my cheeks, his fingers reach towards my hair, "Brianna, why are you crying?"

"I'm crying because I've missed you so much I could die. I wanted so badly to be with you tonight. I can't believe I was so stupid and fell asleep. I'm a complete idiot."

"Brianna, you are not stupid and you're not an idiot. You honestly did fall asleep? That isn't some lame ass story you came up with on the fly?"

"Sean, I seriously did fall asleep. I don't know why, I'm not even tired. I was bored waiting, I guess."

He can appreciate a shadow of humor in my story and begins to laugh. Part of his laughter makes me want to cry harder, because I feel humiliated. The other part wants to laugh with him, relieved.

"Wow, Brianna. Hold on a sec."

Sean turns to wave his friends on. Encouraged, my racing nervous heartbeat begins a beat I recognize. Sean opens my back door and motions for me to climb in. I slide over, so he doesn't have to go around. He follows closely behind me.

"I don't know what to say. I don't want you to cry, *ever again*. You're killing me here. I'm sorry. I was humiliated, which made me angry. I thought you decided not to come—something better came along. They all tried to rile me up...burn dude...loser...sure you have a girlfriend. It was fairly embarrassing. I waited in the back room for twenty minutes and paced the floors. After I calmed down I was worried. I thought something happened to you...or whatever. If you were in a wreck coming to see me, your parents would never forgive me. Worse, I would never forgive myself. I seriously didn't know what to think. I just knew I waited and waited and nothing. No Brianna, no phone call, no anything. I poked my head out and scanned the parking lot several times. I thought I would see you, or you would see me. Nothing."

"Sean, I flew out of the house as soon as I hung up the phone. That is why I was ridiculously early. I didn't know which door to park by, because there were two back doors. I parked between them and hoped I would see you poke your head out. I guess it's hard to see anything when your eyes are closed. I'm so sorry. I just wanted to be with you, that's—"

"Brianna, shhhh!" and his fingertip falls against my lips. Sean, again places his palms on my face. He looks into my tear stained eyes. His expression is sincere and loving. "None of this matters. Let's not waste another minute on what if's."

He brings his face closer to mine and gently kisses my lips. His face pulls slowly back away from mine. He wraps his arms around my shoulders and pulls me in tight against his chest.

"I guess we should talk about next weekend before we are too preoccupied and forget," he grins. "What are you wearing, so I can attempt to look at least a fraction as good?"

"A long dress," I reply.

"Haha ...do you think you could elaborate a bit," Sean smirks.

"You want to know what my dress looks like? I can't tell you, because I don't have one yet. Even if I did have one, I think I would want you to be surprised."

Sean studies the back of the seat in front of him. I see he is unhappy and I hope it's not because I haven't bothered to shop for a dress yet.

I attempt to explain, "Sean, I will buy my dress tomorrow. I have a date planned with my mom and grandmother. I'll tell you what color it is, but I won't explain what it looks like. That's like bad luck or something."

"We're not getting married Brianna, its prom. I thought I would order your flower tomorrow before I have to be at work. I want to make sure it matches, that's all. Plus, I don't want to rent a suit that totally clashes with what you're wearing."

"Sean, black and white, keep it simple. All that matters to me is that I'm with you."

He was lost, "Black and white? What do you mean?"

"Black suit, white flower, then what I wear doesn't matter," I explain.

"Ok yeah, I like that. I want to wear black anyway," he smiles again.

"So ok Brianna, prom starts at like six and they feed us dinner. It's over at ten thirty and then we have post prom at the Lamar Youth Center from eleven until seven. Do you think your parents will be ok with all of that? It's totally chaperoned."

"Seven? Like seven in the morning?" I exclaim.

"Your parents won't go for that, will they?" Sean questions, with a long face.

"No, no, that's not a problem, I'm sure they'll be fine. No, are you kidding, I'm excited because I will spend like thirteen straight hours with you. Sweet jeezus!" I scream.

"Yeah, that is pretty rockin' I agree. Actually, more than thirteen. We have the whole annoying picture drama, which you know will take at least an hour. Plus drive time from Joplin to Lamar; I may have to pick you up at seven in the morning."

"Fine by me!" I shout, a little too loud.

"Kidding aside, I'll probably pick you up about four thirty. We can do the picture thing with your mom, while I spoon feed her my charm. Then we can go back to Lamar and my mom can do the picture thing. We should be able to be at prom by six. Are you sure your parents won't have a problem with you staying out until seven thirty, or eight in the morning?"

"Post prom is sponsored by the school, right? Chaperones, and all that?" I pump.

"Yeah, I guess that's who sponsors it," he answer.

"They won't have a problem. I still can't believe I will spend that many hours with you. All at once! Please pinch me and tell me this isn't another one of my dreams."

"You have those too ...dreams I mean?" Sean stares out the window with a satisfied smile on his face.

Curious, I press, "What are you thinking?"

He turns his head and smiles, "Nothing, can we be done talking now?"

I smile back ...and slide into his lap.

CHAPTER TWENTY-THREE

Today is the day. My quest begins, for the perfect prom dress. I have a clear image of what I want, so today will be a disappointment. I make an irritating habit of pre-visualizing my outcome, only to be let down by my reality. Sean is my only exception to this dreadful habit.

My mother is dressed and ready to go by the time I make my way downstairs. I swear you would think she is the one going to prom, as giddy as she is acting. Her amusement pulls a smile from my lips.

Grandma Harris, my mom's mom, is picking us up at nine-thirty. She wants to be at the mall when the doors open. That's my grandmother, always early ...never late.

I watch while her Navy Blue Buick pulls into our driveway. I see her climb from her car and move towards our sidewalk. My grandmother Harris is short by today's standards, but probably average for her era. Her short hair is light charcoal gray and styled every week. Today she wears some bright red slacks with a red and blue silk blouse. She always looks enormously well kept.

"Hi Grandma! How have you been, I haven't seen you in forever." I say, when she walks through the door, adorning a huge red lipstick smile.

"Hello Bri. I'm glad you called. I've missed our little shopping trips. Are we ready to go?"

"We're ready," my mom and I say in unison.

We arrive at the mall ten minutes before the stores open. We have a great parking spot, but have to sit in the car and wait for the doors to open. Once in, our only mission is to find the perfect dress. We start at the far north end of our mall and hit every store in pursuit of my mental snapshot. My mom and grandmother continue to fill the dressing room with gowns they think are cute, but none are the dress I have etched into my mind. By the end of the second hour, I never want to hear the word cute, ever again.

I see the impatience build in my mom and grandmother with each rejected dress I toss back at them. My mom finally speaks out, "Bri, what is wrong with this dress? You look beautiful in it."

This particular *cute* dress is royal blue, with a blue toile skirt. The toile is streaked with silver glitter. It reminds me of a constellation full of shooting stars.

"Mom, it's *cute* I guess, but it's poufy and the sparkles make it look like a Barbie doll dress. I'm sorry, this is not me."

I hear way to much air pass through her nostrils while I ogle myself skeptically in the full length mirror. I know they're growing impatient, but I know what I'm in search of and I'm not ready to give up my quest. Not yet.

"Why don't we break for lunch and regroup," my grandmother suggests.

"That sounds like a great idea," I answer. *Maybe my mom will suck the air back in her lungs she let out five minutes ago.*

"Yes, it might help if we know exactly what you're searching for, Bri," my mom adds snarkily. *There you go, mother dearest. Breathe...breathe.*

We head south towards the buffet in the mall and pass several stores on our journey. I glance in each window we pass, but see nothing except the same mundane dresses I have rummaged through all morning. I concede I may have to settle for something other than my mental picture. I'm running out of options.

"STOP!" I yell out to my mom and grandma, who are now ten paces ahead of me.

"What Bri? What's the matter?" my grandmother questions.

"Here it is! I found my dress!"

My mother rushes back, "Where?"

"The burgundy and silver one, right over there," I point the dress out to my grandmother.

As we make our way over to the rounder the dress is displayed on, my mom narrows her eyes, "This is the dress you like?"

"Yep, this is the one, it's absolutely perfect."

"Go try a couple of them on Bri," my grandmother suggests.

I head into the dressing room with a size five and a size seven, pretty sure I'm somewhere in between. I grab the size five off of its hanger. I slide the pale silver satin over my head. It skims my body and brushes my curves in a shimmering dance. The base of the dress is a simple A-line with a scoop neck and narrow straps over my shoulders—plain, yet elegant.

I pull the overlay from the hanger next. The overlay is crimson chiffon, soft and flowing. The thin layers of chiffon are split up the front all the way to the high empire waistline. The gleaming silver of the gown beneath shimmers under the layers of chiffon, like it glows. The sliver of silver exposed through the split, radiates like the sun that peeks around a dark cloud. A wide satin band connects the graceful chiffon to an intricate burgundy lace bodice. The three quarter length sleeves gently fall away from my shoulders.

I gaze at myself in the full length mirror and twirl. This is the dress. It is perfect. I open the door to the dressing room and find my way to where my mom and grandmother sit, patiently. My mom's jaw hits the floor.

"Oh my god Bri, I have to admit I didn't truthfully like this dress on the hanger. But now that you have it on—this dress is made for you. You look stunning," my mom chokes out.

"Yes, I agree. That is absolutely beautiful on you. I would never...", she tosses her arms above her head. "I guess you knew what you were after all along, like you designed the dress yourself," my grandmother adds.

I had not given much thought to my quest until now. I did design this dress. This dress resembles the drawing at home in my sketchbook. I had a clear subconscious reason to search for this dress.

I admire myself in the mirror for at least five full minutes and try to picture myself with my hair full of curls and my makeup just right. "Ok, Brianna I love it, will you take it off, so I can pay for it?" my grandmother hints.

My mother and grandmother bicker over who will pay for my dress while I float around in my Sean fairytale. I eventually wander back into the dressing room to take the dress off and put it back on the hanger. After my grandmother makes the purchase, *I knew she'd win...she always wins,* we resume our course to the buffet. Hanging out with my grandmother and my mom today is a pleasant change in my routine.

My mom admits over lunch that she never attended any of her proms. My dad was almost thirty when she was my age. He played in a band every weekend and had no interest in attending a high school dance. This completely explains her giddiness this morning.

After lunch, we set out to accessorize. This is my mom's contribution to the expedition, since she lost out on the dress purchase to my grandmother. We find some silver sandals that are high enough to keep my dress from dragging on the floor, but not so high I will fall on my face. Mom also finds a small silver purse; she insists I have. I don't see the need, but whatever.

My grandmother insists on some jewelry. I don't want to take away from the simple elegance of the dress, but she finds some sterling silver earrings that have burgundy stones that dangle at the end of tiny sterling chains. They are pretty bad-ass, so I give in. I can't wait to see Sean's expression when I flow down the staircase. Princess Jezebel performs her best grand fouette.

I'm exhausted when we return home. I head straight for my room. After I hang up my dress and put away everything else we purchased today, I flop back on my bed. I don't know if Sean will call tonight when he gets off, but a girl can hope. Prom has me as excited and nervous as a child on their first bike ride.

I flip impatiently through the pages of my Teenation magazine and sift through hairstyles for prom. I re-read the astrological love guide first, just for fun—because I have it totally memorized. One little gaze from him is all it took to know. My instincts about him have been so right. He is special, and he is the one meant just for me.

None of the hairstyle I see give me the *wow* factor. I grab my sketch book and study my drawing. That is how I want my hair to look, large loose flowing curls falling innocently down my back.

I begin to dream, I see Sean in his black suit standing at the base of my staircase anticipating my decent. I see the smile on his face and the spark in his eyes when he catches his first glimpse of me. His arm extends and I wrap my arm through his. His eyes lock with mine while he saunters across the floor with me at his side. With one swift swoosh, he whisks me up off my feet and carries me in his arms to a shiny gold chariot. The carriage is drawn by beautiful white horses. He places me in the carriage and the horses gallop out of sight and take us along for the ride. All that is left behind is a cloud of gray dust that drifts in the breeze.

I think to myself ...*Bri, be careful. In your attempt to envision all that is perfect, you will set yourself up for disappointment—again.* There will be no chariot, no horses, no cloud of dust. But, there will be Sean, and that's all that matters. One quest over ...another begins.

CHAPTER TWENTY-FOUR

My school week inches by like solitary confinement. Every minute seems like hours, every hour seems like days. My anticipation of prom night fogs every coherent thought and every subconscious dream.

I need someone to share in my excitement, but feel completely alone.

Natalie doesn't like Sean, for reasons I can't fathom. Her nostrils flair every time his name is mentioned. Her animosity is so blatant, I have to wonder if there is something buried beneath the surface. Adrienne is more tolerable, yet an indisputable part of her doesn't trust Sean. No surprise there—trust is not one of Adrienne's stronger qualities.

Samantha once shared my enthusiasm, but Cory's selfish decision to take an ex-girlfriend to prom has dampened her spirit and left a bitter taste in her mouth, where prom is concerned. This is my first formal, but my excitement will need to remain my own.

I have taken my dress out of the closet everyday this week to gawk at it—like it will magically dance around my room or some other enchanted shit. The dream of Sean and I dancing alone becomes more vivid with each passing night. I'm not sure what my dream means, or why it repeats over—and over—in my brain. I am pretty certain it won't materialize. Dancing, at all, seems like too much to anticipate.

Tonight begins the rituals, the pre-prom preparations. I have my checklist of what needs done tonight, followed by what needs done tomorrow. Time will fly—and land on our thirteen hour's of togetherness runway.

Lunch period, the last one of the week, has finally arrived. I have something special for Samantha, since tomorrow is her birthday. I sit down at the table and pull the wrapped box from my bag.

"What is this?" Sam smiles, and she snatches the present from my hand.

"Sam, I'm sorry I can't spend your birthday with you. I suck as a friend."

"Brianna, quit worrying about my birthday. Tomorrow will be a memory you will hold forever. Oh my god. You have to be so excited. I know you haven't talked about prom much, since the whole Cory calamity. I apologize for that. As angry as I am with him, you're still my best friend. I just wish I was going."

"I wish you were going too. Epic fail Cory!"

"I assume you have your dress. I would love to see it."

"I seriously want to spend some time with you on your birthday. Do you want to swing by tonight or tomorrow?" I wince.

Samantha's eyes question how I can pose something so ridiculous—like the answer is obvious. "I thought you would never ask. In fact, I'm coming over to spend the night tonight. Shoot, I thought I would have to invite myself. I can help you prepare for prom. It'll be freaking fabulous!"

I snatch the present back out of her hand. I'm sure my eyes smile before my lips have a chance to catch up. "In that case, you're waiting for this until your birthday. Tomorrow."

We finish our taco's and finalize our weekend plans. Emily tries to join our conversation, with talk about our schools prom. She is working up the courage to ask Craig Branson, a boy she has been secretly eyeing. Samantha and I encourage her to go for it. The lunch bell rings and we head to class. My afternoon passes much quicker than the rest of my week. Samantha has everything to do with that.

My mother backs out of the driveway when I approach our lane. I pull to the side and roll down my window. "Hey Mom, where are you off too?"

"My cousin Linda was over to visit today. I'm just now off to the store."

"Perfect, Samantha is coming over tonight to spend the night. She's helping me get ready for prom. Her birthday is tomorrow; can you pick up a cupcake or something?"

The smile on my mom's face melts away. I did not consider she looked forward to helping me prepare for my significant day. *God, I'm so selfish!*

An hour after I'm home, Sam shows up at my door. When I open the door, I see she has her arms loaded with an assemblage of beauty shit.

"Sweet jeezus, Sam," I cheerfully greet her.

"Hey," she laughs.

"Here, let me help you take some of this upstairs," I offer, while I grab most of the bags and boxes out of her arms.

"Thanks, actually I have more in the car, so I'll meet your upstairs."

I carry what I can manage up the staircase and sit the load on my bed. She has everything imaginable, manicure and pedicure equipment, curling irons, flat irons, hot rollers, an entire bag dedicated to hair products, skin products and nail polish. *Are you fucking serious!*

I hear Samantha struggle her way up the staircase. I meet her halfway.

"Good lord Sam, please tell me this is all."

"This is everything," she giggles, her dimples dig into her cheeks.

The comforter is literally covered from head board to foot board. Sam starts to separate everything into piles on the floor—by body part.

"Good god Samantha, do I need this much work done, you make me feel a little insecure here," I smile, but I'm not entirely joking.

"Shut the hell up, you know you're beautiful. Tomorrow, you will be, *I bet you wish your girlfriend was hot like me* gorgeous!"

"Sam, you have no idea how grateful I am you're here, but my mom will be heartbroken if we don't let her help too."

"Not a problem, I love your mom!"

Samantha continues to sift through the piles, I sigh. "I had kind of a checklist, but with all of this…" I say and wave my arms around the entire perimeter of my room. "I guess I'm curious to know what your plan is."

"Tonight, we will work on your hands, your feet and your skin. Tomorrow will be hair and makeup. What do you think?"

"I think that sounds like a suck ass way to spend your birthday."

"Ok Debbie Downer, don't be such a buzz kill. This is exactly how I want to spend my birthday. Besides, my parents are taking me out for dinner tomorrow night. My birthday won't totally be about you," she grins. "Now, we have work to do. Go fetch some pitchers of hot water, while I organize. We need to start on your pedi."

"You're so bossy, I swear!"

"You need to change into something less intrusive, too."

I choose not to respond, but roll my eyes instead. I run down the staircase to fill up two pitchers of hot water. While I fill the second pitcher, my mom walks through the door with two bags of groceries. *Uh oh, that was fast.* I finish filling the pitcher and sit it down to help her unload the car.

My mom doesn't say much while we bring in the bags, but speaks up once we finish. "What's the water for?"

"Samantha is giving me a pedicure—and a manicure—and a facial. My friends can be overwhelming sometimes."

"I think that sounds like a lot of fun. Enjoy. By the way, I grabbed a little cake and some pizza for you two." My mom tries, but she can't hide the sadness in her expression

"Thanks, you're the best. Can I ask you another favor?"

"Sure."

"Do you care if we come down to the kitchen to work on my two day makeover, instead of my room? It would be way more convenient, and we could use your help."

"Give me ten minutes to put the groceries away, and the room is all yours," the spark returns to her blue eyes.

I head up the staircase to let Samantha know the change of plans. She gathers up all of the items that will scrub, buff and polish me down to a new layer of skin. She hands me the bag of nail polish to carry and I follow her back down the staircase.

Like a doctor prepares for surgery, she lays out her tools. *She's way to fucking organized.* I grab her a short stack of towels and she pulls a chair out of our dining room and places it behind a tub of now steamy churning aqua water.

"Go change Brianna, what are you waiting for?" she orders.

I run back upstairs and change into some Capri pajama pants and an oversized t-shirt. I bounce back down the staircase and skip half of the steps. As outrageous as this is, a small part of me feels like a celebrity…it's fairly bad-ass.

"Have a seat girlie!"

I stick my feet one by one in the hot bubbling water. The steam and the aroma of menthol are calming—too calming. Sam and my mom chat, while I close my eyes and relax. I'm so excited for tomorrow to arrive, but everything that begins must also come to an end. Prom hasn't even started, but knowing it will end already makes me sad.

After ten minutes, Sam pulls one of my feet from the water and rests it on a towel that is draped across her lap. I let my head fall gently back. My eyes close. I'm nearly asleep when she pulls the second foot from the water. For close to an hour, Sam buffs, scrapes, cuts, files and massages.

My mother jokes with Samantha, "Ok, I'm next!"

"Have a seat Mom," Samantha chuckles.

"Thank you, but I am kidding. Perhaps we can do this another time, when we don't have Brianna to concentrate on."

"Are you sure, we have time, honestly."

"I'm positive, thanks anyway."

I see relief fill Samantha's expression …I smile.

Sam dumps the foot bath water down the kitchen drain and cleans up her tools while my feet absorb the menthol lotion she has drenched them in. She grabs several tubes of ointment and lays them across the counter. *What now?*

"Ok Bri, we need to do something about those hands now. Actually Mom, if you want to join her, we can all do this one together." Samantha spends the next hour going through a four step process on my hands. Total overkill. By the time she finishes, my mom's A.D.D. has kicked in.

"Are you girls ready for pizza? It's late, and I'm starving.".

"Sure," we both answer. When our pizza is finished, Sam carries it upstairs while I grab two sodas and follow behind.

"We're not done, you know," Sam enlightens me. "After we eat, I'll work on your fingernails and we'll polish you up."

I look down at my uneven nails and grimace. Sean will never realize the preparation that went into his prom night. I almost laugh, because if Natalie knew what I was doing right now, she would disown me.

Samantha and I listen to some music and nibble on our pizza. She still nags about her disappointment in Cory. The very fact she still talks about what he did, makes it clear the knife is still lodged in her chest. She wants me to spy and report back after prom. She wants to know if they look *together*, or not. I think this idea sucks, but reluctantly agree.

I want to go to bed uber early tonight and wake up around eight tomorrow morning. Samantha disagrees with my strategy. She thinks we should finish as much as possible tonight. Stay up late and sleep in as much as possible tomorrow. The later I wake up tomorrow, the less tired I will be after the midnight hour. There is some merit to her idea.

Sam finishes my nails; they are salon perfect. I have Samantha pull out the sketch I drew and explain my ideas for my hair. She totally gets it.

"While your nails dry, can I see your dress."

"It's hanging in my closet at the far left in a dark blue plastic garment bag," I answer.

Sam pulls the dress out of the closet and rests the bag on my bed. She slowly pulls the plastic up.

"Wow Bri, this is beautiful. Not what I expected, but pretty."

"What do you mean? Not what I expected?" I look at her through narrow eyes.

"I just mean, I picture you more like the sparkly fairy princess type," she smiles. "Oh wait; this is the dress you sketched into your drawing, right."

"No Sam, I drew the picture of Sean and me, before I found this dress. Weird, right?"

"Holy smoke, are you kidding? You found a dress that matched your drawing? That has an element of creepiness in it. If you ever have a dream about me dying, please don't tell me."

"It wasn't a picnic, but yeah, I found what I was looking for. How's that for good karma ...you know, instead of the creep factor?

"Well, I love the dress Bri, honestly! Especially with the whole sketch karma thing going on. The dress was meant to be."

My cell phone rings, I recognize the name and number immediately.

"Hey!"

"How are you, Miss Brianna. I want you to know, I can't wait for tomorrow to be here. I've done nothing but think about you...and prom...and you, all day. I miss you."

"I miss you too, Samantha says hi."

"Oh, you have company. Tell her I said hello—tell her happy birthday. I won't keep you. I just want to remind you to pack a change of clothes, a bathing suit, and a towel for post prom. I have to go, but I can't wait until tomorrow. I'll see you at four-thirty."

"Oh, ok ...I'll see you at four-thirty. I can't wait either," I say in shock. My mind is stuck at bathing suit. *Sweet fucking jeezus...bathing suit, really?*

"Goodbye Brianna."

"Bye Sean."

I shake the trauma from my brain and glance over at Samantha, "God, I so freaking love him! He said happy birthday, by the way."

"That was nice, that he remembers I mean."

"Sam, he is so ridiculously perfect. My fantasies you all made fun of, they don't hold a candle to him. He is everything to me Samantha, every single breath of my existence."

"You're not planning to …you know?"

At first, I don't understand her question, but then it registers, "Oh good lord, Samantha!"

Sam changes into her night clothes, while I clean up our food mess. I think about her question. Resisting Sean has become harder and harder. This electric chemistry, which pours through our veins whenever we are together, brings on feelings I never knew existed. Can I resist him, yet again tomorrow? I'm not completely sure I can. That is a butt load of time spent together. Yet, there are so many reasons why I think I will. Sean is my first real boyfriend, and this is not something I am ready to explore, not quite yet. Plus, we will be with other people all evening. The temptation won't be as overwhelming if we're not alone.

I stretch out across my bed while Samantha buffs and polishes on my face. She admits to me, she has a light crush on someone at our school. He is the star quarterback of our football team. If you're going to go Sam…go BIG! Samantha is intimidated, like she is beneath him. I don't understand how someone as beautiful as Sam can possess an ounce of insecurity. I work to build up her confidence. She needs to go for what she wants—no holding back. *Tackle it head on—pun intended.* Sean has spurred a new level of confidence in me, this week. I likey.

We talk until after midnight and Samantha falls asleep. I desperately want to shut my mind off. I count sheep. I swat chickens with a tennis racket. I rub my belly, it works for the dog. I listen to my favorite Pink Floyd music. My attempt is futile, the harder I try, the more alert my mind is.

Snapshots of tomorrow flash through my mind—in full radiant color. Flash. Flash. Flash. I glance up at the clock which reads one fifteen, then two thirty, then three o'five. I'm not sure what time I finally fall asleep, but sense it is well after four.

My eyes crack open and allow a fragment of light to slip in. I make out an image walking around my room.

"Sam?"

In a whisper she answers, "Oh, I'm sorry. Go back to sleep, it's only eight. You have a long night ahead of you; you have to try to sleep a few more hours."

I watch her ghostlike figure tiptoe around my room and gather together small piles. I hear her tread lightly down the staircase to the level below. I know I should go back to sleep, but my mind buzzes again, ready to begin my day. Hundreds of thoughts bounce through my brain, things I need to do, preparations that need made. I consciously try to fall back to sleep, but can't. Samantha quietly walks back into my room to find me wide awake and sitting up.

"What the heck are you doing! You have to go back to sleep Brianna, I don't want dark circles under your eyes when I try to make you dazzling today! This is not a freaking option!"

"Too late Sam, I have way too much on my mind to sleep."

"Ugh, Brianna! You are looking at twenty four hours before you can sleep again."

I smile, uncontrollably now. This time tomorrow, I will be in Sean's car next to him, returning home from spending over fifteen solid hours with him. I couldn't sleep now if my life depended on it.

I remember Sam's birthday is today. I pretend to go to the bathroom, but instead grab the little cake from the fridge. I scurry through the junk drawer and search for candles. I finally find a partial box in the far back corner. I don't have seventeen candles, so I use one. I grab the candle lighter and lite it, then head back up the staircase.

As I reach the top landing, I start to sing, "Happy Birthday to you, Happy Birthday to you, Happy Birthday dear Samantha, Happy Birthday to you!"

"What is this? You didn't have to do this! Wow— you are the best freaking friend ever," Samantha chokes out.

"Of course I am," I reply. I reach into my book bag and pull out her present. It's wrapped in shiny yellow paper with lime green polka dots. I passed the gift over to her and she begins to unwrap it, careful not to tear any of the paper. She pulls out the box and rests it in her lap before opening the lid. Inside the box is a journal. The word *FRIENDS* is written across the cover.

"Thanks Brianna, you didn't need to buy me anything."

"I thought this would be nice with our senior year coming up, you know, to write your thoughts down and save them forever. It has a few pages in the back you can store a few photo or music discs—pretty badass."

"This is perfect. Hopefully my life will be more exciting next year. Thank you!"

Samantha and I carry her cake downstairs, pour some milk and devour the entire thing. After we're done, I take my shower and pack my bag for post prom. I skeptically grab my bathing suit. Temptation to leave it behind nearly overtakes me.

Samantha and I sit around for a few hours and talk while my mom steams my dress and makes sure there isn't a wrinkle, anywhere. Right after lunch, Samantha begins her final steps. She pulls all of my hair back and begins another facial. This one isn't gritty. Thank god, my face is still a little red from the buffing she did last night. She covers my face with a funky green mask, just like the movie. At least the mask is soothing and not eating off what is left of my skin. *Sweet jeezus, this better not stain my face green or I will have to fucking kill her!* Princess Jezebel glares at me over her flute of bubbly, while she sinks deeper into her hot tub.

"Sam, I don't want too much makeup. I don't want to look like a slut. No glitter or sparkles, please."

"Dang it Bri, this is a princess kind of night. You're not giving me much creative freedom here! But, you're the boss, so whatever." The clock reads nearly two, by the time my makeup is finished. Samantha and my mom refuse to let me look in a mirror.

My hair is a cooperative effort. Samantha works one side, while my mom works the other. They have to heat the rollers three times to finish my entire head. My mom pulls back some hair from the crown of my head and my temples and secures it with a comb, while Samantha pulls out a few strands to fall around my face.

Samantha picks up my sketch and carefully studies it. She attempts to make every detail as precise to the drawing as she can.

"Where are the ribbons?" Sam asks.

"I never bought any. That's ok, we don't need them."

My mom interrupts, "Oh malarkey, I have all kinds of ribbon in my sewing tuffet. Let me see what I can dig up."

She returns with some pink ribbon. This is the thick kind, in cotton candy pink. The kind you might put in a small child's pig tails. In fact, this ribbon is probably left over from my toddler years. Totally not the look I'm after.

"Mom seriously, it's ok. I don't want the ribbons." *Fuck. Please put that shit away.*

The clock reads three thirty; Sean will be here in one hour. *One. Fucking. Hour.* My heart begins to beat faster.

Samantha and my mom wait while I shuck off my clothes and slide the shimmery silver satin over my hips and up onto my shoulders. I approach my mom and have her zip the tiny zipper that leads from my lower back to my waist where the material ends.

Samantha gathers the layers of dark chiffon away from my hair and face while my mom finagles the outer layer of burgundy lace over my head and arms. Funny I don't remember this dress being overly complicated when I tried it on. After several minutes of tugging, twisting, and tweaking, everything falls into place.

Samantha blurts, "Oh my god Bri, you look gorgeous ...you glow!"

I stare at my mom. Tears stream down her face, *Oh sweet jeezus! Don't do this! You'll ruin my makeup!* "Samantha is right. You are straight out of a fairytale."

"Yes, that's it, like she should ride off into the sunset, or grasp a magic wand," Samantha adds.

I put on my shoes and jewelry while my mom digs out her camera. She wants a few photos of me, alone.

Samantha goes upstairs to grab the bag I packed that contains my change of clothes, *bathing suit*, and towel. I go into the bathroom and toss anything else I might need overnight. I think about how that sounds. *Overnight. With Sean. Sweet jeezus.*

I peek at myself in the full length mirror, for the first time. I don't recognize the image in the reflection. This cannot be me. My mother and Samantha have done an incredible job. I never thought of myself as beautiful, but on this night I have to admit, I look pretty fucking awesome. I can't stop the smile from building.

I sit my bag on the breakfast bar and wait for Sean to arrive. Waiting. Waiting.

Samantha scurries to collect the rest of her stuff and loads everything into her car. I want to help her, but she highly objects.

The preparations are all complete. Samantha is loaded, my mom has her camera ready to aim and I—well I am ready to begin the most memorable night of my life. I am totally and completely prepared for what comes next.

CHAPTER TWENTY-FIVE

My mom spent so much time making my dress perfect, I don't dare sit down. Instead, I watch out the window like a lighthouse beacon. Beep...beep...beep. A car finally pulls in the drive, but the vehicle is not Sean's. My eyes fall to the hardwood floor. I didn't know we were riding to prom with another couple. The smile creeps back into my expression when I glance up to see Sean close the driver's door of this fancy white Cadillac.

"Oh my jeez, it's time! Where's his boutonniere?" Sam barks.

"Boutonniere? What are you talking about?"

"You didn't pick him up a boutonniere? Oh well, never mind. Sean doesn't seem like the type who would care about a stupid flower anyway."

My mom apologizes, "I'm so sorry Bri, I never went to any formals, I didn't know or I would have ordered one."

"Mom, it's fine. Sam's right. Sean won't care."

"HURRY—HIDE! Stand in the staircase, GO— GO," Samantha orders. *Bossy!*

I stand on the landing, just out of sight, while my mom answers the door.

"Hello Mrs. Hart, how are you this evening?"

"I'm terrific Sean, and you?"

"I couldn't be better. Is Brianna ready?"

My mom pretends to yell for me, but knows full well I can hear Sean perfectly. I'm not usually this dramatic, but prom…come on. Some things just deserve a production. I take a deep arduous breath and step off of the landing and round the corner. I'm prepared for his smile. I'm not prepared for my jaw to fall off of my face. Sean is gorgeous, dressed in a black tux with a silver grey vest. *Sweet jeezus!* He's so fucking hot!

We both stand in shocked silence and size each other up. We're so weird. My legs begin to fold, which is not comforting while pencils prop up my heels. My hands quickly grab the edge of the counter to steady myself.

Sean slides a small white box across the counter with one hand and his other arm wraps my waist to steady my wobble. I lift open the lid and in the box is an exquisite trio of orchids, two white with a touch of burgundy in the center; one a deep purple, almost black in color. The orchids are attached to a silver hair comb with tiny silver satin ribbon streamers.

"Oh my god Sean, this is absolutely beautiful," I whisper, because I'm not fully able to speak. "Beyond beautiful, this is perfect, how did you…"

"I'm glad you like it. I was worried you would be upset that I didn't bring a corsage, or one of those stupid wrist things. This just seems more *you*. Please don't make me put this thing in your hair, because I don't have a clue."

Samantha and my mom both peek into the box, now. I see their eyes grow wide. *Uniquely perfect, just like us—awesome and shit!*

Sam looks at me and nods towards the box, "Shall I?"

I smile at her, but shake my head no, "Sam, I think I want my mom to do the honors, if you don't mind."

My mom's hand shakes gently when she lifts the hairpiece out of its box. She studies my hair like it is a sculpture. I lose myself in Sean's eyes while she contemplates. The comb slips into my hair, close to my face. The orchids cascade from the top of my head down the left side towards my ear. She weaves the tiny silver ribbons through my dark curls.

"Well, what do you think?" she asks Sean.

"Mrs. Hart, I think your daughter is gorgeous in old T-shirts and sweatpants, obviously she is breathtaking."

"Picture time!" Samantha reminds us.

Mom pulls Sean and me into the living room and takes four hundred and twelve shots— that might be an exaggeration, but not by much. Sean grows anxious.

"Ok Mom, that's enough!"

"Ok—ok. Go have fun." She's so giddy, I'm sure if we invited her to go with us she would pounce on the opportunity. *Sorry Mom—not this time.*

Sean is nervous, and so serious. *So cute.* "Mrs. Hart, Brianna went over our plans with you, correct? Prom is at Lamar High School, then we will attend post prom at the Lamar Community Center. The event is totally supervised and they lock the doors until seven a.m. I should have her home by eight thirty at the latest, and that is only if we decide to stop and eat breakfast.

Chances are it will be sooner. I promise to take good care of her."

"I have no worries Sean. You two have a great time."

I am glad my mom has this discussion with Sean, versus my dad. Randy would make the situation awkward. My dad raised his concerns and reservations with the post prom arrangement, before he left. My mom debated his objections. She found our plans to be positive. We are doing something structured, versus ending up at an alcohol party or parked alone in some vacant parking lot. Dad finally had no choice but to agree with her argument.

I quickly hug my mom and Samantha goodbye. They both tear up when I walk towards the door with my arm wrapped through Sean's. Sean and I lock eyes and I slip through the passenger door, he has held open. He doesn't pull his eyes from mine while he makes his way around the front of the car and climbs into the driver's seat. I want to look away, but it's no use. His voice finally breaks my trance.

"Now we have the pleasure of doing this all over again," Sean states impatiently.

"Your mom won't be as ridiculous as mine was. It'll be alright."

"I wouldn't count on that Brianna. My entire family is waiting for us."

I laugh.

"What's so funny?"

"Nothing, I feel like a rock star. I'm not used to this kind of attention."

"Brianna, you are always my rock star. Tonight, words can't begin to describe you. Do you realize you are luminous and glow like a fucking angel? I can't assume this is real, because this all feels absurdly dreamlike."

"Sean, you are not the only one in a dream state. Can I tell you something silly?"

"Silly is good, let's hear it."

"I had these weird dreams about you and me. We are a prince and a princess. Stupid, I know, but what's crazy is my dream is slowly becoming my reality."

Sean cocks his head to one side. I continue. "I had a picture in my head of the dress I'm wearing, almost exact. I even sketched it in a drawing I did of us, before I bought it. Your suit is exactly what I drew too. In my dream, you pick me up and whisk me away on a beautiful white horse. Now we're in this beautiful white car, horsepower ...get it? Isn't that weird? I feel like I'm living in a fairy tale I never want to escape."

"Brianna, we are special—far from ordinary. Don't every question that."

Sean and I continue our chat to Lamar. We fight the urge to touch each other until the paparazzi are finished with us. We fully recognize the potential consequence of our desire.

Sean pulls into his driveway. I have never been to his house before. His home is a simple white two-story, similar to my own. I nervously stare forward while he circles around the car. He opens my door and holds my trembling hand.

Once inside, Sean introduces me to his family. They all are tremendously welcoming, and his dad is funny, which calms my uptight nerves. His mom snaps several shots with her camera and then we're off.

As we walk out his front door, his sister blurts, "Good luck tonight Sean, I know you'll win." He doesn't comment, but a scowl builds on his face.

My eyes silently question him while we walk to the car. I barely notice his parent's wave in the background. "I'll explain," he nervously whispers when he opens my door.

Our drive to Lamar High School is quiet. *What just happened?* I wait for his explanation, which obviously isn't coming. Finally, when I see the school in my view I question, "Sean, what are you winning tonight?"

"These questions aren't going away, are they?"

I answer, "I'm afraid not."

"Brianna I should have told you before now, but I wanted this to be a surprise for you. I was nominated for Prom King." *What?*

I'm sure my jaw disjoins and bounces on the floor board of his car, *Prom King?* I want to congratulate him, but the words won't come. Instead, my mind crashes into the possibility that the Prom Queen is his girlfriend, the girlfriend that haunts my happy thoughts. I've never been to prom before, but I am aware who typically serves on the prom court. Couples…cute, popular couples. I doubt his school is any different.

"Brianna, will you please say something?"

"Umm, congrats." *Great. Fucking Fabulous. What do you want me to say?*

"Wow, I guess I should have warned you, but I thought this news would make you happy."

"Sorry, I am happy for you. Just a little surprised, I guess. Wow, I'm dating the Prom King, that's just choice," I say, with too much unintentional sarcasm in my voice.

"I'm not the Prom King, I was just nominated. That doesn't mean I'll win. I hope I don't fucking win. Can we go in and forget the whole thing, please?"

I'm not expecting what I see when we walk through the gymnasium door. Nothing about the room feels like a high school gym. Twinkling lights and golden stars dance around the room and sprinkle their reflection everywhere. Red satin walls cover the bleachers, that are folded and hidden away. Long tables line up in rows, covered in white linen table clothes. Each table is adorned with dozens of candles and a sparkly red and gold centerpiece. My eyes wander around the room and admire the effort that obviously went into making this night magical.

At the end of the rectangular room is a stage. I recognize the center table as a DJ setup, but off to each side are four chairs—chairs that will steal my boyfriend away from me tonight. In front of the stage is an area free of tables, surrounded by a ring of colorful lights that hang from the ceiling. All of the colors bounce from the pale wood and give the room a pleasant aura. I know this dance floor is something I won't see much of tonight.

When my mind absorbs my surroundings, I notice the eyes that all lock on me. I immediately feel awkward and out of place. My focus is forced to my painful shoes. I am an outsider. I am intruding on their space? I'm the stray wolf that tries to enter a new pack. They will either accept me, or they will eat me—alive. All I can do is submit.

Sean has a tight grip on my hand and this is my only security. I have never been a fan of social gatherings, and this one tops my awkward list. If I were here alone, ten seconds would have put me square in a stall in the restroom—for the night.

Sean leads me to a table up front near the stage. His choice surprises me. He has always been more private, more intimate in his choices. Among his peers, I may see a completely different Sean.

We take our seats, side by side at the table. Most of his classmates still wander about and mingle. I am confused why we sat down so soon, but I am out of their scrutinizing eye, so I don't question him.

Sean turns in his seat to face me, "Brianna?" he takes my hands into his. "I need you to know that there is nothing in this room more beautiful than you. I am so grateful you are with me tonight."

A tear wants to escape, but I clamp my emotion. Samantha has worked far too hard on my makeup for me to blow it in the first five minutes. Speechless, I pull on a smile.

"Will you be ok if I leave you here for a few minutes? I would like to find Jon and Victoria, so they can sit with us."

Apprehensively I reply, "Yes, I'll be fine."

Jon and Victoria, I remember them from the gig at the park. Jon is tall with dark hair, rather nice looking with exception to a slightly oversized nose. Victoria, on the other hand, makes Adrienne look plain. She is tall, very slender, with long dark hair and a deep complexion. I don't know what exotic plant she bloomed from, but the plant has to be tropical. If I sit with her all night, I will disappear. This is bad where Sean is concerned, but good where the rest of the wolves are concerned.

I canvass the room full of people I don't know. I feel stupid...and small...and totally vulnerable. So many eyes. I feel them stare with a wary intensity. Their intense gapes surround me and suffocate me. My chest grows tight. I try to pull enough oxygen from the room to take a breath, and turn my focus to the stage and the dance floor where the faces are hidden.

Eight chairs sit empty on the stage—four stage left, four stage right. Sean will sit in one of those chairs tonight, without me. Once again, I will be left alone. If he wins, then what? He will dance with his queen...not me. *This totally sucks ass!*

I am selfishly aware I should be proud of Sean, honored even. I just can't be. Watching Sean dance with someone else tonight and live out my dream, will be irrationally painful. My gut aches just thinking about it.

"I'm back," Sean's voice steals back my sanity.

"Good," I say relieved.

He sits down next to me, while Jon and Victoria join us across the table.

With a warm and friendly smile, Victoria reaches out her slender hand to me, "Hi, Brianna right?"

Surprised someone like her even remembers my name, I return the gesture and shake her hand gently, "Hi, yes that's right."

"You and Sean look fabulous tonight! Evidently the competition is on," she grins.

"Competition?" my brows pull together.

"Prom King and Queen, didn't Sean tell you?"

"Oh that, yes he told me."

"Well, I guess I should wish him luck, but then again, I would much rather win myself."

"You were nominated?" *Thank fucking god! Please win!*

"Jon and I were nominated," she corrects me and reiterates this is indeed a couple's competition. Victoria continues her pointless chatter. Not that I'm listening. My mind is still working out my purpose for being here. This night is not turning out to be the fairy tale I envisioned.

Sean and Jon engage in conversation, so Victoria begins to tell me old stories about Sean. She has known him her entire life. This makes my eyes more green than blue, but I want to know everything I can about Sean, so I hang on her every word. After thirty minutes, I excuse myself, "Sean, I need to find a restroom, I'll be right back."

"Would you like me to go with you, not in the restroom I mean, but walk with you?"

Victoria interrupts before I answer yes, "I'll go with her Sean. I need to freshen up anyway."

I am thankful not to have to make the grand waltz through the gymnasium alone, but I would have much preferred Sean at my side. All of this time together I anticipated begins to feel painfully lonely. Victoria leads me out of the crowded room, slightly in front of me, like she is protecting me. I feel the wolves, they circle their prey. Every single eye tells me I don't belong here.

"They're staring at you," Victoria smiles—like this is a good thing.

"Yes, I see that," I reply, when we walk through the gym doors into the corridor. "Why are they staring at me, is what I want to know?"

"Why?" she laughs. "Well first of all, you are beautiful, and I for one am extremely jealous, that dress is the fucking bomb! You aren't from Lamar, so they're curious. Plus, everybody loves Sean. He speaks of you like you're some angel sent down from heaven. So naturally, everyone wants to see this girl who finally captured his heart."

Caught off guard by her comment, I ask, "He talks about me?"

"Well yes, to the point of annoyance. You don't realize how ridiculously into you he is?"

"I guess not."

"Brianna, I don't say this to hurt your feelings, more to make you understand. Sean is the only guy nominated for prom court that isn't here "with someone", if you understand what I mean. *What the hell am I—chopped liver?* This girl in our class, Alexa, really likes him. Don't be mad, but we all conspired to help her out by nominating the two of them—big mistake. Everyone, of course, assumed Sean would ask her, he'd have no choice. When he found out he was nominated, he tried to withdraw. He knew everyone would be disappointed in him if he wasn't with Alexa."

"So, I am the enemy. No wonder."

"No, it's not like that. Sean had no intention of coming here with anyone except you. He made his stand on that clear to everyone, including Alexa. None of us had any idea how serious you two were until after the nomination. Of course we're not mad, we're happy that he's happy. We care more about him than who he's here with. Don't get me wrong, everyone loves Alexa too. She is one of the nicest girls at this school, she deserves to win--way more than me. We talked Sean into staying in the competition, even though they would come with separate dates. Shoot, I would have voted for them myself, if I hadn't voted for me and Jon," she snickers. "Point is, he is totally into you and he's a great guy. Sean is special, consider yourself lucky."

"You have no idea how lucky, Victoria."

I head into an empty stall, then wash my hands after I come out. I am glad Victoria came with me. This little chat has cleared up a lot of questions. I feel better, except for that ache in my gut, knowing I could be watching Sean dance his only dance tonight with Alexa. Plus I know she's into him—wrong answer. *He's mine! All mine whore!*

By the time we sit back down at our table, the food has arrived. Sean looks over at me and smiles nervously. He leans into me, "Well that took a while, are you and Victoria getting along?"

"Yes, thanks for asking, but I would much rather spend time with you," I remind him.

"We have oodles of time. In fact, by the end of the night, you probably will be sick of me."

"Impossible," I respond and shake my head, pushing the food around on my plate.

He pats my leg gently and begins to eat.

I swallow down a few bites, because in reality I should be hungry, but the anxiety of tonight has swallowed my appetite. Sean finishes his plate and glances over at the mostly untouched food on mine. "Brianna, are you ok? You haven't touched your food."

"I'm fine Sean, I'm just nervous."

"What on earth are you nervous about?" he studies my face and tries to understand my apprehension.

"I don't know. I'm not used to hanging out under these circumstances. I'm used to having you more to myself, I guess."

The servers clear the plates from our table. He glances at me with troubled eyes, "Let's take a walk."

I don't argue when he pulls me from my chair and leads me out of the gym. We walk to the far end of the corridor and sit down on a wooden bench. The corridor is dreadfully ordinary compared to the dreamlike ambiance the gym has been transformed into.

He turns to face me on the bench. My palms rest in his and he rubs the back of my hands with his thumbs. I feel the heat of his palms absorb into my skin. The black rings around his iris have my complete attention. Down...down...down I go.

"Brianna, I want this night to be perfect, special, something you will remember forever. What can I do to make this better?"

I look down at my hands without answering.

He continues, "I know you're upset with me for not telling you about the nomination to prom court. I'm truly sorry about that. I tried to weasel out of it, I honestly did."

"I know, Victoria told me in the restroom. She told me about Alexa."

"Great, thanks Victoria," he mutters under his breath.

"Sean, it's ok, I understand. I know you are special, I should never have assumed that you are only special to me. This is my mistake, not yours."

"Brianna, you have to believe that you're the only one I want to be with, tonight. Please believe this."

"I believe you. I'm fine. I just need a few moments alone with you. I am happy for you. What an honor, to be looked up to by your peers like that."

"The only honor I feel, at this moment, is the honor of walking in with the hottest girl in the room," and he leans in and allows his warm soft lips to brush against mine.

My breathing slows and my heart races—all at once. Now he really kisses me, and sucks the life completely out of me until I'm an empty shell, unable to move.

Three minutes later, we are interrupted by Cory. "Hey lover boy, move your ass to the gym. They've already announced your name."

Sean slowly stands up and grabs my hand, this time I'm the one that leads.

"Come on Sean, this is it! You need to hurry!" I exclaim, suddenly surfing on the excitement of winning.

We crash through the gymnasium door and every eye falls upon us. I pray my lip gloss isn't smeared across my face like a cheap whore. All seven members of the court are already on stage. *Embarrassing.* Sean drops me at our table and finishes his runway walk.

One of their teachers—or maybe a principal, I don't know, approaches the podium and begins to speak in a grating tone. His blah blah blah speech lingers on for a perpetually long time, while I fist my hands in anticipation.

Finally, the moment has arrived; the DJ puts on some soft slow music, the theme song to their prom. The MC for the evening approaches the podium. He names all of the nominees in pairs like they are all couples. The words Sean Gentry and Alexa Hammel fall from his lips. They both stand and the gymnasium roars with applause.

Alexa is sort of cute with deep dimples and shoulder length blonde hair. Someone I could probably be friends with.

I was glad I didn't eat much, because my stomach is about two somersaults away from puking. He pulls an envelope from his pocket. My heart begins to beat faster. He breaks the seal and reads the name.

"This year's prom king and queen are, Sean Gentry and Alexa Hammel. Ladies and Gentlemen, your king and queen!" He signals with a swooping motion of his arm for them to share their royal dance.

My stomach shrinks into a tight knot. I feel like I'm breathing through a straw. I continue to fill my lungs until they burn. Tears begin to build on my lower lid. *Do not cry! Do not fucking cry!*

Bri, you can do this. It's just a fucking dance.

They descend the staircase to the dance floor hand in hand. I fight off the nausea—I am ready, I am mentally capable of not crumbling. They approach the center of the floor and wave at everyone. I let all of the air out of my chest at once.

What are they doing? They unlock hands and Sean approaches my side of the room and Alexa walks to the opposite side ...I am completely confused. Sean stands before me and extends his hand. I place my fingers in his palm and he pulls me to my feet. He leads me to the dance floor and wraps his arms around my waist. My dream flashes before me. We dance alone ...as the wolves close in on us. *Sweet jeezus!*

We continue to dance in slow motion, like no one else is around, just he and I, cheek to cheek, pressing our bodies tightly together. Out of the corner of my eye, I spot Alexa wrapped in someone's arms in the opposite corner.

The MC invites the rest of the court to join us, then the rest of the student body. When the dance floor begins to fill in with other students, Sean leans back. I sink into his deep espresso eyes, that reflect the tiny diamonds of light that adorn the room. I smile. He pulls his hand from my waist and places it on my cheek.

"I love you Brianna," he confesses, and he leans in to kiss me.

I. Love. You. These words are even better than girlfriend. I melt; my mind is a wad of used chewing gum. I stand and stare at him blankly. I want to tell him I love him too, but I somehow swallowed a big fat toad. As much as I try, I can't force any sound past my lips. I just hold him tight, like I'll never let go.

After our dance we mingle and bounce from table to table. He introduces me to the wolves, while he catches countless congratulations tossed his way. Clearly, my prince doesn't only charm me; his peers are quite captivated by him, as well. He has made this night unparalleled, a memory I will never let go ...ever.

CHAPTER TWENTY-SIX

As the evening spirals to a close, more and more of Sean's classmates head to the dance floor. This allows us the perfect opportunity to escape, without being noticed.

Sean pulls me into the corridor for the final time of the evening, "Let's get out of here."

"I thought you would never ask."

He quickly scopes out the corridor to make sure we're alone. He grabs my hand and like a bullet we are out the door and into the parking lot. I smile as an image of Sean and I escaping from the ball flashes through my mind.

We laugh and catch our breath while he holds open the passenger door of tonight's makeshift white chariot. I sadly realize, while the school fades from my view, that the fairy tale portion of our magical evening is over—now a memory.

I am excited to spend the next eight hours with Sean, but the dress that made me look like a princess will be hidden away in a locker, or thrown in a bag somewhere. Once we hit the pool, there will be no more perfectly applied makeup ...no more long dark spirals of curls that flow over my shoulder and down my back ...no more mysterious orchids that frame my face ...no more prince and princess, or in Sean's case, King and Queen.

Sean has taken my unattainable dream and created a reality that is mystically similar, but this is where my dream ends. No more prophecies are left to fulfill.

I see Lamar Community Center ahead. Sean's come kiss me eyes smile at me, while he circles the building in search of a parking spot. Not because finding a spot is difficult, the parking lot is pretty much empty. We could easily park by the front door, but being the first one in the building isn't what he has on his agenda.

As he pulls the car into a dark corner in the back of the lot, I want to tell him how much I love him, "Sean."

"Yes, Brianna."

I sit in strangled silence. I can't put my feelings into words ...or maybe my nerves won't let the words escape. Once again, intimidated by his existence, I am silent. What seem like full hours go by, before I muster up the courage to blurt, "I want you to know I had a great time tonight. I really like you."

"You like me, hmmm. Well I like you too."

I like you, good god Bri. Embarrassed, I change the subject. "So what is this place?"

"It's like a fitness center. They have a pool, and a gym where we can play basketball and volleyball. They have work out equipment. They have exercise, tumbling and dance studios. I don't know it's a sports complex...or whatever."

"Hmm ...great, sports. Well if you want to win, don't pick me for your team."

"I think I've won enough tonight." He leans in to kiss me. I'm pretty sure he is trying to shut me the fuck up.

No other students are here yet. Only a few vacant cars sit to the left of the front door. I assume those belong to our chaperones, or maybe to employees of the community center.

Sean cups my cheeks in his palms and gently rests his lips against mine. The heat from his lips makes it hard to concentrate, or breathe for that matter. Although my kissing portfolio only consists of a few pathetic pages, I can't imagine a kiss any better than Sean's.

He backs away to catch his breath. His eyes climb into the pit of my soul. I could wander around in these eyes forever. His fingers slide through his hair and push it out of his face. *God, please stop that.* His eyes are full of desire, and they take a tour of my body—every inch of my body. "You are so beautiful," he proclaims.

Cars begin to stream steadily into the parking lot. "I guess we should go in," his lips pull tight.

"We don't have to be the first ones in the door," I smile. *Go Bri!* Hell, I could sit in this parking lot all night, with no discontent.

"No, I guess we don't."

He leans in and begins to rub his warm soft lips against my cheek and then works his way down my neck. The heat of his breath makes the tiny hairs on the back of my neck stand at attention. I feel his teeth gently tug at my earlobes and he fists my hair behind my head. His full

269

beautiful lips work their way down my neck and follow the silver strap of my dress down my chest. *Sweet jeezus!* The earth spins, I'm so dizzy. His fingers slide to my waist. His grasp on me is so intense; I believe he may literally rip the skin from my body. His lips continue to follow the scoop of the silver satin towards my heart, which now pounds so hard, I see my chest move with each beat. His hands gently slide the lace away from my shoulders and down my arms. He coaxes the overlay down my rib cage and runs his palms down the outside curve of my breast. I feel the heat of his breath flow through my cleavage, every muscle in my body is tense.

I don't have the strength to push him away—maybe because I don't really want him to stop. I want him, I want to feel the heat of his bare body next to mine, but my conscious pulls me back. *Slow down Brianna, slow down.* When his hands inch their way to the center of my breasts, I gently place my hands over them. Slowly, I slide his hands back down to my waist. Right now, I need to be content with his kisses. I place my hands on his face and tenderly pull his lips toward mine. We lock together with a flaming passion. He swallows me whole, like a snake consumes its prey. His arms wrap my body so tight, not even dust can come between us. I love this man.

Sean shocks me when he suddenly shoves me back, "Shit Brianna, we need to go. Everyone is inside and they lock the doors at eleven, it has to be eleven by now."

We don't take time to catch our breath or regroup, we grab our bags from the floorboard and rush towards the door. An older lady with short grey hair turns the key in the lock when we approach. Sean waves his arms frantically to catch her attention. Finally she spots him and unlocks the door to open it. We bolt in.

"You cut that one close Mr. Gentry, her croaky voice scolds."

"Yes, Miss Taylor. Thanks for letting us in."

We wander down a long hallway towards a voice emanating from the gymnasium. It is the same boring announcer that thanked us for coming to prom. We slide our way into the back of the room, while he goes over the rules for the lock in. Like we can't read.

A wave of fatigue washes over me; while I stand and listen to his redundant voice explain how to properly behave tonight. *As if.* The normal shit, don't fight, no foul language, no disrespecting the chaperones, teachers, community center workers, or other students ...blah, blah, blah. No wandering off by ourselves and absolutely no one leaves the building.

It is clear that making out will be totally out of the question the rest of this evening. A night filled with sports— *fucking fabulous.* I think the beer bash may have been the better option.

The speech is over, finally. Sean and I stand in the back of the room and watch the people exit. They still throw their curious glances in my direction. *Stop it!* I see Jon and Victoria inching their way towards us.

Someone I know, good.

"Dude, where have you been? We tried to find you at prom. They announced for you and Alexa to come back out at the end of the night and finish with a closing dance and no one could find you. Alexa looked like a fucking idiot, standing out there by herself. She will fucking murder you, you better hide dude!" Jon snorts.

"I wouldn't have danced with her anyway. I'm glad we left. We talked about this and agreed we would be with our own dates, if we won. So she has no grounds for fucking issues with me."

Jon continues, "I don't know dude, I think she wanted to take a whirl with you. She had that cocker spaniel look in her eye when no one could find you. Finally, dude wait for it, she stomped off of the dance floor like a spoiled brat and sat back down. She's a little huffy brother, just sayin."

"Well, if she is pissed it should be at Kyle. Why did he leave her standing there, fucking idiot? You know, whatever, not my problem, not my drama ...let's go have some fun."

Victoria's perky voice abruptly changes the subject, "Let's go swim first, since we have to change clothes anyway."

"That sounds good to me," Jon answers, his eyebrows bounce up and down on his forehead.

Sean flashes me his dimple grin, "Do you want to go swimming, Brianna?"

About ninety eight percent of me wants to scream NO! The other two percent, can't quit staring at his dimples. I would run naked through the gym for him if he asked right now. My time in the pool is inevitable, I may as well get it over with.

"Sure, swimming is fine." *Fuck! Did I just say that?*

We walk to the locker room doors that lead to the indoor pool. Sean plants a quick kiss on my lips as he lets my fingers slip from his, "I'll see you in a few minutes."

Victoria blurts, "It will be more than a few minutes; we have to wash all this shit off of our face before we get in the pool. We'll see you in twenty minutes, if you're lucky."

"Well hurry," Sean reiterates.

Panic claims its rightful territory. Victoria and I walk into the locker room. It is a typical locker room with rows and rows of metal lockers. The shower is one big concrete room with stalls separated by thin curtains. The shower heads are spaced evenly in a horseshoe. In between the lockers are long wooden benches with names, and hearts, and choice words carved into the petrified wood.

Victoria rests her bag on a bench and starts to strip. Her slinky red gown falls to the floor. I didn't need to see Victoria half naked to know she is tall and slender. She is the type who will feel comfortable …scratch that, proud to parade around in a bikini. *How fucking ratchet!*

"I'm going to jump in the shower," Victoria informs me, and she grabs a small plastic bag and her towel.

"Yeah, me too," I reply, while I sort through my bag to lay out my bathing suit and anything else I may need. My body will not stand naked any longer than it needs to.

Victoria is out of the shower by the time I have my dress off and folded. I'm already wrapped in a towel. I head off to the shower with my shampoo and body wash in hand.

The hot water feels good while it streams across my face. The curls slide from my head like they never existed. I try to cope, but this feeling of panic edges its way to the stage. I wash my hair twice and lather up my face. When the water has me in a comfortable shade of calm, I turn it off and wrap my towel tightly around my chest.

Victoria already has her hair brushed and her bathing suit on by the time I cautiously creep my way out of the shower room. She straddles a bench and weaves her long silky black hair patiently through her fingers. Her lips pull into a smile when I approach her. "I'm sorry, I'm slow. You don't have to wait on me. Go on out to the pool, I'll be there in a few minutes," this suggestion is my reprieve. If I can avoid strutting my average pale body next to the Bain de Soleil model, I will.

"No, that's ok. The guys can wait."

Damn it!

"So Brianna, how long have you and Sean been dating?"

"I met him about two months ago, but we've only been seeing each other a little over a month, I guess." Weird it seems much longer, like forever actually. "How about you and Jon?" I ask to be polite.

"This time, about six months. Although, we've dated off and on all through high school. Jon is great or at least great compared to what Lamar has to offer. I'll miss him when we break up next month."

"When you break up? Why would you pre-plan to do such a thing?"

"Jon is going to school in Texas next fall and I'm going to Illinois, so obviously, it won't work. We've talked about this, and we're both good with the decision. I'm sure we'll always be friends."

"Wow, that's a bummer. Sorry," I express my sympathy.

"Don't be sorry, it's not a big deal. We knew this day was coming. It's not like we plan to get married, or anything. Jon is my high school boyfriend. Now I'm moving on to college boys ...thousands of college boys," she expands, with a smile that fills her entire face.

I drop my towel to the floor, uncomfortably, while Victoria continues to talk, like I'm not completely naked. I only half listen, because now she has planted the college seed in my head. I have to wonder if this is why Sean keeps some distance between us. He doesn't want a commitment, because he knows he will move on to bigger and better things?

I finally finish dressing and have my bag stuffed in a locker. I wrap my towel around my waste to cover my legs that are literally half the length of Victoria's and follow her towards the pool. My heart races with fear, but equally with anticipation.

I hear the thunderous echo of voices when we approach the huge dome. We walk through the glass door and a dozen people are in the pool, mostly guys. All eyes are on us when we approach the edge. Ok, let's be honest here, not us in all likelihood, but rather Victoria. I just happen to be standing in close proximity. I scan the water to find Sean, but don't see him anywhere. *Yes!* I slip off the towel and slide into the water as quickly as possible. Victoria continues her runway walk to the end of the pool. She climbs onto the diving board and does a perfectly executed backward dive into the water.

Figures, with her body she probably lives at the pool.

I watch while Victoria gracefully swims up to Jon like a mermaid. I dog paddle over to join them.

"Where's Sean?"

"Umm ...he'll be back shortly," Jon answers, his eyes shift nervously.

"Ok, thanks for that bit of information, but that isn't what I asked," I parrot the question.

"Oh man, don't make me snitch on my best friend."

Snitch? WTF. I remain calm, but stare into Jon's eyes without blinking.

"Ok—shit. Alexa is here and she's completely pissed off. She barges in here, right...and makes this big scene, so he went to straighten her ass out. I wasn't supposed to upset you; he will be pissed."

I'm proud of myself. I keep my cool. I suck in enough oxygen to keep from breathing for the next ten minutes and I maintain, "Ok, that's all I wanted to know."

I turn away from Jon and Victoria and dive under the water, I thrust myself clear to the opposite end before I come up to breathe. I wasn't entirely sure, but I had a pretty good idea it would be impossible to cry underwater—and it is.

I am safe in my underwater world. I swim from one end of the pool to the other. I don't stop, and only come up to breathe. When I suck in my eighth breath, I poke my head from the water and Sean is kneeled in front of me.

"Hi beautiful," he hums, while I wipe the water from my eyes.

"Hi," I snap.

"Oh great, I see Jon opened his fucking big mouth."

"Only because I made him. Was he supposed to lie?"

"No, but it wasn't a big deal and I don't need you upset all night."

"Who says I'm upset? Did you straighten it out?"

"Well your tone tells me you're upset. Can you please get out so we can talk?" *Get out? Of the water? Fuck me.*

"Grab my towel on the chair over there and I'll meet you by the ladder."

After he walks away, I suck in another laborious breath. I will not let this beautiful night end badly. I glide over to the ladder and climb up the rungs into the towel Sean holds out for me. He wraps it around me, like a mother that swaddles her child after a bath. The warmth of his arm cradles my shoulder and he leads me to a lounge chair.

"Sean, I want you to know I'm not mad that you went to straighten out this thing with Alexa," that is a little stretch of the truth, but the story I am sticking too. "The reason I'm upset is you left me here alone ...with no one ...stranded ...not knowing where you were. I felt like crawling under a rock, but I couldn't find one."

Sean starts to laugh, but see's the contempt in my eyes and sucks it back in. "I'm so sorry, Brianna. I thought you and Victoria were like besties by now. I thought you'd be ok with her."

"Well I wasn't, so don't do that again ...ever."

He can't contain his laughter this time, and coughs, "I won't, promise."

"What's the scoop with Alexa, do you think you could tell me the whole story ... the version that contains the most truth."

His laughter instantly exterminates, "I have not lied to you about Alexa, Bri!"

I approach from a different angle, "Ok, let me rephrase. Do you think you could tell me the rest of the story about Alexa? I sense there is more to this than you two being nominated for king and queen. I'm treading on her territory and she doesn't want me here, does she?"

"Ok, that's a fair question, I guess. Brianna, you need to try and understand. I'm from a small school. We've all pretty much grown up together. Now that we're older, we date each other. It's the same shit we dealt with in grade school and junior high. I pick you, and then you break up and pick someone else. It's not fucking real; it's all to pass the time. What you and I have is so far beyond their high school bullshit, it's not conceptual to them. In Alexa's eyes, I simply picked someone other than her. She has no idea that fate gave us no other choice." A sincere smile creeps onto his face. His dimples are so close I can touch them...and might. "So, you weren't the slightest bit jealous, I'm disappointed."

I have no other choice than to smile with him...this man I love. "So the bitch is seriously upset?" I glance at my hands, to make sure my skin hasn't turned green.

"Only by her own devise," he maintains.

279

"I don't follow."

"Brianna, I told her several months ago I had no interest in dating her, or anyone for that matter. My excuse was justifiable ...in my mind. I'm leaving for college in a few short months. Getting involved with anyone was pointless."

A lump regurgitates itself into my throat and chokes me. My hands tent my eyes to hide any tears that may escape. I feel his fingers gently wrap around my wrists and pull them away from my face. He expands, "Then I met you and everything changed. Maybe my excuse to Alexa was fake; maybe I'm simply not into her. She would have been a girlfriend, just to have a girlfriend. I didn't see the point. Maybe my excuse is real. Maybe starting a relationship right now *is* really fucking stupid. Regardless, my better judgement was left in the bleachers at the game the night I met you."

Sean caresses my hands gently and stares down at the floor. After two long breaths he looks up and continues, "So, to answer your question, I told her the only way I would accept this stupid nomination for King and Queen was if she understood my night belonged to you ...my dance belonged to you ... my heart belonged to you. I guess my proposal didn't sink in, or she still clung to hope ...or some shit. Regardless, had we still been at prom, it wouldn't have changed a damn thing. Her delusional expectation of a last dance with me would not have materialized. So, is she still mad at me, probably, but I don't plan to let it affect *our* time together tonight. I have nothing to feel guilty about. If she wants to turn this into drama—it will be her drama, not mine. Now, can we go swimming and have some fun?"

I look away and struggle to pull my lips into a smile, I mutter, "Sure."

Sean and I walk towards the edge of the pool. His warm hand rests on the small of my bare back. I notice for the first time of my irritatingly preoccupied night that Sean is built. Like really built. *Sweet jeezus!!* His body is as beautiful as his face. An image of his solid firm body pressed against mine swallows up my thoughts—I smile.

Sean slides into the water, "Well, come on in."

"I'll be there in a minute ...go, have fun!"

His eyes narrow, "Ok."

I turn to head into the locker room. I sit on the bench for a moment to collect my thoughts. I'm satisfied with Sean's explanation concerning Alexa ...yet there is something more that clouds my mind like a thick dark fog.

Sean leaves in four months. I never put any thought into him leaving for college until tonight. It is already unbearable spending so much time apart; this added distance will surely make matters worse.

Brianna, you are such a fucking idiot. Snap the hell out of it. You have Sean tonight. You should be out there with him. Enjoy every minute of him, instead of sitting here alone feeding your insecurity!

I stand up and open my locker; I grab my toothbrush and proceed to the sink. It is nearly midnight. I push my qualms behind me, at least for now, and rejoin the air that fills my lungs and the fire that warms my soul. I slip back through the door that leads to the pool and into the brisk water unnoticed. My arms slide around his waist from behind. He turns to face me, startled.

"I'm glad you're back. I need you. Jon and Victoria are pounding me."

"Sports. Me. Not so much." I admit.

I start to embellish when the ball rockets straight for my head. I hold out my fist to stop it, and incredibly it flies over the net and scores a point. I couldn't do that again if my life depended on it. Sean high-fives me and lifts me above his shoulders until my head towers way above his own, effortlessly.

I'm weightless. #waterfuckingrocks!

We continue with the game, but lose. Some nerdy looking student drifts into the pool area and announces, "The pizza is here!"

More food?

Everyone is excited, like the ice cream truck just showed up. One by one they exit the pool. Sean hangs back and reveals a naughty, bikini dropping grin. He creeps slowly towards the ladder, behind all of his classmates. His fingers lace with mine. When everyone has left the area, including the chaperones, he sings, "Finally!" *What the hell?*

He releases the rungs of the ladder and turns to face me. He wraps my legs around his waist. His finger rests against my lips, silently asking me to stay still. He slowly glides backward to the corner of the pool, next to the locker room door. We both sink down, as low as we can go—our lips skim the surface of the water. He pulls me in tight—we don't move. We barely breathe.

Minutes later, someone opens the door at the entrance and flips off the lights. Alone in the dark, illuminated only by the pallid light that shines from beneath the water, Sean leans in to kiss me.

My arms cling tightly around his neck and my legs wrap securely around his firm body. We are so close; I feel his heart beat through our bare skin. Sean presses my body firmly against the edge of the pool. His arms unwrap from my waist and caress my face. His tongue invades my entire mouth. *Oh. My. God.*

Sean pushes away; his eyes plead. *Don't look at me like that—damn it!* The reflection of the dimly lit pool makes them sparkle like black diamonds—if there even is such a thing. If not, there should be—because they're fucking beautiful.

His wet full lips shine a deep crimson in the twilight of the room. I run my wet finger back and forth over his bottom lip, while the ache below my waist grows more intense. Sean grabs my hand and kisses my fingertip gently then slides it slowly into his mouth. The heat of his tongue gently caresses it. Princess Jezebel swallows hard and sucks in a deep breath.

I feel the pressure build in my body; I am on the verge of exploding. I lean forward to kiss him with my lips slightly parted. My tongue slides in when my finger pulls out. I fist his hair and begin to pull gently, trying to release some of the pressure that has built up inside of me. *It's no use, I can't fight this.*

This is it; I don't have the will to resist him any longer. I don't have the strength to stop this from going further—the lights flip on.

Sean and I both gasp. *What the fuck!*

"Sean Gentry, what in the hell do you think you're doing? Just because you were prom king doesn't give you the right to break the rules. Get your ass out of the pool—both of you get dressed and join the rest of your classmates," a gruff voice of authority demands. He towers over us, his fists clenched tightly over his chest.

"Yes sir, Mr. Clark," Sean responds politely.

Sean grabs my hand and we creep our way to the ladder. I am pretty sure I know why the sluggish pace is necessary. He takes my hand to help me up the ladder. I eye my towel and walk over to grab it while Sean quickly wraps his towel around his waist.

Mr. Clark stands in between both locker room doors. His finger and thumb stroke his chin nervously. His poker face is amusing, because through his stern stance I have an odd feeling that on the inside he wants to throw Sean a high-five.

Sean drops my hand when we approach the girl's locker room. It is completely empty. *What a fucking relief.* After I drift back down from the cloud I am floating on, I pull my clothes out of the locker, along with my shampoo, conditioner and body wash.

With no one around, I stay in the shower longer than I need to. Mr. Clark and Sean give me an impatient glare when I finally meet them in the hallway. We follow silently behind Mr. Clark. Sean braids his fingers with mine and winks at me with that sexy dimpled grin while we walk down the hall towards a room full of chatter. The noise escalades with each approaching footstep.

I'm not prepared for our reception when we enter the tiny mint green room. Every eye is glued to us—most of them smiling. I swear they are ready to applaud—like we are the heroes of their high school comic book. Of course, there are also the scowls that project across the room, like I should wear a scarlet letter, be burned at the stake, or stoned. One of them I recognize, Alexa. *Fuck that bitch!*

Half eaten pizzas are scattered randomly over a long banquet table. Sean runs all ten of his fingers through his hair. His lips pull up in a gratified grin. "Are you hungry?"

I didn't eat much of my dinner tonight and the energy consumed in the pool has left me famished. However, the thought of eating in front of all of these quizzical eyes is not appetizing. "I'm ok."

"Well I'm starving, and you, young lady, haven't eaten jack shit tonight. I think you can choke down a piece, or two. It will be a long night."

"Yeah, ok," I mumble and pull myself into his arm so he can protect me from the silent whispers.

Sean heaps a stack of pizza on a paper plate and leads me to the corner where Jon and Victoria sit.

"So where have you two lovebirds been?" Jon probes.

Victoria adds, "Come clean, what have you been up to?"

Sean confesses, "We weren't doing anything wrong, I wanted to spend some time alone with my girl."

"So where were you?" Jon continues.

"We never left the pool."

"You are the fucking man, Seanly!"

"Whatever ...shut the fuck up so I can eat!"

Sean hands me a piece of pizza. I glance around the room and most of the eyes have lost interest in our soapbox drama. Alexa has even turned her focus to her friends, although she looks like she is ranting, likely about us ...or me in particular.

I scarf down three squares of pizza while Sean finishes the rest of the plate. Jon rushes him to finish so we can go to the gym and play basketball.

We follow Jon and Victoria to the gym. Obviously, basketball isn't one of my fortes either. I hope Sean and Jon will play some one on one, or join a game, while Victoria and I cheer on the sidelines. We enter the gym to the thunderous rumble of bouncing basketballs and occasional squeaks of tennis shoes skidding on the wooden floor.

Sean smiles down at me, "Ready to whoop some ass."

Victoria *thank god!* saves me, "Why don't you two go play, Brianna and I will sit on the bleachers and talk."

A crease runs the full width of Sean's forehead, "Yes, go ahead. I'll be fine with Victoria," I add.

I don't want to be away from Sean, but I also don't want to expose my pathetic attempt at basketball skills to him either.

"Ok, if you're sure. I don't want to leave you alone again," he taunts.

I insist, "I'm fine ...*GO* already!"

Victoria and I straddle the bleachers and face each other. With no makeup, her deep skin is still model perfect. I wonder if Sean ever dated her. Since apparently Lamar boys bounce from girlfriend to girlfriend.

"Thank you, thank you!" I sigh.

"For what?"

"For saving me from basketball hell."

She chirps, "No problem. So Brianna,"

"You can call me Bri, everyone does except Sean."

"Ok, Bri ...what's the scoop, tell me everything!" She coaxes.

"The scoop?"

She mouths softly, "Yeah, what were you and Sean really doing when Mr. Clark found you?"

"Oh. That." I suck in a deep breath through my nose, "We were completely naked on the diving board," I tease.

"Shut the hell up!"

I giggle, "I'm just kidding Victoria. We were making out in the corner of the pool, just kissing, nothing major. *Five seconds later may have been an entirely different story.* They turned the lights out on us, so it was really fucking romantic. It's probably a good thing we were busted," I laugh again.

"Wow—jealous."

"Jealous, because you didn't stay in the pool?" I ask and tilt my head to one side.

"No, fuck no. Trust me; I've had my fair share of pool sex. I'm jealous of what you two have. The way you look at each other, it's pretty fucking amazing."

We continue our conversation while Sean and Jon finish their game. Victoria's dad is a doctor. Her mother is from Argentina, originally. She is going to college for her Bachelor of Science degree and then will pursue med school herself. Our conversation is pleasant. I could be friends with Victoria.

"Where are Jon and Sean?" Victoria questions, scanning the gym floor.

My eyes do a quick once-over, but I don't see them either. "I don't know."

About that time Sean walks through a doorway on the other side of the gym.

Seriously, he better not be consoling Alexa again, this is fucking ridiculous. She wants consoled, I'll show her fucking consoled. Stupid bitch.

He approaches the bleachers, without Jon.

"Do you have a pen in your purse?" he whispers in my ear.

"Yeah, I think so, why?"

"Go grab it and I'll explain when you get back. Victoria, go with her to the locker room. Keep all the crazies away from her."

Completely baffled, I do what he asks. Victoria takes her protective lead to the locker room. I dig through the locker for my little silver purse and pull out a black gel pen. We head back to the gymnasium.

"I have the pen, now what is this about."

"Follow me, both of you," Sean motions.

He grabs my hand and pulls me behind him. We cross the gym and head for the hallway on the other side. This hallway is surrounded by small meeting rooms with an exit door that leads to the parking lot at the far end. We keep walking, until we arrive at the exit.

"Sean, what are you doing?" I grill.

"Hand me that pen. Jon found a way for us to get in and out of here. No one will use this hallway tonight, so no one will be the wiser. We are sneaking out of here for a while."

"SHUT THE FUCK UP!" Victoria blurts, too loudly.

"Shhh," Sean whispers, his fingertip pressed against his lips.

I think I like this bad boy side of Sean. Scratch that, if we leave sports hell ...I love this side of him. Sean holds open the door while Victoria and I escape. He places the pen in between the door and its frame to keep it from latching. Jon already stands at the end of the building, out of sight from the roadway. We all walk down the side of the building to join him. My hair is still damp, so the night air feels colder than it should.

"So what now?" I ask. *Ditching Jon and Victoria and heading to your car?* I smile.

Sean suggests, "We could go to the parking garage next door and sit on the roof for a while. No one will see us up there."

"Perfect!" Jon agrees. "Let me grab a couple of things out of Victoria's car."

We stop at a shiny red Mustang and Jon opens the door. He reaches in the back seat and pulls out two blankets.

Thank god!

He hands one to Sean carefully and coddles the other one in his arms.

Victoria and I follow them to the parking garage. It has to be close to two in the morning, so there is no traffic to catch our escape. We climb the six flights of stairs that lead to the roof of the garage. No cars are parked in the garage and we are high enough to tower above the street lights. The stars light up the night sky.

It is dark, but my eyes begin to adjust. I see Jon pull something carefully out of his folded blanket and place it on the raised sidewalk that surrounds the perimeter of the garage. He spreads half of the blanket onto the sidewalk, against the outer wall, and motions for Victoria to climb in.

Once she's on her butt, he climbs in next to her and pulls the other half of the blanket over them.

I'm closer to Sean. He pulls a bottle of something out, and a small red box and places them on the sidewalk. His back slides down the wall and he straddles his legs. I tuck in directly in front of him and press my body into his chest. He wraps the blanket securely around us. The warmth of his body surrounds me like a glove.

Jon speaks first, "We brought a little refreshment. I hope you girls don't mind. It's not enough to get us trashed or anything, but enough to liven up this party a bit. You don't have to partake, if you don't want to."

Victoria scoffs, "Give that here! ...Jager, hell yeah."

Sean's breath fills my ear, "We don't have to drink this, if you don't want to. I just want to be here with you. This was Jon's idea."

"No, it's fine, really." *Geez, I'm not a total fucking prude.* "What's in the box?"

"Um ...I guess I'll share all of my dirty little secrets with you tonight. I smoke occasionally, but it's rare. Mainly if I drink ...which is also rare, and NEVER when I drive. There, it's all out."

He is nervous, which makes me chuckle. "Sean, I'm not a prima donna. I drink occasionally, too." Obviously, I won't tell him it's only with my parents ...on Christmas Eve ...when they allow it. "I also sneak a cigarette, now

and again, with my friend Adrianne." *Not since Jr. High,
but what the hell.*

"So, you're not upset with me? I have been freaked
out about this for days! I just want you to know, I wouldn't
have pushed any of this on you if you weren't comfortable
around it. Please know that."

Jon interrupts, "Sean, shut the fuck up and give the
girl a drink ...geez!"

We lean back and peek at the stars. The Jager
warms its way down my throat—but it kinda tastes like dog
shit—not that I've ever actually tasted dog shit. While the
bottle empties, the conversation loosens. *And the flavor
improves.* Victoria feels like an old friend, and what's
crazy is she feels like the perfect combination of Natalie,
Adrienne and Samantha. Our little half pint is empty. Sean
suggests we head back before they miss us. That way we
can sneak back out later. I am perfectly content right where
I'm at, but I get what he says. We don't need the post-
prom-police looking for us.

We fold up our blankets and stash the empty bottle
in the trash can next to the exit before we head down the
stairwell. Jon tucks the blankets in Victoria's car while
Sean stashes the remainder of his cigarettes in her console.
We head back to the door Sean rigged with the pen.

As we approach the door, the same female teacher
that let Sean and I in the building tonight, walks out.

"What are you doing out here! You are not to leave
this building Mr. Gentry and Mr. Wells. Come inside this
instant," she shakes her stubby finger like a club.

Sean, by means of his intoxicating charm, grovels, "I'm so sorry Miss Taylor. This is entirely my fault; I wanted to stick some of my stuff I didn't need any more in the car, so I won't forget it. We were coming right back."

"You are not above the rules Mr. Gentry, and it appears you attempt to test the limits tonight. You all come with me until we see what we want to do with you the rest of the night." *Busted by the PPP—drag.*

We follow Miss Taylor through the gym into a hallway near the front door. These rooms, although dimly lit, appear to be dance studios, obvious from the mirrors and bars that line the walls. She stops at one of the rooms and points her chubby little finger inside.

"Wait here!" she demands, through clenched jaws.

Several minutes later she returns with Mr. Clark, still with his arms folded in an authoritative stance, but a smile his eyes can't conceal.

"Well Sean, it appears we're seeing a lot of each other tonight. Jon, it appears you have decided to follow Mr. Gentry on his journey."

"Well, actually Mr. Clark, going out to put stuff in the car was all my idea," Jon slurs proudly.

"Great," Sean mouths under his breath, while he pinches his forehead with his fingers.

"Jon, have you been drinking?" Mr. Clark grills.

"No sir, not me," then Jon snorts laughter through his nose.

"Oh fuck!" Sean mumbles.

"I'm not blind. I've been around the block a few times myself. I know for a fact that you've been drinking, my guess you all have. I have no choice but to confine you to this room, alone. You will not be allowed to join the rest of your classmates until you sober up. I'll be back in two hours to check on you."

When the sound of his footsteps fade to nothing, Sean blurts, "Mr. Clark fucking rocks!"

I bust out in laughter. "Are you kidding, our punishment is being alone with each other for two hours! Sweet jeezus, we should have done this when we first got here!"

"No shit! Damn it, I should have kept my cigarettes."

"I still have mine," Jon spouts and looks at Sean like he's from another galaxy.

"I'm glad you're an idiot Jon! Now pass them over."

Sean walks to the far corner of the room furthest from the door and cracks the window.

Jon rummages the room and finds a TV and turns it on. "Damn, it's not hooked up to cable."

Victoria, who obviously took dance divulges, "That's because it's just a monitor and DVD player, they probably use it to work out dance routines.

Jon thumbs through the DVD's that are scattered on the tray underneath. "Sweet, these are all like music videos and shit," he reports and slips one in.

"Hey, turn the lights out and shut that door!" Sean wails from across the room.

"So, how about a dance?" Jon asks and extends his hand to Victoria.

Jon and Victoria cuddle in each other's arms while the music plays. I watch them with covetous eyes. When the tempo speeds up, she motions for me to join them. I smile, but hold up a finger that insinuates I'll be right back.

I slide across the floor to Sean and place my arms around his waist. The breeze that blows through the window is cool and damp, but the warmth of his body is comfortable.

"What are you over here thinking?" I pry.

"Oh, nothing major. I'm just enjoying all of the time we have spent together tonight. I don't want to go back to reality. I hate being apart and that's really scary."

"Scary ...why?" *Buzz kill alert!*

"Nothing Brianna, we'll talk about it later. Tonight, let's enjoy."

Shit, now what? Just when things move forward. Never mind, he's right ...not tonight. "Ok, two conditions, one ...we *will* talk about it later, and two ...since it's only the four of us, you will dance with me tonight. I'll show you a few moves," I tease, while I grind my body into his.

His eyebrows bounce happily across his forehead, "Let's get started." The four of us dance for over an hour, not the kind of dancing we would do in public, but I have Sean moving—that in itself is a major accomplishment.

The tiny buzz we had going wears off quickly. When it fades, it sucks every ounce of my energy with it. If this was a tumbling studio instead, I would have found a mat and went to sleep. All of us wear down. One by one we slide down to the floor. Jon flips on the light and turns the monitor off. We place everything back where we found it. Sean relocks the studio window he and Jon used to blow smoke from.

This last two hours has been the best part of our entire night. I made new friends. I spent my entire evening with Sean, sportless. I seriously want to give Jon a kiss for his bad behavior. We lean back against the wall; my head rests on Sean's shoulder. Victoria's head rests on Jon's lap. When Mr. Clark walks in, I'm sure it appears we sat here all night, bored to the point of demise, because he smiles ...pleased he's taught us a lesson.

Apparently we look sober, because he allows us to leave. When he turns his back to walk away, we all smile at each other. Our special night is our own little secret. Too exhausted to play any sports, we head to the music room. I assume it will be empty, but instead it is full. No one plays music. They all just sit around and talk, tired themselves.

The four of us sit at a table for a few minutes and contemplate if we want to go to breakfast when this is all over. Sean addresses Jon and Victoria and suggests, "You two figure it out. Brianna, come with me."

I follow him to the piano. He sits down on the bench and pats the area next to him. He wants me to sit too. I fall in next to him. He begins to play some random stuff at first, but then takes a breath and starts to sing. To Me. Fucking Cool.

I feel the tears cling to my lower lid. One escapes the other I catch. Sean sings to me in front of his entire class. I can see green ooze from all of their pores, including Alexa's. His love for me has never been more apparent than this particular moment. I lean in to kiss his cheek when he finishes. His face turns to meet my lips.

Night turns to dawn, and Sean drives me home. We are too exhausted to talk, or even make out. We kiss and say our goodbyes.

CHAPTER TWENTY-SEVEN

I wake up in a cold sweat. What time is it? What day is it? Why did I have that dreadful nightmare? I sit on the edge of my bed, shake my head and hope the images will somehow fall out and roll out of my room.

Sean and I sit at a small mosaic table and face each other, a bistro maybe. His warm hands massage the back of my palms. The sky outside is dark—pitch black. I see the reflection of other patrons arched over candlelight in the window we sit against. We inhale the scent of fresh basil, oregano and baked bread. Our lips pull up in an endearing smile while we wander around in each other's eyes—like we do in real life. Like a bolt of lightning, there she is—the woman with long black hair. She claws her way into my dream. Her long bony fingers snatch Sean from his chair and just like that—he is gone. *Whew, she really needs to quit that!*

I feel like I have slept for days, but then maybe I have. I can't catch up from the twenty four hour marathon called prom. My reprieve, this is a four day weekend. I welcome the restful extension with open arms.

I already know, from a prior conversation that Sean works extra-long hours this weekend to make up for hours he took off for prom. My Saturday and Sunday are well planned. Grams is attempting to pull together Easter dinner. She hasn't had dinner for the family in almost a year, so this may be a challenge. Saturday will be spent in Grams kitchen, helping her prepare.

Friday and Monday are purposefully left open on my schedule. Sean said he worked all weekend, but he didn't mention Friday or Monday. A girl can hope. Today I should clean my room, but sleep is all I can focus on ...and food. I'm freaking starving! After I stuff my face full of cereal, I lay around on my bed all day and flip through magazines I've already read. I read Sean's zodiac connection with signs other than Pisces, but none of them are as kick ass as ours. He's completely mine, bitches!

By midafternoon, I'm exhausted, from doing absolutely nothing. If I stay in this bed ...I will be asleep. My parents are downstairs watching Almost Famous, my dad's favorite movie, so I go down and join them. I end up watching three movies before I pull myself from the love seat and head back upstairs.

As I fluff my pillow to hold in my arms and pretend its Sean, my cell phone rings.

"Hello."

"Hey," Sean's voice chokes out.

"Hey, hi, how are you?"

"Ok I guess ...still tired."

"Yeah, me too ...prom did a number on us. I miss you," I admit and hope the hint will force him into his car, on a road to Joplin.

Sean questions, "Do you?"

"Well yeah, implacably," I reply and catch the sharpness in his tongue.

"Cory wants to come down Monday to talk to you about Samantha ...whatever. Do you have time for us to stop by Monday afternoon Bri? It shouldn't take up too much of your time."

Something is wrong, he said Bri again. I address his question, "Of course you can come down. If I had my way you'd be here every day, all day, *tied to my bed!*"

His voice is hurtful, "Hmmf, yeah I'm sure you'd love me to drop everything, jump in my car, and travel to Joplin every day."

What the fuck? "Ok, what's the deal Sean? Have I done something to upset you, 'cause you're kinda being a jerk?"

"Don't worry about it—I guess you haven't, you know what ...I'll see you Monday, I'm tired," he responds in a hard tone, and adds under his breath, "of a lot."

"No! Hold the fucking door. I need to know why you're mad at me."

"Brianna, if you can't see anything wrong, then I guess it is all me. Maybe this exhaustion has my negative brain cells working overtime. I'll talk to you Monday and I'm sure everything will be fine. Happy Easter."

"Happy Easter to you!"

We say our goodbyes, and although he lightens up a bit at the end, I can't stop the tears. I cry myself to sleep ...and I don't even know why.

My eyes are still puffy when I wake up the next morning. I think about the premonitions I had of our beautiful prom night ...how nearly all of the vivid dreams came true. Will these stupid nightmares come true, too? Will Sean be snatched away from me...just like that? I suddenly remember something from prom, my exhausted memory blocked. Maybe Sean is trying to push me away because he knows he leaves for school in a few months. *This totally sucks!*

His curt conversation with me last night disturbs me. I can't think of one viable reason he has to be mad at me? Our conversation last Sunday night was amazing. We haven't seen or talked to each other since, so what's his deal. Did this have anything to do with Cory ...or Samantha? I can't find any relevance. Cory's trip Monday will be a waste. I could save them the gas, but I won't. I need any excuse I can find to be with Sean.

My mind is too foggy to think, I head to Grams. My tires screech to a halt in the loose gravel of their drive at ten AM. Aunt Jenny isn't here yet. She was supposed to be my replacement when Grams lovingly relieved me of my Saturday duties. My visit today is completely unannounced. If Grams tries to send me away, she will have one hell of a fight on her hands. And where the fuck is Aunt Jenny?

I march into the kitchen ready for a fight.

"Brianna, what are you doing here today?" she asks cheerfully.

"I knew you would have tons to do. I figured you could use some help," I reply, still ready for an argument.

"Well, thank you dear, that is very kind. Are you hungry?" *Ok...cool.*

"No Grams, I ate a bowl of cereal this morning, I'm stuffed."

"What would you like me to do to help?"

"You can roll up the noodles on the dining room table and slice them up. You know what to do."

For the next two hours I help Grams roll out pie crusts, boil eggs, chop vegetables. I haven't snuck in to see Gramps at all. I don't want to remind Grams why she banned me. I hold my breath and slither into the living room.

Gramps is asleep; I stand over his bed. His face is thin, thinner than the last time I was here, which seems impossible. His body is so frail and weak, I'm afraid to touch him. He looks like a skeleton. His mouth is gaped open and his breathing is labored. I sit down on the bed next to him and gently touch his hand. His eyes open...

His lips pull up in a weak fragile smile. I'm sure its reflex, but it still makes me feel warm inside. He picks up his free hand and rests it on the back of my palm. Does he recognize me?

In a breath no more than a whisper he speaks, "Riny."

I nearly fall to the floor, he actually said my name. A tear falls from my already tear swollen eyes. I lean down to his ear and whisper, "Hey Gramps." I'm in such shock, I don't even know what to say, I offer to make him a milkshake, since they're his favorite.

He replies with barely a whisper, "That would be great."

I race into the kitchen and let my grams know he recognizes me.

"Brianna, you're imagining things, he hasn't spoke for weeks now."

"Honestly Grams, he knows who I am, and he's talking!"

Grams rushes to the living room to see for herself. Her weary golden eyes immediately fill with tears. I give them some space and head back to the kitchen to make Gramps a shake. When I finish, I bring in the mug and hand it to Grams.

I miss my gramps so much that I would give anything to have this time with him, but Grams misses him even more. I gladly offer this precious time to her, because I don't know how long it may last. I stand back ...waiting, watching. Grams looks so happy that I finally turn and go back into the kitchen and clean up the mess we created in our prep work. I leave them alone for over an hour. I hear Grams soft voice whisper to Gramps. I can't hear what she says, but her voice is full of love. I am so thankful I am here to give her this time with him.

As I dust the flour from the table and finish up her dishes, a nagging thought comes back. Where in the fuck is Aunt Jenny. I have to wonder if she really helps Grams on Saturdays, or if this is just a fib my grams concocted to keep me away

All of the prep work is complete. The pie crusts are ready to fill, the noodles are ready to toss in their broth and all of the meat is beautifully prepared to stick in the oven. Everything is clean and ready for tomorrow's final preparations.

I walk into the living room and stand at the foot of Gramps bed. I offer to help Grams clean Gramps up, but she refuses. "Brianna, I want to enjoy this time with your granddad. We'll work on the rest tomorrow."

"I'll come over in the morning and help you finish."

"That would be delightful. Thank you so much for everything today."

I hug Grams goodbye. I walk around her to give Gramps a kiss on his forehead.

"Bye Gramps."

"Bye Riny," his voice is stronger now.

As I walk to my car, I smile because I know Grams may still be sitting on the edge of that bed tomorrow morning. She will embrace this gift as long as she can. This is a day we will hold in our hearts forever—our Easter miracle.

When I put my car in drive, my thoughts shift to Sean. What the hell is he mad about? I don't appreciate this part of my Easter very much. I should call him tonight, but I'm sure he's at work.

Gramps still has his wits about him when I arrive Easter morning. Aunt Rachel and I work to clean up Gramps and prepare him for his company. After he falls asleep for his morning nap, we help Grams prepare for the enormous feast. All of my family begins to show up at two. One by one they pile in. Some bring sides, some come empty handed. Easter dinner goes off without a hitch, like we haven't missed a single week. *We Rock!*

After dinner, the parents all congregate in the living room. They expend every ounce of Gramps precious energy and take turns talking with him. My cousins and I head off to the barn and climb up in the hayloft. We sit in a circle on staggered bales of hay and share memories and funny stories of our childhood. Amanda tries to speak of the ghost encounter, but I play it off, so the subject changes quickly.

One by one, we all leave …and although no one says the words, we all realize what a gift today was. Not only a day to spend time with family, but one more day to come to terms …to tell our husband, our father, our grandfather that one last sentiment …to say our goodbyes.

CHAPTER TWENTY-EIGHT

It is a perfect Monday morning. The sun illuminates around fluffy white clouds staggered across a periwinkle blue sky. I loaf on the patio most of my morning and soak up every ounce of vitamin D I can absorb. While I sit with my eyes sealed, my face pointed in the direction of the sun, I mull over Friday's weird conversation.

My relationship with Sean sometimes feels so natural, so in sync. We are on our own narrow bandwidth, connected. Other times, like Friday, throw me completely off guard. Sean's thoughts are his own and I can't begin to interpret them. Cory will be with him today. This is not my preferred scenario, yet a small part of me knows this is the only motivation for his visit.

I call Samantha to enlighten her about Cory's concern. I want to relay back her true sentiment. Assumptions can get you in trouble. Samantha reiterates what I already knew. She is done—finito. Samantha will be attending Joplin's prom with our star quarterback in two weeks. Cory is nothing more than a pothole on her journey to love.

Sean pulls up in Cory's car around one; my heart begins its expected race ...it beats faster with each approaching step. I toss down my magazine, stand up and prepare for my hug. Instead, he parks himself in a chair across the patio and disregards me. *What the fuck?* I shake my head and scoff under my breath, before I sit back down.

Silence…and it's not fucking golden. I finally glance up at him through my long lashes and break the awkwardness, "Hi Sean …hey Cory."

Sean doesn't have a chance to respond before Cory jumps right to the point. "What's up with your friend, Bri? I have called her like fifty fucking times and she won't answer my calls. Is she trying to punish me—because point taken? Or is she that fucking mad? Not talking will just perpetuate the problem."

"Cory, I don't disagree with you. This conversation should be with her—not me. I don't want to be the bearer of bad news, but she's over it. What you did to her at prom is inexcusable in her eyes—actually, in most people's eyes. I understand your dilemma, in a way, yet you have to see how wrong it was. I mean really, who takes their ex-girlfriend to prom? So not cool."

"So, I'm wasting my time."

"Don't take it so hard …you were doomed anyway," I chuckle.

"What's that supposed to mean," Cory's brow furrows.

I pull up the magazine and turn to the page that details their love connection and hand it to Cory.

As Cory reads, I shift my focus to Sean, "So what did you do this weekend?" *I'm trying here!*

"I worked."

I smile nervously, "I know that part. What else did you do?"

"I did nothing else. It appears you've had a busy weekend."

Cory hands me the magazine back. He cocks his head, confused, "So this is why she won't see me anymore?"

"No jerk, she won't see you because you took another girl to prom. I am just trying to point out that you two aren't meant to be anyway."

"I'm the jerk? After reading that, she's the fucking prima-donna."

"Cory stop, Sam is great. She's selfless and will do anything to make people happy. She is probably my closest friend. You hurt her enough she had to boot your ass and move on. I can't say I blame her."

"She moved on? Like she has another boyfriend already?"

"Yes. She already has a date for Joplin's prom in two weeks. You snooze, you lose."

Sean jerks his head towards me in one swift motion. His eyes burn a hole into my heart, "Joplin's prom is in two weeks? So, do you have a date, too?"

"Of course not! So do you want to read what it says about us?" I plead and pounce on this epic opportunity.

"About us, what is it?"

"It's an astrological love connection guide."

He laughs callously, "No Brianna, I don't believe in that shit. I don't need the stars to tell me if I'm compatible with someone."

The way he puts it makes it seem really fucking stupid. I need him to read it, we're special—and I don't feel very special right now.

"It's really good, are you sure?"

"I'm sure."

My plan fails. My puppy dog pout doesn't even work on him.

Cory interrupts my focus, "I guess today's trip was a total waste of time."

"We can go if you want to," Sean adds.

What, NO! I grasp, "Sean you haven't met my dad yet."

This will hopefully buy me some time to think. I know my dad will ramble for a while, because he is good at that. "Hold on, I will go get him," I state while I bolt through the door before he has time to refuse.

I introduce my father to Sean. Their conversation immediately turns to music, this is promising. My dad can talk about music for hours.

I have to devise a way to keep Sean here. I need to talk to Sean alone, but what will I do with Cory? Maybe Natalie or Adrienne is home. We can all go for a walk. Cory has to be on board, he is the key. Sean is along for the ride today.

While my dad and Sean chat, I approach Cory. I recommend under my breath, not to draw Sean's attention, "Cory, you drove all this way. I don't want you to leave yet." Cory smiles a full white teeth smile. *Yes!* "I have other friends you know. I can call Natalie or Adrienne. It's a beautiful day; we can all go do something together."

Cory beams, my plan is successful. He winks and grabs my arm, "I know what you're trying to do. I'll play along."

I grab my cell phone and call Natalie. "Natalie, Sean and Cory are over here, we thought about going to the park. Do you want to go with?"

With Natalie, sports immediately possess her sporty little brain, "I'll grab some Frisbees and be over in a bit."

Success—I smile. I look over at Cory and he's still staring at me, "Natalie will be over in a few minutes. We can go to the park and hang out."

Sean glares at me when I give Cory the news. He obviously overhears this part of our conversation. Fortunately for me, Sean is respectful and won't interrupt my father's lengthy recall of his rock and roll life. Cory and I joke around, while Sean and my father end their conversation.   At least twenty minutes pass since the conversation began.

"Well it is nice to meet you Randy; yeah ...we'll jam sometime."

Sean turns to Cory, "I thought we were leaving?"

"Dude, I didn't drive thirty minutes to turn around and go right back home. We can go to the park for a while, it's not like we have anything better to do."

Before Sean has a chance to rebut, Natalie walks up with two Frisbees.

Sean isn't happy, but I know once we arrive at the park we can sort out whatever is on his mind. I haven't done anything wrong—how hard can it be.

The drive to the park is quiet. Even Natalie doesn't say much. Sean won't hold my hand; he barely looks at me. We climb out of Cory's car and head to an open field. I stop in my tracks, now is the time. This awkwardness needs to end, so we can enjoy our day.

Everyone is several paces ahead.   I yell out, "Sean...Stop. Cory and Natalie, go on ahead. Sean let's go for a walk, please."

He doesn't argue with me, which I partially expect. He follows behind me, his fists clenched in his pockets. I continue to walk towards the lake. The air smells like dead fish, but I don't care. It is quiet and it is private. I take a seat on a small hill that faces the water. Sean slides in next to me and leaves just enough distance between us not to touch me.

He sits in silence, so I begin, "Can you please tell me what is going on. I am completely lost right now. Where does this heartless attitude come from?"

He stares ahead in silence. I'm ready to speak again, but he finally blurts, "Well, if I'm heartless that's because you've destroyed what's left of my heart. Brianna, I can't do this anymore."

Can't. Do. This. Anymore. My eyes immediately begin to pool, *hold it together Bri.* "Can't do what anymore? I thought you enjoy being with me."

"Enjoy being with you? I think it goes beyond enjoyment, on my end anyway. I can't be the only one that makes an effort to make this work."

"What on earth are you talking about? How do I not make an effort?"

"Answer this for me Bri ...what are you doing to make an effort."

His question confuses me. I don't understand what I'm doing wrong, but I don't know what I'm doing right, either. I don't have an answer. My back is against a wall, I am speechless—yet I can't *not* respond. Our relationship obviously teeters on my answer. Not finding the words, I cry harder.

His expressionless face turns away, "I didn't think you could answer that question."

"What do you want me to do to make an effort? I don't understand what I'm doing wrong."

"Anything. Everything. I don't know. Jeezus Brianna, just forget it," he urges and wipes the tears away from my eyes. "I'm probably over reacting to a lot of mixed emotions I have right now. I can't expect you to be as absurd as I am. *But I am absurd!* Can you just try to meet me in the middle on this—that's all I ask."

Sean wraps his arms around my shoulders and pulls me against his body. I sob harder. All of the pinned up fear floods through me like water through a broken dam. The love in my heart for this man would be unbearable to forget. The stain in my soul—impossible to remove. I see he has doubt, or is finding an excuse to doubt us. *Meet him in the middle ...what the hell does that even mean. He needs more of me? Like sex?*

Sean carefully moves to a less intense subject. He asks about my Easter. I suck in my emotions and recap my day with the family, although there is far too much on my mind to appear enthusiastic. Sean has no story to tell, he worked the entire day and evening.

The change of subject harbors my emotion, but not my deep bed of concern. I push my hair behind my ears and stare breathlessly at his full lips. I need their warm comfort against mine, but he doesn't offer. His fingers, however, find their way to my thigh and reflexively dig in. Shock waves pass through my body. I rest my head on his shoulder. We both gaze out over the lake in silence—and think.

I muster up every ounce of courage I have to mumble softly, "I love you, Sean Gentry."

I'm not sure he realizes his fingers have a death grip on my leg. I feel his breath flutter, uneven and shaky. I turn to look in his eyes, my head still against his shoulder. His eyes are as accepting as I have ever seen them. They are a cesspool of emotion ...full of depth, desire, love, mistrust and sorrow. I feel his breath on my cheek. He whispers back, "Well, that's a start," then he leans into me, his lips slightly part.

I am a flood of emotion; I want to cry again, this time in relief.

Sean eases me backward and rests my back on the cool, fresh-cut grass. His fingers gently trace the neckline of my tank top and slide slowly towards my chest. He lifts my arm and runs his fingertips down the inside where the skin is overly soft and delicate. The hairs on the nape of my neck dance when his fingers trace my side. His palm slides across my abdomen, just above the waistband of my low cut jeans. My ribbed tank top masks the fire from his touch...not acceptable. With one swift move I yank the tank top out of my jeans and fold it up, over my chest and expose my belly.

His eyes plead when he climbs between my legs on both knees and leans over me. He begins to softly kiss my abdomen and works his way from one side to the other. His hot lips and moist tongue run along my waist band. His palms lift my back and pull my abdomen up, like he's pulling a palm full of water to his lips.

The world around me spins in slow motion. He works his way up the center. When his lips reach the edge of my bra he sucks in a deep breath and slides my shirt back down.

Princess Jezebel throws the ice cube she used to cool her flushed face at her mirror and it shatters…falling in chards to the ground. I sigh and ache for him more than I ever have before. He breathes slowly while his lips rub my shirt lightly over my breast. They make their way to my neck. *Sweet fucking jeezus!* My body is in full spasms.

His strong arms push him into a seated position and he pulls me onto his lap. I face him with my legs wrapped around his waist. His palms cloak my neck like a scarf. He pulls me towards him and rubs his lips along the edge of my tank top. I want him, all of him—this time, I am ready.

Sean works his lips up my chest onto my neck. My head falls back limp under its own weight. His fingers braid through my hair and he gently pulls my lips back to his. He stares into my eyes with a look of desperation. Does he want me to save us from our craving, or does he want me to give into this inevitable passion we share for each other?

He answers this question for me. His lips meet mine with an untamable, unstoppable fury. His hands choke my waist and pull me into him. I raise my arms, when his hands begin to pull my tank top up slowly. I hear Natalie's voice.

"Jesus Christ, put your clothes on. I didn't come out here to hang out with Cory by myself all day. You're being rude."

Sean pulls the front of my shirt back down. We both steal a deep frustrated breath.

"This is a predictable outcome for us," Sean complains, under his breath.

I smile and take another deep breath, "We should probably go join them."

We follow Natalie back to Cory. He sits on a park bench with his head resting in his palms—bored. We start a game of Frisbee football. Although there are no real teams, or rules, it is clearly girls against boys, because the entire purpose must be to tackle. I am much slower than Sean...or Cory, so I am tackled a lot.

Natalie and Cory hit it off. Cory recovers quickly from his bleeding heart. Honestly, Natalie and Cory are a much better fit. Cory's not like a jock, but they are both fun loving, outgoing, and both apparently ate paint chips as a kid. They are far less awkward than he and Sam. I decide to back away and let them figure this out on their own.

Sean and I end our day on a good note. He, in spite of our day, still has deep seated issues, but for now, he wants me ...and I want him, more than ever.

Cory dumps Sean and me off at my house. He asks Sean to meet him at Natalie's in a few minutes. My educated guess, Cory wants to ask Natalie out and maybe sneak a kiss in private. A few more minutes with Sean, plainly, is acceptable to me.

Sean leads me to our front stoop instead of the patio. He fondles my fingers while we sit on the concrete step. His torn eyes carefully study my face. "Brianna, I love everything about you ...about us. You need to recognize we have a difficult road ahead, if we keep this going," he hangs his head and studies the ground. "I know I can't expect you to feel what I feel, because it's fucking crazy and absurd and ridiculous," he looks back into my eyes. "I do, however, wish I could read you—just a little. You're so fucking confusing. If you feel even close to how I feel, we have to work together on this. We both have to do everything in our power to keep this together. To spend time together. To build this into something that will endure these obstacles." His fingertips run down the length of my face. his dimples are so close I could lick them, "Do you understand?"

Endure is the only word I focus on. Yep, he wants sex. I want to answer, but his lips steal my concentration and swallow my rational. I shake my head yes while his body leans in to kiss me. *Sweet jeezus!*

CHAPTER TWENTY-NINE

The basketball game was our blossom and prom was our bloom. I always thought that a flower symbolized life, a fresh start...but I was wrong. Flowers symbolize death. The final stage, the end of the road before you wither away and die...and slowly decay back into the ground you spawned from.

It is Saturday. Nearly two weeks have passed since I saw or spoke to Sean. My delusion that everything was fine—yeah, not so much.

Tonight is Joplin's prom. All of my friends are pre-occupied with preparation today. If I was any kind of a friend, I would offer to help Samantha prepare. At this moment, I can't be a friend to anyone, that includes myself. Samantha is so much better at prep work; my thought that she somehow needs me is preposterous anyway.

Over and over I recap our last conversation. Sean seeks middle ground, which is just dandy—if I knew what the fuck that was. Middle ground? Are there too many highs and lows? Personally, the lows seem self-inflicted, and not by me. *Right!*

I need to put forth more effort ...those were his words. I am blind to what more I could be doing. Does he not recognize how completely in love with him I am.

For two weeks my stomach has been tied in a knot, which makes it difficult to walk and impossible to eat. My room is my sanctuary, my prison ...my chamber of torture and pain. Alone I sit, night after night, and grip my gut, and pray for my phone to ring, while it sits silently on my nightstand. The only sound that bounces from these four walls at all is the agonizing cry of pain I allow to escape when my head sinks into my pillow each night.

Sean isn't just a high school boyfriend. He is inside of me, he is a part of me. Nothing can erase him from my soul and nothing will ever fill the void he has slowly escaped from. Without him I am lost and confused like a child that wanders through the damp cold forest at night. I am petrified I may never find my way and be whole again.

Summer is almost here. With summer was the hope of more time spent together. That hope is gone. The hardest part, I don't know why. I want to fix us, but I don't know what he believes is broken. I don't understand what went wrong...not this time.

My Saturdays once again belong to my grandparents, like he never existed. But he does exist. A huge hole in my heart and the knot in my stomach confirm that, every minute of every day.

Gramps has stumbled back to his unconscious world. I pray for him to come back to us, I pray for him to leave us. This state of limbo just makes the shovel of loss dig deeper. To mask my own pain is easy around Grams. She is a victim of her own misery.

I arrive back home after a day with my grandparents, ready for the solitude of my room. My mom stops me when I walk through the door.

"Something came in the mail for you today. It's on the end of the breakfast bar."

I pick it up and notice the weight. It is a square white envelope; the expensive kind wedding invitations come in.

My mom continues, "And another thing, it is a beautiful day. You are not going to spend the entire afternoon in your room. I don't care if you sit on the patio and wallow in whatever it is you wallow in, you are not rotting in your room. Not today."

"Thanks mom, your loving concern overwhelms me."

"Briana, I do love you. That's why I'm pissed. I don't want to be mean, but enough is enough. You have sat in that room for days. I don't know what's going on with you, because you never talk to me. I can only assume it has to do with the boy you were seeing. You need to fix this, or move on. Maybe whatever he sent you will make you happy."

"He sent me?" I question.

"I assume it's from him; A Lamar return address is on it." *Wedding invitation...no he wouldn't...I feel sick.*

I rip into the envelope and yank out the red card that is stuffed inside. On the outside is a picture of his school embossed on the paper with the letters LHS stamped in black above it. I open the card and something falls to the floor. I bend over to pick it up. It is a picture of Sean, his senior picture. Inside is his graduation announcement.

I want to bleed myself dry. He knows graduation is inevitable. He knows leaving is inescapable. He knows our certain demise is unavoidable.   This so-called compromise is just an excuse to obstruct the gears in our perfectly oiled machine ...to bring us to a screeching halt. Why didn't I see this before. Nothing is wrong with us. Sean needs an out.   I don't need reminded of his graduation. I begin to weep.

"Brianna, sit down and tell me what's going on ...please!" My mom insists.

I gasp for breath and respond, "Mom, there is nothing you can do to fix this. I can't do anything to fix this. My destiny with Sean is debilitated and shackled."

"Bri, that's a little dramatic don't you think? What could possibly be so bad that you can't work through it?"

I flash the announcement at my mother, "He's leaving, don't you understand!   He's going away to college."

"Oh..."   She stalls, but regroups and continues, "Brianna, couples work out obstacles in their relationships all of the time. Look at me and your dad, he's on the road more than he's home. How far away is he going?"

"To MSU."

My mom snorts laughter through her tiny nose. "To Springfield? That's an hour from here, Bri."

"I understand that," I clip my words, irritated by her amusement. "He obviously believes it will be an issue, because he tries to stay away from me and tries to find excuses to be mad at me. He wants to forget about me, I can tell. I can't stand this; I miss him so bad I could die."

"Brianna, don't say things like that," my mother's eyes lock in a serious stare down. "You two didn't ...well, you know?"

I shake my head to absorb her question before I answer, "NO, of course not!"

My mom sucks in more air than she needs. "So what exactly is going on? I see in front of you an invitation to his graduation, not something I would think would upset you. He obviously wants you to be there."

"Mom, people send these to everyone to let them know they are graduating so they get checks in the mail. That doesn't mean you're supposed to go to the graduation."

"So, he sent you an invitation, but you're not supposed to go?"

I explain further, "No, not unless he actually asks me to go."

"He wants you to send him a check...then?" she poses.

"No, I doubt he wants money from me. That's for people like uncles and aunts and stuff."

"Let me see if I understand. He sent you an invitation to an event you're not invited to, that you already knew about, and he doesn't want a gift. So what is the invitation for again?"

My head begins to throb from all of the thinking, "I don't know ...maybe he had extra's."

"I don't know Bri, are you sure he doesn't want you to go? That makes the most sense."

"Mom, he hasn't called me for two weeks."

"Oh…" she mutters, again.

"If he wanted me to go don't you think he would call and talk to me about it? I mean, what am I supposed to do? Show up at his gymnasium, by myself, and sit in a corner. That might make sense to you, but it doesn't make sense to me."

"Ok Bri, you know the situation better than I do. Maybe you're right. If you haven't heard from him for two weeks, that is odd. Why don't you put on your bathing suit and I'll fix us some iced tea. We'll go soak up some rays."

My mom doesn't bring Sean up anymore. Maybe she is just as confused as I am. She is right about one thing. The weather is beautiful, now that I've climbed from the dark murky depths of my personal hell. This is a day I probably needed, not only for my sanity…but to give some sign of my beating heart to my lifeless pale skin.

Tonight, I curl up in bed and stare at the invitation. His graduation is less than two weeks away, on a Friday at six pm. Maybe, just maybe, he will call me and he will invite me. I am lost in his senior picture for close to an hour. When I place it on my nightstand, a single tear rolls down my cheek and disappears into my pillow. This will be the last tear I shed for Sean Gentry.

CHAPTER THIRTY

Three months I sit on my bed and stare at four walls. I half expect my mom to call the white van with little bald men and strait jackets—but she doesn't. Maybe she knows I already live in a padded cell of my own design. All of my dreams have turned to nightmares. The woman with long black hair and a pallid face follows me and lurks over me like a vulture waiting for my last breath of life.

I am fully aware the pain I feel is self-inflicted. I might be able to move past it, but there is one thing that holds me back. The severance isn't justifiable. There is no explanation of the force that disjointed us limb by limb, piece by piece, and burned us until nothing remained but ash. Nothing makes sense.

I analyze every part of our relationship, because I have nothing left in my life, except time. I dissect every shared moment, every conversation, every kiss ...what went wrong? What gaffe did I commit to turn him away? I need a reason to bring a closure.

I am alone in my pain, left to suffer in silence, because no one can possibly understand the importance of what I have lost. More of Sean's soul lingers in me than my own. He is not something I can replace like a pair of tennis shoes, or a lost cell phone. He has been ripped away from me, which leaves a deep unbearable wound that refuses to heal. Instead, it festers and becomes more and more intrusive ...more and more painful.

I decide—today will be a better day than yesterday.

It is Sunday. Summer vacation is nearly over. I haven't seen any of my friends. I have barely seen my parents. Grams is the only person I can muster up the strength to be around, because we agonize together silently.

I pick up my cell phone, which hasn't been used over the last few months and dial a number.

"Hello."

"Natalie, this is Bri. Are you doing anything today, because I could use some company?"

"I was going to lie out; you're welcome to join me," Natalie offers, with more compassion than I expect.

She continues, "Adrienne is coming over too, in about an hour."

"Perfect, I'll see you in a little while."

I fish through my drawers to find my bathing suit, which is buried deep. It hasn't been used since post-prom. This makes me want to cry. I sling it out of my drawer and throw it onto my unmade bed. I head downstairs to take a shower.

As the hot water drenches my face, I reimagine my time in the pool with Sean at post prom. I shake my head to snap myself out of my reverie. After I finish my shower, I dry off and wrap a towel around my chest. I head back upstairs and sit on the edge of my bed.

I suck in all of the oxygen the room has to offer, stand up and let my towel drop to the floor in a wad. I pull on my bathing suit and walk over to the mirror. I don't recognize the body I see. I'm thin, almost bony. Before my demon of solitude talks me out of it, I grab my towel and my suntan lotion and head down the staircase.

"Are you going swimming, Bri?" my mom asks, with a smile that fills her entire face.

"Nope, I thought I'd go catch some rays with Natalie and Adrienne."

"That's wonderful!" Mom cheers, with more excitement than she should be forced to have for such a simple task.

I walk across the street to join Natalie on her patio. Adrienne is already there. They both appear happy to see me, I'm relieved. I pull out a lounge chair and listen silently while they continue their conversation about school starting.

Adrienne pulls me into their conversation first, "Hey Bri, I'm going to go apply for a job tomorrow at the mall. Would you like to come with? Natalie can't work because of her sports."

"I probably should have done that months ago, but sure, why not."

"Yay! Are you ok now Bri?" Adrienne asks with concern.

Natalie adds, "Yeah, I think it's terrible what Sean did to you. Cory told me about it."

"Cory told you about what?" I pump, troubled yet curious.

"About Sean, hooking up with Kylie Smith at their graduation party. What a loser."

Kylie Smith? I know her. She was the ex-stalker-girlfriend of a guy I went out with once. I assumed the excruciating pain I felt over the last three months could never be surpassed ...I was wrong. The softball sized knot in my stomach now tries to regurgitate itself. I start to gag, while my hands clutch my gut to hold in the pain.

"Oh no, you didn't know, did you?" Natalie covers her gaping mouth, mortified.

"No, I haven't spoken with Sean since the day at the park."

"The day I went with you?" Natalie pries.

"That's the day," I admit.

"Oh my god, I had no idea. Cory never said a word about you two until after graduation."

"Are you dating Cory?" I prod, and pray she is. Maybe I can find some answers.

"I *was* until a few weeks after school was out. He's not really my type, so I ended it. Plus, *your friend* Samantha acted a little irritated. I don't know why, I would have happily traded her boyfriends."

"Wow, I didn't know that either," I divulge.

"Well Bri, you have been a little out of touch lately," Nat suggests, with a soft smile.

"So is Sean and Kylie dating now, or what?" I ask and wish I could suck the question back through my lips. The thought of Sean touching someone else, kissing someone else makes me want to puke.

"I have no idea. I haven't spoke to Cory in a long time. All I know is she majorly hit on Sean at their graduation party. I guess at first he tried to ignore her, but by the end of the night, Cory said they appeared to be together. Cory thought you two were still together, so he was kind of pissed at Sean. He never mentioned anymore about it, and I'm sorry, but I didn't ask."

"So why did you break up Bri?" Adrienne prods. "You two were perfect together, that whole zodiac bullshit was ultra-cool. I was jealous ...and I don't get jealous."

"Adrienne that's the thing, I don't know why. He just stopped calling."

"And you didn't ask why?"

"No. All I know is everything was fine until after prom. The day Natalie went to the park with us, he acted weird, but we talked and I thought everything was ok. The only thing he said was I need to meet him in the middle and I need to put forth some effort. I don't know what he meant. I still don't understand what I did wrong. I thought we ended the day on a good note, but that was the last time I heard from him."

Natalie has a completely confused look painted on her face, "You have not called to talk to him about this?"

"No, he obviously doesn't want to talk to me, or he would call me."

"Bri, have you ever called him?" Adrienne digs.

"Once or twice, maybe."

"Oh my god Bri, no wonder he quit calling," Adrienne deducts.

Natalie embellishes, "Girl, we should have taught you better. I can't believe you never called him. Did you ever go visit him?"

"I met him at work once," I admit, my head hung in shame.

"Well that explains his comments at the park ...jeesh! Brianna, you nutcase! Guys want to know you care about them, too. They are more insecure than we are. I wish you would have come to us with this, months ago. You might have been able to salvage this, but now it's been so long, especially if he's still seeing Kylie."

My throat is sealed tighter than a drum. My gut aches so bad, my only reprieve is to curl up in a ball like a fetus. The tears I haven't shed over the last three months have apparently just accumulated into a reservoir. Now, they have broken through their dam and they all rush down my face at once.

Natalie and Adrienne hover over me and try to comfort me. I feel guilty for ruining their plans today. My room is where I need to be, alone with my demons ...where I belong.

"I have to go home. I'm sorry I ruined your day," I apologize and stand up to snatch my towel.

Natalie jumps in front of me and throws her palms against my chest, "You are not going anywhere. First of all, sit down. Second, dry it up and pull your shit together. Third, and listen close, we WILL fix this. If he is important to you, why would you give up without a fight?"

Natalie begins to push me backward with force. Adrienne grabs my arm gently and turns me around. She pulls me back down into the lounge chair.

"Well there's step one," Natalie rallies.

"Natalie, why don't you go fix her something to drink. I won't let her leave, I promise."

"Vodka preferably," I call out after her.

"Yeah right!" Natalie jokes, completely miscuing my seriousness.

Adrienne pulls up my chin up, "Bri, look at me!" Her voice is softer when she continues, "I wasn't kidding when I said I was jealous of what you and Sean shared. Do you have any idea how hard it is to find something that special? I saw the way he looked at you, like he looked straight into your soul. I saw the way you looked at him. If you lose him, you may live your entire life trying to replace him. You have to pull yourself together, so we can figure this out. He loves you, I know he does. It's the same for him as it is for you. He's probably broken. By never calling, he probably thinks you don't care about him ...at least not like he cares about you. You see that, right?"

My voice wobbles, "I guess that could be true. God, I am so lame. Why couldn't I see what he was after? I am so selfish. I would give anything to have him back, but what if he's still dating Kylie? He won't take me back if he has a girlfriend, he's too morally decent."

"Brianna, stop that! Do you want him back, or not?"

"Obviously I want him back. That doesn't mean he will take me back."

"If you want him back, you need to fight for him. You have to do whatever it takes to win back his heart. There is no rule that states you must play fair and who gives a rats tit about Kylie Smith—slut. If he is dating her, wipe her out of your mind like she doesn't exist. Sean does not care about her the way he cares about you, no way ...and if he does, he's all kinds of phony anyway." She pauses a few seconds while I absorb her advice before she continues. "I won't give you false hope. This won't be easy ...or fixed with one phone call. You better be prepared to fight. "

"That's right! You have to fight for your man. The good one's anyway," Natalie giggles, while she hands me a glass of Coke.

As I ingest the hope they spoon feed me, the tension in my gut eases. The breathless sobs diminish to single tears that stream down my cheeks. I take a sip of the soda and rest the glass on the concrete next to my feet. "I need you, please tell me what I should do."

Natalie starts, "Well, the first thing you need to do is call him, and I don't mean next week. I'm talking about immediately. Like now."

Adrienne adds, "Question him about graduation. Call him out on Kylie quickly, so you know what you're dealing with. Will she be an obstacle or not?"

"Absolutely!" Natalie agrees.

"And what if she is?" I ask.

"Then you work around her. You work twice as hard to win him back. Listen up—this is key! Guys are fairly easy to manipulate, but you have to know how to work it. First of all, don't blame him for anything. He'll just get defensive or stop listening. That will get you nowhere. Instead, you accept responsibility for what you've done wrong, but toss out little hints that let him know he is also partially to blame. If he sees how sorry you are and how you have placed all of the blame on yourself, in the back of his mind he will see where he faulted," Adrienne advises.

"But he didn't do anything wrong. It was all me," I argue.

Adrienne protests, "Not true. He could have talked to you about his issues. He could have asked you to call him. He could have invited you over to see him. Instead he walked away. He did plenty wrong."

Natalie adds, "I agree, except for that no blame bullshit. This is just as much his fault as yours. He needs to know where he fucked up. Not with a sprinkle of seeds, but with a slap across the face with a tree."

I suck in a deep shaky breath. I still feel nauseous, "Ok, then what?"

"That's easy," Natalie smirks. "You tell him you're coming up to see him."

"What if he says no?"

"You show up anyway," she smiles.

"I totally agree," Adrienne adds. "It is much harder for him to ignore his feelings if you're in front of him."

"Ok, worst case scenario ...what if he doesn't care about me anymore."

"Then you move on Bri, you have to let go. Don't assume that he doesn't care after one visit. Give this some time. Key...key...key...don't let him lose sight of you. Make a huge presence so he thinks about you—constantly. Calls...visits...notes...whatever."

"He's going to leave for school in a few weeks, how will I stay in his thoughts if he's not here?"

"You call him, even if he doesn't answer your calls. You go see him when he's home, even if he doesn't want to see you. Do this for at least a month. If he still doesn't respond, you let go and move on," Natalie offers.

"Be careful, if you take it too far, you become the psychotic stalker, ex-girlfriend. You don't want that," Adrienne snickers.

Nat finishes, "Sometimes it's after you back away that they finally come around. Jealousy takes over when they think you've given up and moved on."

"I had no idea this was all so complicated. How did you become so smart about all of this?"

"We talk to each other when something goes wrong or we need advice. Something you should have done several months ago. You can't hide from the world Bri, it's not healthy," Adrienne concludes.

All of their advice makes perfect sense. I'm not sure why I kept my pain hidden. I didn't even talk to my mother about it. Inflicting it on others seemed selfish. I had no idea anybody would understand. It seemed impossible that anyone could identify with what I felt. The truth about love is, we all go through heartbreak of varying degree. Advice doesn't have to be custom made for me to be good advice. They don't have to stand in my shoes to understand how our relationship works.

I continue to lay out with my friends all afternoon— and talk, or listen. Like a dose of good medicine, I feel their words heal my wounds. I have a long dark tunnel to crawl through, but at the end is a flicker of light. For the first time in months, I hear my heart beat and feel myself breathe again.

Tonight, I will call him; I will take a leap of fate...

I sit on my bed and stare down at my phone. I wish I could just pick it up and dial Sean's number, but it's hard. So hard. Sean's phone number lights up my screen so many times, I finally have to plug it into my charger. It is seven o'clock, three hours since I came home. What am I waiting for? I start to piss myself off.

My phone rings and breaks the silence. Is it Sean? Yeah, right. I pick up the phone and glance at the number, it's Adrienne.

"Hello," I croak, in a thick voice.

"Well, what did he say?"

"I wouldn't know, because I haven't called him yet."

"WHAT? Brianna, do I have to come over there and dial his number for you? I will if I have to."

"No, that won't be necessary."

"Seriously, what are you waiting for? If he is horrid with you, which by the way is entirely possible, you can't feel any worse than you already feel. You need to be confident in what you shared enough to crawl past this fear, or intimidation, or whatever the fuck you feel. Consider this, he has been hurt as much as you, he may actually be happy to hear from you."

"I don't know Adrienne, I suppose you're right. Please realize my confidence is nowhere near your level. What if he tells me it's over, and he's in love with Kylie? I'm so fucking scared—I'm shaking."

"Brianna, you're making excuses. Be assertive, have faith that his feelings for you are real. If nothing else, you will be in the forefront of his mind after your call. You will haunt his dreams. If he blows you off on the phone, show up at his house. Let him gaze into your eyes and tell you he doesn't love you anymore. I've seen how he stares at you. He won't be able to do it. Just sayin."

"Ok, ok, I'll call him."

"Brianna, I will give you one hour and I'm calling back. If you haven't talked to him, I will come over, dial his number and throw you the phone. You've got this." She pauses, "I'll call you later anyway and figure out what time works for you to go to the mall with me tomorrow. We're still filling out some applications. Right?"

"Right. Sounds good, thanks Adrienne. I'm glad you called."

"I'm going to hang up now ...don't think about it, put his number in and hit dial. Ready. Set. Bye."

I hang up from Adrienne and immediately pull up Sean's number, before I lose my nerve. I suck in a deep breath and before I stop myself I hit "dial". The phone begins to ring in my ear.

"Hello," a woman's voice answers.

"Is Sean there?"

"No he's not, whose calling?"

"This is Brianna, Mrs. Gentry."

"Brianna, well hello. Sean's at work, but he'll be home soon. I'll tell him you called."

"Thank you, Mrs. Gentry."

This was not part of the plan, and I don't like it. Leaving a message takes away the element of surprise and gives Sean an out. He doesn't have to call me back. Now prepared, he can have his mother screen his calls and avoid me altogether. *Damnit...I should have hung up.*

Twenty minutes pass and I stumble over to my stereo to put on some quiet music. My glimmer of hope has opened my sealed eyes. I glance around at the disorder of my room and feel ashamed ...not enough to do anything about it. Not tonight.

My phone startles me when it rings. I race back to the bed to pick it up. I see its Natalie, so I ignore it and throw it on the bed. It's still bouncing when it begins to ring again. Damnit Natalie, she's so impatient. I answer and spit, "What?"

"Brianna?"

My hands immediately tremble while my mind processes the voice on the other end of the phone, "Yes."

"Oh, it didn't sound like you."

"I'm sorry; I thought you were Natalie being OCD."

Sean is rigid, not unpleasant, but guarded, "So, you called me?"

I take a deep breath to clear my head and gather the thoughts I have rehearsed in my head all evening. "Yes I did, I hope that's ok."

"Its fine Bri, I just wonder why?"

Bri? I hate it when he calls me that.

I know in my head the speech that I practiced, but the words are stuck, they won't come out. My throat feels like it is full of marbles. Unable to swallow, unable to breathe, unable to speak, there's nothing left to do except cry.

Sean commands, "Look, I have plans tonight, if you don't have anything to talk about."

I think about Adrienne's words, stay confident, believe in us ...believe in him.

My voice somehow chokes out, "Sean I'm so sorry, for everything. What we had was so special, and I single handedly destroyed it. I don't blame you for hating me and I don't blame you for seeing someone else now."

His voice is silent while my heart pounds out a dozen loud beats. He finally begins, "First of all, I don't hate you. I've never hated you. That's not even feasible. I know this, because believe me, I've tried.

I confess, "I need you to know I have never been so miserable. I can't believe it took until today to figure out what you meant by putting forth effort and meeting you halfway. I am so stupid sometimes."

"You're not stupid, so excuse me if I have a hard time buying into your sudden revelation. How fitting, you figure it all out right before I leave for school. That conveniently freed up your summer to do what you wanted, didn't it?   ...and, what on earth are you talking about? Who am I seeing?"

"I heard you hooked up with Kylie Smith at your graduation party. Why? I don't understand. Why didn't you invite me, I would have went with you."

"Why?   Seriously Bri!   I sent you a fucking invitation, how much more invited can you get! You never showed up. That was my final blow. I was already tired of feeling for you something you obviously will never feel for me.   You didn't even acknowledge that you got the invitation. I prayed you would call me and at least ask about it. Nope. Nothing. I kept thinking graduation night you would walk through the gym doors, but you never did. It was my high school graduation Brianna, something meaningful that your girlfriend should attend. Yes, I hung out with Kylie for a while at the party and talked, but we've never dated.

"Sean, I'm sorry for everything I've done to hurt you. I'm sorry I never called you. I'm sorry I didn't drive to Lamar. I'm sorry I was scared and insecure. I'm especially sorry I didn't come to your graduation. It was not because I didn't want to be with you, you have to know that. Do you honestly not see how much I love you? How can you possibly believe I don't feel the same way?"

"Sometimes actions speak for themselves. I can give you an entire list of reasons. First, you knew I didn't have a cell phone. You also knew I had to pay for long distance charges every single time I spoke to you. I know you knew this, because we discussed it, more than once. Still, you refused to call me. I finally decided after our day at the park to see how long you would go without calling, if you didn't hear from me …a test of your commitment to our relationship, I guess. What's it been Brianna, over three months?

I came to see you, several times. How many times did you come to see me? With exception to prom night, you've never been to my house. I was on limited time and it would have been nice to come home and see you in my driveway ...for that few hours I had, between school and work. Everything we had was because I made it happen. If this relationship were up to you, there would never have been a relationship.

Then, let's talk prom. When I told you I loved you, you sat there. Do you understand how stupid I felt for sharing my feelings with you? That is when it became obvious to me, I am much deeper invested in *us* than you are. Oh, I almost forget ... your prom comes around. Did you know Cory went with your friend? I tried so hard to figure out why you didn't invite me. I still don't understand, but decided it wasn't worth the torment anymore.

As if all of this isn't enough to slap me into realization, graduation rolls around. I want so desperately to call you, but I can't. I have to hold my ground. Plus, I just know after you get the invitation you will call. I'm sure of it. I wait and wait for a call that never comes.

Brianna, that day by the lake when I told you I couldn't do this anymore, I wasn't kidding. I have my future to think about and you are an unpleasant distraction in my life."

My mind races to try and come up with a logical explanation for my behavior. What he thinks is not at all how I feel. As Adrienne eloquently put it, I have to plant some seeds, but still accept total blame.

"Sean I'm sorry I didn't call you. You're right, I'm not stupid. But I am ignorant when it comes to relationships. You are my first real boyfriend, so I don't know how any of this works. Night after night, I sat by the phone and prayed for a call. I don't know why I didn't dial your number and call you. Half of me was scared. It took me three hours and a life threat to dial your number tonight. The other half was insecure. I thought you would call me when you had time and wanted to talk. Why didn't you ever say anything to me? That would have made such a difference. If I knew you wanted me to call, I would have called ...every day.

I'm also sorry I never came to see you. My reasons are basically the same. I didn't know you wanted me to. You always were so busy, and the one time I did want to come up to Lamar to hear your band; you made such an issue. I didn't know it was an option. I would have hopped in my car at your beckon call. I just needed the invite. I will come to see you now, if you'll still let me.

Why didn't I tell you I love you at prom? I was so touched I couldn't speak. I told you at the lake, but even before that, you had to know when we touched, when we kissed, when we looked into each other's eyes. It was all right there.

Why didn't I ask you to my prom? I have no idea. You're not into the whole dance scene, so I didn't think you would want to go. Also, I've never asked a guy to a dance. I've never even been to a formal until I went with you. That is also why you didn't have a boutonnière. Samantha didn't tell me about that step until you pulled in my driveway. I felt so lame and completely humiliated."

Sean laughs quietly, "I did wonder about that."

I take a deep breath and continue. "Graduation, what can I say except I am genuinely ashamed. My mom told me you probably wanted me to be there ...I argued with her. I hadn't heard from you in two or three weeks. You sent the invitation to me, but you never called. People send graduation announcements out to a lot of people that they don't expect to be there. Since I hadn't heard from you, I assumed I was one of those people. I was petrified to walk into the gym all alone and sit by myself. I'm not comfortable enough with your parents to show up and intrude on their space. If we talked about it, I would have felt totally different.

Sean, I have completely botched up everything. Right now, I can't even stand to look at myself. I hate myself. I hate the weak, shy, scared person that I am. If there was only one do-over in life I would use mine up at this precise moment. I just wish you would have been more specific than, *I need to put forth effort*. I thought you meant I needed to be more physical with you."

    "Are you serious? You thought I meant sex? Wow. If anything, we needed to slow down. I never needed anything more from you than what you were comfortable giving. You honestly didn't understand what I meant?"

"I seriously did not understand what you meant. For the record, this has been the worst and loneliest summer of my entire life. Today was the first day I have seen, or talked to any of my friends."

"What the hell have you been doing?"

"Sitting in my room and wishing I was with you."

"All summer?"

"All summer."

I can't be positive, but Sean's breathing becomes labored. I have to wonder if a tear might escape his beautiful dark brown eyes. It is time to step up my game.

"Sean, can I please come up and see you tomorrow?"

"No, I'm sorry Brianna. I have to work tomorrow; it's my last day. The rest of the week I need to pack. I'm not sure how to break this to you, but I'm moving to Springfield this weekend. I'm glad you called, I sincerely mean that. At least I understand what went wrong. These are not words you want to hear, but I don't think I can travel back down that road again, it's too painful. College starts soon and I need to focus on my goals. I just became resigned to you not being part of my next chapter. Now you want to come back on the last page. I'm afraid it may be too late for us." He sits in silence a few seconds; he hears my gentle sobs in the silence. "Brianna, please quit crying ...how about Tuesday at noon?"

Before he can change his mind I accept, "Sean, thank you for calling me back, it means everything to me."

"Brianna, thank you for calling me ...I think," he squeezes out a laugh. "Good night."

"Good night, I'll see you Tuesday at noon."

"Ok goodnight ...then. Sweet dreams."

CHAPTER THIRTY-ONE

Adrienne picks me up at noon, on the nose. We fill out applications at restaurants and clothing stores all afternoon. A job might be the distraction I need to avoid my dark solitary hell. Plus, my parents won't balk at the gas bill when I travel to Springfield, if I foot my own bill. *Yes, I need a job!*

My day with Adrienne is heartening. She understands how significant tomorrow is to me. Sean isn't merely some high school crush. This bond we share plunges much deeper. Her encouragement throughout the day helps build my confidence. The fact that he is willing to see me, at all, is hopeful.

I go to bed early, mentally drained and exhausted from our day at the mall. My heart begins to reawaken from its deep lifeless slumber. My breaths are not as painful. Even the knot in my stomach is not as intrusive as it has been over the past few months. If I could only rid myself from the endless nightmares, my life might feel almost normal again.

This nightmare is different, more vivid and realistic. I sit on the edge of a creek. Choirs of frogs croak. A gentle summer breeze blows my hair away from my face. I feel the single ray of sunshine that shines down on my cheek through the thick canopy of leaves that hover over my head. Gramps is there, he is normal again. He stands a few feet in front of me and smiles, with his toothless grin. The bib overalls he wears are stained with dirt. His rough calloused hands reach out for me. I want to hug him, but when I stretch my arms out, he's out of my reach. My eyes narrow when Gramp's face slowly morphs into Sean's. His deep soul piercing eyes and full warm lips smile down on me. His hands reach out, just inches from my grasp.

"I love you Brianna, but I have to go," softly escapes from his lips. I stretch my arms further and desperately try to touch his fingertips.

The face slowly fades back to Gramps. "Riny, it's time for me to say goodbye. You will always be the song in my heart."

Once again Sean's face appears, "Don't forget me. I'll never forget you."

I see the woman with long black hair as she walks up the bank of the creek. Her face glows white in the tiny rays of sunshine; her long black hair shimmers, like satin. She gets closer and closer. I frantically extend my reach and try to touch the fingertips that are so close to me. It's too late, she smiles down on me, but her beauty is false. Her smile is menacing and evil ...her teeth are sharp, stained, and broken.

The face in front of me changes back and forth from Gramps to Sean to Gramps to Sean. She grabs his wrist and pulls him behind her and slowly walks away. I want to stop her, but I can't feel my legs. I am paralyzed. I sit there unable to do anything except watch while she slowly leads them away. They disappear into the forest. *NO!*

I wake up, shake off the nightmare and realize it is only a figment of my insecurity. While I sit on the edge of my bed, I hear the sweet sound of birds outside my window. This is the first time all summer I actually took the time to listen. My curtains whip in the cool morning breeze. They gently dance over my bed. The sheer flowing fabric reminds me of my prom dress, the way it floated while I moved across the floor. I smile.

Today is possibly the most important day of my life. My future happiness and sanity depend on its outcome. I need to be rational and composed. Sean has to be reminded that he can't live without me ...because I can't live without him.

I spend most of the morning preparing, both mentally and physically. I decide to wear the ivory eyelet blouse that Samantha and I picked up on our shopping trip. The same blouse I wore to Parazzo's the first time I went. I ease into my favorite pair of faded jeans. The waist on them falls down around my hips now.

My mother wishes me luck and I set out for Lamar. Millions of scenarios speed through my mind on the way to his house. I want to be prepared for anything. No matter what his question, or argument may be, I need to be ready with an answer. If he still loves me and wants me, I know exactly what I will say and will hold nothing back this time. Adversely, if he tries to reason his way out of our relationship, I have an argument for that also.

My nerves are on edge when I pull into his drive and catch my first glimpse of him while he sits on his front stoop. I pull in at ten minutes before twelve. He doesn't smile which crushes a portion of my confidence. He stands up and moves towards my car. Even Princess Jezebel twirls her hair nervously around her bony fingers. I suck in every ounce of oxygen my car has to offer.

My heart beats louder and harder than it has ever beaten. The echoes of thunder that pound in my head just make me more nervous. He is more gorgeous than I remember. *Sweet jeezus!* His deep dark eyes glare through me while he approaches my door and lifts the handle. I never take my focus from his while I step out of my car. His eyes look me up and down slowly, he smiles. I let the air seep from my lungs, like I'm breathing through a straw.

"Wow, I guess I forgot how beautiful you are," Sean comments.

"Whatever. I'm so nervous right now, can I please have a hug."

Sean wraps his arms around my trembling body. He holds me tight until my shakes subside. I feel tears build up while he holds me, but I fight hard to suppress them. I don't ever want him to let me go, but he does.

"I hope you don't mind Brianna, but I invited Jon over today, too. He wants to hang out for a while before I leave this weekend, and this is the only day I can afford to slack off. I still have a ton of shit to pack before Friday morning."

My heart nose-dives into the pit of my gut. This is not a scenario I prepared for. We aren't spending our last day together in each other's arms, like I envisioned. Chances are good, we won't even have an opportunity to talk about anything meaningful. My heart screams this is intentional. He doesn't want to let me in. More of my confidence erodes out of existence. Princess Jezebel climbs under her covers and buries her head under a pillow.

"I hoped for some time alone, but I guess I will take what I get. Maybe if you need help packing I can come up tomorrow or Thursday and give you a hand." I can't believe I come up with such a kick-ass idea.

Sean's eyebrows pull together, "Yeah maybe, we'll see."

Jon pulls in the driveway and jumps out of his truck. His enthusiasm is a bit overwhelming for today's somber mood. "Hey Brianna, long time no see."

"Hey Jon," I reply with a smile that never makes it to my eyes.

Jon looks over at Sean, "So, what are we doing today, my friend."

"I thought we'd go for a drive, cruise the miracle mile, maybe head down to the railroad right of way."

"Sounds like a plan to me."

I stare at the ground while we make our way to Sean's car. Maybe he notices, because he suggests, "Hey Jon, will you drive?"

"Yeah...sure."

The entire situation sucks ass, but at least, this is the best possible scenario. Sean holds open the door and helps me into Jon's truck. His truck has a small backseat, but I don't offer. I fold up the console armrest in the middle of the front bench seat and sit down. Sean climbs in after me and slams the door shut.

Sean has Jon pull in a gas station so we can grab some sodas. I'm not thirsty, but he grabs me one anyway. Since I folded up the console, there are no cup holders. We have to hold onto our sodas. He never offers to hold my hand. He just clings to his cup ...like I do.

I don't have much to say in this awkward situation. I listen while Sean and Jon reminisce about some of the crazy things they have done throughout the years. Once we're in the country, Jon turns the stereo in his truck up loud and rolls down the windows. My hair weaves itself into a huge knot on the side of my head. I feel my heart stop beating while I become more and more invisible.

Jon talks—non-stop. I feel Sean's eyes locked on me. I stare straight ahead. I turn to face him and he looks at me with such intensity, like I'm a complicated set of instructions he can't quite figure out. Maybe he reads the misery on my face, or maybe I look emotionless, like I don't care? I don't know. I just pray he knows this is not how I planned to spend possibly our last day together.

His arm stretches in front of me; I feel his shoulder rub lightly against my breast. He turns down the radio. *Better.* "Jon, why don't you head down to the right of way now ...down by the creek."

Creek? A vision of my nightmare flashes before my eyes, I gasp. Sean looks at me puzzled.

"Sure thing, man I wish we had some brewskies."

I think to myself, *man I wish we did too.* Maybe they would numb some of the pain I feel.

Sean grabs my leg with his hand and squeezes gently. I nearly jumped out of my skin and about drop my soda.

"Brianna, are you ok? I didn't mean to scare you," he grins his flirty dimpled grin.

352

I shake my head and smile back, "Yeah sorry, I didn't see that coming."

"Sorry, I can let go if you want."

In a whisper, I answer, "No, please don't." My eyes lock with his, and for the first time in a long time I feel the connection between us. He lets me wander through his secret world again.

Jon is now the one out of place. He continues to drive while we stare at each other, like the first night. We can't pull our eyes apart, maybe because we don't want to …maybe because we can't. I feel Sean's hand grip my leg with more strength. I'm not sure he's conscious of this.

Our concentration is broken when we travel down a steep decline of loose gravel. When we reach the bottom, there is a narrow path between tall weeds and grass barely wide enough for the truck to fit through.

Sean releases my leg and hands me his soda. His upper body flings out the window. *What the?* His arms reach out for something, but I can't tell what he's doing. A full minute later, Jon stops the truck, the path has ended. In front of us is a creek, I see the outer bank. Sean climbs back through the window with a bouquet of wild flowers. A smile touches my heart when he hands them to me.

Sean opens his door and climbs out, he motions for me to follow. Jon already wanders towards the creek.

He grabs my hand this time and turns to face me. "Brianna, I'm sorry. I know you came down here today and expected more …you thought we could put everything back together. I shouldn't have made plans with Jon. But, I figured it would make the day more comfortable, less

353

intense. I see you're not happy, and that wasn't my intention. Try to lighten up and have some fun, we will have some time to talk later. I promise."

His words give me comfort. I smile and look down at our hands clasped tightly together. His arms are cut and bleeding.

"Your arms Sean, is that from picking my flowers?"

He looks down, "Yeah, I suppose it is."

"Wow, I'm sorry. Now I feel bad."

"Why would you feel bad Brianna, this pain is minor. I've grown immune to pain."

His words gouge me. I have no response.

We spend an hour down by the creek, we talk, we joke and we tell stories. Actually, they tell stories—I listen. The Sean in the stories is so far removed from the Sean I know, I feel like we're speaking of someone else. Our time passes quickly. Too quickly.

On our drive back to Sean's house, Jon hints that he will be hanging out with us for a while. Sean corrects his assumption. "Jon, why don't you swing by later this week and help me load all of my crap. Brianna and I have to catch up on a few things, this afternoon."

"Oh, no problem. I get it, I don't wear a bra ...whatever," Jon jokes, while I glare up my nose at him.

We do have a lot to catch up on. Issues need resolved. My confidence builds again, but I can't read Sean and know with certainty what he thinks.

Jon drops us off around two. It is hot and arid, not like the cool damp air we felt in the woods by the creek. Sean gives Jon a guy hug—the type of hug where they don't overly touch, but rather slap each other reassuringly on the back with some force. They say their goodbyes.

Sean grins at me sheepishly and he grabs my hand to lead me into his house. His father isn't home yet, but his mother greets me from the living room.

"It's nice to see you again, Brianna. What have you been doing all summer? I expected to see a lot more of you, once school was out."

Awkward! I'm not sure how to respond. I don't need to. Sean takes control of her friendly interrogation.

"Mom, stop. Brianna has a life. She's here now. Let's focus on that ...shall we."

His answer is a blatant lie. I would not describe my summer as life at all. More like putrid rotting death—until today.

I avoid her question and politely address her, "It's nice to see you again, Mrs. Gentry."

"Brianna, please don't call me that, you make me feel old. My name is Sheryl."

"Ok, thanks Sheryl."

Sean tugs on my arm to avoid any further interrogation. He swiftly leads me away. We climb up a noisy wooden staircase that leads to his bedroom. My heart pounds furiously with each upward stride. My hands shake like a junky when we approach the landing. I can't be sure if my anxiety is a result of the demons of destruction we need to face ...or if I anticipate our kiss. *God please let him kiss me.* Princess Jezebel pulls the pillow off of her face. *Kiss? What kiss?*

Sean looks down at my hands. The shaking is completely noticeable—I'm so embarrassed. His smile flattens when we walk into his room. He sits on the edge of his bed and pulls me down next to him. I can't stop my leg from bouncing.

I think back to the one and only time he was in my room, and a nervous giggle escapes.

"Is something funny?"

"Yes. No. Maybe. I just thought about the time you were in my room and you refused to sit on my bed. Hell, you barely looked at it." *Brianna, why did you say that? That was really stupid.*

"First of all, I tried to be respectful to you and your parents, secondly I think our relationship is a little beyond were it was at that time," Sean argues defensively.

"Sean, I'm not making fun of you. It's a cute memory, that's all."

He smiles. *Whew, good save.* "I guess we should probably talk about the last few months," his statement more of a question than a fact.

"Probably," and wish we could skip the bullshit and turn back the clock. *Do Over!*

Several silent seconds go by, so I begin. It's not that hard, I've practiced. "Sean, is there any chance you can forgive me for the mistakes I've made? I regret all of them, horribly. I really screwed everything up."

"There's nothing to forgive, Brianna. We both made mistakes, we both jacked this up." *Adrienne is right, planting the seed of blame works.*

"Sean, I promise I will do everything I can to make this right. I will drive to Springfield to see you. I will call you, every night if you want. Whatever it takes to fix us, I'm willing to try."

"It's not that simple, Brianna. The entire summer escaped us, and we needed that time to build *us* into something stable and secure. We're basically starting from scratch. I leave in three days. I don't think this can be fixed in three days. And, I'm sorry, but with everything that will be on my plate, I'm not sure I want to add this crazy, fucked up, confusing, beautiful, long distance relationship. Don't be mad, I'm trying to be realistic."

Wrong answer, buddy! I've memorized the counter-attack for this predictable argument. I rebut, "Sean, we are special! What we share isn't some childhood crush, or high school romance. This is real. I don't want to waste my entire life trying to find what I already have, with you. I will not give up without a fight. I can't stand to be away from you. This summer has made that painfully obvious."

"Brianna, that's just it, you *will* be away from me. I won't be home, hardly ever. You thought the school year sucked, this will be ten times worse! My parents are spending their life savings on this education, I can't take that lightly. I'll have full time classes and studies and

357

homework and working part time to have spending money. I don't see this being a situation that will be easy to overcome. Not to mention the other problem that exists."

"What other problem?" I protest.

"You have to see, our ability to communicate is treacherous. We have this unique ability to connect on some bizarre sub-conscious level, but when we need to talk ...we have serious issues. Lord Brianna, I know you realize this! Why do you think we've spent the last several months apart? We rely too much on this inner connection. Everything we read, or feel from each other, however real that may seem, is still left to interpretation. That isn't healthy."

"But we're talking now! We can work on this. I was scared ...of everything, because I never knew how you felt, but I can try harder."

"I'm not sure I can. I'm not an open person, especially when I need to share my feelings. I wish I could tell you I would do better, but it's an obstacle I may not overcome. I'm a private person, it's just my nature."

"Sean please, we have to try. We have no other choice. I can't picture my life without you. It's too late for me. I can't breathe when you're not around."

"Oh Brianna, you can and will breathe without me, as I will without you. I wish I could tell you what you want to hear, but I can't give you a definitive answer. I don't know, without a doubt, that I want to travel down this road again. My head tells me I need to walk away and leave it alone, but my heart doesn't ever want you to leave this room. I promise I will give it some serious thought this week, that's all I can promise. If you want to spend some time with me while I pack, I would like that. I do have to pack though, as long as you understand that."

"I do understand, and I would love that."

"Can we change the subject now at least for a while? I have missed you like crazy. It would be nice to spend some time with you that isn't strained."

"I would like that, too."

Sean gives me a genuine dimpled smile. He breathes a heavy sigh and walks over to his stereo to pick out some music. While he thumbs through his CD's, I catch a glimpse of myself in the mirror that hangs on the wall, behind his dresser. My hair is a tangled bird nest. *Thanks Jon.* I notice a brush that sits on his dresser and ask if I can use it.

"No, you can't." I gape at him. "But if you ask me to brush your hair, I would agree to that."

"Ok ...Sean, will you *please* brush my hair?"

Sean turns on some music I don't recognize—soft and romantic. He grabs the brush from his dresser and sits on the bed next to me. I turn with my back against his chest while he gently pulls through my tangles. I feel his palms slide softly behind the bristles. In slow even strokes I feel him work around my head until the brush falls through my hair, effortlessly. When he is finished, he turns me around to face him. His fingers slide along the edge of my hair and pull it back away from my face. The hairs on the nape of my neck do their happy dance.

Sean's breath is labored and sporadic. His eyes take their rightful place in my soul. Talk is so overrated. Our lack of communication is a negligible hindrance compared to this connection we share when our eyes meet. This feeling, I already know, will never be found with anyone else. EVER.

Sean's fingertips slowly trace the edge of my face. My legs tremble uncontrollably and shake the mattress on its frame.

"You are so beautiful," Sean whispers softly, while he gently lowers me back on his bed.

"Turn over, I want to hold you while I listen to this song," he continues.

I turn my back to him and slither my body up towards the headboard. Sean inches his way up, until his head is just above mine. He wraps his arms around my waist and pulls me against the crescent moon shape of his solid body.

His body fits perfectly against mine ...like a foot fits perfectly into a favorite sneaker. I feel the heat that radiates from his body. My tremors finally seize. I close my eyes and listen to the music while I bask in his embrace. This moment can remain frozen in time, forever.

When the song finishes, Sean's arm gently pulls my side towards him. I gently rest on my back. He props up on one elbow and towers over me. He seriously needs to stop looking at me like that, or kiss me already. I feel the lingering path his fingers tread up my side. The backs of his fingertips gently brush over my abdomen. I turn my head to look in his eyes. *Please kiss me!*

"You make this decision very difficult for me," Sean confesses.

"Your decision was already made before I arrived, wasn't it?" I press, calmer than I should be.

"It was, but now I'm thoroughly confused. A huge part of me knows I will be much better off without this distraction. I already have a huge adjustment to make going from a small school like Lamar, to a school the size of MSU. You have taught me the difficulty and frustration of a long distance relationship. So, why do I even consider this possibility? My head told me not to let you come over. I probably should have listened. My heart, however, tells me an entirely different story. I think our hearts share a single soul. No matter how hard I try, I can't shake you. What the hell do you do to me, Brianna?"

"Sean, *please* listen to your heart. Our destiny is fulfilled by our heart, not our head. There is no logic in love. We don't choose love—love chooses us. I have felt it since the moment I met you. Don't walk away from something we may never feel again. Besides, listening to your head wouldn't have done any good anyway."

His eyes narrow, "And why is that?"

"Because, I was going to come and see you whether you wanted me to or not," I confide.

His full white smile spreads across his face. "You were, were you? Hmm ...I'm not sure how I feel about that," he teases and begins to tickle me.

No, no tickles! I turn irrepressibly mean when I'm tickled, like a murder victim that struggles to survive. Within seconds his friendly tickles turn into a full blown wrestling match. He has me pinned against his bed and locks my hands above my head. His entire weight is on me, restricting any movement.

I could fight, but I don't. My eyes drift slowly from his lips to his eyes. His playful gaze turns serious and finds its way back home. I can actually feel him wander through my soul. A place he is unlikely to escape from.

"You do this to me every time," he argues.

"Do what?"

"Pull me in, with those big beautiful turquoise eyes of yours. Damnit, it's useless."

He hesitates only briefly and loosens his grip while he pulls my arms back down towards my body. My elbows bend with my palms face up under his on each side of my face. He slides his fingers in-between mine and weaves them together tightly. He leans in, his breath escapes through his slightly parted lips and he begins to kiss me.

I feel the electricity flow through his lips into mine. The world around us fades out of existence. My hands are now the ones that death-grip his, like I'm dangling one hundred stories in the air. I use all of my strength to slide his hands as far as my arms will reach and hope this will lower his body onto mine. The plan works until he climbs off. *What? No! Princess Jezebel scowls at me over her glasses. What did I do?*

I want to grab his lips and pull them back to me. I plead, "Please don't stop."

Sean rests his face in his palms and covers his eyes. He mumbles to himself, "I promised myself I would not do this."

I have to find a way around his inhibitions. I sit up in front of him and gently pull his hands away from his face and kiss his palms softly. My eyes focus on his lips, but I know it would be a mistake to kiss them at this moment. Instead, I caress his face and run my fingers through his hair gently. I climb onto his lap and hold the union our eyes have made. His hands dangle at his side for at least twenty beats of my heart. He is blatantly fighting the urge to touch me.

I slide my fingers down his neck, then back up again towards his face and trace his warm full lips. I feel his hot breath. My body aches for him.

His hands wrap my legs around his body and he presses into me. I feel his lips touch my forehead. We are eye to eye with no space between us. His arms wrap around my waist, my legs wrap around his. I will never let anything come between us. Ever. Three months of pinned up frustration and built up pain rushes out of our bodies when are lips meet again. I want to crawl inside of this man and live—I want to crawl inside of this man and die. I need him, I want him, and I don't care what the consequence might be.

Sean lowers my back onto his bed and climbs on top of me. He doesn't miss a single kiss. His palms slide up my sides and caress my bare skin. A fire spreads through my veins. That familiar ache is back. His lips work their way down my neck. My back reflexively arches. His arm slides into the gap and pulls me up to lock us together. We are in a two dimensional world, pressed flat by the weight of our own desire. His head slides under the loose layers of material that cover my abdomen. Goose bumps swathe my stomach when his lips work their way down the center to my waist band. I want to scream, but his parents are below us, instead my fingers twist and claw through his hair.

My breath is heavy and fast. There isn't enough air in the room to fill my lungs. His tongue traces the edge of my waist band, which now hangs much lower than it used to. I feel him, all of him, through our clothes. I want him so desperately, it's torture.

"Sean!" his mother yells up the stairwell ...our overheated passion once again auspiciously interrupted.

CHAPTER THIRTY-TWO

Sean sits up and throws his hands over his head. He grabs my hand and pulls me up while I work to catch my breath. I'm so dizzy; my head sinks back onto Sean's pillow. He lets out one heavy breath sigh and yells, "Just a minute Mom."

"I'll be right back," he gripes, through clenched teeth.

I stretch across his bed for a few minutes and replay each passionate moment. Sean brings me to a world that doesn't exist without him—a world where the sky burns shades of pink, orange, yellow and red ...like a perpetual fiery sunset.

I climb off of his bed and wander through his room, glancing at the newspaper clippings and photos pinned to his bulletin board. I thumb through his extensive CD collection. I notice a book that rests on top of a box that is already packed. The box sits on his desk chair. The cover is navy and grey, the edges of the pages are leafed in silver. I run my fingers across the leather texture of the cover and wonder what's inside. Curiosity claims me. What I find is more than I bargained for. It's a journal—about me ...or us, more specifically.

My rushing heartbeat exposes the guilt my conscious creates, but the temptation is too great. I flip through the pages quickly.....

February 15th – What on earth just happened? My P's and Q's are all in a row. I have no room for obsessions. No time for distractions. But who is she? This girl who piques my interest ...captivates my psyche? I have never seen anyone so beautiful, so full of mystery. My eyes were locked with hers only a few minutes, but it's like she is burned into my soul. A permanent scar. Damn Jon just had to take a cigarette break. I asked her to wait—but she didn't. I should have known she wouldn't. She is so far out of my league; we're not playing the same sport. I have to find out who she is.

My heart explodes with each word. I quickly read on.

February 18th *– I never realized, until this day, that euphoria and desolation are capable of feeding each other. This mysterious girl has invaded my soul. I can't concentrate on anything except her. These fantasies bring me a joy I can't describe, yet her memory haunts me and makes me cringe at her image. What the hell! How will I ever erase her out of my head? How will I ever find her?*

I almost cry when I realize the torment we shared. I speed read through the pages and pull out the parts that pertain to me. This isn't hard, they are always the first thought he shares.

February 28th *– It's been two fucking weeks! My mind is stagnant, not moving forward – not capable of forgetting. I have to concentrate on my future. College is only a few months away. Yet somehow, I can't imagine my future without her – a girl who touched my life for mere seconds. This is completely ridiculous.*

March 11th *– Relationships…getting involved…having a girlfriend. However you label it, the idea is bad. Bad. Bad. Bad. Today, Cory hands me a number of some cute blonde he met at some club in Joplin. She wants to meet me. I have no clue who this girl could be, and truthfully have absolutely no interest in her. What I do have interest* *in is a distraction, even if it's temporary. I have to rip this mystery girl out of my head. She haunts my dreams day and night. Just like I knew she would. Tomorrow, I will throw caution to the wind and pay a visit to Cory's little blonde.*

March 12th – Thank god I'm stupid. And selfish. I set out today to meet my distraction. I knew full well it was a temporary fix and I would never see this girl again. I knock on the door of the cute little blonde only to find what I craved all along. This girl who haunts my dreams stood before me. I believe my heart stopped beating briefly. How odd fate is. She is far more beautiful than I remember. If she spoke two words, I don't remember them. But that was ok; I just wanted to absorb her into my pores. I didn't need small talk to know I'm completely captivated by her. This is completely fucking insane!

March 14th – I had to know if my instinct was right. Is this girl Brianna, the girl of my dreams or an empty shell of my overactive imagination? I spent four hours with her on the phone, more time than I could spend with anyone else. The way she thinks intrigues me. Her voice coaxes secrets out of me I thought I would never share with anyone. One truth will remain a secret. The truth of how absurdly into her I am – this girl I barely know.

March 17th – Waiting and wondering – will she ever call. It has been days since my four hour call to her. I need her to want me like I want her. My feelings are completely insane—of course she doesn't feel the same way. I want to believe she has some interest. Maybe. I don't know. Maybe she is just nice ...or whatever. Tomorrow I have a few hours free. I think I will pay her a visit. Yes, I'll pay her a visit. I will.

March 18th – I made a trip to Joplin tonight before work. She was in the bathtub when I arrived, according to her brother. Adulterated thoughts floated through my mind when I pictured her bare body drenched in steaming hot water. God, she's so fucking beautiful. When she finally appeared in front of me she had nothing on except an old worn grey tee-shirt that hung right above her knees. It was sexy as fuck! Her damp hair was piled on top of her head. I followed the tiny droplets of water that slowly traced her cheeks and her neck. They slid down her chest and soaked into the ragged gray cotton. I wanted to sip them from her skin. She invited me to her room—which scared the shit out of me. If she knew the thoughts that ran through my mind, it would have scared the shit out of her too. Her room is simple and conservative, no posters, no piles of magazines – nothing to clue me in on what makes her tick. Except the music...this girl is into music.

My nerves made me come across like a jerk. I hate it when that happens. Not that our conversation was unbearable, or even uncomfortable—but, it was agitated. Definitely agitated. I wanted her to kiss me so I'd shut the fuck up.

As she pulled in close to me and conformed to my chest, I sucked her scent deep into my lungs and prayed it would stay there forever. She was so close I had to touch her, so I slowly slid my hands onto her face. The fire started in my fingertips and worked its way through my arms, and finally engulfed my entire body. What the hell. I have never had a girl do this to me before. I have to wonder if she's even mortal.

Her eyes are a striking turquoise. I have never seen eyes this color. I want to dive into them and swim to some far away deserted island with only her. I needed my fingers to be surrounded by her long thick silky dark hair, so I carefully undid the clip on top of her head and let her hair fall down around her face. She is the most beautiful human I've ever seen.

I hear footsteps climb the wood staircase. I gently close the journal and place it back where I found it. I move over to the pile of CD's and pretend to read the back of one.

"Kings of Leon, that's a good one," Sean clues me in, while he makes his way across the room.

"Yeah, I like them. I don't have this one."

"You can borrow it if you want. Hey, sorry about that, I had to take out the trash for my mom. She wants you to stay for dinner tonight, if you don't mind hanging out that late."

"Sure, that would be great. I'm here until you kick me out."

"Cool! You may never leave then. My dad needs me to run to the store with him to pick up a few things. Do you want to come with?"

I decline graciously, and seize this opportunity to learn more of Sean's private thoughts. "If it's ok, I'd rather stay here and look at your cd's some more. I'll wait right here for you," I offer, with a wink.

Sean's eyebrows wave across his forehead, "Well ok then, I'll see you in a few."

He pecks my cheek and heads back down the staircase. I immediately grab the journal and find the spot I left off.

I moved in to kiss her cheek and read her signals carefully. A soft floral aroma seeped from her body in strong waves, which calmed me. My heart was swollen like a red balloon, ready to explode. I moved my lips to hers slowly. This is a first kiss that assures me everything I thought about her is real, beyond even my overactive imagination.

My hands shake and I grasp the book tightly. How did I not see how he felt? Why didn't I drive to his house and read these months ago. Maybe I wouldn't have destroyed us. I read on.

March 20th – *Today, I took Brianna to Shoal Creek Falls. Cory and her friend Samantha tagged along. The falls are pretty fucking cool, but pale in comparison to her. The mist clung to her skin like tiny diamonds that glistened in the sun. I wanted to lick every drop from her delicate skin.*

We ditched Cory and Samantha and hiked up the river. At one point, we stopped at a small pool in one of the rocks. The way she took in nature intrigued me. She embraced each tiny frog like they were her long lost friend.

I sat her down and used fatigue as my excuse. Of course, I had other motives on my mind, like twisting my fingers through her long dark hair ...or feeling her lips pressed against mine.

She sat between my legs with her back against me. I peeled the pale blue oxford from her, one arm at a time. Every muscle in my body was tense. I softly slid her hair to one side and let my lips run down the nape of her neck. She turned to face me, and I fell into her turquoise ocean. All I could picture was lifting the white camisole gently over her head and sliding her jeans gently off her hips. I

completely suck as a human being. If I would have kissed
her at that moment, it definitely would have ended in
embarrassment. I had to call time out ...I had to breathe.

I don't know if she was tired, bored, or sick of my
company, but her mood turned south, she became
withdrawn. I did something to make her reject me, but I
don't know what it was. I was there, right beside her
...and then I wasn't. She was quiet when we ate. No not
quiet...gone. That is a much more accurate account. Is
there someone else she dreams about? I don't know what
happened, and I didn't know how to fix it.

Then she did the unthinkable. She drug me to some dance
club she knew I didn't want to go to. Is this even the same
girl I was with earlier today? I was totally confused.

I must admit, I didn't want to go, but seeing her return
from the dance floor moist with heat, her hair haphazard
and sexy, clinging to her wet body...it almost made it all
worth it. She was hot and stripped off her shirt, leaving
only that damn white camisole. Her breasts are like the
most beautiful thing I've ever fucking seen. Firm and
soft—all at the same time. God, I wanted to touch them,
so bad. I wanted to kiss them even more. My mouth was
so dry, I couldn't swallow.

She promised me I wouldn't have to dance, and I almost
held her to that, out of spite ...but I needed her body
pressed against mine. I pulled her from her chair and
held her close while Bruno Mars blared through the
speakers. She fit perfectly into my space.

I was shocked, excited and nervous when she told me she
wanted to go to Cory's car to be alone. All I could think
about was pulling that fucking white camisole off and
running my tongue over those perfect breasts. That wasn't

371

in the cards—not tonight. She stopped me, but her rejection wasn't harsh. She didn't make me feel awkward or ashamed ...she was gentle and passionate and showed me where her line is drawn. Truthfully I am grateful she has a line. One of us needs to.

I look down at my breasts and smile. *They are kinda fucking perfect, aren't' they?* Princess Jezebel flaunts them proudly. There is so much to read and not nearly enough time. I decide to skip ahead and come back if I have time.

March 26ᵗʰ My week is irritating. Between work, school, and band practice, I have had no time with Brianna. I haven't heard from, or seen her all week, which too is frustrating. Not once over the last two weeks has she offered to come and see me. She hasn't even called me, and she has a fucking cell phone. I just don't understand. I think she likes me, but I don't think she is into me the way I'm into her. This will not end well, I'm afraid. I break down and call her this morning, she doesn't answer. I wonder who she's with.

March 28ᵗʰ When it comes to Brianna is anything ever painless? She did call me back while I was at work. I don't head straight to practice, I give her a call. She is short and to the point, like she doesn't want to talk to me. I am so fucking confused. I think her interest in me may be all self-imagined. I'm too nervous to let her see me play, but her lack of interest cuts deep. She doesn't act like she would be there even if I wanted her to be. I'm a complete idiot.

Then tonight, she paints a completely different picture. She is upset I haven't invited her, mad even. I have to wonder if that is because her friends now want to go. I just don't know. My plan was to ask her to prom tonight, but she definitely had me second guessing. The more time I spend with this girl, the more invested I will be...and the more pain I will feel later.

I have already been foolish enough to allow myself to be completely absorbed by her, when what I should concentrate on is my next chapter. College. Her feelings aren't strong enough for me to endure a long distance relationship. I can't keep investing. I already know in my heart if I don't call her, I will never hear from her again. But then, maybe Prom will be that fall in love moment for her. It could work. I played her the guitar tonight. I think she was touched. I asked her to prom. She accepted.

He will never hear from me again, those words slice through my heart like it is strawberry jello. I don't need to intrude on his private thoughts to know where I fucked up. I ruin everything. I am a terrible—terrible person. He loves me, he truly loves me. This could have been a beautiful relationship; instead I destroyed it with my immaturity and insecurity. My only prayer is there is enough spark left to rekindle the scorched fragments of our hearts.

I quietly shut the journal and place it back where I found it. I sit on his bed and relive the words that are now carved into my mind. I need to shake them, so he won't be suspicious—but it's hard to un-know something you are now privy to.

Several minutes later I hear footsteps, once again, ascend the staircase. My revelations into Sean's inner secrets fill me with mixed emotions. Fear, guilt and love all fight their battle in my head while I attempt to appear composed.

"I'm sorry that took so long. I think my parents might have heard us wrestling around. I guess they think we were having wild sex...or whatever. My dad asked for us to come down, we're making mom nervous. We can go down and hang out on the deck."

"But I can't kiss you on the deck," I complain. Princess Jezebel hisses and stomps around, like a spoiled child who had her favorite toy taken away.

"Wanna bet?" he taunts.

I cling to his arm and follow him down the staircase and out the sliders to the deck. It is shaded, away from the torrid heat of the mid-day sun. Sean plops back in a lounge chair, black metal with a thick tropical cushion. He pats between his legs and offers a place to sit. I grin and straddle facing him instead.

"Ok Brianna, I think we've done enough damage to my sanity for a while, turn around and let me hold you...*please*."

My lips pucker up into a pout, and I slowly turn around. I lean my head back against his chest. He wraps his arms around me and pulls me against his body. "It's ok you know," he assures me and rests his head against mine.

"What's ok?"

"We can enjoy each other without making out."

"Oh...," my voice is small. "I hoped you meant something a little broader."

"Such as?"

"I thought you meant *we* will be ok. You thought about it and you're so into me you can't possible stay away from me. You are undeniably and completely in love with me and can't picture your life without me kind of broad."

"Oh Brianna ...if you only knew."

"I think I do," I confess.

CHAPTER THIRTY-THREE

Sean walks me to my car at nine pm. I don't want to leave, but he wants me safe at home before it gets too late. I promise to call him when I get home. Today is a great day.

My drive home grants me time to contemplate our fate. The day spent with Sean reassures me, overall. I sense his will towards salvation, yet I also feel the lingering doubt that hovers over us, like a heavy dark storm cloud. I think one more day with him, before he leaves, will boost our chances.

Prying into his private thoughts was dissolute, yet the insight revealed secrets which are essential to our survival. Looking at our relationship from his perspective turns on the flood lights to my unforgivable mistakes. I don't blame him for questioning our relationship. I don't blame him for walking away. I have two days to win back his love and overcome his doubt, before he is gone.

When I left his house for the evening, he placed in my palm a folded up piece of white paper, scribbled with his new address. This is all he could give me, either by choice or necessity. He didn't elaborate ...and since I was busy kissing him, I didn't ask.

I mull over every word he wrote and each fragment of our conversation while I travel the long road home. When my mind totally relapses into subconscious thought, an image juts across my path in the roadway. I gasp and slam on the brakes, out of instinct. My car skids sideways before it comes to a complete stop. *Sweet jeezus!* My heart pounds through the walls of my chest. My pulse is in my throat, which makes it hard to catch my breath. I sit in the middle of the road and count out thirty loud beats of my heart, until I gather my senses. An image of the woman with long black hair, floating across the roadway, flashes through my mind. I shake my head to erase her haunting image and shift the car back into drive.

I pull in my driveway at ten pm. No lights are on, which is odd. When I walk in, the house is eerily quiet. I flip on the kitchen light. On the end of the breakfast bar is a note.

Brianna,
We are at your grandparents. I tried to call you, but you must not have your cell with you today. I'm afraid your granddad doesn't have much time. The family is over spending his final hours with him. Call me when you get home.
Love Mom

"NO!! This can't be happening!" I scream.

I run back through the door and jump in my car. The drive to my grandparents feels much longer than usual. I have to say goodbye to Gramps one last time.

Please God, don't let me be too late. You fucking idiot ...why didn't you take your cell phone today! I chastise myself.

I fly into the gravel driveway and skid to a stop for the second time tonight. Several cars are parked in the driveway, I still have a chance. My heavy steel car door slams and I race towards the house. Light from the windows burns through the darkness, like a Thomas Kinkade painting. I can see my family gathered around the dining room table when I approach the well-lit house.

I crash through the door recklessly and command the attention of the room. Grams sits in her usual spot, tears fill her red swollen eyes. I ignore everyone's glares and run to the living room. He is gone, the bed is empty.

I collapse to the floor; my face falls into my hands, and I sob. I feel arms wrap solidly around me. I look up, it's my father. He sits on the floor next to me and cradles me in his arms. I didn't notice he was home when I bolted through the kitchen.

"When did you get here?" I manage to choke out.

"Late this afternoon, I'm so sorry, Bri. You have to understand your granddad is in a better place now."

"When did he pass?" I ask, my throat barely able to spit out my words.

"Tonight, about seven. I guess he was conscious earlier today, but fell out of consciousness about two, or so I hear. He left peacefully, in his sleep.

"I should have been here. I should have had my phone. I'm so sorry."

"Brianna, don't beat yourself up. You couldn't have known this would happen today. Your mom told me you were trying to patch things up with your boyfriend. How did that go?"

"Better than expected I think, but he's hard to read, so I honestly don't know."

"Well good. I don't like to see my little girl in pain. Why don't you come in the kitchen now."

"Give me a few minutes, please Dad."

"Sure thing," he climbs up from the floor and heads back to the kitchen.

I sit and stare at my Gramps empty bed. Tears stream continuously down my flushed cheeks. I make my peace with his passing, but my gut cringes with pain. I wasn't with him to hold his hand, to say goodbye. That is a moment in time I will never get back.

This could have been any other day, and I would have been here. I rarely leave home without my cell phone, why today? My thoughts are muddled and confused. Life is making me choose between the two most important men in my life. If I would have remembered my phone, I would have left. Sean and I would not have reconnected. A clear chance at a future would not exist. What force throws this uninvited decision in my direction? Whatever it is, it needs to stop—because it sucks.

I can't help but recall last night's dream. This iniquitous black haired woman with the hideous forged smile pulls them both away from me ...or was she? How do I rationally interpret this dream? The face faded from Sean to Gramps. Maybe it was a choice, my choice ...and I chose my future, instead of my past.

I suck in a deep shaky breath and head to the kitchen. I approach Grams, who sits in her chair with pink swollen lids. I bend down to hug her. Her breath is uneven and labored. She struggles with her loss.

"Grams, I'm so sorry I wasn't here today. Please forgive me."

"No repentance is necessary, Brianna. He loved you and he knew you loved him, whether you were here today or not."

I kiss her cheek and take a seat. That must be a cue. After I sit, the room buzzes with conversation again. I sit silently, numb to my surroundings, until midnight. I follow my parents' home.

I climb in my bed, too exhausted to sleep. Tears form a never ending river down my cheeks and into my hair. Gramps is gone. I will never see his pale blue eyes again. The anxiety of my fate with Sean does not comfort me either. He is noticeably apprehensive, all with good reason. My ridiculous insecurities have stolen something that mattered ...a lot.

I weep for hours before I finally drift to sleep. I don't dream, or at least that I remember. Maybe the wicked woman with black hair is finally gone. Maybe my nightmare is finally over. Or maybe, I am simply not asleep long enough for her to find me.

My father's voice carries through the stairwell and calls my name. I groggily reply, my voice hoarse, "Yes Dad!"

"Bri, can you come down here?"

Still foggy, I slide out of bed. I still have on the clothes I wore the day before when I stumble down the staircase. "Yeah Dad, what do you need."

"We're heading to the funeral home with your grandmother this morning. Will you stay at her house in case anyone drops off food, or plants, or cards, or whatever?"

"Sure Dad, do I have time to jump in the shower first?"

"We need to leave in thirty minutes, so make it a quick one," he forces a smile through his overly white, perfect teeth.

I run upstairs and grab a change of clothes. I wash my salty, tear stained face and hair and head to Grams. She has already left with my parents.

Over the next several hours I sit and stare at Gramps empty hospital bed ...and hope he will magically appear. Occasionally, a memory will come to mind that makes my sadness fade, briefly. Smiling feels good, appropriate. He is in a better place; I know this, yet I still have to cope with the realization I will never hear his voice. I will never smell his tobacco. I will never see his beautiful eyes.

Every twenty minutes or so, someone interrupts my memories, or my mourning, to drop off a casserole, or a card. *Amazing how something this private spreads so quickly, it's not even in the obits yet.*

After several hours, I lay down on the couch to rest for just a minute. My eyes close, my mind shuts down. I dream. I sit on the ground with my back against a huge tree. I see a strange meadow in front of me, filled with neon yellow flowers. The grass and the tree leaves are a vivid electric blue. The sky is a water color of red, orange, yellow and lavender. Treading through the tall grass, he approaches me slowly. It's Gramps. He is younger, slightly chubby and so healthy he glows. Still wearing his bib overalls, he squats down in front of me. He grabs my hands with his. I feel the gentle strength his hands possess. These are not the feeble weak hands I held lately. He smiles at me and kisses my forehead.

"Riny, don't cry for me, someday you will see me again. We'll walk through this meadow together. Tell your grandmother I will wait for her. Tell her the sky here is a perpetual sunset that never disappears. Tell her the grass is vivid blue and the sea is as pink as her delicate lips. Riny, there is no pain. Tell her there is no pain, only beauty. Tell her I will miss her every day, until she comes home. But tell her not to rush, because we have eternity to share."

"I will tell her Gramps, I promise. I miss you and I love you."

Gramps fades; I see the neon color of the flowers leaking through his image. "Gramps wait! Don't go. How do I hold on to Sean?"

His voice fades to a whisper; his image becomes more and more transparent. "Riny, only you can choose your path in life, only you can m..." that is all I have and he's gone.

My eyes fly wide open and infuriating tears fill them again. Gramps is happy—and pain free. The last thing I should do is cry. Maybe the reason for my tears is the realization that my destiny is up to me. Something as important as my future happiness with Sean should not be left in my hands.

Grams and my parents return in the late afternoon. Grams doesn't want a big to-do. They plan a simple visitation and funeral with just family and close friends. The funeral will be tomorrow. I give Grams an update of today's visitors and explain their generous offerings. She can't believe all of the food that has already shown up, but she wants to fix a few items herself. She has no reason to cook, but I don't argue. She needs the distraction. As long as she keeps busy, she won't dwell on her loss.

Although I'm dizzy from exhaustion, I offer to hang out and help her prepare something for tomorrow. I need to tell her about my dream, anyway. I think it will make her happy—even if it was just a dream.

After my parents leave, I sit her down at the table and tell her everything my dream had to offer, from the color of the grass to Gramps exact words. She smiles and hugs me. She must believe the dream holds some truth.

By the time I help Grams fix three pies and her famous chicken and noodles; I don't arrive home until almost eight pm. I manage to strip out of my clothes and throw on my oversized pajama pants and a tee shirt. I grab my cell phone from the night stand to find Sean has called three times. The log displays his name at eleven last night, again at ten this morning and finally about two this afternoon. Samantha and Natalie have also called, but for now, Sean is my only real concern. With all of the confusion, I forgot to call him when I got home last night ...he is probably worried sick.

I dial his number, with no hesitation by the way, but no one answers. I try again an hour later. His mother's kind voice answers, "Hello."

"Mrs. Gentry, or I'm sorry, Sheryl ...is Sean home?"

"Bri, he's already in bed—asleep, I'm sorry."

She called me Bri, which tells me Sean called me Bri in front of her—his *I don't like you right now* name for me. I have to explain everything to him tomorrow, I pray he understands.

Tomorrow is Gramps funeral. His visitation is scheduled for ten o'clock, his service immediately follows. The family will meet at my grandparent's house afterwards. Maybe Sean will be done packing and he can be here with me, to keep me from emotionally crashing. Not a beautiful way to spend our limited time together, but I need him. Tomorrow will be hard.

My mind is too troubled to sleep, but exhaustion wins the final battle. I wake up at seven. I don't want to call Sean's house and wake his parents yet, so I dress first. About eight-thirty, I dial his number, but no one answers.

384

I climb in the car with my parents and head to the funeral home. Several cars already fill the parking lot, many I recognize. Some I don't. I stand outside before I enter the building and dial Sean's number. Still no answer. *What the hell.*

I enter the funeral home and join my family in a long hallway. Some woman I don't recognize announces for us to go into the viewing room. Her words smack me awake from my numb stupor, viewing room, suddenly I am nervous. I have never seen anyone dead before.

I slowly enter. The room is cold and the sickening sweet aroma of flowers overwhelms me. The overpowering odor and my shaken nerves have me two seconds from losing my cookies all over the dark blue carpeting. I already see my grandmother and some of my aunts and uncles huddled together…bound by sorrow. This is far more emotional than the previous two days at Grams' house. I can't do this.

I stand frozen in the center of the room when I turn to leave, at least for a while. My father spots me and calls my name. My body turns to face him, but my mind is already out the door. He walks briskly over to my side and holds me. My mind slowly returns to my body and I begin to cry.

"Brianna, it will be ok. Come on, I'll walk with you."

My father walks by my side with his arm around my shoulder until we reach the casket. I stand over the casket and feel as lifeless as the body in front of me. This has to be a bad dream. My grandfather looks thin, but well-groomed with more color than normal for him lately. He is still, almost plastic. His eyes and his smile—the two things I love the most about him, locked away for eternity. These are the things I want to remember, the grandfather that came to me in my dream, not these inert soulless remains. I walk briskly away.

I sit in a chair in the back of the room. My parents bring several relatives over to introduce to me, ones I've never met, or ones I don't remember. Honestly, I can't tell you any of their names when it's all over. My mind is so far away, it's in an entire other dimension.

About two, everyone takes their seats and the minister begins to speak. He shares kind words about my grandfather, though there is so much more to him than he has time to reveal. After he finishes, an uncle by marriage stands up at the podium and reflects on the grandfather I want to remember ...the silly, blue eyed, hard working, bib overall wearing, tobacco chewing grandfather that was mine.

When the service concludes, we all walk by the casket once more on our way out of the funeral home. My parents stand outside and speak to a few family members; I head straight for the car. I sit on the hood in my black dress until my tears dry up.

I try hard to picture my dream, where Gramps stood before me, happy and pain free. This makes me smile. This is when I realize my tears are not for my grandfather; my tears are for me ...for *my* loss and *my* pain. I am suddenly reminded of Sean. All of my attempts to call him today have been futile. I certainly don't need him to think I

386

blew him off. I dial his number again ...still nothing. I start to panic.

He's mad, he has to be mad. He called me Bri for god's sake, of course he's mad. I bet he's screening my phone calls and refuses to talk to me. Tuesday, I offered to help him pack yesterday and today, he has to be home. It is now three o'clock and will be four before the graveside service is over. Then there is the dinner at Grams with family and close friends. The timing of this could not be worse. I have to get a hold of him. I have to see him before he leaves tomorrow. I have to spend time with him to secure our future. I have to go to the graveside service, but then ...I have to go to Lamar.

My parents finally make their way to the car. We approach the front section of a very long line of vehicles and follow patiently while we drive across town. The graveside service is brief, thank god.

"Mom, Dad. Will you drop me off at home before I come to Grams' house? My head is pounding. I think I need to rest a while, before I come over."

"Sure Bri, that's fine. Try not to linger too long or you'll miss out on the food," my dad answers.

"I'm not all that hungry, anyway."

"Brianna, you need to eat something, you're getting too thin."

"Dad, I'm fine," I lie.

My parents drop me off at our house and pull out of the driveway. I wait for them to pull out of sight and I try Sean's number again. I still don't receive an answer. I jump in my car and head to Lamar.

I don't tell my parents, because I don't think they would understand my need to drive to Lamar on such an important day for our family. I understand the importance, but I also understand the importance of this time to mend with Sean before he leaves. He won't be mad, once I explain. Sean is insecure, but he's not self-absorbed. If he is finished packing, maybe he will come back to Joplin and eat with my family. All I know for sure—I have to see him.

The trip seems distinctively longer than it did Tuesday. Yet everything today moves in slow motion. Finally I spot his house and pull in the drive. His car sits in the driveway. I don't know if I'm talking to God or Gramps, but I look up and mouth the words thank you.

I knock on the door, but there's no answer. My hands block the glare, while I peek through the glass on their front door, but I don't see any movement. I pound on the door this time...still nothing. I walk to the backside of their house to see if I can catch any movement in Sean's room, but the curtains are drawn.

Did Sean offer to hook up with Jon today? I can't remember their conversation. Maybe they drove around again.

I pound on his door again, more frantic. His parents are obviously not home. I turn the handle of the door to see if it is unlocked. It's not; this tells me Sean isn't here, so he must be with Jon.

I jump in my car and search for Jon's truck. I drive all over town. I follow the country roads that we traveled on Tuesday. I almost pull down the rock lane to the creek, but I don't want to get stuck or stranded by the creek—especially if that creepy woman with black hair still hovers around. She's taken enough from me. I pull over on the side of the road and walk down instead.

Funny the path seemed short in the truck. On foot, it goes on for miles. About halfway down I hear voices, I'm encouraged. I walk faster, almost in a jog. A van is parked at the end of the lane, but Jon's truck is nowhere around.

I'm not close enough to make out features, but I'm close enough to know that none of these guys are Sean. I quickly turn to walk the other way.

"Brianna, is that you? Stop!" rings behind me. I stop dead in my tracks. Is it Sean? I don't think so. But the voice??

I turn slowly around and walking up the path towards me is a tall blonde. When he approaches, I see that it's Cory. Thank God.

"It is you? What are you doing here beautiful?" he prods.

"Looking for Sean, have you seen him?"

"Sorry, no. Come have a beer with us. I haven't seen you in a long time. You look different, is your hair longer?"

"Yeah, maybe."

A full white smile spreads across his lips, "Great, come on." He grabs my hand and starts to drag me behind him.

"No...no. That's not what I meant. Maybe my hair is longer. I can't have a beer with you. I need to find Sean."

"Fuck Sean. You were mine, first," he grins. I'm not sure if he's kidding or serious, but I don't have time to figure it out. I have to find Sean. Time is running out.

My parents will kill me. Grams will be disappointed in me. But I have to do this. I decide to drive back to Sean's house and sit on his steps until he returns home. Even if it takes all night. I jump back in my car. His parents pull in the driveway while I speed down their road and approach his house. "Thank fucking god!"

They are almost to their stoop when I skid in behind them. I jump out of my car quickly, "Do you know where Sean is?" I press, my voice desperate.

His dad walks up to me calmly. His fingers dig into his temple, "I take it Sean didn't get a hold of you."

"No, I've had serious family issues to deal with."

"Oh honey, Sean moved today. We drove him down to MU and moved him into his dorm room. He's gone. I'm sure he will call you soon."

"He told me Friday. Why is he gone?" I panic.

"He packed everything yesterday. He thought you planned to come down yesterday, but when he never heard from you, he assumed you were too busy. He asked us to move him today instead. I tried to tell him to wait."

"Do you have his phone number?"

"No, he doesn't have a phone yet. Sorry Bri, I'm sure he'll call when he's settled." *I'm not sure of that.*

"Ok, thanks Mr. Gentry."

I climb back in my car and sit for a minute while his dad walks into the house. As soon as he is out of sight, a flood of tears pour down my face. I can't lose both of them. Blind, I back slowly out of his driveway. I don't want his dad to come back out and check on me. I can't see anything through the tears, so I pull over by the park Sean's band played in. I sit there for a full ten minutes and let the tears flood—until none are left. I stop crying, just like that. It's almost like someone flipped a switch. The pain is gone. I feel nothing. I am numb.

My demons are back, and they are stronger and more powerful than they have ever been before. They pull me back down to the shadowy depths of my personal hell— and there is nothing I can do, but let them.

My car is on autopilot, all the way to Grams house. When I pull in her driveway, it is nearly seven. Some of the family has found their way back home, but a lot of them are still here, assessing the driveway. I suck in a deep breath and step inside.

"Brianna! There you are. I tried to call you, I was worried."

I check my phone and there is a missed call from Grams' number, "Sorry, I fell asleep and didn't hear it." I didn't fall asleep; I fell into the pits of hell, but Grams doesn't need the gory details.

"Sit down, sit down, let me fix you something to eat," she offers.

"Grams, I'm quite capable of fixing my own plate."

"Brianna, sit down and hush it."

Grams wants to feel needed. No, she needs to feel necessary ...essential ...indispensable. Isn't that all any of us truly want?

CHAPTER THIRTY-FOUR

As I sit silently on the edge of my bed, I mentally prepare for yet another week of my solitary torment called school. I can't escape from my loss; it has once again possessed me—like a demon.

The loss of Gramps stole my purpose—and left me useless and unneeded. God, I miss him so much. This loss is painful, but seems appropriate, the way it was always meant to play out ...with months to prepare. The loss of Sean, however, is like wearing a thick wool sweater on a hot humid day. There is nothing comfortable about it. It is constant nagging torture. He loved me, I loved him. Unnecessary circumstance kept us apart. Not even the job I have now will occupy my mind enough to release me from my torment.

At work, I am surrounded by a smorgasbord of self-proclaimed "hot" guys. Although their interest is blatant, they offer nothing I want. A few of the girls I work with, however, have been let into my dark circle of fun. These girls are far more reckless and rebellious than say, Natalie, Adrienne and Samantha. My weekend jaunts with these new friends are filled with parties and drinking. They are my escape—and allow me to drift away from my world of detachment.

A month has passed since Sean left. He never did call with his phone number, which I knew he wouldn't. Every day for three weeks I prayed for a phone call—that never came. Finally, I quit praying. Even if I hadn't fucked everything up beyond repair, how am I supposed to compete with a sea of college girls? I'm not that delusional. The only thing that prevents me from moving on is closure. If I knew he didn't love me. If I knew there was no chance for us. If I knew when he would be home so I could pay him a surprise visit.....

As I sit there and choke on my misery, a revelation hits me. Cory works in Joplin, I remember this from a conversation he had with Natalie the day we went to the park. Cory is Sean's friend. Surely he has talked to Sean, or knows when Sean will be home next.

I push myself off of the edge of the bed, resolved. I will pay Cory a visit after work tonight. This epiphany gives me some peace.

School edges along at a snail's pace. I only spend half days at school this year, which is a blessing. It is painful enough getting through three classes. My afternoons are spent taking a class at Joplin's Jr. College, which I skip most of the time. Today is one of those days.

I drive to the park alone and sit on the hill that overlooks the lake, where Sean and I sat five months ago. This is not the first time I have sat here, but today feels different. I am comforted to know Cory may have some answers I desperately need. Maybe he's talked to Sean. Maybe he will have some advice; after all, he's known Sean far longer.

I sit on that hill for hours, lost in my reverie of beautiful memories. That line on my lips wants to pull up; while I stare at the exact spot he gently lowered me to the ground and kissed every inch of exposed skin on my body. The smile just won't come. Finally, I stand up. I brush the grass from my ass and head to work.

I leave work at eight pm and head straight to where I think Cory works. I pray he still works there. I pull into the parking lot, nervous. Not near as intimidated as I would feel if I was meeting Sean, but still nervous. I climb from my car and walk inside. Not knowing where to find him, I approach customer service.

"Can you tell me where I can find Cory Fletcher?"

"He should be back in the warehouse, go to the back corner of the store, there will be a set of double doors," she explains, while she points me in the right direction.

"Thank you," I reply, and I turn to follow her instructions.

It isn't hard to find Cory, his voice towers above all of the noise.

Catching movement, Cory's eyes bug in my direction, "Brianna? What are you doing here?"

"Do you have a few minutes, to talk with me?"

"Sure, yeah, let's go outside where it's quieter." He opens the door for me and motions for me to move forward.

We sit down outside, on a picnic table. Vapor lights that tower over us cast a soft glow around us. He is nervous, and fumbles with a cigarette. I bum one and try to calm my own nerves. Cory lights them both and I begin, "Cory, have you heard anything from Sean since he left for college?"

Cory's eyes fall to his lap and he sucks a long draw from his smoke, "Nope. Sorry Bri, not a word. So, what's up with you two? I thought you broke up or some shit?"

"I don't know, Cory." My eyes fall to my black Converse, "Everything became misconstrued, and messed up, mostly because of me and my stupid insecurity. We had a painful summer, but we were trying to work it out right before he left. Then my grandfather died, so the week Sean left was even more botched up. All I have is an address; I've written him a couple times and asked him to please call me…but nothing. I don't know what to do anymore."

"Wow Bri, I don't know what to tell you. You have more than I do. I don't even have his address. I will ask around and see what I can find out if you want, but…" the conversation ends.

"But what?"

He signs, his breath heavy and continues, "Bri, don't take this the wrong way, but have you ever considered …nah, forget it."

"No Cory, I don't want to forget it, just tell me. You know him much better than I do. I need to understand."

"I was just about to say; maybe he met someone else at MSU."

"Yeah, that's crossed my mind, more than once," I admit. My forehead rests in my palms now.

When I finally look up, Cory is staring at me, "Brianna, I know you two had some special shit or something, but I don't think you ever met the real Sean. The real Sean is moody and unforgiving. I don't know what happened over the summer, but if you did something to hurt his ego, he may never forgive you. Just sayin'."

"So what should I do? How do I win him back and make him forgive me?"

"I'm afraid you won't like my advice, but if it were me, I'd forget about him. Move on. If he wants you back, trust me, he will be in touch. If there is one thing I do know about Sean. He goes after what he wants, no matter what the obstacles are."

"Cory, I can't move on, not until I know for sure. We had no closure. One day we are working on us. The next day...well, there was no next day."

"I'll see what I can find out, come see me a week from tonight."

"Ok, thanks Cory," I say and work to swallow the knot in my throat.

I drive out of the parking lot not feeling any better as a result of Cory's candid advice, yet a small part of me now feels reconnected to Sean's life in some small, insignificant way.

The following week is torture. Every day I fight the urge to visit Cory at work, to see what he's found out. This isolated darkness I am not living, but merely existing in takes its toll. My honor roll status is now that of an average, or below average student. My friends...what friends? They all abandoned me, and I can't blame them. The innocence of my youth has been corrupted. I drink and smoke as a means of escape. Still with all of these changes, one thing remains constant, unchanging ...my heart aches for Sean Gentry, every minute of every day, every sleepless minute of every night.

I recall my pathetic begging letters. I begged him to forgive me. I begged him to call me. I begged him to love me, when I should have explained the situation. I should have told him about my grandfather in one of my letters. At the time, I didn't want pity or sympathy—I still don't. I also don't want to guilt him. I just want him to love me. The way he once did—the way I believe he still does, deep inside.

Tonight I can meet Cory again. That was the longest freaking week, ever. Surely, someone has a number or knows when Sean will be home next. I pull up to the grocery store Cory works at. This time I don't ask for him, I head back where I found him last week.

I walk through the double swinging doors and I don't see him, so I ask a co-worker, "Is Cory here?"

"Brianna yeah, he's out stocking shelves. Sit here while we go find him for you."

They all scatter and head in different directions. While I sit and wait, I wonder how they know my name. Odd.

Cory busts through the doors with his entourage that follows close behind. "Hey Brianna, let's go outside."

"Ok," I follow while Cory and another co-worker lead the way. We sit, once again, on the same picnic table.

"So, what did you find out?" I ask anxiously.

"Brianna, I think you need to give this up. You are far too beautiful to waste your time like this."

"I didn't ask you what you thought; I asked you what you found out."

"Bri, nobody will tell me shit. No one will give me his phone number, if he even has one. I honestly think they were pre-warned to not give you any information. I guess I shouldn't have said it was for you. Everyone pleaded the fifth and didn't know jack shit, at least that they admitted. It's like he fucking vanished. The way I see it, if Sean doesn't want you to have his number, he has probably moved on or doesn't want you back. You need to let this go and move on yourself."

If Sean doesn't come back, I need the closure and the brutal honesty, but Cory's words are like daggers that pierce my soul. I sob, for the first time in a long ass time. I don't want to cry; my emotions have been locked away and hidden for so long I forgot what it is like to release them. It sucks.

Cory slowly pulls in beside me and comforts me. He wraps his arm around me while I cry and try desperately to catch my breath.

When my over dramatic sobs wane to a quiet shedding of tears, Cory's friend speaks up, "You know

Cory, this girl could use some fun. You should bring her to my wiener roast this weekend."

"What do you say, Bri? Do you want to hang out by a fire, throw back a few brews …and shit? No hold up. Let me rephrase, be ready Saturday at seven, I will pick you up and we will hang out! No isn't an option."

"Cory, I don't think that's a good idea."

"Why Bri? Because Sean might get mad. Come on, you've wrote him with no response. He hasn't contacted you in a month …wake up! Besides, from what I see, you need this. You need to pull out of this funk you're in, and what better way than to hang out with a bunch of fun, kickass guys!" he smiles so big, his teeth swallow his face.

Cory's friend introduces himself, "By the way, I'm Tyler." He shoots Cory a glare for his lack of introduction, before I blubbered like a baby. "Bri, I don't know you, and I don't know this Sean guy, but I will say what Cory is trying to tell you makes sense from an outsider's perspective. If I want to blow somebody off, I ignore them. It really is that simple. They finally take the hint, and I avoid the drama. Forget him. You need to have some fun …and this party will be fun."

I feel the painful tingles start in my fingertips and work their way through my body. The numbness returns. I respond, "Well, you should have said it was a party, I'm in."

Cory clasps his hands behind his head and leans back. "Good. Finally! I'll pick you up Saturday at seven."

Cory hugs me again and whispers, "Bri, it will all be ok, you'll see."

I pull back and glare at him, like he's stupid. "It will never be ok, until Sean comes back to me ...but, whatever. Saturday."

"Bri, you don't listen ...oh, never mind. I'll see you Saturday."

The pendulum of my week swings at a pace you can barely see... moving slightly, but never changing direction. Complete numbness has returned. I feel nothing. I don't cry, but I never smile either. I exist.

It is Saturday; I work the lunch shift which is my new Saturday routine. My grandmother Harris stops in to see me, like she does every week. My job at the buffet has given her a newfound reason to shop at the mall, her second home. Every visit has its bonus. I have a kick ass wardrobe. This week is no exception. I take my break when she arrives and join her while she eats her usual fried chicken and bread pudding. She hands me a shopping bag filled with sweaters and shoes. I thank her for the gift and finish my shift.

As I drive home, I still have reservations about the party tonight. An enormous part of me is reluctant. I know Cory is simply trying to lift my spirits. Tyler is nice, too. He would have to be to invite some basket case girl he just met to his party. Still, there is this aching feeling in my gut that tells me Sean would not approve. *Pfft. Like he will ever care enough to find out.*

I jump in the shower when I get home, this must surprise my mother.

"Do you have plans tonight, Bri?" she asks optimistically.

"I'm going to a wiener roast with Cory, Sean's friend."

"Oh, I see," her eyebrows furrow. I watch her mouth twitch. *What the hell.*

"What? I thought you'd be happy, I'm getting out of the house."

"It's nothing, I am glad to see you go out. I just wish it wasn't with someone associated with Sean. I see what you're trying to do, and it won't work."

"What exactly am I trying to do?"

"You're trying to stay connected to him through his friends, and that won't work. Trust me on this, it will backfire on you. You need to put this boy behind you and move on. I don't see that this is a good way to accomplish that."

"Mom, I'm going to a wiener roast I was invited to, that is it ...nothing more."

"Ok Bri, whatever you say."

"Whatever," Princess Jezebel hisses and casts her snake tongue towards my mother.

I stomp off to my room irritated, like a spoiled child. It isn't like my mom to confront me, she usually doesn't meddle. She must feel pretty strongly about this, or she's just in a pissy mood. I don't know, what if she's right? Do I cling to anything I can to stay in Sean's life? Is my newfound friendship with Cory a way to keep connected to his circle? Probably, but I don't honestly see the harm. Sean is part of me. Nobody understands we share one soul. Nobody. When he left, he took part of my soul with him. Or he still lingers inside me. I'm so numb to pain I can't even tell anymore. All I do know is I'm not whole without him.

I dig through the shopping bag my grandmother handed me today and pull out a sweater. It's cute …whatever. I throw it on with a pair of blue jeans. I don't particularly care what I look like, so I pull my hair in a ponytail and coat my lashes with some mascara. I still have an hour before Cory picks me up, so I sit on my bed and flip through the drawings of Sean that now fill my sketchbook.

A million questions, I want to ask Cory, rotate through my brain. Would his parents relay a message to him if I gave it to them? Will Cory go see Sean and talk to him for me? Could I pay Sean a surprise visit, or is that a bad idea? I need answers, so I can move forward, with or without him.

Cory pulls in my driveway at seven on the nose. I think to myself, *maybe I should have fixed him up with Adrienne.* I climb into his car still uncomfortable with the arrangement. I should have drove myself and met him. *God, why didn't I think of that sooner!*

"So where does Tyler live?" I ask, while I buckle my seatbelt and try to calculate how much time I have to question him.

"Here in Joplin, not too far from you actually."

I realize my time is limited, so I shoot Cory the first question. "So Cory, I need your opinion. You know Sean better than I do...

"Brianna ...STOP! We will not spend our evening discussing Sean. This night is about you, having fun, hanging with friends. This night is to prove to you there is a life beyond Sean Fucking Gentry, who by the way blew you off, if you haven't noticed. I don't want to hear his name the rest of the night. Agreed?"

"No not really, but I'll shut up."

"Bri, I don't want you to shut up. I want you to take your mind off of "*him*" for a while."

My lips pull in a straight rigid line. After a few minutes, I change the subject. "So, how long have you worked at Save-A-Lot?"

"About two years. I also work for the Joplin Globe."

"What? Doing what?"

"I'm the one that bundles all of the papers, so they can be distributed to the drivers. I've done that for about two years, also. In fact, I called in sick tonight so I can go to this party."

"I'm confused Cory, how do you do both?"

"I work at Save-A-Lot from four until eleven and then I work at the newspaper from midnight until five."

"And you've done this for two years?"

"Yep."

"How did you go to school? When did you sleep?"

"I had days off here and there with both jobs, I caught up then."

"So there were days you had no sleep at all? Why would you do that?"

"Well Bri, it's actually kind of embarrassing. My parents built a new house, then my dad was laid off and had to find a different job, which didn't pay near as well. He couldn't afford the house anymore and wanted to sell it, you know, to find something smaller. My sisters and I wanted to keep our house, and our friends, and our school. We didn't want to move, so we all got jobs and chipped in. We were all responsible for a bill. Mine was the power bill; my sisters paid the phone and cable."

"Wow, I seriously am spoiled. *"He"* made me feel that way sometimes, but when I look at your life, I seriously am."

"Bri, you're not spoiled, you're fortunate ...and thanks for the *"he"* thing by the way. That's progress," he smiles.

"We're here," Cory proclaims.

I see a number of cars that line the road. This really is a party. I was worried it would be a few guys from Cory's work.

"Ok, let's roll," I rally, while I crack a forced smile.

I open my door and climb out. We proceed down a hill to the fire. Tyler is there and greets me immediately.

"Hey Bri!"

"Hey."

Tyler pulls me around and introduces me to some of the people around the fire. I imagine he knows Cory probably won't. Introductions are not one of his fortes. When he finishes, he offers to grab me a beer.

"Do you have anything stronger?"

"I think there's some Jack Daniels on the table."

"That works."

Tyler toddles off to fix me a drink. I sit down on the straw bale next to the fire. Cory mingles with friends, so I sit in silence and stare into the flames. Sean's face dances in the glow of the fire. *I know. I know. I can't help it.* The warmth I feel on my face reminds me of his hands that cup my cheeks, ready to kiss me. I want to close my eyes and fantasize, but everyone would think I am weird, so I zone. I would give anything to have him with me right now.   Pulled in next to me.   Fondling my fingers. Squeezing my thigh. Warming my soul ...the one he stole. *Fuck you Sean.*

"Bri, here's your drink," Tyler offers and interrupts my evaporating fantasy.

He sits down on the bail next to me. Cory glances over at me. He approaches and sits on my other side. I feel claustrophobic, like I'm held here against my will, at gun point. *Don't try to escape, we're watching you!*

"You don't drink, Bri?" Cory asks and stares down at my cup of ice and what looks like soda.

"Oh, she's drinking!" Tyler enlightens him.

"I will likely out drink you this evening!" I scoff.

"Is that right? Well that's my girl!" Cory cheers.

My girl? What is that supposed to mean. I suck down the drink quicker than I should. It's not to dull the pain. I don't feel pain, just an achy numbness, like a foot that has fallen asleep. The alcohol replaces the emptiness, the void; it gives me the ability to feel something ...anything.

The more I drink, the more I open up and release my demons. Unfortunately, they always find their way back home. I suck down number three in no time. My inner diva must emerge, because I have a circle of guys that surround me. They cling to my mindless babble ...like what I have to say is important. Idiots.

One of the guys in the circle fires up a joint and passes it around the circle. I've never smoked pot before, but there's a first for everything. I toke on it like I know what I'm doing, every single time it comes my way. After a few minutes, even the fire is funny—and I'm fucking starving!

"Cory I'm hungry!" I laugh. "Like really, really, really fucking hungry."

"Well, let's go see what's left."

He helps me stagger to the table. It's pretty empty except a casserole dish filled with red Jell-O and fruit cocktail. I pick up the dish and a spoon.

"Here let me grab you a plate," Cory offers.

I stare at him blankly, "Plate? I don't need a fucking plate." I carry the entire container back to the fire with me.

"Wow, I didn't know you had such a sailor mouth on you," Cory admits.

"Pfft ...when I drink, I use fuck as a fucking comma."

I sit down with my Jell-O and eat the entire dish. Everyone stares. *What?*

"Ok, that was really fucking good!" I hand Cory the dish. "Can we go to McDonalds now?"

The whole group cackles like lunatics while Cory makes our exit speech. I think he understands it may be in his best interest to get me the hell out of here, before I do any real damage. He guides me to his car, with his fingers pinching my waist. It's hard to walk a straight line, because the line moves under my feet. It really does. On our drive home, I start to feel nauseas.

"Do you still want McDonalds?" he offers.

"No, I think I need to go home. I don't feel so good." I lean my head against the cool window.

The fun part of my buzz dies. Now I'm just zoned out ...like a zombie. Drinking really sucks ass. My eyes can't focus on anything, so I stare out the window and reflect on memories of Sean. I miss him so fucking much. Why did he leave me? I want to understand. When he was in my life, I didn't need to drink, or do drugs to feel alive. He was my high, he was my drug. I want to cry, but can't.

Cory pulls in my driveway and eyes me, "Are you ok, Brianna?"

The sound of his voice intrudes on my thoughts. His question sifts through me like sand through a crack, "What, I'm sorry?"

"Are you ok?" He slides over in his seat and wraps his arms around me, pressing my cheek against his chest.

In the darkness of his car, for a brief delusional moment, I feel Sean's arms. I hear Sean's heartbeat. I close my eyes and snuggle into the embrace. I feel his warm lips touch my forehead. I feel the heat of Sean's lips while they work their way towards mine. I feel the fire and passion of his lips against mine. I feel alive. Something isn't right, he doesn't taste right. I taste alcohol and cigarettes and ...oh my god! I push away. This isn't Sean, this is Cory.

"I have to go," I shriek.

"Will you come see me this week Bri?"

I'm so confused, what just happened, "I don't know, I have to go."

I push my way out of his car and run for my back door, for a multitude of reasons. I climb my staircase on my hands and knees and fall into bed. My head sinks down in my pillow and the room spins in circles around me.

"Shit!" I slur. I stagger my way down the staircase to the bathroom.

CHAPTER THIRTY-FIVE

When I wake up Sunday morning, my head throbs to each perfect beat of my heart. The smell of sausage pollutes the air trapped in my room and makes me feel nauseas all over again.

"Sweet jeezus, what did I do?"

As I pull myself up slowly and sit on the edge of my bed I recap my prior evening. It's hard to focus with the drum that bangs in my ear, but bits and pieces slowly pull together.

"Oh no. No. NO. **NO.** What the fuck did I do?" I repent and grasp my face with both hands. *This is wrong on so many levels.*

I should have listened to my mom. By now, I should realize she's always right. In an attempt to stay connected to Sean and find a way to make things better, I made things one hundred times more complicated. I kissed one of his best friends. What the fuck did I do? Who was the dumb-ass who fed me pot?

My hands shake when the realization of my actions sinks in. Or maybe from the alcohol withdraw, I can't be sure. Sean already has serious doubts about us ...his faith in me, badly bruised. Now this kiss, I know enough about Sean to know this is unforgivable—irreparable. Only I could single handedly kill an immortal, fate driven love. And I did ...one regretful feat at a time.

I search thoughtfully for a solution. The kiss was a simple mistake and a lack of sober judgment. It meant nothing to me, I barely remember it. I have to talk to Cory; he has to keep our dirty little secret—forever and always.

I spend the majority of the day in bed. Nothing I try will ease this pounding in my head, or the ache in my heart. At four, I drag myself out of bed and clean myself up. I have to talk to Cory, before he blabs his mouth to anyone.

His car is parked in the back of the parking lot. I let the stale air seep from my lungs. I head back to the storage room, but don't need to go that far. Cory is in the isle that leads to the double doors, stocking items in the frozen food section.

"Cory!"

"Bri!" he replies, with an of-course-she's-here smile plastered on his face. "I'm so glad you're here. I was going to call you tonight. My uncle has a band that is playing Saturday night. They've asked me to sit in with them. Will you please come with me?" He cocks his head and eyes me like a cocker spaniel.

"Cory, I don't know. We need to talk."

"So, talk," he suggests, still smiling.

"Not here. This is important."

"Bri, I just came back from break and I need to have this done before I leave. I'll stop by after work. I'm off in two hours."

"I thought you worked until eleven?"

"Not on Sundays. I work until seven. I don't have to be at the Star until midnight, so I have all the time you need. Now how about this Saturday? It would mean the world to me if you showed up."

"We'll talk about it. I need to go."

Cory's smile begins to melt away. The seriousness of my expression must finally register in his brain. *Keep up Cory!*

"Ok ...I'll see you in a couple hours."

I leave as quickly as my feet will carry me. Cory is sincerely happy to see me ...this completely sucks. Instead of driving straight home, I turn off by the lake and pull into a parking spot next to the boardwalk. I walk and walk and walk, to clear my head.

I consider the situation I have created with Cory, and although pot apparently makes me momentarily stupid, I can't place the blame on him. Cory is just trying to be nice to me. Maybe we both were caught up in a moment that ran away from us. A kiss is all it was, nothing more. How bad can this be?

I dig through the shattered pieces of my memory and try to remember exactly what happened. I was nauseas, I remember that clearly. Cory was holding me— or hugging me, although I can't remember why. I remember Sean kissing me, but it wasn't Sean ...it was Cory. I'm so confused. I wanted Cory to be Sean. I wanted to feel Sean kiss me again. I probably came onto

Cory. Fuck. Then again, maybe I'm blowing this entire indiscretion out of proportion. Cory probably hasn't given two thoughts to it. It was just a kiss. He didn't appear embarrassed or concerned. Yes, that's it. I'm making a big deal out of nothing. Let it go.

I reach the end of the boardwalk and sit on a park bench. My eyes wander out over the water that reflects the setting sun. Ducks drift by and wait patiently for their hand out.

One possibility lays buried I refuse to think about it. Has Sean moved on? He's been gone almost two months and that is plenty of time to develop a new relationship. I haven't sent him a note for over two weeks. Maybe it's time for one last letter ...for one final plea. If he doesn't respond, I have to let him go. I silently make myself this promise.

I head back to my car. I know there is a notebook and pen in my backseat from school. I turn on the dome light in my car. I don't think, I just write.

Sean,

In your words...we didn't choose this love. It chose us.

Soul-mate, what a ridiculous term. The correct term should be soul-merger. I once believed there was so much of you in my soul that I didn't exist anymore. I was wrong, you didn't invade my soul, our souls combined. We share a single soul that can never be pulled back apart. You can't mix fire and gasoline and expect to return them

414

to their original state. Instead, you linger in each other's souls for the rest of your pathetic life—never to break free.

It has been seven weeks since you left. There was no explanation. There was no argument. You were there ...and then you were gone. You sang to me once that you would never give up on us. Is that what you've done? Have you given up?

I fully understand I have been a disappointment to you, from the very beginning. I mutilated everything beautiful we once shared. My stupid insecurity made me feel unworthy of your love. I was intimidated by your very existence. You were perfect in every way; how could you possibly love me? Because of this, I was uncomfortable and afraid to tell you my honest feelings. I am sorry, but I am not afraid anymore. I love you Sean! I've always loved you, with every beat of my heart ...with every breath that I take.

I know I have made mistakes. I should have been there for you, I wanted to be. I should have showed you how I felt, because the feelings were, and still are, overwhelming. If you could only feel what I feel you would understand how much I need you.

Although our summer was entirely fucked up, I thought our last visit would begin to mend our broken pieces. I haven't had an opportunity to explain what happened the week you left. Apparently, you don't want to hear my excuses, or you would have called. I don't blame you, but I have to explain, for my own selfish reasons. I need redemption, or I need closure ...and there are too many loose ends for either.

When I left your house that night, I arrived home to a note on my counter. My grandfather was dying and not likely to make it through the night. I'm sorry I didn't call, but at that particular time, all I could think about was getting to him as fast as I could, to say goodbye one last time. My efforts were futile because he was gone by the time I arrived. The next twenty-four hours are a blur. Once the shock wore off, I tried desperately to call you Wednesday night. I called several times Thursday, and made a trip to Lamar between the funeral and the get together at my grandmother's house after the funeral. Your parents will verify. You were already gone by the time I could leave. I don't tell you this because I want your sympathy. I don't want you to feel bad. I just need for you to understand why I wasn't there, when I desperately needed to be.

Sean, I can't make you love me again, I am painfully aware of that. What I can do is tell you how much I love you. My life is full of regret and things I would like to forget—but, you will never be one of them.

But, as much as I love you, I can't continue to love someone, who doesn't reciprocate. This will be my last letter, unless I hear from you. I can't pretend you will come back to me, if you won't. If you have even an ounce of love for me left in you, please let me explain...in person. If I don't hear from you, I will have to assume you don't love me. I will sadly accept our story has played its final scene. I will move on and leave you alone...regretfully.

I Love You,
Brianna

I re-read the letter before I close my notebook. The sun sets and the evening air cools off quickly. It is time to head home to prepare for Cory's visit. My head needs to be clear. He has to understand and agree to keep our secret.

I can't concentrate on Cory, my thoughts are on the letter, while I drive the winding roads that surround the lake. I feel like I am manipulating his feelings by telling him about Gramps death. I don't want to pull out the sympathy card. Sympathy is an easy emotion to attain. His love is what I'm after. Sympathy and love are two completely different emotions. On the other hand, he needs to understand why I didn't return his phone calls. Sorry, obviously won't cut it. He needs to realize the magnitude of what I was going through, to make me risk what we were attempting to salvage. Hopefully he will not only understand, but forgive me. I need this from him.

I'm not entirely confident about the ultimatum I give him—or myself. It's so final. This is my last letter ...can I honestly hold myself to this threat? As harsh as the option sounds, it is imperative to my future mental stability. I need a breaking point, a place where I concede. I have to stick to this decision.

I pull into my driveway and Cory's car is already there. I glance at the clock on my dash and it read six fifteen.

I climb out of the car and Cory opens his door. "You're here early," I suggest.

"Yeah, I've been here for like an hour," he explains, while a warm smile creeps onto his lips.

"An hour! I thought you didn't get off until seven."

"I didn't feel good after you left, so I told them I was going home."

"You don't feel good?"

"It was an excuse Bri, relax. I just wanted to see you."

I choke on my breath, "Cory, that's what we need to talk about. Let's go up to my room, it's chilly."

"After you," he offers and motions me forward with his arm.

I lead Cory through the kitchen and up the staircase to my room. Unlike Sean, Cory has no problem plopping down on my bed. I sit in front of him with my back against the headboard and my knees pulled into my chest.

"So before you begin with your *serious* discussion, we need to talk about this Saturday. Will you please go with me? Your opinion means a lot, and this is my first real gig. I even get paid for it. Please Bri. I won't discuss whatever it is you want to discuss, until you agree."

"That's complete bullshit Cory—and blackmail. Which, by the way, is illegal. But whatever, I'll go watch you. I *will* drive myself, and I *won't* stay the entire evening."

"Deal!" He pulls in to awkwardly hug me, but I don't let go of my knees.

"Cory, we seriously need to talk. You do understand why I came to see you?"

"Because you wanted info on *him*."

"*Him* is Sean, Cory, *he* has a name and I will say *his* name out loud. This is all about him."

Cory's icy blue eye's narrow. "Why do you do this to yourself, Brianna? I don't get it."

"What's not to get Cory? I love him."

"You've seen him one day, in the past five months. How is that love? What will it take for you to realize?"

"Realize what?"

"He doesn't want to be with you anymore, or he would be here. I do want to be with you, that's why I am here. Plus, you were mine first."

"What the fuck are you talking about? I was never yours! You have known from the start it was always about him. God Cory, he's your best friend—your words, not mine. You don't think this is totally fucked up?"

"No Brianna, I don't. I think the way he treats you is fucked up. That's all I see."

"You don't understand Cory. You can't possibly comprehend certain aspects of our relationship."

"You use your big fancy words, but let me tell you what I do *comprehend*. I care about you, and have since

419

the first night I met you …pre-Sean. You are beautiful, and one of the coolest fucking people I've ever met. Since you came to visit me, all I have done is think about you, non-stop. You are vulnerable right now. You're just in pain, and scared to let go. I completely understand. But, you deserve better than that. You deserve to be loved, you deserve to be happy. You deserve to be with someone who will be there for you. I guess I also understand that I'm obviously not that person. You've created this fairytale romance in your head. I hate to tell ya sunshine, love isn't happy endings. Your relationship with Sean is far from a fairytale. You need to take a step back and look closer at what you have with him …because from where I sit, it ain't much. It was *never* much."

His truth chokes me, like a wad of cotton. I'm choking on emotion, but Cory doesn't comfort me. He sits like a statue and glowers at me. Everything I want to spew at him is ludicrous and delusional. I'm not sure I even believe myself anymore, but I have to try to make him understand.

My voice comes out in shreds, "Cory, I appreciate what you did for me, I really do. I also understand why you see things the way you do. I see how ridiculous this must look. What you don't get …what nobody gets …I love him. I love him so much, I came to you for answers— not to form some half-ass relationship with you. What happened the other night was wrong. So fucking wrong. It was wrong of me …and it was wrong of you. I need you to understand this."

"Oh, I understand perfectly. Bri, you hold on to your little love story. You hold on to your memory of this guy who is holding someone else in his arms tonight. This guy who isn't giving you a second thought. You dream of kissing him, while his tongue is down someone else's throat. You do that for as long as you like ...just know, I won't wait for you to get over it. I work hard to make my life better, all on my own. I would love to be in college right now, instead of working two worthless fucking jobs, but hey, my parents can't pay the bills, so college ...yeah right. If I'm not good enough for you, I get that. But do me a favor; don't live your life based on illusions and whatifs. I may be chasing my tail, but you are far more delusional than I am, sunshine. *Quit calling me fucking sunshine!*

Even though my head is buried in my hands, I hear the mattress squeak and feel his weight lift from my bed. I hear his footsteps stomp down the staircase. He is gone.

The floodgate to my emotion opens wide. My face falls into my pillow. I can't breathe, but it doesn't matter. There isn't enough oxygen in the room to keep me from drowning anyway.

As my pillow soaks in a river of tears, Cory's words hit me head on—like a Mac truck—speeding down the interstate at eighty. Not that what he told me never crossed my mind, but to hear it spoken—out loud, is ruthless. I see a vivid picture of Sean wrapped in someone else's arms. They braid together, skin on skin and gaze into each other's eyes—then they kiss. I want to barf. He looks happy and content like her, this nameless ugly face. I hate her. They go further, in my mind, than we ever did. I never shared this intimacy with him. I never had him completely. In my heart, I know Cory is right. I know we are over. I hold onto my delusion because it hurts to bad to set it free. Maybe I'm addicted to the pain, because the pain is better than erasing him completely. I need to erase him. This needs to end. This needs to end, tonight.

I gag on my tears with my face still buried. The release feels oddly comfortable when it oozes from my veins. I feel a hand tenderly rub my back and my head. It calms me as I continue to sob. Ten minutes pass and I push out my last tear. I slowly turn over. Cory is next to me with tears that pool on his own lids. He really does care about me.

"Brianna, I'm so sorry. The last thing I want to do is hurt you. I just get so frustrated; please forget everything I said. It was hurtful and mean. I hope someone, someday, loves me the way you love him. I'm never good enough for anyone. Part of me is jealous. Please forgive me," he begs and wipes the tears from my eyes.

I choke on the words, "Don't apologize, you're right. I'm having a hard time accepting it. Two kinds of love exist, the kind you seek and the kind that finds you. The kind that finds you is rare. I can't even explain it. We did have something special, but he walked away from it …with good reason. It kills me to face that."

Cory's grabs my hands. His thumb begins to massage my hands. His blue eyes lock with mine, "Brianna, what you shared with Sean was special, because you're special. You will find this love again, I promise. You have to open your heart and let others in. You will create this magic again with someone who appreciates what you have to offer."

Cory releases my hands and wraps his arms around my shoulders and pulls me into his chest. He doesn't let me go, because the faucets turn back on—and saturate his white tee-shirt.

The more I realize how right Cory is about Sean, the harder I cry. I wanted enlightenment, and Cory hands it to me on a fucking tarnished silver platter. Cory does know Sean better than I do. He tried to sugar coat the truth, but I wouldn't listen. I had to have the truth thrown at me like a grenade before I would listen. Sean is in a different place and a different time in his life now. What we shared was special, yet juvenile at the same time. The reality of our situation is he's outgrown me. He knew this would happen before he ever left. Sean didn't want this to work, because the further it progressed, the harder the inevitable would be.

I choke back my tears a few foggy minutes and pull away from Cory's chest. I stare at him with puffy, tear stained eyes—so attractive. "Cory, thank you for your honesty. I did need a wakeup call. Thank you for trying to be a friend. I know I've made that difficult. I'll come and watch you play for a while Saturday I promise, call me later this week and let me know the details. For now, I need to be alone. I hope you understand."

"I understand," he assures me, while his fingers peel the tear drenched strands of hair from my face and slide them behind my ears. His lips meet my forehead and he hugs me on last time.

"Saturday," I clarify, with a forced smile.

"Saturday. I'll call you tomorrow, or Tuesday with the times and stuff."

"Thanks Cory. Sorry you had to miss work for this."

"Awe, don't worry about that. I think I'll go park at the Globe and catch a little shut eye, before I have to go in."

"In your car?"

"Yeah, I do that all of the time."

"Cory, you are not going to go sleep in your car for four hours, that's ridiculous. It's cold out. I need quiet and time to think, you need to sleep. Crash here. I won't be sleeping anytime soon, so I'll wake you up at eleven-thirty."

"Are you sure Bri, because that would rock. My car isn't exactly the most comfortable sleeping quarters."

"Yeah, it's fine."

Cory unlaces his tennis shoes and kicks them across my room. One of them leaves a scuff mark on my wall before it tumbles to the floor. He spreads out on top of the covers and fluffs up his—my pillow and folds it under his head. I turn off the light and sit quietly in the dark in the corner of my room.

An hour passes. I sit in silence. I pull my legs into my chest and hug them tightly. I have so much to think about, but I am so mentally drained ...so tired.

Cory's voice whispers quietly, "Will you lay with me. I promise to be good. I could use some comfort right now, what an emotional night."

I know in my mind it is wrong, but I'm cold ...and I'm tired. So tired. My body shivers from the stress. I don't answer Cory, but I stand up and walk towards the bed. I fall on top of my covers, and ease back onto my other pillow. One million and four thoughts spin through my head, but I'm so tired. I reach over and set my alarm for eleven-thirty, in case I fall asleep. I stare silently at the numbers that glow on my clock. I watch them change with each minute that passes. My mind chews on everything Cory threw in my lap tonight. I wish I could spit it all back out—but I can't.

Sean has a freedom he's never had before. I'm not completely naïve. I know what this freedom will mean for us. We are over.

I'm still cold and wish I could slip underneath my covers, yet I know that movement won't go undetected. I feel the warmth of Cory's body just inches from mine, so I carefully edge backwards until I suck in his radiant heat without touching him.

From the sound of his breathing, I think he's asleep, but his arm lifts and wraps my waist by instinct. He pulls me closer to his body. I want to push away, but the warmth and security is comforting. I listen while he breaths hard and slow into my ear.

His body edges closer and closer as the minutes tick by. First, his leg wraps through mine and pulls my hips in against his. A few minutes later, his other arm slides under my neck and cradles my breast bone. I know deep down this is bad ...this is really bad. But I'm so tired ...and oddly, it doesn't feel terrible.

Cory cradles me like this for nearly an hour until my arm begins to feel prickly and tingles from lack of circulation. I try to ease slowly onto my back, so the blood will return to my numb fingertips. When I turn, Cory's arm slides under my shirt. His hot, calloused hands begin to caress my skin. The glow from the clock shows me his eyes are still sealed, but I'm fairly certain he's at least somewhat awake. He grips my hip bone and pulls me towards him, facing him. His lips touch mine, and they're warm ...so warm. His rough hands are determined; they start to slide towards my breast. I quickly push them away and back to my waist. He wraps them around my back and slides them up to my bra strap. The clasp is undone before I even realize they are there.

I whisper, "Cory, stop. Please stop. I don't want this."

He doesn't listen; his hands began to slide under my bra, onto my bare skin.

"Cory, stop," I plead and grab his wrists trying to pull his hands away.

"Brianna, relax. I won't hurt you. Ever."

Cory turns me again, onto my back and climbs over me. I tug at his wrists while he pulls my tee-shirt up and exposes me. He leans over me and kisses me. He has my wrists locked above my head and he works his lips down my neck to my chest.

"CORY, STOP IT! NOW!" I beg.

"Bri, don't be a prude! Samantha and Natalie enjoyed this." Even Princess Jezebel is ready to kick him in the nuts—and she's a slut.

I use all of my strength to pull my arms from his grasp and push him off of me. "I think it's time for you to go to work now."

"Seriously? What the fuck Bri, I guess I'm not *Sean*, what was I thinking," his tone sarcastic.

"No, you're definitely not, but what does that have to do with anything?"

"Are you telling me you two never did anything?" He laughs hysterically, "Are you a virgin?"

"Cory, it's time for you to go to work," I snap.

"Brianna, I'm so sorry. I had no idea," he chuckles some more and makes me want to fucking punch him.

Cory leans in to hug me, but I shove him away. I feel ashamed that I let it go this far, but equally humiliated that I'm still a virgin.

"Just go, ok Cory. I have school tomorrow."

"Ok, I'll call you this week and let you know about the gig time. I truly am sorry Brianna, don't be mad at me."

"I'm not mad," I spit and reset my alarm, shunning his gaze.

Cory plants a quick kiss on my forehead before he heads down the staircase. I sit on my bed and struggle with the clashing and conflicting emotions that spin through my confused head. All I want is Sean ...and Cory is a real threat to this desire.

CHAPTER THIRTY-SIX

I wake after what feels like a brief nap, to the buzz of my alarm clock. My eyes are on fire from the tears I shed throughout the night. My reflection in the mirror is hideous; my eyes are nearly swollen shut. The idea of staying home from school today is attractive, but I know that will just feed this vicious cycle and lead to more tears. I dig out my makeup and try to mask as much puffiness as possible.

School predictably moves like a slow leaky faucet, one tiny irritating drip at a time. It is a challenge to keep my eyes open and focus during class. During first hour English class, all I can swallow is my evening with Cory. My moral character has been violated and disrespected. Unlike Sean, Cory didn't stop. He ignored my gestures. He even disregarded my commands. That is so wrong. I should have been more pissed last night—I should have punched him in the face. What the fuck's wrong with me. I should never allow myself to be the victim.

Cory caught me off guard. I've never had a guy disregard my boundaries. Sean would never do such a thing. Weirdly, a small part of me wants to thank Cory— and that is really fucked up. Because I hate him. I hate what he did, but he pushed me beyond my fear. Because that's what it is. I'm not some moral princess, I'm just scared of the unknown—and what Cory did last night was unknown to me. Fear is what kept me from an intimate relationship with Sean. A more mature connection may have salvaged our fate. The underlying issue wasn't the push ...as much as the pusher. What the fuck am I thinking? Like sex would have saved us. If we made love, somehow the demons wouldn't find us? *Bri...you are an idiot, and Cory is a pig!*

I struggle with Cory's perception and opinion of my relationship with Sean. My common sense shouts that he's right ...still, my heart can't help but feel I remain in Sean's soul, somewhere. He needs a gentle reminder of where he locked me away.

My feelings for Cory are contrite. I let him kiss me again. Why do I keep doing that? I don't love him. Hell, I'm not even sure I like him.

By second hour, my head wins. I accept that Sean and I are, by all practical accounts, finished. I open my writing tablet to take a few notes and there, smugly staring me down, is my all too brave letter to Sean. I forgot I wrote it after the drama with Cory. My acceptance of fate, once again shattered. I can't go on. I can't give up.

I read the letter to myself, and debate whether to send it. Once more, the battles commence in my head. Do I attempt, or do I relinquish? I examine everything and cling to any sign to continue my fight, but find nothing. I rip the letter from my notebook and start to crumple it up, but I stop. I can't bring myself to destroy it. I place it neatly back in the notebook and close the cover. I read my letter on twelve different occasions that day.

Tuesday night, Cory calls like he said he would, a quality I wish Sean possessed. He plays at the Moose Club in Joplin at seven on Saturday. As much as I want to hate him, because my life would be far less complicated, I crave his friendship. I need that trivial connection to Sean.

"Cory, I'm not promising, but I'll try. I have to work until four, then I need to spend some time with my grandmother, she's not feeling very well," I lie.

"Oh, I'm sorry. Well, I hope you make it. I've never played for a real audience before, so it would be nice to have a familiar face in the crowd to look at."

I talk to Cory for several minutes. He is dejected, not himself. Or…he's just treading light on soft ground.

The remainder of my week edges by slowly. The only highlight of my monotonous day is opening my notebook to Sean's letter, over and over. And over. My daily debate to send it gives me something meaningful to contemplate. By Friday, I decide I will. Once the truth is rendered, I will accept his decision, either way, and move on.

Friday night, when I arrive home from work, I stuff the letter in an envelope and address it to Sean. Saturday morning, my heart pounds when I place it in the mailbox and lift the flag. You would think I handed it directly to him …as scared as I am. There is also something therapeutic. I know this is it, all or nothing. I pray a silent prayer.

My grandmother Harris meets me for lunch. I enjoy her visits, but find myself running out of things to talk about, as the weeks go by. If I had a life to discuss it might help, but I have nothing—nothing except my drama with Cory. That isn't a subject to share with my grandmother.

We chat about school and family to pass the time. My breaks are only twenty minutes, so we manage to fill the time.

Tonight is Cory's gig ...probably another mistake in my ever growing list of fuckups. I understand Cory's need for moral support. But why me? I just hope he doesn't read anything into my presence...because the pages are blank. I will drive myself and leave before he's done, so I don't see what can go wrong.

I arrive at the Moose Club at seven-thirty, purposefully after Cory starts playing. I arrive and fully expect to curl up in a dark corner of the room alone. Instead, I look around and realize Cory must have invited half of his school. I recognize many of the faces from prom and post prom. I recognize a few more from their gig in Lamar Park. Cory doesn't need me here; this is just another one of his manipulative ploys that I keep falling for. I turn to head back out to my car, but someone stops me.

"Aren't you Brianna?" a girl with short blonde hair grills.

"Yes, I am," I shoot her a dopey grin.

"Cory told us to keep an eye out for you. Why don't you come and sit with us."

I force a puff of air from my nostrils and follow her to the table full of Lamar kids. When I sit down, she introduces herself, "Hi, I'm Caly, Cory's sister."

Oh great. "Nice to meet you, Caly."

Several other people introduce themselves. I don't *know* any of them, but *recognize* several of them ...including Alexa, Sean's prom queen. *Perfect.* She doesn't introduce herself.

All of his classmates do their best to pull me into their conversation. I feel like a fish out of water, choking on air as I gasp for oxygen. I don't know these people, and Alexa's watchful eye isn't easing my inhibitions. She gloats in the idea that Sean is no longer with me—I can tell.

Cory takes his first break and sits down with me. He shoves a drink in front of me, on the table.

It doesn't look like a soda. "What's this?"

"A seven and seven," he offers.

"Cory, I can't drink this, I'm not old enough to drink in a bar. Plus, I'm driving."

"Fine, I'll take it back," he taunts.

"No, that's alright." I pull it back from his hands. "Are you sure it's ok?"

"Its fine Bri, they'll never know the difference. I'm so happy you decided to come."

Cory puts his hand on my leg and pulls me in closer to him. I unclench his fingers and dig my nails into his skin. I throw his hand back into his own lap. He rolls his icy blue eyes at me and smirks.

"So, what do you think? Do I sound ok?"

"You sound great, actually."

His smile beams from ear to ear, "*Good*, because they've ask me to join them full time. Now I can quite that stupid job at the newspaper. I'll make more money playing two nights a week than I did working there five nights ...and I'll be home earlier! I have to work it out with Save-A-Lot, but I think they'll work around my gigs."

"That's great, I'm happy for you Cory."

"Are you having a good time?"

"Yeah, just peachy," I lie. *Remove Alexa from the premise and I might stand a chance.*

"Good, I have to get back," he announces, and jumps out of his chair. His lips assault mine so quick I don't even know he's landing. A quick peck was all it was, but it was enough to piss me off. He's done it again. By the time his assault registers in my brain, it is too late to stop. He spins around and catches my enraged wide-eyed glare, and struts to the stage. He looks over his shoulder when he climbs onto the stage. A cheesy, pearly white grin is glued permanently to his face. Princess Jezebel crosses her arms over her chest and smiles. I want to slap her. I want to punch him.

I guzzle down my seven and seven quickly; ready to exit. When my glass slams to the table, Caly strikes up a conversation with me, "So, you know my brother totally likes you, right. He talks about you non-stop. He is so much happier than he's been in a long time, thank you."

"Caly, I'm not seeing your brother. We are friends. If he doesn't quit trying to kiss me, we won't be that for much longer."

"I don't think my brother thinks that you're just friends. Don't hurt him Bri, please. He really, really likes you."

Caly's soft expression tightens. I'm no longer Cory's savior, in her eyes, I'm the demon who will rip his heart out and eat it for breakfast. I don't belong here. I push myself up and head towards the bathroom. I sneak out the side door while Cory is playing, and hope my disappearance goes unnoticed—at least until I escape the parking lot.

Three days pass with no word from Cory. I'm glad he finally gets the hint, but I have to admit, I miss having someone to talk to. I don't miss him long, because tonight, my cell phone rings. "Hello."

"Hi Bri, its Cory," he mumbles in his deep voice. Silence falls over the phone; I don't know what to say. He continues, "Why did you leave Saturday night, without saying goodbye?"

"I was tired and it appeared you had plenty of people there to cheer you on. Plus, you need to stop fucking kissing me. I'm not your girlfriend."

"You were the only person I wanted there. I don't care about any of them. I'd say sorry about the kiss, but I'm not."

This conversation has departed down the wrong track. Apparently it's time for some brutal honesty. "Cory, you have to quit misreading my feelings for you. You are my friend, that's all. We are not a couple; we will never be a couple. Your sister was under the impression that we are dating. We are not dating Cory! Get that straight."

"Ok, in your eyes we're just friends. In my eyes, you are a girl I'm pursuing, that I want more than friendship with. This is all quite normal—really. What would you say if I asked you to be more than a friend? I really like you Bri; I would be so happy if you would give me a chance."

"Cory...NO! How many times do we have to go over this?"

"I'm stopping by Friday and we will talk about this. I need to understand what I'm doing wrong, because I know there's something there. I feel it—and you feel it too."

"Cory, No. I'm busy Friday; it's my dad's birthday. You don't do anything wrong. *Except for forcing yourself on me.* I just don't feel that way about you. Nothing is there—trust me. I still have feelings for Sean, I can't control that. You're his friend. It's all too weird."

"Are you fucking kidding me? This is still about Sean. After everything we've talked about. Seriously, get the fuck over it! I give up; have a pleasant life with your fairytale!"

"Cory, stop!" my debate is futile, because he hangs up.

436

I sit on my bed; my fists grab wads of hair and pull. I try to figure out exactly how I created such a mess. *You should have listened to your mom, stupid!* Princess Jezebel stabs her long, thin, accusing finger into my chest.

I have another perspective to consider. Cory gives me everything I desperately wanted from Sean. He calls, he spends time with me, *and he works two jobs*, he tells me how he feels about me. Maybe Cory reads our situation correctly, and I'm the illiterate one.

But ....there's always a but. I don't love Cory, and truthfully I don't trust him. Not completely. His moral character is shady.

My final letter to Sean went out with Saturday's mail. I am consciously aware he has it by now. It is painfully obvious my final plea didn't warrant a phone call.

I sit on my bed and hold my face, deliberating my predicament; I hear footsteps march up my staircase. *What the? Sean?* Natalie and Samantha waltz into my room, their expressions are pure smugdom. I'm already on defense. "What a shocker! When did you two become such good buds?"

"Don't worry about it," Natalie snaps, her lips pursed tight. "We need to talk."

"Sure, what's up?"

"I heard a rumor, and I want to know if it's true."

"Me too," Samantha adds, while her mouth twitches nervously.

"Rumor? What rumor?"

"Are you seeing Cory?" Natalie blurts.

Samantha stands behind Natalie and twists her fingers through her hair. I almost laugh.

"Ok, that is a weird question, but no, I'm not seeing Cory if you mean is he my boyfriend. Have I hung out with Cory a little, yes. We're friends. Why are you asking this?"

"Well everyone I've ran into lately in Lamar tells me you are dating Cory. I just think that's seriously crappy if it's true." The tone in Natalie's voice is pretentious. She has no right to ask me these questions.

"First of all Natalie, if I was seeing him, what's it to you? You haven't been dating him for months. I do believe Samantha dated him before you did, and you had no problem leaching on to him after her breakup, so what exactly is your issue?"

"The *issue* is Brianna, you are supposed to be my friend, and Samantha's friend. Samantha and I weren't friends when I dated Cory."

"Oh, but now you're best buds? Whatever Natalie, your arrogance entertains me. Samantha, what is your take on this? Are you mad at me too?"

438

"I don't know what to think about our friendship anymore …if there even is one. You've completely changed this year, Brianna. It's like you're three gallons of crazy in a two gallon bucket, and I don't want to keep cleaning up your left over crazy"

"Nobody asked you to," I fume.

"You are not the same person anymore. I don't honestly like the new version of you. I guess I would be upset if you were dating him. I mean, that would be like me and Sean going out, just weird."

Samantha's comment shoots across the room like an arrow from a crossbow and plunges to the center of my heart. "That isn't the same thing," I spit.

"Why isn't it Bri? Are you special?" Samantha barks.

"No, I'm not special …however, the relationship I have with Sean is special and you are fully aware of that."

Natalie rejects my argument, "So your boyfriends are off limits to us, but its ok for you to date ours?"

I continue to invalidate their comments, "Ok, this is totally fucking stupid. First of all, I'm not dating Cory. We've hung out a few times because he's trying to help me get back together with Sean. *Liar!* Secondly, I wouldn't have a problem with you dating an ex-boyfriend of mine, if I wasn't still completely and madly in love with them. Neither of you are in love with Cory, to my knowledge."

Samantha's expression softens, "I'm sorry things didn't work out for you two? Is he worth all of the heartache Bri? It seems to me that since you've known him, you've been more miserable than happy. This breakup has turned you into someone I don't even recognize. I would appreciate my friend back. Please let this go."

"Brianna, we talked about this a few months ago. You can't chase him if he's not interested. You look like a psycho stalker, give it up." Natalie frostily adds.

My vision blurs while tears swell up in my eyes. *Who woke up these fucking emotions? I'm so sick of tears. And salt. And snot. I want the numbness back.*

"Natalie, I can't. It's not a matter of his interest anymore. We have unfinished business that we need to work through. He loves me too, I know he does." I shift my eyes to Samantha, "I miss you too. Someday I hope you feel for someone what I feel for him, but until that day, please don't judge."

Samantha responds considerately, "I just miss you, and I hate the person he has forced you to become."

"I'll second that," Natalie scoffs.

"He hasn't forced me to become anything, or anyone. My actions belong to me alone. Who I am now is someone I chose to become. Don't blame any of this on Sean. I never see any of you anymore, not by choice, but because of my schedule. I hang out with different people now, so obviously, I'm going to be different. I do miss you both, very much …and sometimes, I miss the old me, too."

"Well sorry, but it is about choice …everything is a choice. I truly hope you and Sean work things out, I honestly do. A point comes where you need to surrender, I hope you find that point …and soon," Samantha finishes.

Tears escape my water logged eyes and drip from my chin, "Actually, I wrote him a final letter. I needed to explain a few final things. I've already promised myself this is my final attempt. If I don't hear anything from him in the next few weeks, I will call uncle. I promise. It's time, I agree."

"Thank god! Bri, there are other fish in the sea, seriously," Natalie blurts.

"Yeah, I know." I agree verbally, but Natalie still doesn't get it. Boyfriends are disposable, in her eyes …something to pass her time and keep her busy. Samantha understands.

"Well Sam, are you ready to go? We're going to be late," Natalie smirks and presses salt deep into my wound.

"Where are you two off to?"

"We're going to a movie with Blake and Trevor; they're picking us up at Natalie's." Ah, now I understand the connection. They're both dating football players. Happy fucking day

"Ok, have fun."

"What are you doing tonight?" Samantha asks.

"Nothing, but I have gobs of homework to finish up," I pretend, because I have no desire to tag along on their date.

"Oh, ok ...see you around. Call me sometime, maybe we can hang out," Samantha smiles.

"Come on Sam, they will be waiting on us if we don't get back," Natalie is as impatient as ever. She turns to me, "See ya around, Bri."

"Yeah, later." *P S, Is that all you got bitches? Nobody likes you. And your shoes are fucking ugly.*

Wow, I think to myself while they scurry down the staircase. *Did they seriously just come over here and chew me out, for hanging around Cory?* I shake my head. This is far more complicated than I thought. If Samantha and Natalie are mad, Sean will be livid. I need to keep my distance from Cory, beginning immediately.

I already know Cory has no intention of helping me renew my relationship with Sean. I don't think that was ever his motive. He won't be satisfied remaining friends. I'm weak and vulnerable, and honestly, don't need the temptation. It is far too easy to let Cory into my world. My world is lonely. It feels good to have attention from someone who cares. Hell it feels good to have someone to talk to, period. Unfortunately, this relationship is a time bomb waiting to explode. I don't care about Cory, not really. He's just someone to fill the emptiness. He could be anyone and achieve the same results.

Friday night arrives. My mom has planned this ginormous party for my Dad's fiftieth birthday. The entire family is here, including Grams.

The party, at least for the night, is a decent distraction from my Sean-Cory clusterfuck.

Cory won't stop calling. I haven't answered any of his calls or texts. It's hard to disconnect myself from the one thing that held me in Sean's world, but it's necessary. Apparently, Sean will never be part of my world anyway. My final attempt brought nothing. A big part of me, the part that doesn't want to believe the inevitable, truly believed my letter *would* change everything. I knew in my heart Sean still loved me. Once he knew the truth he would understand and come back to me. How could I be so delusional?

Several hours into the party my family is jamming in our garage while the non-musical guests, like me, watch. I look up to catch Cory stumble into the garage. His bloodshot eyes skim over the faces that now stare back at him. The room is dead silent. Cory has been drinking, a lot.

I stand up and drag him out of the garage as soon as my feet will carry me and try to avoid further embarrassment. "Sweet jeezus Cory, what are you doing here? I told you I can't talk to you today! It's my dad's birthday."

He slurs, "I know what you told me. You also won't answer your fucking phone. We need to talk. Let's go to my car."

I suck in a heavy sigh and walk towards his vehicle. I climb into the front passenger seat and close my door. Cory climbs into his seat and digs out his keys.

"No, fuck no! We are not leaving this driveway," I scold.

"I just want to talk to you Bri; we're not going far so chill the fuck out."

"First of all, you are trashed! Clearly you aren't driving me anywhere. Secondly, we can talk right here. We don't have much to talk about, anyway."

"Fine Bri, that's just fine …nothing to talk about, isn't that some fucking shit."

"Cory, listen to me, and try to absorb it over the alcohol. My friendship with you was *never ever* about forming a relationship with you. It has always been about Sean. I have said this from the start. I know you don't want to hear this, but you need to listen. I needed your help to get him back and that is all. Apparently, you have no intention of helping me, which is ok—whatever. I get it."

"No…I won't fucking help you try to hold onto something that isn't there. Let it the fuck go, already."

"I know I need to let go. Regardless of when I can accomplish that, starting a relationship with you won't happen. Neverfuckingever. That is wrong...and you're not my type, anyway."

"Not your fucking type—hilarious. Wrong? …wrong, yeah! Sean wouldn't like that very much, would he?" He snorts drunken laughter and I'm two breaths away from punching his face. "You know Bri, you are totally fucked up. You won't ever have Sean, you understand that don't you. He doesn't want you anymore, he's like so done with you ...or that's the impression he gave me."

"What? When did you talk to him? What did he say to you? What did you say to him? Please tell me."

"Listen to you! Sean ...Sean ...Sean, what a fucking joke. Who will save you when I'm not around? Who will pick up all of your scattered pieces ...your friends? What friends Bri? You've managed to cut everyone out of your life, oh except the one person who has cut you out of his. Congratulations on your epic ability to care about the people who don't give a fuck about you— and shit on the people who do."

I can't argue his point. I shift my focus to the ground between my feet. Cory is silent, while tears drip in between my legs. Who will pick up my damaged pieces? The answer is obvious.

"I am Cory. I have to be the one to put the broken pieces back together. The only person who can fix me...is me. I have to be ready to be fixed. You are a constant reminder of what I have lost. I should have never involved you, I'm sorry."

"That's all I am to you," he scoffs. "I'm nothing more than a reminder of Sean. Fuck Cory, he doesn't exist. Thanks Bri, you really know how to make people feel good. I would have done anything to make you happy. But that's me, always the loser."

445

Cory has this undeniable way of making me feel guilty, probably because I should feel guilty. I have to keep my guard up; he's trying to break down my armor.

I glance over, and through the darkness I see his eyes focus on his thumbs between his legs. I have hurt him. Why do I hurt everyone? *God I hate this!* I reach over his console to awkwardly hug him. "Cory, you're not a loser." I have to delicately phrase what I'm about to say. "Cory you have been there for me when I needed someone. You have to know, I appreciate that. You've tried to pull me from this darkness, which has surrounded me for months now. You *have* been that light that has pulled me to the surface."

I reflect carefully how to continue "the but part" while I rest my head on his chest. How do I explain my feelings for Sean, devoid of hurting his severely bruised ego? While I process my thoughts, Cory's grip on my neck strengthens.

Cory shoves my head forcefully towards his lap and his other hand slides in to unbutton his pants. I free myself from his grip and scream, "What in the hell do you think you're doing?"

"What Bri, you don't do that either? Your friends do, just so you know. What the hell good are you? No wonder Sean left; you're nothing but a tease. If you're going to throw me in the trash, the least you could do is give me one for the road."

"Get the fuck out of here, Cory! Leave and *don't ever* come back."

446

I open the door to his car and jump out. I slam it shut and flee. I don't bother to look back, but I hear the gravel fly when his tires spin from our driveway.

With my party mood hindered beyond repair, I head to my room. Cory's expectation was disturbing. He is a manipulating jerk. Sending him on his way became effortless.

What did he mean by *the impression Sean gave him*? Did he honestly have a conversation with Sean? If this is true, it changes everything. Or, was Cory grasping at straws, making shit up to force me to let go?

How will I ever let Sean go? I know in my heart I need to let him go, but how is that even possible? He is imprinted on every tiny fragment that remains in me. The missing pieces are gone, stolen by him when he disappeared. Can I honestly put back together these jagged broken pieces by myself and move forward. I don't know, but it is certainly time to try.

CHAPTER THIRTY-SEVEN

My constant dream state has taken me through endless days of torment and regret while I desperately try to wake from my eternal nightmares.

Tonight, Sean stands and faces me with a look of contempt, arms folded, and dark eyes cold. Cory stands behind him with a smirk of satisfaction tattooed across his face, like he has stolen valued treasure.

I escape their condemnation, and run through the dense forest aimlessly. Suddenly, claws dig into my ankles and yank me to the ground. The woman with black hair rises from the ground, covered in muck and sand. She grabs me by my hair violently, and pulls me into a pool of loose wet quick sand. I sink slowly into its damp cold bowels. My lower body is paralyzed by the weight. The sand presses hard against my chest and makes it difficult to breathe. I reach out my arms desperate to be saved.

Cory catches up to me, his arms are easily within reach, yet Sean's hand is also extended, but too far away to touch. I study Cory's hand, merely inches from my head, while I continue to sink into the dark depths of the pit. I struggle to reach Sean's hand that moves closer, but is still beyond my reach.

I feel the powerful grip of the woman with black hair. She pulls me deeper, and the light fades to black. Suddenly a strong grip locks around my wrist. It pulls me from the heaviness that surrounds me. I can't see anything. My eyelids are filled with sandy sludge. I feel gentle fingers scrape the muck from my eyelids. Gentle music plays faintly in the background. I wake enough to realize my cell phone is ringing.

"Hello," I choke out groggily.

"Bri, its Cory. Don't hang up! I'm so sorry for last night. I'm so sorry for *everything* I have done to you. I know you will never forgive me, but you need to know that alcohol betrayed my brain and I'm embarrassed and regret everything I did."

I shake my head, to gather my senses. I fully absorb what Cory refers to, the memories rush back like a vivid nightmare. "Cory, don't ever call me again. I'm done with this charade; I'm done with all of it. My future will not include anything to do with Lamar."

"Ok, I understand, I won't call you ever again. I am sorry, I don't know why I do the things I do sometimes. Yesterday is not a day I'm very proud of. I'm sorry I hurt you. I'm sorry I destroyed everything important to you. Sean's right, I'm a self-centered prick. I want you to know, it has been great getting to know you. I truly do care about you. Always remember that."

"Cory stop. Goodbye."

"Bye Bri."

I hang up the phone with some satisfaction that he at least apologized, yet not enough to make up for his inexcusable actions. He embarrassed me in front of my family. His comments were cruel, and his vulgar expectations and forcefulness was totally unacceptable.

As I begin to wake up, I revisit some of his comments in the car. The comment that stands out, insinuates that he spoke with Sean. When did he do this, and what did he share? I can't trust that he spoke with Sean, at all. But add that to his comment on the phone, *I'm sorry I destroyed everything important to you.* Did this mean he did talk to Sean, and if so ...what on earth did he do?

I think back to my nightmare and wonder whose hand pulled me from hell. I wish Cory wouldn't have called, so I would have my answer, but now the moment is over. The dream is gone.

I head down the staircase to grab a glass of juice before I attempt to get ready for work. Today is a new day and I have every intention of greeting it with a new attitude. I think I meant what I said to Cory. I'm done with everything Lamar. Sean is gone from my life, now Cory is too. I need all of this bullshit behind me. Fuck a bunch of love bullshit.

Both my mother, in her robe, and my father, in his night pants, sit at the breakfast bar when I stroll into the kitchen. They both glare at me.

"What?" I ask, confused and still groggy.

My dad, unshaven with bloodshot eyes, leans back and crosses his arms over his chest. "Brianna, I don't know the young man that showed up here last night, but he is not welcome here ever again. Is that understood?"

"Bri, how could you invite someone like that over while we had company? Do you know how embarrassing that was for me and your father?"

I totally understand, because I too was embarrassed, beyond words, but for some unknown reason I feel the need to defend Cory.

"He called and apologized this morning. He had a seriously bad day. He works very hard mom, you don't understand. He has to help his family pay their bills, which is crazy."

My dad argues, "No Brianna, that is called responsibility. His actions last night, however, were not responsible. My guess, he's not even old enough to be drinking, let alone be behind the wheel of a car when he's drunk. That is not anyone I want my daughter in a vehicle with. I don't want you to associate with him."

"We mean it Bri!" my mom adds.

"Ok, enough. I get it. I told him last night not to come back, and I told him this morning not to call me anymore. It won't happen again, I promise."

"Well good. I knew I raised an intelligent daughter. Whatever happened to the guy you were dating a few months ago? I liked him, he seemed like a great dude," Dad probes, running his fingers through his wavy mop, while my mother blows poisonous darts at him.

"It's ok Mom, I'm coming to terms. He went away to college. We haven't seen each other for quite some time now. I miss him too, but it wasn't meant to be, I guess."

My mother's eyes are about to fall out and roll across the counter. I think she actually believes me. If I can convince her, maybe I will convince the rest of the world. Convincing myself will take some work.

"Well that's too bad; he was a nice kid. Glad to hear he's doing something with his life though. School is a must these days," Dad finishes while my mother's eye continue to beg him to shut the hell up. She might have bought my performance, but she understands a relapse isn't out of the question.

I discontinue my confrontation and return to my room to get ready. I call Samantha when I finish and see if she wants to hang out after work. Can I convince her too, and try to rebuild what is left of our tattered friendship. She has plans with her boyfriend, so I won't be able to test my mad acting skills—at least tonight.

Work is cumbersome. Someone called in sick, so I am stuck on the steam table. The moist heat makes me nauseas. It doesn't do much for my hair and makeup either. The only good thing about today is working with Madison. She is fun, and probably one of my closest friends from work. She knows all about my drama, unlike most of my co-employees. After two hours of heat, I am ready to pass out, or throw up. I need a break. I turn to let Madison know where I'm going, when an image appears before me. This has to be a dream. Sean is on the other side of the counter with his arms folded over his chest. The corners of my mouth turn up, uncontrollably. My smile is more painful than usual; these muscles haven't been used for a very long time.

"Can we talk?" his voice is flat.

I stutter through my answer, "Umm ...yes ...absolutely. I was just going on break." I turn to Madison with puppy dog eyes and don't have to ask. I can tell from her expression, she knows exactly who stands before me.

"Yes, go ...go! I have this; take all the time you need, I have it covered."

I go back to my locker and grab my purse. When I exit the mall corridor, Sean is at my side. He asks, "Where are you parked, because I'm a million miles away from here."

"I'm not too far. We can go to my car."

"Good."

I want to see his dimples, or feel his fingers wrap through mine, but nothing. He won't even make eye contact with me. I am barely able to breathe from the weight of fear that stacks up on my chest. Is this it; the resolution I need to move on. Is he here to tell me he has someone else in his life now? Was Cory right all along? Or did Cory talk to Sean and obliterate any sliver of chance we had? I look down at my feet while I continue to lead him to my car. He walks at least two paces behind me.

I unlock the doors and Sean climbs into the passenger seat. I climb into the seat next to him. It is cold, so I start the car to knock off the chill. The stereo blasts out old Aerosmith when the engine starts. I quickly turn it down.

"You don't have to turn it all the way down, I like Aerosmith," he conveys with eyes I don't recognize. His eyes are shallow and cold. They force me to look away.

He reaches over and turns up the music, slightly. I try to cast a glance at him again. His eyes fill with so much emotion. Anger, pain, hatred, even a little crazy.

I suck in breath like I'm breathing through a straw. "I'm sorry Sean, I must look awful. I had to work over those damn steam tables all day. You look great though. I can't believe you're actually here. It's so good to see you! I've missed you so much."

"You look fine Brianna, but cut through all the small talk and bullshit."

I bite at my lip, "Bullshit, what bullshit?" He could be upset with me for so many reasons right now; I don't even know which one to choose. "Did you get my letter?"

"Yes, I got your letter; I received all of your letters. I don't understand why you waited so long to tell me that your grandfather died. Did you think that wouldn't matter? I would have been there for you Brianna. It would have made all of the difference in the fucking world. Instead, you made me believe for two months that you didn't give a shit. Nobody can make that many mistakes unless they're somewhat intentional. I seriously don't understand you. I feel like a pawn in your cruel game of life."

His harsh words cut through my skin. This pain is real, and not self-inflicted. "I'm sorry, stupid decisions are my specialty," I admit. I shake my head, because this isn't

454

entirely my fault—and I'm kind of sick of taking all the blame.

I suck in a heavy breath and continue, "I didn't want to explain it all in a letter. I begged you to call me. I honestly needed to talk to you, that wasn't up for negotiation. The problem is you never answered my letters. You never called or gave me your number so I could call you. You never came to see me. Instead, you simply disappeared. I felt like I was writing to fucking Santa Claus, who doesn't really exist. Personally, I don't think it should have taken my grandfather's death to finally drum up a response from you?" *Fuck planting seeds!*

"So you want to pin this on me? You knew we were fragile. Your words have always said one thing, yet your actions say another. All I knew is you begged for me to consider our relationship, and then *you* disappeared. What was I supposed to think? God if you would have only explained!"

Sean stairs at his hands and shakes his head in disgust, before he continues. "By the time you finally called back, I'm sorry …but I was pissed. You made my decision easy. I was in no hurry to work on us. I felt like our day together meant nothing to you. I understand now, but you have to see how your ambivalence looked through my eyes.

Even with all of that said, I missed you every shitty fucking day. I seriously considered ways to make this fucked up relationship work, but I needed time. I moved to a much larger city with a much larger school and it took time to adjust to all of it. College is hard and it's all I can do to keep up with my studies. Shit, it took me two weeks of pounding pavement in my free time to find a job within walking distance of campus.

I was finally ready to come and see you. Then I received your letter and felt even better about the situation, because I totally understood. I counted the days until I could come home so we could work this out in person. All I wanted was to taste your lips and hold you. Instead, I come home to find out I will never taste them again..."

Tears pool on my lids, ready to make their escape. I was right all along, he did still believe in us. He did still love me. I should have followed my heart and drove to Springfield to find him.

"So you didn't meet some girl in school, or Springfield, and forget about me?"

"No, I didn't, but it appears I'm quickly forgotten."

"Forgotten, you've never been forgotten. I have been miserable for months. Sean, I love you. All I want is to be with you. When you left you took my heart and my soul with you. I'm empty and alone. My friends won't talk to me anymore, because I'm so depressing. Do you know how many times I wanted to jump in my car and head to Springfield to find you?"

"Jeezus Bri...stop with the fucking lies! If that was the case, why didn't you? You had my address ...too busy dating Cory, or what?"

Those words might as well be his fists, which wring what life is left out of my heart. He knows. He knows, and he will *never* forgive me. "Dating Cory? I am not dating fucking Cory. I was never dating Cory! I tried to befriend him, but that didn't even work out well. I want nothing to do with him."

"When is the last time you talked to Cory?"

"This morning, but he called me while I was asleep, or I wouldn't have answered. I told him not to call me, ever again."

"So when is the last time you saw Cory?"

"Last night, but he came to my house uninvited, drunk and I made him leave."

His words pollute the air between us, "The friend's only thing is total bullshit Brianna. I know this for a fact. I came home this weekend for no other reason than to see YOU! We needed face to face time to discuss your last letter and our future.

My first time home in months, and what a great reception it was! How do you think it feels to hear everyone I know talking about Cory and Brianna? How do you think that set with me, Bri? Welcome home, and by the way did you know your girlfriend, you know...the one you've agonized over the last couple of months, now dates your best friend.

I truly thought this whole time we had something special. I fell for all of it, because I wanted it that bad. I needed to believe in you, and trust in us, even though my gut told me it was all an illusion. Every time I convinced myself to let you go and move on, there you were, sucking me back in like it is all some sort of mind game.

457

I have nothing left to say to you. You are nothing to me. You don't exist. Thanks for making it easy for me this time."

I cry the ugly cry that sounds like you're regurgitating your own heart, "Sean you have to believe me. I love you, Cory is nothing to me. We were friends, in my eyes, and that was all. He saw us differently than I did. When I found out he told people we were dating, I called him out and stopped hanging out with him. I avoided his calls all week last week. He showed up uninvited during my dad's birthday party. It was awful! You have to believe me, there is no one—except you!"

Sean throws me a seething glare and turns away, "Friends? Did you kiss him?"

"What?"

"You heard me Brianna, and don't lie to me, because I will find out the truth. Did you kiss him?"

I take my time answering, and hope he forgets his question. I try to change the subject, "Why did you wait so long to contact me Sean? I honestly thought you wrote me off. Why couldn't you answer even one of my letters, or gave me a quick call. I'm so sorry for everything. But you left me with no hope. Please give me a chance, please give us a chance."

"By not answering my question, you answered it clearly. No there won't be another chance. Everything I heard is obviously true, although I didn't want to believe it, I couldn't believe it. I gave you the benefit of the doubt, which is more than you've ever given me. Now that I know the truth, I can't possibly ever look at you the same again.

The pain I have been feeling is nothing compared to the pain I am about to endure. Do you have any idea how regrettable it is to walk away from a love that you know in your heart you will never find again?"

I grovel, "Then don't ...don't walk away. I can't bear to live without you, we do belong together. Can't you see that?"

His voice is thick with hate. I cower under his penetrating gaze until I have to look away. He finishes, "No, I don't Bri. I don't see that at all, or you wouldn't have done what you did. You know, I used to believe there was no one but us. The rest of the world faded to black around you—or even the thought of you. But, there is a world out there, it does exist and I have to live in it. We've both made bad choices, we both have regrets that will haunt us for years to come, but this? You're my girlfriend, he's my friend. I just can't do this anymore. Our story ends here. I will always love you, but I can never forget what's happened ...it's unforgivable. Stay away. Don't call. Don't write. Don't visit. I'm done. Really done." He opens the car door and slides out.

I yell after him, "The rest of the world only exists to destroy us! Please don't go, please. I'm begging you." I should run after him, but I already know it won't do any good. I watch through puddled eyes while he moves across the parking lot and disappears out of site. My heavy head falls to the steering wheel and I cry longer and harder than I have ever cried in my life. I have no hope to cling to; there is no delusion of a fairytale ending. It's over ...end of story.

Everything I should have said dissolved into silence. Why can I never find the words? He is gone ...I sat there and let him walk out of my life.

I grapple with my emotion for thirty minutes before I gain enough composure to return inside. I know I can't stay at work any longer, I can't even see—my eyes feel like two balloons. I need to let Madison know I'm going home.

"Oh no!" she cries sympathetically, when I approach her. "I'm so sorry, Bri."

"I need to go home. Can you tell Jeff I was sick to my stomach?"

"Sure Bri, I'm so sorry! Call me tonight if you feel up to it. We'll talk."

"Thanks Madison, I owe you one."

I turn away and head for the front door, only to run into Jeff. "Where are you going?"

"Home, I don't feel well at all. Madison has it covered."

"No, you're not going home. You will finish your shift or you can forget about coming back to work permanently."

"Well I guess it's been nice working for you ...whatever." I walk out, and could care less that he yells obscenities behind me. The loss of my job is pathetic and insignificant in comparison to the real loss I just suffered. *So fuck you back!*

I drive home with my eyes to blurry to see. I stay on the country roads as much as possible, and try not to kill some innocent bystander.

I head straight for my room, but my mother stops me. "Now what? Brianna, I thought you were better when I saw you this morning."

I can't turn off the tears. I need an emotional plumber. I explain, "Sean came to see me today. He knows about all of the time I've spent with Cory. It's over."

"So he came to tell you it's over. Really? I would say it's been over for a while, when you consider what my daughter has went through for months. Glad he finally cleared that up for you. Asshole."

"Mom, don't blame him. I'm the one who has continually screwed everything up with him. This isn't his fault. It's mine."

"Well I don't happen to agree. You have cried over this boy for six months and he hasn't been here. In my opinion, good riddance."

"Mom, please don't ever say that again. You don't understand. Nobody understands. How can you understand something too beautiful to be real? I just want to go to my room. It's over, I'll put this behind me, I promise." ...and that is exactly what I do.

CHAPTER THIRTY-EIGHT

For several months I live under a dark shadow of gloom. Nothing can hold my interest, or touch my heart. Existence is an obscure motion through a dimly lit tunnel. The wraith of my deeds has fallen upon me.

Today, however, is my eighteenth birthday. I only remember this, because Sean showed up on my doorstep one year ago, today. Today is the unwritten deadline I allowed myself to grieve. I still miss him, every day. I'm fairly certain I will always miss him, because without him, there are pieces of myself that are missing. Not tiny little chips that you barely notice, but big structural beams, which weaken your entire framework. I haven't completely collapsed, but I'm very careful to not carry much of a load.

Today is the day, the day of a new beginning—the dawn of a new age. It is time to start a new chapter, or maybe an entirely new novel. I am nearly done with school, only two months to go. I head to the bathroom to brush my teeth before I leave. For the first time in months I see the sunshine that beams through the kitchen window.

I smile at my mother and give her a hug. She pulls her head back and squints. *What?*

"What was that for," she vocalizes.

"Just because."

She smiles and remembers, "Happy Birthday Brianna. It's nice to see you in such a good mood." My mother is beautiful; it's been a while since I noticed.

463

"Thanks Mom. I think today is a great day for new beginnings."

"Wow, I wish you would have had a birthday a long time ago. Now I feel bad that we're leaving town this weekend. To be honest, I didn't think you'd notice."

"Mom, don't worry about it. You, Dad and Ben will have a great time in Florida."

"Well, we still have tonight. Is there anything special you would like to do for your birthday?"

I think about her offer for a few seconds and respond honestly, "I think I want to eat dinner and watch a movie with my family tonight."

My mom nods her head in approval, "Well then, that's what we'll do. I'll make some lasagna for dinner and pick up some movies today."

"Mom, you don't have to go to that trouble. I know you have a lot to do to get ready for your trip. Chinese takeout is fine."

"Ok, if you're sure. It's your birthday."

"I'm sure." I kiss her cheek and slip out the door.

School is pleasant for a change, not the typical doldrums that add to the conflict in my head. I make a conscious effort to smile at everyone I pass by today and to my surprise, most of the faces smile back. The ones that don't smile stare at me in confusion, like I'm a new kid in school. They probably never noticed me before today.

It's like I put a new battery in my life clock. Even time pushes by at a more acceptable rate today, compared to my ugly months prior. I smile at the sky when I walk out of the building. One last thing needs done before I totally close the Sean chapter of my life. It's kind of stupid, but symbolic—it's something I need to do, for me.

Instead of heading directly to the Junior College, after third hour, I head towards the lake. I park my car and take off on foot towards the lake edge Sean and I sat that warm spring day last year. Today is not as warm, the sun is out, but the breeze has a chill.

Along the way I find a single yellow flower that grows next to a rock, so I bend over to pick it. It's delicate and beautiful, like love. It reminds me that things do die, but bloom once again.

I find the exact spot and sit on the cold ground, my legs pulled into my chest. I hold the stem of my flower between my thumb and finger while I watch a pair of geese swim by. I make peace with my past.

I place the small yellow flower on our spot, like I'm placing a flower on a grave. I kiss my fingertips and touch the earth where we once sat. I stand up and take a deep breath while a single tear drops from my eye. I turn to walk away, my dark suffocating shadows left behind.

I pull into the parking lot at the Junior College, and realize I'm late to class. No one is in the parking lot except one other person. He walks before me and holds the door open.

"Hi," he smiles, his eyes a soft green. "I'm Ryan."

"Hi, I'm Bri," I smile back, a flush of color heats up my face.

I don't hear his footsteps, so I know he stands and stares at me while I head to class. A nervous smile pulls up on my lips. Now I'm curious, have people noticed me over the past several months and I just didn't see them? Or, did the dark gloomy cloud that shrouded me keep me well hidden from the rest of the world? I guess I will never know.

I end up dating him, that boy who graciously held open the door for me and smiled that day. Although we have an awkward start, he is fun …and fun is what I need at this particular time. This gift of time allows me to grow…and to heal …and to love again.

Over the next year, our relationship blooms. Neither of us leap right into college. We decide to take a year and have some fun. My parents completely support our plan. I have to wonder if "the plan" is actually their idea and Ryan just plays along. Over the summer we swim and boat and go to concerts. In the fall, we camp in the mountains. During the winter we vacation on a beach in Mexico. We enjoy our time together, and that is good enough.

Ryan is my very best friend. We do everything together, we are inseparable. I can't lie, I still think about Sean, more often than I should. Ryan doesn't have that connection with me that Sean did, but Ryan gives me something Sean never could …his time.

It is my nineteenth birthday. Ryan and I have been together almost one year. My house buzzes with celebration. Mom and Dad try to make up for leaving me alone last year on my birthday. All of my family is at my house, and so is Ryan and a few of our friends.

"Brianna, there is someone here to see you," my father bellows from the kitchen.

I excuse myself from the endless paparazzi to see who it is. When I make my way from the dining room to the kitchen, I see Cory standing at the door. *What the?* Behind him, I see Sean with his arms folded neatly over his chest.

My legs grow weak under their own weight and I gasp. Ryan grabs my hand, "Are you ok?"

"I'm fine; give me a minute, please."

Ryan's eyes glare vivid green at Cory, a look I have never seen from him before. What he doesn't realize, the real danger lurks behind Cory.

I slide open the patio door and step outside.

"Hey Bri," Cory beams cheerfully.

"Hey Cory," I answer and lock my focus on Sean. "Hi Sean."

"Hi Brianna. Can we go talk somewhere?" Sean asks.

I lead them both from the patio, down the sidewalk to the steps of our front porch. I sit down on the steps and stare up at both of them, confused. Why are they here, and for that matter, why are they together? Not-at-all-awkward. "So, what's up?"

Sean answers first, "I want you to know I didn't forget your birthday."

He's not here for my birthday. This is just weird—but good weird. An ache swells in my chest—like a heart orgasm. I haven't felt this for so long, I forgot how euphoric he makes me feel. All of my feelings for him, that were safely tucked away over the past year, now rush out to the surface and pour over me, like the falls we once stood and admired. My hands begin to shake while my eyes trace the outline of his lips.

Cory's voice comes through in waves, because I could care less what he has to say. "Bri, we wondered if you might go for a ride with us. I think we all need to talk."

I study Sean's face while these words fall from Cory's lips. Sean looks guarded; this visit is Cory's idea. Cory is trying to set things right …maybe …maybe not. He continues to talk, but I can't absorb a word he says. I want Sean to speak, but he doesn't. Does he want to talk? He just stares at me, with tension that tugs at his features.

I want him to hold me and tell me that he misses me, but I know he won't. He stands stiff, with his hands tucked deep in his pockets.

Cory repeats himself, "So what do you say Bri, will you go with us for a while?"

Go-with-you. I snap back to reality. My mouth is suddenly dry. My legs bounce nervously while my mind goes through spin cycle. *Sweet jeezus, what do I do? This is wrong on so many levels!* My mouth betrays my heart and the words spill out before I can stop them, "Cory, I can't leave. My family and friends are here. This party is for me."

Sean observes, "Cory, she has a boyfriend. This was a bad idea. We need to go and leave her to her celebration."

My heart wants to scream, *No, please don't go Sean. Please don't leave me again.* But, everything I want to say is blanketed by silence. Cory is too late—the irreversible damage is already done.

"Ok, I guess. We'll see you around Bri," Cory concedes. *No you won't.*

They both turn and walk away. Every muscle in my body wants to chase after Sean, but I'm paralyzed. I watch when Cory climbs into the driver's seat. I barely notice his beaming white smile through his window. Sean walks around to the passenger side. He stands and gazes in my eyes for several seconds. He finally sucks in a deep breath and a soft smile touches his lips. His dimples are still there. *God I love those dimples—god, I love him.* When he opens

469

his door, his voice whispers into my soul, "It was great to see you Brianna. You still haunt my dreams."

"It was great to see you too, you will always haunt mine." I don't know if my words fall upon his ears, or if my confession blows away like a feather in the wind, because his door seals shut.

Cory's car backs from my driveway slowly. Why don't I run after Sean, why don't I stop him? I don't care what my family thinks. Truthfully, I don't even care what Ryan thinks. Sean is my soul, and without him I will never be whole.

Yet I don't run after him and I don't stop him. I'm not sure why. I watch while the car fades out of sight. I stand up and brush off my ass, and I walk back into my party—like the world didn't just change.

I will not be given another opportunity with Sean Gentry. I know this. My decision will someday haunt me. The truth about love, opportunity only knocks once, so you better grab it. The innocent notion that love will last forever erodes with the loss of your first true love. My one true love will be nothing more than a memory—a memory that may fade, but will never disappear.

My heart may belong to another, but my soul will always be his, hidden from the world. My biggest regret …which one?

The End

EPILOGUE

We do not always choose who we love, sometimes love chooses us. That's what I told her once. What I failed to explain is this love is not patient and kind. This love is powerful and consuming. It fingers its way through your mind, body and soul, like a wisteria vine that oozes through cracks in a weathered barn. It strangles your emotion and overpowers your logic, leaving behind scars you cannot see—but, scars more painful than those that once bled.

From the moment I fell into her eyes I knew. She invaded me, she became everything I could feel …touch …taste …smell …hear …or see. She is everywhere. She is everything. She is thunder and rain, powerful, exciting and destructive. She is wind that wraps her comforting arms around me and beats me to the ground. She is sunshine, warm and kind until she scorches my soul until I blister. She is pain. But, I still desire to hold her every painful day.

I know I still want her, because she won't leave. She dances in my head all day. Every day. All night. Every night. I know I still need her, because I can't picture any part of my future without her. I know I still love her, because I can't breathe when I hear her name.

They say love hurts. Love doesn't hurt. Loss hurts. Rejection hurts. Loneliness hurts.

For ten fucking years this has been my life. I walked away, sure—but with good reason. She offered to take the blame, so I let her. It was easier to believe this was all her fault. But it wasn't her fault. It was entirely my fucking fault…every stitch of it. She never would have walked out on me, but I walked out on her with every complication. I see that so clearly now. It was all just fuckery.

I tried to get her back once, but it was too late. I walked out on her, what did I expect—for her to wait? Actually, I kind of did. I guess I'm just a sick perverted asshat—I mean I should wish her a life of fucking happiness …with butterflies and shit. But I can't. I kick myself every time I think about how many times I walked away from her. At the time, it seemed like the right thing to do, we were complicated. And I was fucking stupid. But, I should have listened to her. I should have believed her. I should have killed fucking Cory.

Yeah, it was over a year later when Cory finally fucking confessed. He told me he forced himself into her life—the self-centered egotistical little prick. In his eye's I stole her from him, because he saw her first, at some club. How fucked up is that? He admitted her true motive was me. He manipulated her. She came to him when she was weak and he made her believe the worst possible scenarios. He told me she repeatedly fought him off and finally told him to take a fucking hike. He came clean with me, finally—but, that didn't stop me from punching him in the face …and breaking his nose.

We had a plan. Actually it was more Cory's plan, because I was too scared. We would kidnap her and talk everything out. Cory, Mr. Manipulation, would help me convince her. We would do it on her birthday, since it was our anniversary. Fucking stupid. There was a flaw in our plan. She didn't want me back. She was in a relationship, probably far healthier than we ever had. I blew it.

So, I got married. Yeah, I pushed her aside and pried open a crack in my heart. Sounds good on paper. My wife was beautiful, and fun, and probably a great catch—for someone else. She gave me a gift more precious than life—a great fucking kid. I couldn't escape the dreams about turquoise eyes—the color of the ocean. In the end, my wife wasn't the one who wandered through my soul and danced through my dreams, because I would never let her in.

We failed, and it's entirely my fault. I never gave her one hundred percent, because I didn't have one hundred percent to give. After the baby was born, what little I had left all went to my daughter. There was nothing left for my wife, so she left—me and the kid. I didn't even cry.

Since then, all I do is think about this girl who stole my heart ten years ago. I don't want to think about her. In fact, I wish she never existed. But she does, and she just had to become famous. She just had to make something of herself. That way, I can't even escape the image of her. She's out there, for the world to see. I don't have to wonder if she's still fucking beautiful—or a big fat cow, because I know. Photos of her are everywhere. And yes, she's even more beautiful than I remember.

She was here in Boston last week. God, I wanted to meet up with her…but I couldn't. When we get together, bad things happen. Someone always gets hurt. Usually me. We don't try to fuck things up, but somehow that's what happens. If the world would disappear, we might have a chance. But the world won't disappear—and I have a daughter.

I am proud I resisted the temptation. I went to her signing, but I stood in the background and watched. Yes—like a fucking stalker. I lurked in the background as her deep ocean eyes glanced up at her fans. I distillate her every move while she smiled at each and every one of them, with a smile so sincere my heart oozed out of my chest. I fantasized that each smile was for me, and only me. It took every ounce of self-control in me, not to walk up and kiss her.

And then ...I left. I walked away. I had nothing left to do except drown myself in a bottle of bourbon. So, that's what I did.

I thought I was in the clear until my entertainment editor decided to do a story on her. I offered to take the assignment myself. What the fuck was I thinking???

50458602R00263

Made in the USA
Charleston, SC
27 December 2015